UNTAMED SHREWS

UNTAMED SHREWS

NEGOTIATING NEW WOMANHOOD
IN MODERN CHINA

SHU YANG

CORNELL EAST ASIA SERIES
AN IMPRINT OF CORNELL UNIVERSITY PRESS
Ithaca and London

Number 213 in the Cornell East Asia Series

Copyright © 2023 by Cornell University

First published 2023 by Cornell University Press

Library of Congress Cataloging-in-Publication Data
Names: Yang, Shu, 1983– author.
Title: Untamed shrews : negotiating new womanhood
    in modern China / Shu Yang.
Description: Ithaca : Cornell University Press, 2023. |
    Series: Cornell East Asia series ; number 213 |
    Includes bibliographical references and index. |
    Summary: "Untamed Shrews traces the evolution
    of unruly women in Chinese literature, from the
    reviled 'shrew' to the celebrated 'new woman.' Yang
    shows that the violent, jealous, and promiscuous
    shrew archetype of imperial times transformed
    into a symbol of empowerment in Republican and
    Communist China"—Provided by publisher.
Identifiers: LCCN 2022042681 (print) | LCCN
    2022042682 (ebook) | ISBN 9781501770616
    (hardcover) | ISBN 9781501770623 (epub) |
    ISBN 9781501770630 (pdf)
Subjects: LCSH: Women—China. | Women in
    literature. | Sex role in literature. | Chinese
    literature–History and criticism.
Classification: LCC HQ1767 .Y3594 2023 (print) |
    LCC HQ1767 (ebook) | DDC 305.40951—dc23/
    eng/20220921
LC record available at https://lccn.loc.gov/2022042681
LC ebook record available at
    https://lccn.loc.gov/2022042682

CONTENTS

ILLUSTRATIONS

Acknowledgments

My interest in the new woman goes back to the time when I was pursuing my master's degree in Beijing. In 2007 I translated an article by the Swiss sinologist Raoul David Findeisen (or Feng Tie, 1958–2017) on Zhang Zhaohe, the wife of one of the most celebrated modern Chinese male writers, Shen Congwen. This experience opened my eyes to the compelling life stories of Republican Chinese new women who gained control over their marriages and their husbands. My excitement, however, soon turned to consternation when I studied in the United States years later for my doctoral degree. In classes, the assigned scholarship on the new woman focused on images created by the leading May Fourth male writers. These new woman characters either are objects of male criticism or are too perplexed and stymied to move ahead on their chosen paths, starkly different from the historical figures about whom I had read earlier.

Upon noting this divergence, I started to browse broadly beyond May Fourth canons to trace depictions of the new woman in multiple genres and by various authors. When I increasingly encountered descriptions pertaining to the shrew of traditional Chinese literature in portrayals of the new woman, I came to realize that current scholarship might have lost sight of the connection between these two seemingly unrelated female types. This discovery prompted me to conduct research on such a nexus, which finally took the form of a doctoral dissertation and then this volume.

My research has received tremendous support and assistance from my mentors and colleagues, as well as scholars I have crossed paths with at various times and in various ways. The graduate seminars offered at the University of Oregon by Maram Epstein and Tze-lan Sang on late imperial Chinese novels and the modern new woman, respectively, gave me early insights into associations between old and new female models and the changing commentary on them. I am greatly indebted to Maram for her meticulous reading and revision of my academic writings of all kinds, her late-night and weekend emails, and most importantly her belief in me over the years. I thank Tze-lan for continuously directing me on my research and career choices even after her departure from Oregon. I thank Bryna Goodman for her insights and rigor as a historian of modern China, which have helped me reshape my writing. I thank Alison Groppe and Roy Chan for serving on my dissertation committee and helping with resources and interpretations.

I also owe a debt of gratitude to other scholars. Gail Hershatter read my dissertation and gave much-appreciated feedback for turning it into a book. Louise Edwards reviewed the article version of chapter 1 and encouraged me to strengthen my argumentation, sharing her perspectives on the material on the Chinese suffragettes. Christopher Rea offered his reading on examples of the popular media in modern China, inspiring me to take a more expansive view when approaching the Republican period. In addition, Gail Hershatter, Xueping Zhong, and Emily Honig chaired conference panels I organized related to the topic of this book and made valuable critiques.

This book would not have been possible without a positive workplace environment. First at Sewanee: The University of the South and then at Western Michigan University, I have been fortunate to enjoy supportive colleagues, solid funding, and self-reliant students. I thank the Department of Asian Studies at Sewanee and the Department of World Languages and Literatures at WMU for fostering my growth as a junior faculty member. I thank the Timothy Light Center for Chinese Studies at WMU for always assisting with publicizing my work in print and through conference presentations.

This book has benefited from award competitions and fellowships. The Oregon Humanities Center Graduate Research Support Fellowship at the University of Oregon funded my overseas travel for locating archival sources. The European Association for Chinese Studies accorded me a great honor in the form of the Young Scholar Award in 2018 for a piece of writing derived from earlier versions of chapters in this book. The Women's Caucus in the College of Arts and Sciences at WMU granted me the Gender Scholar Award in 2020, which provided further support for my research on Chinese women.

I thank three academic journals for their rigorous reviews and their permission for me to reuse published material in chapter 1, chapter 3, and the epilogue: *Modern Chinese Literature and Culture,* now published by Edinburgh University Press; *Nan Nü: Men, Women and Gender in China*, published by Brill; and *Chinese Literature: Essays, Articles, Reviews*, published by the University of Wisconsin–Madison. I thank the two reviewers for Cornell University Press for their detailed page-by-page comments on my manuscript and their recognition of the contribution of this book to Chinese and gender studies. I thank my editors, Alexis Siemon and Ellen Labbate of the Cornell East Asia Series (CEAS), as well as copyeditor Amanda Heller for editing my work and guiding me through every stage of the publishing process that brings this work to fruition. I thank Mia Renaud and the marketing team of Cornell University Press for helping with the promotion of the book. I thank Katherine Thompson for revising multiple rounds of the manuscript and providing constructive suggestions.

Lastly, I thank my family members in China and the United States for understanding and indulging my need for plenty of time and space to pursue my dreams. I thank my mother for being a model of a resilient woman; and my husband and my son for riding life's roller coaster with me.

FREQUENTLY CITED NEWSPAPERS AND JOURNALS

Beijing Women's News (*Beijing nübao* 北京女報)
Central Daily News (*Zhongyang ribao* 中央日報)
China Daily (*Zhongguo ribao* 中國日報)
Daily Learning (*Rizhi bao* 日知報)
Drama Daily (*Xi bao* 戲報)
Eastern Miscellany (*Dongfang zazhi* 東方雜誌)
Eastern Times (*Shi bao* 時報)
Enlightenment (*Jue wu* 覺悟)
Fiction Daily (*Xiaoshuo ribao* 小說日報)
Grand Evening News (*Da wanbao* 大晚報)
Ladies' Journal (*Funü zazhi* 婦女雜誌)
Liberation Daily (*Jiefang ribao* 解放日報)
L'Impartial (*Dagong bao* 大公報)
Masses' Strength Daily (*Qunqiang bao* 群強報)
National Herald (*Shenzhou ribao* 神州日報)
National News Weekly (*Guowen zhoubao* 國聞週報)
New People Daily (*Xin min bao* 新民報)
New Youth (*Xin qingnian* 新青年)
Patriotic News (*Aiguo bao* 愛國報)
Patriotic Vernacular News (*Aiguo baihua bao* 愛國白話報)
Peking Daily (*Beiping ribao* 北平日報)
People Daily (*Min bao* 民報)
People's Literature (*Renmin wenxue* 人民文學)
People's Stand (*Minli bao* 民立報)
Qiqi Monthly (*Qiqi yuekan* 七七月刊)
Republic Daily (*Minguo ribao* 民國日報)
Shanghai Daily (*Shen bao* 申報)
Shengjing Times (*Shengjing shibao* 盛京時報)
Shing Wah News (*Xinghua bao* 醒華報)
Shuntian Times (*Shuntian shibao* 順天時報)

The New Woman (Xin nüxing 新女性)
The News (Xinwen bao 新聞報)
The Times (Shishi xinbao 時事新報)
Torrent Flood (Benliu 奔流)
Women's Eastern Times (Funü shibao 婦女時報)
Women's Life (Funü shenghuo 婦女生活)
Women's Vernacular Daily (Nüzi baihua bao 女子白話報)
Women's Weekly News (Funü zhoubao 婦女週報)

UNTAMED SHREWS

Introduction
The Shrew–New Woman Nexus

In 1992 the pop star Madonna claimed: "I'm tough, I'm ambitious, and I know exactly what I want. If that makes me a bitch, okay." Her remark challenged male privilege and the custom of containing powerful women through demeaning epithets. It demonstrated how women themselves could intervene, turning insults into badges of honor. Almost two decades after Madonna's reshaping of "bitch," the transnational "SlutWalk" movement shed critical light on the term "slut." Protesters, both women and men, took pride in this word as a rhetorical weapon against gender shaming and regulation. In a similar vein, the writers and critics of various backgrounds examined in this book revalued the concept and label of the Chinese "shrew," using it to describe newly desirable behaviors of Chinese women in the early and mid-twentieth-century environment.

This book examines the hitherto unresearched connections and continuities between the traditional shrew and the modern new woman in China. Public interest in the long-standing trope of the shrew did not disappear with the advent of modernity in the early twentieth century. Rather, this pejorative imagery presented itself in new contexts suited to the changing social milieu and evolved as part of an emancipatory process for women. Building on a corpus of repeated yet repurposed vocabulary, imagery, and allusions, this book shows why and how the shrew archetype shook off its negative connotations and acquired value in the Republican and Communist eras.

Shrew

"Shrew" is a day-to-day denigratory term, a social reality or historical agent, and a narrative trope resulting from male writers' misogynistic anxiety. Shrew stories permeated literary and historical texts in premodern China and reached peak popularity during the seventeenth century with full-blown comedies, satires, and novels on this theme.[1] The best-known shrews in Ming–Qing literature include Pan Jinlian in *Plum in the Golden Vase* (*Jin Ping Mei* 金瓶梅), Xue Sujie in *Marriage Bonds to Awaken the World* (*Xingshi yinyuan zhuan* 醒世姻緣傳), and Wang Xifeng in *Dream of the Red Chamber* (*Honglou meng* 紅樓夢). These characters are all strong women who are textually discredited for their ambitions, desires, and cruelty. Their fierceness is represented in the texts as a foil for ideal womanly behaviors prescribed by the Confucian ethos.

Despite the shrew's prevalence in late imperial literature, there is no single Chinese term that encompasses this very common character type. She is the unnamed inversion of the *jiefu* 節婦 (the chaste and virtuous woman), and traditional texts typically pair her with a "wife-fearing" or henpecked (*junei* 懼內; *pa laopo* 怕老婆) husband, keeping the focus on her male victims. The lack of a single native term to denote related characterizations of women gone rogue does not delegitimize the use of the English concept of the shrew as an analytic term. This book follows the current scholarly paradigm in using the term "shrew" as a shorthand way to refer to this disparaging type.[2]

On the basis of premodern writings, the Chinese shrew includes three main categories: *pofu* 潑婦, the unconstrained, transgressive, and polluting woman; *yinfu* 淫婦 (or *dangfu* 蕩婦), the promiscuous woman; and *hanfu* 悍婦, the violent woman. While *pofu* can be understood especially in terms of a woman's "scattering" actions as indicated by the word *po* 潑 (to scatter, spill, or splash), it is often a broadly inclusive term used to refer to all types of shrews.[3] Compared to the Western concept of the shrew, which is mainly used for comedic effect, the Chinese shrew is more threatening and culturally repulsive. Within the logic of neo-Confucianism—a medieval offshoot of classical Confucianism highlighting "a form of moral metaphysics" that prescribed Confucian values as an instrument of social control—improper desires and behaviors open the door to disaster.[4] The Chinese shrew, with her fearless defiance of all gender norms, is the foremost threat to Confucian social structures. She is the ambitious woman who desires to displace patriarchal authority and pursue her own interests; she is the jealous woman who wishes to control the men and female rivals in the family; she is the ruthless woman who schemes to overpower her opponents and opposes polygamy even if it means the extinction of her husband's lineage; she is angry and abrasive, employing verbal and physical violence on a regular basis; she is lustful and sexually dangerous, knowingly using her attractiveness to seduce, dominate, and kill.

Scholars of Ming and Qing literature have written about "the demise of shrew literature" after its heyday in late imperial China.[5] Calling attention to the unsuitability of the negative shrew character type given the new position of women and femininity in modern China, this argument creates a divide between tradition and modernity regarding their differences in coding feminine identity. It has also been widely perceived that the construction of a modern China at the turn of the twentieth century was largely contingent upon the elimination of the shrew. For example, in a 1906 article on building vocational training centers for female criminals, its author criticized the wicked aspects of women's nature (*e'gen xing* 惡根性), including brazenness (*hanxing* 悍性), jealousy (*duxing* 妒性), indolence (*duoxing* 惰性), and promiscuity (*yinxing* 淫性).[6] In echoes of the discursive trend beginning in the 1890s with regard to the "woman question" (*funü wenti* 婦女問題), the article treats shrewish attributes as the root cause of the national decline, and thus a target for reform as well as the starting point for revolutionizing Chinese women and the state.[7]

Chinese male intellectuals and politicians have never ceased to censure women's jealousy, violence, promiscuity, and other "vices" for the sake of their advancement. Yet it cannot be denied that they also tolerated and even encouraged, in quite open terms, conventionally demonized female qualities when navigating tumultuous modern changes. For many New Cultural figures, the shrew did not require discipline, and should even be held up as an iconoclastic force against tradition. Under the chaotic status quo of Republican society, reform-minded intellectuals and Communists recognized that Confucian modes of female virtue would never allow women to break out of their prescribed roles. They instead suggested that some degree of shrewish behavior and discourse was needed for women to achieve substantial progress in social, cultural, and gender reform.

Shrewish traits were being seen in a new light in certain intellectual circles, reconfigured as symbols of the modern rebellious spirit. Even when male intellectuals formulated women's unruliness as problematic to claim their roles as enlighteners and guardians of social order, they also urgently needed that disruptive energy for strengthening their revolutionary profile. The face of femininity was changing. According to the historian Henrietta Harrison: "By influencing and changing the norms which had been used to define elite status, the new ideal of citizenship came to affect the whole definition of femininity, and thus the construction of gender. In the past the delicacy and weakness of women had been their defining characteristic. Generations of young men sighed over such weak and sickly heroines as Lin Daiyu in the *Dream of the Red Chamber*."[8]

Refined, vulnerable femininity gave way to fiery womanhood. Although Lin Daiyu might have still held strong appeal within male fantasies, critical discourses had set out to characterize her as a model of all that was wrong with traditional femininity.[9] She was never referred to as an ideal for modern femininity, nor did writers ever mention her, even with nostalgia, when denouncing the vulgarity of the new woman. As David Strand points out, "Modern-minded Chinese were coming to expect that women, like men, would be physically more active, assertive, and even vulgar in the role of citizen."[10] Reformers valued the ability of women to defy norms, even if this required the appropriation of behaviors conventionally considered uncouth for women. The modern ladies wore immodest clothing, which in the past had been deemed "a mark of low status." They "had natural feet" and made a "loud sound" when proudly walking in their high-heeled leather shoes. "Instead of sitting quietly at home, they were to be seen in schools and walking through the streets, even on occasion taking part in sports."[11] Some women made their way into male preserves and "brandished things that men tended to use, like revolvers and cigarettes."[12] The changing views on what constituted female vulgarity suggest how the modern construction of desirable femininity recuperated aspects of the shrew. While modern cultural figures claimed to invent their models of new womanhood as distinct from traditional female types, many of the constructions either were based on existing shrew figures in premodern texts or had integrated recognized qualities of this prototype.

The modern use of the term *pola* 潑辣 (sometimes written as 潑剌)—meaning feisty, pungent, and forceful—also indicates the change of attitude toward shrewish traits. In premodern texts *po* was widely used to describe a quality of unruliness. For example, the Monkey King in *Journey to the West* (*Xiyou ji* 西遊記) is referred to as a *pohou* 潑猴 (wanton monkey). *La* (literally, hot, peppery) was associated with ruthless characters. When describing female figures, it predominantly concerns shrews known for their peppery personality, pungent language, and cruel behavior. By no means were *po* and *la* sanctioned as qualities of desired femininity. In *Dream of the Red Chamber*, the shrew Wang Xifeng is immediately introduced as a *popi* 潑皮 (ruffian, villain) and *lazi* 辣子 (hot pepper, peppercorn). When Daiyu first meets her, she is taken aback by her "brash and unmannerly" introduction.[13] Xia Jingui, the shrewish wife of Xue Pan, is also described as *pola* (translated as "a spoilt shrew").[14]

In the modern context, the *pola* model of womanly behavior came to take on positive meanings. In "A Woman from the Liu Village" (*Liutun de* 柳屯的; 1934) by Lao She (1899–1966), one character refers to the disruptive shrew in the story in relatively favorable terms as a *pola* woman who is good at household management.[15] In "The Way of the Beast" (*Shou dao* 獸道; 1936), Sha Ting (1904–1992) depicted "a cursing shrew" whose tirade (*pola de zhouma* 潑辣的咒罵) is presented sympathetically as a woman's last resort to survive wartime hardships.[16] This treatment complicates female victimhood and creates a model of tough resiliency.

The quality of being *pola* was also linked with the Chinese Nora, or the leftist revolutionary woman who dares to be transgressive to empower herself. Ouyang Yuqian (1889–1962) staged a *pola* protagonist in his new woman/Nora play *The Shrew* (*Pofu* 潑婦; 1925). Lan Ping, the stage name of Jiang Qing (1914–1991)—later famous as Mao Zedong's (1893–1976) wife and the figurehead of the Gang of Four—asserted herself as a *pola* female who was unwilling to diminish herself to please men. Mao Dun (1896–1981) in "The Road" (*Lu* 路; 1932) called upon the new woman to abandon shyness and adopt *pola* so as to merge into the masses (*buyao haixiu, pola xie, zuandao qunzhong zhongjian qu* 不要害羞，潑辣些，鑽到群眾中間去).[17] These modern texts reclaim the potential of *pola* strength and identify *pola* women as being unconstrained, independent, and willing to take on leadership roles—qualities that were expected for the new woman, who had to stand up to a society that was less enlightened than she.

New Woman

At the dawn of the twentieth century, a series of national crises in China heightened social demands on Chinese women, necessitating their transformation into capable and patriotic citizens. Women's education and the women's rights movement gave rise to new roles for women. It was against this reformist backdrop that terms such as "modern woman" or "new woman" began to appear in intellectual discourse to designate a novel type of woman. The modern or new woman was not a temporal notion neatly differentiating herself from the premodern or old woman in traditional China. A woman living in modern China did not naturally qualify as new or modern. Instead, the modern woman or new woman was an intellectual and ideological concept with an emphasis on espousing social and political reform. On such instrumentalist grounds, the new woman in reformist discourses of late imperial and early Republican China centered on the revised notion of the traditional "good wife and wise mother" (*liangqi xianmu* 良妻賢母) ideal.[18] "Some commentators saw women primarily as the mothers of citizens and opined that they should be educated—preferably at home—in a modicum of modern housekeeping and child-rearing skills so that they could raise the next generation properly."[19] In society, this reformist gender conservatism faced increasing challenges from women themselves as they grew more publicly visible "as teachers and students, contributors to a women's press, revolutionaries and suffragists."[20]

The tension between discourse and reality continued in the ensuing New Culture or May Fourth era from the mid-1910s to the mid-1920s. Images and social practices of the new woman became more multifaceted and nebulous. In the leading May Fourth journal *New Youth*, women's subordinate status within the Confucian family system was attacked as emblematic of the repression of individualism in traditional society. The May Fourth new woman enjoyed independence and personal autonomy: "She was represented by educated women who strove to save the nation while seeking their own sexual and economic autonomy."[21] Career women and female writers negotiated with the May Fourth call for women's emancipation through their lived experiences and fictional or (auto)biographical explorations.[22]

It was during the May Fourth era that the term "new woman" gained currency. Hu Shi (1891–1962), a leading New Cultural liberal figure, delivered a lecture in 1918 at the Beijing Women's Normal School which was later published in *New Youth*. Hu coined the term *xin funü*

(新婦女: the new woman) to signify some American women he had met abroad.[23] He commented that "'new woman' is a new word, and it designates a new kind of woman, who is extremely intense in her speech, who tends towards the extreme in her actions, who doesn't believe in religion or adhere to rules of conduct, yet who is an extremely good thinker and has extremely high morals."[24]

Hu's conception of the new woman maps onto the stereotype of the shrew for such outstanding qualities as biting language, offensive behavior, and defiance of decency. Morality was considered a prerequisite, but it was dissociated from the Confucian moral doctrines and instead marked a woman's sensitivity to the times and the state. Progressive ideas of the day on women coincided with some long-standing charges against women's unconventional actions. The same cluster of descriptions of a vocally, physically, and spiritually threatening woman was repurposed from discrediting the shrew to lending credibility to the new woman. As Hu Shi intuited, feisty and indomitable women would be great advocates for the iconoclastic ideology of the new times.

Japanese sources also inspired the Chinese advocacy of the new woman. The term first appeared in Japan in 1910. Tsubouchi Shōyō (1859–1935), an influential modern writer and educator, gave a series of lectures that year on the theme of "The New Women in Modern Plays." Using modern plays of the West written by Henrik Ibsen (1828–1906), Hermann Sudermann (1857–1928), George Bernard Shaw (1856–1950), and others, Tsubouchi introduced the concept *atarashii onna* (the new woman) together with an alien female identity to the Japanese audience. The women characters studied in his classes "rejected the conventional roles of wife and mother in favor of self-discovery and egalitarian relationships."[25]

A year later, Tsubouchi's literary society staged Ibsen's 1879 play *A Doll's House* which made the protagonist, Nora, synonymous with the Japanese new woman and feminist. In the play, Nora is a happy and caring middle-class housewife living with her lawyer husband, Torvald Helmer, and three children. To treat Torvald's illness, she secretly borrows money by forging her father's signature. She then saves up on her own to pay the debt. Later, when the secret is exposed, her husband, contrary to Nora's expectation, treats her like a child and attacks her even though she has done everything for his benefit. Nora becomes disillusioned with her marriage. After a turbulent conversation with Torvald, she leaves the house with the iconic gesture of slamming the door. Those associated with the *Seitō* (Bluestocking) society considered themselves "Japanese Noras," while the Japanese press used terms such as "Japanese Nora" and "new woman" only to denigrate these independent women.[26] The case of Lan Ping, discussed in chapter 3 of this book, in which the Chinese press and the awakened woman took contrasting approaches toward the Nora label, resembles this clash in modern Japan.

Beyond external influences, few studies have traced the effects that earlier Chinese female types had on the composition of the new woman.[27] Little scholarship exists on the inspiration drawn from traditionally negative models.[28] This book is the first to provide a historically contextualized analysis of the shrew–new woman nexus. It argues against the fall of the shrew and refuses to treat the new woman as a stagnant and fixed category dating from and hence belonging only to the early twentieth century. Rather, the new woman had an impact on a much broader period of history. She was not only repeatedly revisited in later decades as a major New Cultural legacy but also came to denote revolutionary Chinese femininity at different points of ideological fluctuation.

This book draws material from literary texts, the press, theater, political documents, and film. Only an inclusive framework could do justice to the spirited, sweeping, and sustained discussion of the new woman held throughout the first half of China's twentieth century. The book claims that the many guises of the new woman, from the early Republican suffragettes to the Communist and socialist radicals, are female images grafted onto the violent, sexualized, and transgressive models of the traditional shrew. The chapters are accordingly arranged by types of new woman/shrew images and their associated qualities, rather than by a rigid chronology.

Chapter 1 sets the stage for the confluence of the two female images in the early Republican era by presenting the prevalence of the shrew trope in depicting the radical suffragettes in the mainstream male-dominated media. Chapter 2 and chapter 3 center, respectively, on female jealousy and promiscuity, the two principal sins of the shrew, to map out twists and turns in her fate once she became connected with the May Fourth new woman, the Chinese Nora. Chapter 4 and chapter 5 take on the classic character type of the shrewish wife and analyze her repurposed presence in modern popular writings and revolutionary renditions. The epilogue continues the exploration of the tacit collaboration between politics of the party-state and the shrew. In interpreting gender-based reform of the Great Leap Forward through the lens of *pola* womanhood, this concluding section of the book poses questions about the shrew's legacy, the use of female unruliness, and the status of Chinese-style feminism.

Authorship

By focusing on male voices, this book, rather than being "male-centered," presents how the shrew, as a male-authored trope, underwent shifts in meaning and orientation in the modern era while still at the hands of male authors. It therefore works more on literary and discursive constructions than on the treatment of the shrew as a social reality. One might argue that in real-life Chinese society there have indeed been many shrews; however, even if many women may seem shrewish at various moments in day-to-day situations, the term "shrew" that is attached to them is essentially a patriarchal creation. Except for a few incidents, this book does not engage with women's voices on this subject. Women would likely approach this term differently or would forgo the term altogether in their discourse. They may affirmatively reject the textual tradition of writing or wronging the shrew. Their perspectives may also appear veiled, mediated, or ambivalent. Hence, we can only guess at the heterogeneity of female voices on the Chinese shrew.

In sticking to the male literary convention, this book displays a spectrum of male voices: some are feminist while some are misogynistic; some are assertive, and some are more skeptical and uncertain. Just as these voices vacillated on whether to be sympathetic or disparaging toward shrews or new women, I often find myself struggling to understand the textual ambiguity of the men's works. But as it stands, it is precisely this ambiguity that rendered the shrew image so polysemic and fruitful in modern China. No matter whether the male critics hated her, feared her, or loved her, they needed her. The shrew was useful in advancing revolution, new culture, and ideology, and she was versatile, satisfying miscellaneous needs of different social actors. The media's habit of piling on her and the authors' lingering interest in her demonstrate that this old trope achieved continued yet renewed, and even augmented, strength in its new environment.

Rather than meeting her demise, the shrew morphed into a symbol of empowerment in many representations of the new woman. This connection makes one wonder: To what extent does the old and negative category have to renew or purge itself before becoming usable, useful, and desirable? According to common assumptions, for models of problematic women to be integrated into a righteous purpose or simply to fit into the new, they normally must undergo reshaping. In the various cases this book examines, however, shrews remained intact when they were recruited into modern progressive or revolutionary causes. While there existed reservations and reproaches surrounding the women's manners, modern shrews were *not* reeducated, reformed, or removed by men, patriarchy, the state, or supernatural forces.

Unsurprisingly, given their tenacity, shrews have prevailed and will continue to do so in men's constructions. The motif of the taming of the shrew exists exactly because she *cannot* be tamed. Her persistence compels men to continue thinking and writing about her. In other words, the shrew seems to have written herself, through man, by dominating his pen/penis/phallus and phantasy. The shrew's story, in this light, is less a *history* of male manipulation than a sustained *herstory* against temporal and textual tides of men's writing of challenging women. Readers of this book will still see shaming, but the power of the Chinese shrew certainly shines through the murky discourse on virtue, femininity, propriety, and progress.

CHAPTER 1

The Shrew Is Back

*Media Representations of the Early
Radical Chinese Suffragettes*

On April 21, 1907, the *Beijing Women's News* published a short piece in the column "Beijing Local News" about a fight between an elderly scribe, Mr. Chen, and his wife. Under the title "The Expansion of Women's Rights" (*Nüquan pengzhang* 女權膨脹), the story playfully depicts the fierceness of the wife, who knocks her husband to the ground, rides on him, and dramatically cries, shouts, hits, and curses. Amazed by the spectacle of female strength, the reporter gasped, "What an impressive, strong wife!" and commented that news of the incident had widely spread, turning Mr. Chen into a laughingstock.[1]

To a reader in late imperial and early twentieth-century China, this story would have seemed familiar. The pervasive shrew stories in Ming and Qing literature included similar ferocious women and their henpecked husbands, aiming to proclaim to the public what behaviors and gender relations were inappropriate and thus deserved derision and condemnation. This 1907 piece, however, in addition to provoking laughter, also poses challenges regarding how to redefine the shrew and reinterpret shrew stories as China engaged with modernity.

First, Mr. Chen's story points to the persistence of shrew literature. It does so by inheriting readily recognizable patterns of the shrewish wife and the henpecked husband and employing stock phrases such as "rolling on the ground and throwing tantrums" (*dagun sapo* 打滾撒潑) to describe the wife. More importantly, published five years before the establishment of the Republic of China in 1912, the story indicates the direction that shrew literature would take in its engagement with the new era. Shrew stories, previously concerning domestic strife and husband-wife hierarchy, now began to be used in public discussions of the rising status of Chinese women because of the women's rights movement. Through a seemingly trivial incident of marital conflict reported in the news section, the newspaper suggested the shifting meaning of the shrew in early twentieth-century popular perception.

Second, the way this piece of news was presented altered readers' expectations of a typical shrew plot. Linking women's rights with a wife's shrewishness, the story illustrates progressive concepts in mundane images in order that the old theme of the shrew can be revitalized into a metaphor for women's new situation. A reader who had known premodern shrew stories would have had to adapt himself or herself to the novel and weightier meanings that traditionally negative female archetypes came to carry in a modern context. Instead of continuing to read these stories merely as comical or cautionary tales, readers had to come to understand the association between the shrew and the concept of the new woman in public discourse and imagination.

This anecdote, though tiny, inverts norms with respect to class, gender, space, and power. In conventional shrew stories, violent scenes relevant to figures of the elite class were largely confined within domestic bounds. Yet in this news item an elite couple surprises the audience by openly causing a ruckus on the street.[2] The scribe's wife, a woman of the educated class who resides in China's capital city, has defied the prescribed boundaries of wifehood: stepping out of the inner space, she publicly disobeys and disciplines her husband; she shows that women of gentry families can behave badly too, using physical force before the public eye; she rejects the notion of women as victims of conjugal violence, reshaping female insubordination in ways that go beyond the constraints of the domestic sphere.

Even though the content of this news story would have been provocative at the time of publication, it is risky to equate it with the standpoint of the newspaper. Launched in 1905 by Zhang Zhanyun (dates unknown) and his mother, the *Beijing Women's News* was the earliest and most important women's newspaper in the Beijing area at the turn of the century.[3] Within its approximately four years in print (1905–1909), the newspaper published over 1,200 issues and was read widely across

regions and classes. Unlike most of its contemporary print competition, especially the tabloids, which took a superficial, whimsical approach to fashionable ideas, the *Beijing Women's News* was committed to
women's topics. It advocated for women's rights and education while
also introducing new modes of civilized life to Chinese women.

Despite its devotion to progressive themes, the newspaper nonetheless had a limited view of women's liberation. Likely because of the staid
middle-class background of the editors and the less liberal climate in
Beijing compared to that of the coastal cities, the voice of the *Beijing
Women's News* was often ambivalent or self-contradictory. While urg-
ing women to pursue new education, it also reiterated the value of traditionally defined roles for women as virtuous mothers and wives. It
juxtaposed articles advocating women's independence with ones emphasizing women's deep-seated obligations to the family (and, accordingly,
to the nation). In one article women are celebrated for shouting abuse
against Confucian suppression and daring to "smash ancestral memo-
rial tablets."[4] In another note published immediately after, such fierce
women are denounced for exerting excessive power. Given the mixed
views expressed in the newspaper, it makes more sense to simply recognize the frequency with which shrew imagery was adopted to discuss
women's changing condition. The newspaper used the trope flexibly
and strategically, with both positive and negative connotations. This approach accommodated an audience of varied social backgrounds; while
making iconoclastic overtures to the paper's more progressive readers, it
appeased conservatives with its lingering judgments on unruly women.

The case of the *Beijing Women's News* provides a snapshot of changing perceptions of the shrew in modern China. There were incidents
that employed the trope as the ultimate demeaning device for portraying women. There were also emerging ideas that turned shrews and
their outrageous stories into a fountainhead of inspiring narratives
about women's self-empowerment. Although some writers and readers
treated the revival of shrew stories as a literary gimmick for fulfilling
the pleasure-seeking appetite of the masses in transition, some discovered revolutionary elements aligning the shrew with a strong modern
female subjectivity. No matter how varied these uses were, the writings
almost unanimously approach the shrew as an independent disruptive
force, one who was no longer only a reflection of the failures of her
husband or an emblem of "the breakdown of the sociopolitical order
within orthodox discourse."[5] She came to intimidate society in an increasingly direct manner.

This chapter analyzes early twentieth-century public discourses surrounding the early Chinese suffragettes, who emerged shortly after the establishment of the new Republic. This group of women updates the definition of the public woman on temporal, spatial, social, and political dimensions. Mostly educated and trained in Japan, these women had shed blood on the battlefield against the Qing regime.[6] After the accomplishment of the revolution, they transferred their energies from the military to the political realm, asking for equal rights to vote. They even resorted to force, which provoked social controversy. The public reacted to the suffragettes (particularly the radicals) in a way that merged with the discursive trend foreshadowed by "The Expansion of Women's Rights" in 1907. The evolution of the shrew category was entangled with the new image of women who boldly presented themselves in the streets and later in the parliament. The shrew trope flooded the media, allowing the press to capture the shock that these women gave the public through their transgressive advances. Yet it was also through the once disparaged imagery that a feminist negotiation with gender stereotypes and social equality was made possible for some reform-minded men and women.

A Different Public Woman

Prostitutes had made themselves "public" long before other female types, while scholarship normally considers female students the first group of public women in modern China. As a social category born out of the demands of nationalism, female students were closely linked with public space and China's cultural and ideological transitions.[7] Their active presence in the urban landscape aroused both hope and anxiety among social critics. When responding to new opportunities in the public sphere, female students often acted in their own ways without regard for rules or advice from (male) officials and intellectuals.[8] They amazed the public when they autonomously organized women's military activism during the Republican revolution and insisted on joining the army to fight on the front line. Those who had studied in Japan were especially prominent because of their more militant profile. They brought military tactics they had studied in Japan back to China as techniques for use on the battlefield and later on the political stage.

The female militants received public acclaim for their contribution to the Republican revolution and were categorized as present-day embodiments of traditional female warriors such as Qin Liangyu

(1574–1648) and Hua Mulan.[9] Once the new regime was established, these women were immediately attacked for harboring desires beyond serving the nation. As Louise Edwards points out, in the understanding of the Chinese audience, women's public participation in warfare should illustrate "the long-standing conceptions of women warriors in China's past—extraordinary women achieving extraordinary goals during times of national crisis who return to the domestic sphere when order is restored."[10] To everyone's surprise, these women refused to return to their domestic roles as daughters and wives after the revolution; they instead demanded full citizenship and equal rights with men to reinforce their public presence. Their endeavor marked the first step toward women's suffrage.

The women's suffrage movement in China underwent waves of failure and revival.[11] The militants-turned-suffragettes belonged to the short but intense first wave spanning the closing months of 1911 to late 1912 or early 1913. This wave witnessed the forceful public debut of the early Chinese suffragettes (who were variously referred to as *nüzi canzheng yuan* 女子參政員, *nüzi canzheng hui* 女子參政會, *nüzi canzheng tongmeng hui* 女子參政同盟會, *nüzi canzheng tongmeng* 女子參政同盟, *nüzi canzheng tuan* 女子參政團, and *nüzi canzheng tongzhi hui* 女子參政同志會). They began by expressing their outrage at the constitutional exclusion of women as equal citizens in 1911. After constant protests over the course of a year, they lost momentum in late 1912 under the anti-democratic government of Yuan Shikai (1859–1916). The second wave of the Chinese women's suffrage movement coincided with the decade of the New Culture movement.[12]

The radical suffragettes were the main reason behind the intensity of the initial wave. These women had an explicit political agenda and did not shy away from aggression. Unlike moderate suffragettes, who thought women should improve themselves at home before entering the public arena, the radicals adopted a revolutionary approach and advocated for the immediate exercise of women's citizenship in public spaces. They resorted to violent measures when offended by male politicians' indifference, hostility, or betrayal; they stormed the parliament, cursed and slapped male politicians, kicked policemen, smashed windows, and ransacked newspaper offices.[13] Though the idea of violent pursuit of the female franchise was introduced in the earliest years of the twentieth century, it was not until the emergence of the radical suffragettes in the 1910s that the vision turned into a tangible reality.[14]

In October 1911, Song Jiaoren (1882–1913), the leader of the Revolutionary Alliance and later the principal spokesman of the Nationalist Party, wrote the first version of the Republican constitution, the so-called Ezhou constitution (*Ezhou yuefa* 鄂州約法). It states that all people are equal without specifying whether the term "people" includes both sexes. The ambiguity remained in the draft of the provisional constitution. When the senate promulgated the constitution on March 11, 1912, in article 5, Song's original statement was expanded to claim that all people are equal, regardless of race, class, or religion. References to sex are excluded. Three prominent suffragettes, Zhang Hanying (1872–1915), Tang Qunying (1871–1937), and Wang Changguo (1880–1949), submitted a petition to the parliament declaring the urgency of recognizing women's political rights. By this time the three women had transformed the Women's Northern Expedition Team (*Nüzi beifa dui* 女子北伐隊) into the Shenzhou Women's Suffrage Alliance (*Shenzhou nüjie canzheng tongmeng hui* 神州女界參政同盟會), which provided the organizational basis for articulating women's interests. Their request was rejected. The members of the alliance then sent another letter to President Sun Yat-sen (1866–1925) and the parliament, asking to add the phrase "regardless of sex" to article 5. The parliament decided to discuss the petition in its chambers on March 19, at which time "Tang and about a dozen other women requested permission to enter the parliament to speak on behalf of their proposal. They received a flat denial in response."[15]

The suffragettes expressed their anger through acts of aggression. On March 19, Tang Qunying, carrying her pistol, led over twenty women into the chambers, where they seated themselves among the parliamentarians. During the debate, when their proposal was jeered and guffawed at by conservative male delegates, the women protested with "harsh language" (*e'yu dichu* 惡語抵觸) and "unrestrained roars" (*dasi paoxiao/xiaoma* 大肆咆哮/哮罵, *paoxiao kangji* 咆哮抗激, *paoxiao fenxun* 咆哮奮迅, *paoxiao zhenglun* 咆哮爭論).[16] In subsequent days, the authorities were reluctant to take steps; the women's aggressive actions escalated. On March 20 and 30, the suffragettes stormed the parliament again, shouting and cursing, pushing and kicking policemen. Their hands bled from smashing windows (*shou jie yixue* 手皆溢血).[17] In April, Yuan Shikai replaced Sun Yat-sen as the president of the Republic and moved the government to Beijing. The suffragettes continued to lobby the National Congress in Beijing for women's voting rights. In August they twice physically attacked Song Jiaoren during public meetings. From late 1912 the campaign rapidly diminished under Yuan's rule. The last boisterous protest was reported to have occurred on December 11, 1912.[18]

This first wave of the women's suffrage movement did not achieve its political goals but was not a simple failure. The suffragettes presented a new category of the public woman that shook the norms of gender and politics altogether. As pictured by David Strand, "A young woman with bobbed hair scolding a middle-aged male politician standing in the way of her winning political rights conjured up a new brand of politics."[19] Strand here refers to politics on its own terms, yet the scenario certainly articulates a change in gender politics. While the news piece in the *Beijing Women's News* mocks the rise of female power through a shrew story, the early radical suffragettes were literally acting out the popular vision of shrews in public. They took shrewish violence that was originally directed at ineffectual husbands out on disappointing male politicians. Their tongues and palms were used to scold and slap the men who stood against their rights and the professed democratic spirit of the Republic. Shrewish qualities assisted the women in carving out a foothold within the Republican system. The unstable political environment at the start of the new regime further enabled them to upset the gendered temporal and spatial order and to force their way into the public realm.[20]

Gender and politics intertwined at a deeper level after this early feminist movement. "Women's suffrage in China in the 1910s shaped the national politics and the meaning of democracy in China by injecting gender into early republican politics," and through the efforts of the suffragettes, gender became "a founding category in modern politics."[21] The injection of gender into politics, rather than meaning that women appeared in the political sphere, marked women's increased consciousness of their identities as females and citizens, as well as their increased understanding of the reciprocal nature of these identities. Women came to shape terms, missions, and boundaries with growing autonomy in determining whether and how to relate to social prescriptions. Their challenges to gender and social order caused a stir in the press. Criticism centered less on the women's political claims than on the threats they posed to normative gender practices and relations. For example, they "ignored the order and rushed into the parliamentary chambers" (*buting jing ru yishiting* 不聽竟入議事廳); they "seated themselves among the delegates" (*yu zhu yiyuan zazuo* 與諸議員雜坐) and "firmly pulled on the sleeves and jackets of the assemblymen" (*jing jian zhi yiyuan yimei*

竟堅執議員衣袂).²² *Zazuo* (men and women sitting next to each other) and *zhi yimei* (pulling sleeves and jackets) invoke principles of the pre-modern "Domestic Regulations" (*Nei ze* 內則) in the *Book of Rites* (*Li ji* 禮記), which regulate a strict separation between men and women: "Male and female should not sit together, nor have the same stand for clothes, nor use the same towel or comb, nor let their hands touch in giving and receiving."²³

The most vehement responses were leveled at the women's breaking of the separation between the inner (*nei* 內) and outer (*wai* 外) spheres. *Nei-wai* and *yin-yang* are the two traditional Chinese polarities that define gender difference and ethics through the language of spatial order and cosmological schema. The two notions justify "the social and political submission of women to men, the exclusion of women from a direct role in public life, and the assertion that women were intellectually and morally inferior to men."²⁴ *Nei-wai* restricts women to the inner quarters of the house and prescribes the essential distinction between the sexes and the division of labor. As a result of these codes, women were associated with domestic duties including raising children and taking care of household chores, and were accordingly linked with such traits as quietness, placidity, and obedience.

In the traditional conception, the shrew acts in sheer defiance of the *nei-wai* principle. She is loud and short-tempered rather than quiet and peaceful. She upsets the domestic order by abusing her husband, servants, in-laws, and her husband's concubines and offspring with other women. She steps into the *wai* at her will. Her improprieties and willingness to expose her body in public always bring severe humiliation to herself and her family. Much like the traditional shrew, the early Republican suffragettes ventured into the public realm without concern for their vulgar speech, conduct, and intermingling with men. In the press, the ready-made image of the shrew helped social critics find the language for describing these new women. In addition to noting their frequent curses and roars, press reports also employ more explicit terms including "barbarian deeds, shrewish and violent behaviors" (*yeman shouduan, pohan xingwei* 野蠻手段，潑悍行為), "unreasonably troublesome" (*wuli qu'nao* 無理取鬧), "willfully disturbing" (*renyi raoluan* 任意擾亂), and "fierce edge" (*xiongfeng* 兇鋒) to paint the suffragettes.²⁵ When referring to the English suffragettes, the press even used the epithets "bitches and shrews" (*jiannü pofu* 賤女潑婦).²⁶

These terms most prominently invoked the type of the *pofu*, now depicted as shattering windows, spilling blood, and scattering female effluvia. Figure 1 is an example of how the imagery of the leaking female body was used in the press to visualize the *pofu* and her transgression of the *nei-wai* order. On November 9, 1912, the *China Daily* in Hong Kong published an editorial cartoon captioned "Obstacles to Women's Suffrage" (*Nüzi canzheng zhi zhang'ai* 女子參政之障礙). In the cartoon, a bobbed-haired woman is giving a speech at the podium while breast-feeding her baby. She uses one arm to hold the baby and lifts the other arm in the air as if she is speaking with passion. With both arms busy at the same time, she fails to properly cover her chest. Her blouse is wide open, exposing her breasts to the male audience sitting right below the podium (fig. 1). The audience, interestingly, seems to be intentionally avoiding looking at the speaker. Either lowering their heads to look at the table or ground, or hiding underneath their hats, the members of the audience all avert their eyes from the woman.

FIGURE 1. "Nüzi canzheng zhi zhang'ai" 女子參政之障礙 (Obstacles to women's suffrage), *China Daily*, November 9, 1912.
Source: David Strand, *An Unfinished Republic: Leading by Word and Deed in Modern China* (Berkeley: University of California Press, 2011).

The cartoon exhibits the mingling of spheres and categories: the personal and the political, the private and the public, the *nei* and the *wai*, the *yin* and the *yang*, and the feminine and the masculine. A woman appears in the political realm, a long-defined masculine space; she is even nursing, a behavior that is strictly prescribed for the domestic sphere. While the audience of random men feels shame and shuns her, the woman dares to continue breastfeeding. By using the word *zhang'ai* (obstacle), the illustrator conveyed a pessimistic, if not entirely disapproving, message on women's participation in politics. Although the original Chinese word does not specify whether it is in singular or plural form, I translate it as "obstacles" as the cartoon points to multiple potential issues that obstruct women's public and political engagement.

The first issue is the female biological role as mother, which involves giving birth and producing milk. The unnatural presence of the baby at the political podium is jarring to the fictional viewers on-site as well as viewers of the cartoon. It suggests that women's bodily functions (such as the cumbersome breastfeeding routine) preclude them from public activity. Recent twenty-first-century cases have continued to expose the challenges of balancing female biological imperatives with public life.[27] Second, by flagging motherhood and motherly duties, the cartoon expresses a bleak outlook on women breaking down the *nei-wai* division. Spatially and culturally coded as those who stay at home (as reflected by the term for wife, *neiren* 內人, which literally means "the person inside the house"), traditional Chinese women lacked public identities. By playing with an imagined hybrid position, the cartoon laments the future of aspiring Chinese new women: to bring a person of the *nei* out into the *wai* and into the political arena would only seem awkward; to blend the personal into the political would shame women and jeopardize social order. The disgrace, felt by the male audience but unfelt by the woman in the cartoon, speaks to the social hostility and discrimination that act as additional obstacles facing women's venture into politics.

Third, the cartoon's disciplinary message deploys the trope of pollution in association with female bodily discharges, that is, the exposed female chest and the leaking breast milk. Women's effluvia were traditionally linked with sinister omens or catastrophic power. This is especially true for the *pofu* shrew, whose discharges are as unconstrained as her unruly temper. The image of the shouting and nursing suffragette in the cartoon evokes some classic Ming–Qing shrew narratives. In the late Ming/early Qing novel *Marriage Bonds to Awaken the World*, there is a scene in chapter 68 when Xue Sujie, the epitome of the traditional shrew, joins a group of women for a public pilgrimage.[28] The scene depicts the disturbing spectacle of the group of unconstrained women acting wantonly in public. As Maram Epstein analyzes: "The description of the crowd of women preparing to set out on the pilgrimage to Taishan is an offensive scene of pollution: women are running back and forth 'like a pack of dogs,' cursing, defecating, menstruating, nursing babies, and yelling orders back and forth. . . . [T]he unruly, leaking female bodies in this scene are naturalized and foregrounded as emblems of social transgression."[29]

Likewise, the *China Daily* alerted its readers to women's increasing autonomy through imagining the pollution that female bodily functions could bring to the public space. It was made evident that allowing women into the political realm would be not only absurd but also disgusting. To mingle *nei*-associated activities with the *wai* would introduce a threat to the domestic order and a source of contamination to the public. This regulatory rhetoric—polluting, problematizing, and policing femininity—finds fuller elaboration in the following section involving popular indulgence in multifarious forms of female transgression. The sources provide more diverse views on the public reaction to the linkage between suffragettes and the shrew. Far more than a random point of reference, the shrew served as a cultural-discursive repertoire for the public to draw on as they negotiated the challenges of feminist radicalism.

The Shrew in the Mainstream Male-Dominated Media

By likening the suffragettes to the violent *hanfu*, the licentious *yinfu*, and the unconstrained, refuse-spreading *pofu*, the public directed criticisms at the loss of female gentleness, sexual morality, and the ordering of space. Unlike editorials and social commentaries, the sort of fictional and imaginary representations of such linkage meant to impress and entertain readers. Given the different foci of the materials in terms of which shrewish qualities they highlight, and for the sake of analysis, I categorize sources from the male-dominated media based on three main types of depictions—the violent shrew, the obscene shrew, and the unconstrained shrew—although there is of course overlap among types. These texts usually feature less common aspects of events and characters that editorials and debate essays fail to present.

The Violent Shrew

Violence was the most direct threat the public had to deal with from the suffragettes. Female violence at the time was rooted in both reality and imagination. A cartoon published in the *Shanghai Daily* in 1912 is a representation of an actual incident when suffragettes kicked policemen in Nanjing as well as a way of fantasizing the growing feminine violence to the point of horror. With the woman's image looming so large and her big foot in Western-style high heels jabbing the body of a small man (fig. 2), the cartoon visualizes the suffragette as an intimidating, monstrous being with Chinese and Western, feminine and masculine characteristics.[30]

One article titled "Nothing Too Strange" repeats the word "strange" (*qi* 奇) to figure female violence as a bizarre spectacle for public entertainment.[31] Another one copies lines from Li Bai (701–762), the famous Tang poet, to mock the physical strength of the suffragettes in Nanjing: "One fist knocked down the Huanghe Building / One foot kicked over

FIGURE 2. A Chinese suffragette kicking a policeman during a protest in Nanjing in 1912. The caption reads: "If a woman can kick a policeman, this woman must be extraordinarily valorous. I think so and therefore I draw this picture to show it.—[Wang] Dungen." *Shanghai Daily*, March 30, 1912. Wang Dungen (1888–1951) was a leading calligrapher, satirist, journalist, and publisher in Republican Shanghai.

Parrot Island" (*yiquan daping Huanghe lou yijiao tifan Yingwu zhou* 一拳打平黃鶴樓一腳踢翻鸚鵡洲).[32] Even in articles seemingly irrelevant to the suffragettes but published around the same time, women's ruthlessness was still a focus. Zhou Shoujuan (1895–1968), a well-known writer of the Mandarin Ducks and Butterflies school (*yuanyang hudie pai* 鴛鴦蝴蝶派, a genre of popular fiction that included love stories—as suggested by the romantic imagery of paired mandarin ducks and butterflies—but also stories about crime, historical adventures, social intrigue, and more), presented a translation of a Western source in the *Women's Eastern Times* in 1912. The essay lists the raw materials in nature that come together to make a woman, among which are "the brutality of the tiger" (*hu zhi canren* 虎之殘忍) and "the quick tongue of the parrot" (*yingwu zhi diaoshe* 鸚鵡之掉舌).[33] This publication suggests the authorial or editorial acknowledgment of the interest in female violence and, accordingly, the journal's timely attunement to it.

The suffragettes' violence reached its apex in two incidents in 1912. Tang Qunying publicly slapped Song Jiaoren for his failure to support the women's suffrage campaign in a speech he gave on August 25. Another suffragette, Shen Peizhen (dates unknown), thrashed soldier Xiong Zaiyang on the back on October 5 because he had spread the rumor that he and Shen were a couple after they had coincidentally stayed at the same inn.[34] Shocked by the two women's use of force, the public coined the term "Tang's palm and Shen's whip" (*Tang zhang Shen bian* 唐掌沈鞭) to refer to their female power (*ci feng* 雌風).[35] What triggered public shock was not simply the reality of female violence but that it was women of the educated classes who were using physical force in a flagrant manner against men of eminent social standing. Recalling the awe provoked by the 1907 news piece analyzed at the beginning of this chapter, the uneasiness felt by the public resulted from the unsettling fact that elites could riot too, and that gentry women could act like vulgar shrews.

The two incidents became fodder for satire in the press. Using characters from the renowned eighteenth-century novel *Dream of the Red Chamber*, caricatures rework the gender power relationships of the figures involved. Someone commented in the *Shanghai Daily* that "Xiong is more pitiful than the character Jia Rui in *Dream of the Red Chamber*; Huang [Huang Zhenxiang] is more adorable than Jia Rong in the Ningguo House."[36] Huang Zhenxiang was the head of the Bureau of Shipbuilding, known for his heroic character. When Shen Peizhen brought Xiong Zaiyang's case to his notice, he quickly arrested Xiong, interrogated him in front of Shen, and insisted on sending him to a military tribunal to be shot. While the narrative is spiced up to enhance the appeal of the publication, its reference to Shen's attraction to and collaboration with men reflects a trend in stressing the women's lethal power, which can be further observed through the authorial perspective on the relationships between Shen, Xiong, and Huang.

If the author considered Xiong pitiful and Huang adorable, he must have been assuming the perspective of Wang Xifeng, the foremost shrew in *Dream of the Red Chamber*. In desiring Shen Peizhen, Xiong "hankered for the taste of swan" (*yu chi tian'e rou* 欲吃天鵝肉).[37] Jia Rui desires the higher-class Xifeng, which in the novel is described similarly as "a case of 'the toad on the ground wanting to eat the goose in the sky'" (*lai-hama xiang tian'e rou chi* 癩蛤蟆想天鵝肉吃).[38] With the help of Jia Rong, Wang Xifeng sets up Jia Rui and lures him in; he eventually masturbates to death out of an uncontrollable lust for her. The Jia Rui chapter in *Dream of the Red Chamber* (chapter 12, a key *yin* chapter according to the gendered *yin-yang* numerological punning) is a concentrated representation of the violence, pollution, and defiance of Wang Xifeng.[39] Xifeng herself is depicted throughout the novel as having excessive bodily fluids, particularly blood. She suffers "chronic hemorrhaging with an uncontrolled loss of menstrual blood" after miscarriage of a male fetus and has other frequent incidents of "vomiting up quantities of bright red blood."[40] These details add corporeal dimensions to her shrew identity. By this analogy, the article in the *Shanghai Daily* aligns Shen Peizhen with the shrew of traditional literature and indicates that Shen might also have hoodwinked Xiong with her accomplice or unlawful lover.[41] The critic Wang Dungen commented that Shen exceeded the classic shrews including Wang Xifeng (*Shen nüshi fei Wang Xifeng kebi* 沈女士非王熙鳳可比).[42] Whether or not Wang is comparable to Shen, the stock imagery was a convenient model for modern observers to use in interpreting the suffragettes.

Published in the *Eastern Times* four days after Tang Qunying's attack on Song Jiaoren, one text titled the incident "The New Dream of the Red Chamber" (*Xin Honglou meng* 新紅樓夢). It endorses Tang's slapping by drawing an analogy to the smack that Tanchun plants on the face of Wang Shanbao's wife in *Dream of the Red Chamber*:

A newspaper reported that Tang Qunying struck Song Jiaoren. She slapped Song's face wildly, making a loud, sharp sound that shook the roof tiles. One can't help but recall the smack

Tanchun gives to Wang Shanbao's wife in *Honglou meng*. That smack is also loud and clear. After being struck, Wang Shanbao's wife says: "This is the first time I got hit. Tomorrow I will go back to my home." I know this is also Mr. Song's first time being hit. I already heard him saying things like going back home when he resigned as minister of agriculture and forestry. Some said, "This smack might have beaten away many stars of misfortune surrounding Song and he can be expected to become the president in the future."[43]

By equating Song with an old and unctuous female servant in a traditional family, the text inverts the moral structure of this incident, making Song the guilty party deserving of discipline. Tanchun, born to a concubine of the Jia patriarch, is both inside and outside the central Jia line in *Dream of the Red Chamber*. She is often wronged but keeps her dignity and her authority to criticize others. Tang Qunying resembles Tanchun, for she and her suffragist sisters were both included in and excluded from Republican definitions of modern citizenship. She was akin to the daughter of a concubine who could never feel at ease with her relationship to the father/fatherland. Tang's status as a source of trouble and embarrassment was evidenced in her relationships with male politicians including Song Jiaoren, Sun Yat-sen, and Yuan Shikai. She presented herself as a defiant daughter who might have "accepted Sun Yat-sen's authority as leader but not necessarily as patriarch."[44]

The act of slapping exemplifies the unruliness and volatility in both women. Tanchun slaps Wang Shanbao's wife when the servant steps out of line in daring to touch her during a household search for proof of an illicit affair. In a frenzy of rage, Tanchun gives her a resounding smack on the face and shouts: "Who do you think you are? How dare you touch me?"[45] The slap is meant to reposition the old woman, who has gotten carried away, back in her proper position as a servant. Tang Qunying's blow was also aimed at disciplining a servant who went astray. Song Jiaoren, as a government official, was a public servant people looked to for help. Tang and her team had been depending on his support in their campaign until he failed to speak up for them against constitutional inequality when the Revolutionary Alliance became the ruling Nationalist Party.[46] Tang viewed the removal of the principle of sex equality from the party constitution as a clear act of contempt for women and an indication of the loss of the spirit of the Revolutionary Alliance.[47]

Song was unable to respond to either Tang's words or her blows. He appeared to take on the role of a traditional lowly female, intimidated, subjugated, and disciplined. In contrast, the suffragettes on the scene were aggressive and dominant. By inverting gender roles and reversing gender hierarchy, this playful allusion to *Dream of the Red Chamber* humiliates Song and hails Tang's attack as righteous. Even if men still wavered over whether or how they were to evaluate the new woman, previously negative types were making a comeback and exerting a rather different role in public discourse. The unconventional conduct of the suffragettes pushed the public to adjust its understanding of femininity. Some even went so far as to anticipate the appearance of certain unseemly female qualities with the rise of the new woman.

Adding to the changing view on female vulgarity, the metaphor of the "tiger with rouge" (*yanzhi hu* 胭脂虎) also acquired new connotations. The term first appeared in the Song dynasty *Records of the Unworldly and the Strange* (*Qingyi lu* 清異錄) to describe a minister's wife who is politically minded and eager to participate in the business of her husband. In the Qing dynasty, the term became common in shrew stories.[48] "Tiger with rouge" captures the nature of Chinese shrews, who are usually depicted as beautiful but cruel. In amusing articles that compare Tang Qunying to a tiger with rouge, the writers invoked this analogy to portray her as a combination of beauty and beast. In "Straight Heart, Fast Mouth," a regular column in the *Shanghai Daily* featuring sardonic or comic essays, someone with the pen name Hu Chi (literally, "tiger loony") used this device to comment on Tang's attack on Song. "[The slapping] was like a performance of the tiger with rouge that was so wonderfully acted. . . . Because the palms on the cheeks of the Nationalist Party governor Song Jiaoren belong to a young lady, the slapping must be dexterous in skill and clear in sound. I was itching to rush to Beijing to shout 'Bravo!'"[49] At the time Tang was forty-one, no longer a "young lady" (*shaonian nüshi* 少年女士). Such fantasies captivated the wide male readership of the newspaper.

On the same day, the paper published another comic short story titled "The Cheeks of the Hero" (*Yingxiong jia* 英雄頰), written by Wang Dungen. It seems to adopt the long-standing "hero and beauty" narrative exemplified by the story of the warrior hero Xiang Yu (232–202 BCE) and his concubine Beauty Yu. Traditionally the hero and beauty stories celebrate the ideal combination of valorous masculinity and docile femininity. In order to make Tang Qunying the beauty and Song

Jiaoren the hero, the story depicts Tang as young (*shao nüzi* 少女子), petite, and delicate (*jiaoxiao qingying* 嬌小輕盈). The depiction blatantly alters the fact that Tang is eleven years older than Song; and she is "short and plump" (*duan er weipang* 短而微胖), and not agile at all because of her bound feet.[50] These changes helped lure readers into expecting a typical hero and beauty story and to continue reading. "Striking the cheeks of the hero with the hands of the beauty, the two things are equal in high value. Of this kind of rare encounter in the world, what else can surpass it?!"[51]

Yet the story soon exhibits ambiguity regarding Tang's violence, an apparent departure from the model of the beauty. The text dramatizes the slapping scene: Tang "slapped once, twice, six times, numerous times," leaving the audience "in astonishment."[52] Through exaggeration, the story deviates from the narrative of hero and beauty to come closer to the pattern of the beautiful but bestial shrew. Although starting out as a supposedly young and gentle beauty, Tang turns out to be a tiger with rouge—attractive on the outside while atrocious on the inside. By melding the two female stereotypes, the story creates an ambiguous synthesis in which the slap performed by Tang is somewhere between repugnant and pleasurable. This is further disclosed by the textual construction of Song Jiaoren's response to the slap: he feels a sharp pain yet luxuriates in the fragrance left on his cheeks by Tang's palm. Eroticizing the violent encounter and implying masochistic pleasure, the text hints that women's physical ferocity in public could break down bodily boundaries between the sexes and open the possibility for new erotic sentiments and practices.

The Obscene Shrew

The intermingling of the sexes in the public domain was the foremost factor that stimulated concern over women's sexual virtue. In the case of the early suffragettes, the *yinfu* or *dangfu* indictment also involved factors having to do with women's crimes. An increase in crimes related to sexual behavior was a distinct phenomenon in the early Republic, and perpetrators were often married or widowed women.[53] Against this social backdrop, the public had reason to suspect that the suffragettes—for instance, the widowed Tang Qunying, the divorced Shen Peizhen, and the divorced and remarried Lin Zongsu (1878–1944)—might have engaged in illicit or immoral sexual activities.

In the novel *An Unofficial History of Studying in Japan* (*Liudong waishi* 留東外史; 1916), heroic women such as Tang Qunying and Wu Zhiying (1868–1934), who had assisted Qiu Jin (1875–1907) in the Republican revolution, are derided by male characters as vain "tigresses" (*mu dachong* 母大蟲). The women do whatever men want them to do when in need of help; when the men are no longer useful, the women immediately abandon them. The novel criticizes a Lady Hu (whose surname is a pun on the word for "tiger"), who is compared to Tang Qunying in the text. This lady is described as having had many lovers since the time when she was young; her sexual prowess is said to surpass even that of top Shanghai prostitutes. In the story, she unabashedly comments on her lovers one by one to a male character and tells him that she lost her virginity at the age of fourteen to a photographer in a Beijing photo shop.[54]

The linkage between new women and prostitutes was not new in late imperial and early Republican discourses. An often-referenced example involved the warnings that the late imperial press frequently issued regarding the mixing of female students and prostitutes in public, alerting readers to potential dangers that might result from the public presence of the female students.[55] During the 1910s, as the radical suffragettes came to the fore, the analogy between new women and prostitutes became increasingly moralistic. The writers drew this parallel to discredit the women activists as morally unsanctioned and politically illicit. The public tone grew more aggravated when women demanded, beyond educational rights, an equal constitutional footing with men.

Writings in the press fantasize about close interactions between suffragettes and local prostitutes. On November 22, 1912, the *Shanghai Daily* published a playful article concocting a correspondence between the two groups of women. The suffragettes write to the prostitutes first, complaining about the failure of the suffrage movement after a year of all sorts of endeavors. Admitting that "the lionesses have lost their nerve to continue roaring" (*shihou wuli* 獅吼無力), the suffragettes ask the prostitutes to contribute by using their expertise in manipulating men, especially the senator-patrons.[56] The suffragettes believe "the land of the tender" (*wenrou xiang* 溫柔鄉) has the greatest power to move the other sex.[57] Similar terms surrounding sexual force later resounded in an article in the *Daily Learning* in 1913. Metaphors including "the Village of New Beauties" (*xinyan cun* 新妍村), "the Land of the Tender," "the River of Love" (*aihe* 愛河), "the Ocean of Desire" (*yuhai* 慾海), and "the Street of Stealing Men" (*touhan jie* 偷漢街; *touhan* refers to a woman committing adultery) ridicule members of the Women's Autonomous Association (*Nüjie zizhihui* 女界自治會) for being good at flirting (*gongpin shanmei* 工顰善媚) and sleeping around (*neng zuo zhentou zhuang* 能作枕頭狀).[58]

In replying to the suffragettes, the prostitutes urge them to give up the pursuit of suffrage. They reason that if there are truly talented women, they should exert their power in the domestic sphere: "They should shape their husbands into politicians who follow our political opinions; but they themselves should remain in the inner space as supervisors."[59] The use of the word *kunwei* 閫威 (literally, power or authority inside the inner chambers) illustrates the authorial eagerness to resituate women from the public space back into the domestic sphere, even at the husbands' expense. If women must seize some power, the author seems to say, let them have it in the household; a shrewish wife is tolerable if she does not bring her behavior before the public eye.

An article titled "A Wanton Woman Joins the Reform" (*Dangfu weixin* 蕩婦維新) in the *Patriotic News* offers another glimpse into dynamics between modern ideas, women, and empowerment. The story is structured around the strife between a wife and her husband who has studied abroad. Known for her promiscuity, the wife supposedly becomes an even looser woman when she begins to consider herself a reformer. When the husband attempts to discipline her using traditional principles of propriety, she counters by touting the modern concept of gender equality and claiming that he has no right to control her. The man becomes angry, arguing that they are legally wedded (*jiefa fuqi* 結髮夫妻: literally, hair-tied-together husband and wife, a metaphor for legal first marriage) and therefore he has a natural right over her. The wife laughs, retorting, "Now that you have cut your hair [as a modern new man], what is there to tie?" He has no reply. She then declares her intent to leave her good-for-nothing man and start an independent life.[60]

The woman in this story is aligned with the negative term *dangfu*. She is granted positive qualities, however, in that she is able to stay calm and outwit her husband. She has the sort of verbal skills enjoyed by the traditional shrew but integrates new vocabulary into her argument with the man. The use of the term "wanton" in the story title is ambiguous. On the one hand, it seems to condemn how modern culture and education open the door to sexual license and wifely unruliness. On the other hand, the story displays full sympathy for the wife's plight, implying that the label "wanton" might be facetious or, more likely, an unfair charge from the conservative public. After all, the only textual evidence of the woman's so-called licentiousness is a repetition of the Confucian expression "She is not contented with the home" (*bu an yu shi* 不安於室).[61] The author seems to care less about detailing the wife's promiscuity than presenting the modern charges she levels against her husband that eventually strengthen her in the struggle to free herself. In conceptualizing the story under the category of the shrew, was the author trying to demonize a new woman's ambition beyond the inner chambers by calling her wanton? Or was the author calling into question popular biases toward women who are willing to open themselves to new ideas and reforms? In either reading, the text acknowledges the slippery boundary between the shrew and the new woman and shapes it into a stimulating textual ambivalence.

One satire in the *Patriotic Vernacular News* complicates women's liberation through the dramatization of women's sexual appetite. It quips that the first two principles in the proposed Constitution for Equality between Men and Women (*nannü pingquan jianzhang* 男女平權簡章) should be phrased as follows: "First, request the president to allow the establishment of brothels of male prostitutes all over the country so that women can freely visit for entertainment; second, the Republican constitution should allow women to purchase male concubines, with the limit of a hundred."[62] Earlier that year, the same newspaper published an article denouncing the new women as "dissolute" (*fangzong* 放縱) and "common" (*xialiu* 下流) in hiring male prostitutes and patronizing male opera performers.[63]

As dramatic as the public charges might have been, they were not entirely baseless vilifications. Much of the inspiration came from slogans and tenets used in suffrage campaigns. For example, Shen Peizhen at a meeting of the Women's Suffrage Alliance in September 1912 brought forward the concept of "no-husband-ism" (*wufu zhuyi* 無夫主義). How Shen came up with the idea is unclear, yet the influence of Western feminism and some local conventions were both likely sources.[64] It would be arbitrary to treat this corpus of varied materials (spanning literary, historical, medical, religious, and secular sources) sweepingly in claiming an indigenous origin for Shen Peizhen's adoption of "no-husband-ism." But it can be argued that multiple cultural heritage resources were probably in play in influencing the suffragettes' grasp of this concept. The use of the term "no-husband-ism" also adds to queer history for Chinese women, given how it had been fostering public imagination of female sexuality as existing with(out) men and/or with other women.

Shen claimed that if men continued to refuse suffrage to women, women would then adopt a new method: "Single women would refuse to marry men for the next ten years [*shinian bu yu nanzi jiehun* 十年不與男子結婚]; married women should refuse to speak to their husbands for ten years [*shinian bu yu nanzi jiaoyan* 十年不與男子交言]."[65] Shen said "no speaking," but no one missed the euphemism for "no sex." In a later popular text, this line was quoted as "for ten years, seek no land of the tender," which unveils the sexual innuendo and the equation of suffragettes with prostitutes.[66] The suffragettes can also be understood as criticizing patriarchal marriage traditions: the institution of marriage forces even "respectable" women into a situation that is not so different from prostitution, and for that reason, women should take control of the transaction.

Shen Peizhen's claim provoked great controversy. In the ensuing month alone, the *Shanghai Daily* published several articles questioning the feasibility of Shen's plan. One commentator hoped that it was not empty talk, and that Lady Shen would carry out in her personal life whatever she expressed in her words.[67] One observer countered that even if Shen could remain celibate for ten years, she still would not transform those "strong-willed women who stick to the three followings" (*jushou sancong zhi wanfu* 拘守三從之頑婦; "the three followings" refers to a woman's obedience to her father before marriage, to her husband after marriage, and to her son after the death of her husband) and the "chaste ladies who bite down on the corner of the quilt in bed" (*yao beijiao zhi zhenyuan* 咬被角之貞媛). The writer suggested asking local prostitutes to stop serving old customers and reject new patrons for ten years, a method that would force men to beg in tears for women's participation in politics. According to this commentator, his idea was quickly dismissed by his own concubine, who reasoned that even if prostitutes stopped accepting new business, the civilized new women might still fall into decadence and sleep with men: "Although prostitutes are cheap and low, by no means are they willing to be fooled by the female heroes/new women."[68] The credibility of the concubine's voice is uncertain; nevertheless, it muddles the celebrated *nüjie* 女界 (literally, "women's world"). Originally *nüjie* was a male-invented concept referring to the lamentable conditions faced by Chinese women. It came to be reshaped by women themselves during the modern transition. Even prostitutes, who had often been excluded in the past, became more frequently included in public discussions on *nüjie* and the suffragettes' mobilizing appeals to their female compatriots.[69] Here the concubine's point of view suggests an alternative possibility—that the exclusion, or unsuccessful inclusion, of prostitutes in *nüjie* might be a result of these lowly women's choice to distance themselves from radical women's circles.

Many elite educated women attacked "no-husband-ism" as a synonym for sexual wantonness. A woman named Zhang Xiaofen reported that she knew some women in the Suffrage Alliance who followed antimoral and anti-humanitarian views like that.[70] Another woman named Li Jingye equated "no-husband-ism" with the freedom to change husbands without constraints. She denounced Lin Zongsu by name for having changed husbands three times before the age of twenty. Despicable morals (*ruci zhi renge* 如此之人格) overrode other factors, accounting for the widespread dismissal of the suffrage campaign.[71]

The (presumably) lewd personal lives of the suffragettes gave inspiration to popular and folk writings. In fact, one reason for the women's frequent protest against the press had to do with the libels that the newspapers published.[72] Since the decline of the suffrage movement in late 1912, Yuan Shikai had recruited several leading women activists into his government under the title of "female counselor," tempting the public to further imagine the women's illicit sexuality in liaison with political corruption.[73] Shen Peizhen was said to be especially proud of her title and often carried a large calling card showing off her connection with Yuan's regime.[74] In the novel *The Autumn in Nanjing* (*Jinling qiu* 金陵秋; 1914), the character Bei Qingcheng (*Qingcheng* is a pun on the Chinese term referring to the catastrophic "city-toppling" power of the femme fatale) alludes to Shen's networking with political leaders; in the text, Bei Qingcheng is condemned for using her outrageous sexuality (*tedang er wujian* 特蕩而無檢) to pursue fame and social status.[75] Liu Chengyu (1876–1953), a Republican politician, stated that Shen had intimate ties with every significant person in the government and even introduced her female comrades to politically connected men for their pleasure.[76]

The sexualization of Shen Peizhen culminated in an article titled "Shen Peizhen Causes a Ruckus at Xingchun Restaurant" (*Shen Peizhen da nao Xingchunju ji* 沈佩貞大鬧醒春居記). Published in the *National Herald* in 1915, the article, by developing a recent incident between Shen, her girlfriends, and some young men into "erotic fiction," led to a public disturbance and finally Shen's trial in the same year.[77] The incident revolved around a party at the Xingchun Restaurant, located in one of the popular centers of prostitution in Beijing. The party was put together for Shen Peizhen's convenience, so that she could meet the young tycoon Jiang Liangsan. At the party, one of Shen's girlfriends, Jiang Shuwan (who had already acquired a reputation for indecency),[78] made Shen the butt of a game, asking Jiang Liangsan to kneel and smell Shen's feet. Shen was offended: "My feet have long been unbound and look no different from the feet of men. What is the point of smelling them?" Jiang Liangsan smacked the table and shouted at Shen for not following the rules of the game. In return Shen overturned the table and shouted abuse (*pokou dama* 破口大罵) before taking her leave.[79] Later when seeking redress at the newspaper office, Shen and her team mistakenly assaulted an innocent man instead of the targeted newspaper correspondent.

Even though the new women had been irritating to the male-dominated press, it was not until this incident that the papers saw a perfect chance to take the women down. Marking the women's "first erroneous attack," the incident provides solid grounds for criticism.[80] Except for the *Shuntian Times,* which supported the women, Beijing papers including the *Chouhua News,* the *Eastern News,* the *Daily Learning,* and the *New China Daily* were determined to put Shen Peizhen on trial to address "corrupted social mores and disrupted national order."[81] The *National Herald* called Shen "a shrewish and crass woman" (*yi pola zhi chouxing nüzi* 一潑辣之醜行女子).[82] Others bemoaned the "vulgar speech" and "barbaric fighting" exhibited by Shen and other elite women, likening them to "violent shrews in the countryside" (*xiangcun hanfu* 鄉邨悍婦) and "wanton women of the village" (*dangfu cunyu* 蕩婦村嫗).[83]

The incident entered folk songs and vernacular poems, thereby broadening the audience. The *Eastern Times* published a ballad (*xinhua zhuzhici* 新華竹枝詞) which made fun of the foot-smelling farce at the restaurant. Later the same newspaper included a satirical vernacular poem deriding the improper behavior of the Chinese new women.[84] A drum song (*gu'er ci* 鼓兒詞) titled "The Fate of the Angry Females" (*Nu ci yuan* 怒雌緣) by Dan Fu was particularly popular because of its obscenity. The song reframes the assault as an erotic story by fantasizing that the male victim was completely naked when the women attacked him. Compared to other caricatures, which describe him as having wounds on either his head, neck, or belly, this song highlights that his penis was severely injured.[85] The victim cries about his shameful injury: "I never had syphilis in my life, but now I am too damaged to face my wife."[86] The song was so popular in Beijing society that it was said that "ten thousand mouths were circulating it."[87] In another caricature by Dan Fu, the author created an imaginary letter from Shen Peizhen in reply to Jiang Liangsan's apology. In her letter, Shen explains her wrath at the restaurant and in obscene terms tells Jiang that she is quite willing to present her feet to him in private.[88]

To paint Shen Peizhen as shameless, the press also used (or distorted) old court cases against her. The *Shing Wah News* published an article on June 17, 1915, noting that Shen had made brazen statements in a past court case: "Shen unashamedly stated that there is a mole on a man's penis to prove to the court that she was once his concubine."[89] In protest, Shen wrote a letter to the Beijing press accusing the newspapers of misinforming the public. She appealed to the court, condemning the papers for "creating libel out of thin air" and "repeatedly using obscene depictions to impress the public."[90] Stating that she had never been anyone's concubine, nor did she have two sons, as reports claimed, Shen clarified that the lawsuit mentioned in the papers was about debt issues. "If I had sons," she questioned, "why did the man want a divorce but not want to keep the children? Why did he choose to pay the fine instead of claiming his heirs?"[91]

Shen's question reveals the extent of the misogynistic slander that the male-controlled press directed at her. Even her trial on July 2 constituted a cause célèbre for public voyeurism. Tickets sold out a day in advance, and early morning crowds surrounded the courthouse.[92] The audience enjoyed the spectacle of women criminals, and they actively engaged in the trial process. When a witness swore to tell even the ugly truth in order not to violate the law, the people all chanted, "Don't break the law; don't break the law." During the trial, when one statement did get so ugly that the chief judge asked the witness to stop, the mob continued to shout: "Keep speaking! Don't break the law!"[93] The audience had come for the scurrilous details; the personal, the political, and the public were intertwined more openly through the discourse of female promiscuity. The *yinfu*, besides serving as a spectacle and an object of fantasy, also facilitated the formation of the modern Chinese social space and the formulation of public opinion/oppression of the new women.

The Unconstrained Shrew

The *pofu*, literally, a woman who spills or scatters, is another pervasive character type used to illustrate the suffragettes. The aforementioned texts in the press outline the integration of the concept in depicting the suffragettes as splashing blood and spilling breast milk. This section of the chapter focuses on a later text, *An Unofficial Erotic History of the Republic* (*Minguo yanshi yanyi* 民國豔史演義; 1928), which offers a concentrated reworking of the characteristics of the *pofu* shrew in its portrayal of the suffragettes. First published in eight volumes in 1928, the novel was reprinted three times in the eight years that followed.[94] It is recognized in Chinese scholarship today as a "social novel," among the many other categories produced by the Republican popular writers or the Mandarin Ducks and Butterflies writers. Information on the author, Tao Hancui, is unavailable, but this work includes comments and prefaces by some of the most famous popular writers of the time such as Wang Xishen (1884–1942) and Xu Zhuodai (1881–1958). Titled an "erotic history," relating obscene stories of "warlords and bureaucrats" (*junfa guanliao* 軍閥官僚) and "alluring and wanton women" (*yaoji dangfu* 妖姬蕩婦), the text nonetheless does not make the suffragettes explicitly promiscuous.[95] It degrades these women primarily through the *pofu* trope.

The novel features a suffragette character named Sun Beizhen. Her name invokes Shen Peizhen, while her behavior also recalls other radical suffragettes including Tang Qunying and Wang Changguo. Sun is portrayed as extraordinarily fat and often wears a tight outfit of Western women's clothes and a pair of golden-rimmed glasses. She is described as ugly, although her face in an illustration in the novel appears pleasant (fig. 3). She is good at public speaking; whenever there are meetings, she always jumps up onto the podium to shout "Freedom!" and "Equality!" She can insert herself into a crowd of men and speak without feeling embarrassed.

The novel devotes three chapters to Sun Beizhen. One episode starts with Sun inviting two male senators to her hotel room for a talk about women's suffrage. Afraid of Sun's female power (*ci wei* 雌威), the senators call off their dates with prostitutes and show up at her room. The story then goes on to depict in compelling detail her bizarre behavior that shocks the male visitors. Studies of Republican history have noticed the unusual depiction of the suffragettes in this piece of unofficial history. Researchers tend to interpret Sun's unseemly conduct in terms of her transgression of gender codes.[96] No studies have paid attention to the specific method the text adopts to represent the transgression. David Strand categorizes the character as "a vulgar slut," which is a synonym for the shrew, but his study does not examine how she inherits and updates this stock literary type.[97]

FIGURE 3. "Sun Beizhen zhi benlai sexiang" 孫貝珍之本來色相 (The original erotic look of Sun Beizhen). Tao Hancui, *Minguo yanshi yanyi* (Hangzhou: Zhejiang guji chubanshe, 1990).

Sun Beizhen's image as a *pofu* starts to take shape as the senators are entering the room. Her loud, coarse voice welcomes them before they see her. This scenario evokes the first appearance of Wang Xifeng in *Dream of the Red Chamber*: her "very loud voice" that can be heard before she is seen makes Lin Daiyu wonder who could be "so brash and unmannerly."[98] The senators' first view of Sun is obscene: the men see her lying in bed with her legs splayed wide apart (like a prostitute waiting for her customers) and her big natural feet resting high on the edge of the bed. The men feel embarrassed, while Sun rises very naturally to shake hands with them. One of the senators "feels that the palms of the great woman are wettish, which is probably because her hands get sweaty so easily."[99]

The depiction of Sun's damp palms situates her within the norms of the *pofu*, for she starts to spill (*po*) as soon as she appears in the story. This detail associates her with water and the concept of *yin* in Confucian *yin-yang* symbolism. The shrew in traditional literature stands for *yin* excess that manifests in cold, wet, and dark images. As the water radical in the character *po* indicates, the shrew's appearances are often accompanied by excessive water imagery, such as floods or uncontained bodily fluids.[100] In this story, Sun sweats heavily, gulps tea frequently, and must relieve herself repeatedly.

While eloquently protesting gendered differences in social roles, Sun Beizhen suddenly stands up and takes off her Western-style long skirt. She tosses it on the bed and exposes a pair of flowery pink Chinese trousers. The men see her calmly walk to the chamber pot that is placed in the same room. She bends down, throws the pot lid to the floor, pulls her trousers down, and sits on the pot in front of them. As she asks one man to pass her a cigarette, she urinates into the pot, making a loud noise (fig. 4, upper half). Then several plops come from the pot as she defecates and quotes the French revolutionary Madame Roland: "I'd rather die than give up equality and freedom." Just as she shouts out her slogan, there are more plops, "resembling the rhythm of a music box." As she continues to express her determination in winning liberation for Chinese women, the music in the chamber pot goes on (*dingding dongdong dongdong dingding de zouqi yue lai* 丁丁東東東東丁丁的奏起樂來).[101]

The episode sets up a parallel between Sun's oral eloquence and her excretory flow. She does not differentiate between the openings in her upper and lower body. This Bakhtinian display of the suffragette's uncouth natural body inserting itself into political discourse reveals how much the woman disrupts order and discipline through her routine corporeal functions. The parallel climaxes when Sun raises her voice to an even higher pitch and states: "Chinese men always treat women as playthings. We women are too pathetic. When we achieve equality between men and women, I will let rip a bigger sense of injustice [*xie zhe yidakou yuanqi* 洩這一大口冤氣] on behalf of our two hundred million fellow women." Instantly there is a loud percussive noise from the pot. The text comments, "When Sun Beizhen is talking about venting rage from her mouth, the lower part of her body vents air." She continues to declare that she wants to make Chinese men wear powder and rouge, bind their feet, and serve as women's concubines and prostitutes. Another two "plunks" sound in the pot. The men feel repulsed by her absurd speech (*jingren qilun* 驚人奇論) and the emanating stench (*chouqi sizheng* 臭氣四蒸).[102]

The chapter title, "Flowing and Gurgling, Letting Rip Some Hot Air" (*Taotao gugu dafang jueci* 滔滔汩汩大放厥詞), highlights the parallel between the activity of Sun's lower body and her bombastic speeches. She refuses to contain either her speech or her excreta (sweat, gas, urine, and excrement). The upper and lower bodily apertures that signify trouble,

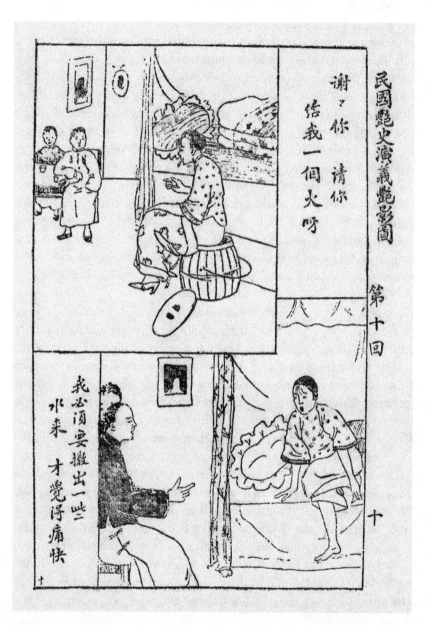

FIGURE 4. Sun Beizhen sitting on the chamber pot and rubbing between her toes when discussing women's suffrage with the two senators. Tao Hancui, *Minguo yanshi yanyi* (Hangzhou: Zhejiang guji chubanshe, 1990).

contamination, and offense in traditional texts serve to reinforce Sun's identity as the loquacious and polluting *pofu*. The commentator in the novel jokes that she is "a monster of the women's world" (*nüjie zhong zhi guaiwu* 女界中之怪物) and "a female evil spirit" (*nü er yao zhe* 女而妖 者), echoing the association between the shrew and animals, fox spirits, and monsters.[103]

After about an hour, Sun Beizhen finally stands up from her chamber pot and sits back on the edge of the bed. She loudly calls in the servant to bring her a small pair of scissors. She then takes off her big black leather shoes and white socks, exposing a pair of fat, swollen feet. On her heels, patches of calloused skin are peeling off like the bark of a tree. The text revels in the exposure of Sun's uncivilized natural body. From her lower body to her feet, she feels no qualms about exposing herself to the men.

Sun rebels against conventional gender codes; her body itself represents defiance against normative ideals. The appearance of her feet contrasts with the traditionally desired image of female feet. Hers are big and rough instead of small, soft, and fragrant. Her toenails are old and thick so that when she cuts them, the clippings jump and spatter (*tanjiang kailai* 彈將開來). One piece of nail lands right on the lips of one senator and gets stuck there in his saliva. The senator hurriedly wipes off the nail with his hand and pulls out a handkerchief to wipe his lips, a reaction once again emphasizing the sense of pollution generated by this *pofu*'s scattered bodily waste. The suffragette is repulsive, and the men are not any better. The presence of the saliva on the senators' lips makes them look bad, pointing to the hidden fact that the men have been experiencing sexual pleasure in viewing the unrestrained Sun Beizhen. The suffragette is being treated as a substitute for the prostitutes the men had originally planned to visit. Instead of privileging the men over the shrew, the text equally exposes their hypocrisy and absurdity.

After all the initial embarrassment, things get even worse. Sun dips one finger in her teacup and uses it to scratch between her toes. She tells the men that she has suffered from an annoying itch between her toes since she was little and must use her fingers to rub those areas very hard every night so that she can fall asleep. To achieve better results, she relates in excitement, "a desperate strength" is needed to break some soft skin between the toes and let pus flow out; if there is also some blood, that is even more comfortable (fig. 4, bottom half). While asking the men for advice on treating ringworm (*wanxuan* 頑癬), she keeps dipping her finger in the tea and rubbing hard between her toes. According to Sun, her mother also suffers from ringworm all over her body, and she must bathe in boiling hot water every day.[104] In the *yin-yang* idea, ringworm is another example of *yin* imagery, associated with dampness, bacteria, and contagion. After the tea, the bathwater, and the watery and bloody effluvia discharged from Sun Beizhen's feet, this ringworm detail adds one more piece of proof to her identification with *yin* excess. The specifics about the critical demand for "boiling hot" water—a *yang* symbol related to heat—also contribute to the portrayal of the suffragette and her mother as *yin*-excessive, polluting creatures.

This foot-rubbing scene is at the same time indicative of sexuality. Western psychosexual theories describe the foot as "a very primitive sexual symbol" and point out the "world-wide association of the foot with the sexual organ."[105] Ming–Qing pornographic depictions of sex describe a man's fascination with rubbing the bound feet of his female lover. In the novel *The Plum in the Golden Vase*, there are terms depicting Ximen Qing's ways of playing with women's bound feet: he can *nie* 捏 (pinch), *wo* 握 (hold), *nian* 拈 (use three fingers to fiddle with the toes), *sao* 搔 (use the thumb to scratch the bottom of the feet), and *kong* 控 (insert the middle finger in between the toes and then rub).[106] These actions are linked with sexual stimulation for both parties.

Sun Beizhen too takes unusual pleasure in scratching her feet, and she requires a lubricant to break the skin to release fluid or blood. These sexual innuendos eroticize the nature of the meeting, making the obsessive rubbing motion an indicator of the mutual sexual arousal between the senators and the suffragette, which is visualized in the illustrations. In the top image of figure 4, in which Sun is seen smoking and slouching over her chamber pot, she points in the direction of the two male voyeurs. In the second image, the men have drawn much closer to her and are sitting at erect attention, pointing at the exposed vulva which peeps out from under Sun's skirt, only inches away from her hand, which is distractedly rubbing her foot. The painting on the wall beside her bed echoes the thrust of the man's extended finger. The exposure of Sun's natural feet is just one more detail reinforcing the shrew's willingness to take unconstrained pleasure in her body.

The senators are finally allowed to leave after showing their support for women's suffrage. In delight, Sun jumps off the bed and writes more than ten letters all at once, inviting her suffragette sisters to come for a meeting the next day. She then pulls out a big jar of biscuits from underneath the bed. After gobbling biscuits, gulping down four big cups of tea, farting loudly, and sitting on the pot one more time, she falls asleep and immediately begins to snore. The next day during the women's meeting, one suffragette jumps up and accidentally overturns Sun's chamber pot. The filth shoots up (*zhichong er qi* 直沖而起) and sprays wildly (*kuangjian er chu* 狂濺而出) all over a suffragette who had been sitting on the other side of the pot. The victim is surnamed Tang, which literally means hot liquid, and is phonetically suggestive of the surname of Tang Qunying.[107]

Since the *pofu* is "both a polluting force and a castrating one," Sun's later attack on a character named Zhong Xiaorun embodies her castrating threat.[108] Zhong is the minister of agriculture and forestry, who is modeled on Song Jiaoren. During the parliament meeting the next day, Zhong starts his speech by acknowledging the significance of suffrage. Then he takes a sharp turn to state that Chinese women are certainly not ready to gain it. The audience applauds; Sun Beizhen "glares in rage." Other suffragettes all turn red from anger. As Zhong carries on with his opposition, Sun gets so irritated that blue veins stand out on her cheeks and the fury in her heart can no longer be restrained. She jumps onto the stage in a storm of anger and tugs tightly at Zhong's necktie with her right hand. The women in the audience all chant, "Hit him! Hit him!" Sun raises her left hand and gives Zhong a solid smack across his face (fig. 5). She intends to slap him one more time when the police swarm in and drag her off the stage. She and the other women stamp and curse (*dunzu dama* 頓足大罵), throwing the meeting into chaos.[109]

"Beating, slapping, and hair pulling" are displaced forms of castration in addition to "actual policing or attempted amputation of the penis."[110] These variations on castration are blatant in this slapping scene. The text details the shrew's uncontained anger that rises, explodes, splashes, and finally takes the form of verbal and physical violence. The slapping is loud, and the curses are crude. The symbolic castration is executed publicly and is therefore more insulting. Even the necktie that Sun grabs is phallic and emblematic of the shrew's classic attacks on the male phallus.[111]

How does *An Unofficial Erotic History of the Republic* view the suffragettes of early Republican China? As a *yeshi* (unofficial, popular, fictionalized history), it aims to entertain the public by dramatizing the new women's private connections with politics and their crossing of gendered boundaries. Nonetheless, despite the entertainment value, the suffragettes in the text also call attention to corruption, defects, and

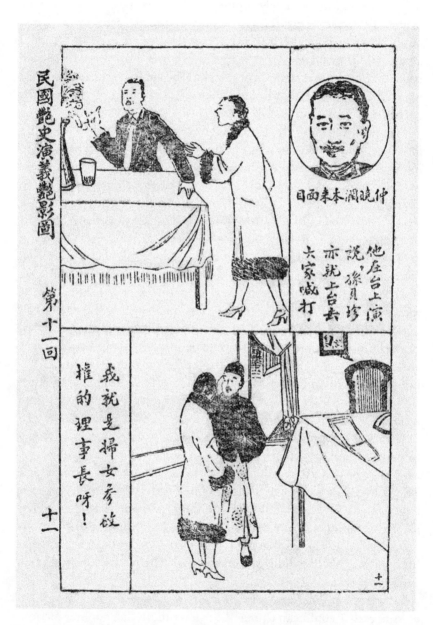

Figure 5. Sun Beizhen jumping onto the stage and slapping Zhong Xiaorun. Tao Hancui, *Minguo yanshi yanyi* (Hangzhou: Zhejiang guji chubanshe, 1990).

failures of the early Republican system, which had opened the door to ruckus, farce, and disorder. In those moments when the suffragettes are depicted as *pofu*, it is possible to see the narrator's delight in how the shrewish Sun Beizhen and others hold power over the flawed male characters. While there is extensive literature on female ugliness, fatness, and transgression in Western queer theory, when situated within the local tradition of the enactment of the shrew figure, the *pofu* depictions in this novel speak particularly to a modern pattern of reactionary male politics in China. The vilification of the shrew goes further compared to Ming–Qing literature, in that textual details are more visceral in exaggerating and super-stigmatizing the shrew's alien body. The fascination or disgust felt by the onlooking men shows that the shrew imagery has become more polemical in the modern context. Whereas in Ming–Qing stories there could be no possibility or indication of actual political change because of women wreaking havoc, the Chinese men during the turn-of-the-century transition indeed saw themselves as being challenged and threatened.

"If such popular representations turn the women's suffrage movement into a farce," notes Madeleine Yue Dong, "they also discursively open up possibilities for women as indispensable actors in an important moment of Chinese history."[112] I further argue that the *yeshi* texts not only recognize women as important players in history but also display their ability to intervene in the rules of the *hi*story. Although *An Unofficial Erotic History of the Republic* did not, and could not, go beyond the limits of social reality to "imagine the Republic as giving women more public power," through the *pofu* trope it empowers women—even if only textually and temporarily—in their fight against a defective society.[113]

With the literary transgression realized through the shrew archetype, the suffragettes appear more resourceful and respectable. This perspective enriches the view of current scholarship on these early Chinese feminists. Historians including Louise Edwards and David Strand have used public discourse to showcase the social hostility facing the women, criticizing media images and depictions as forms of misogynistic disapproval. By teasing out discursive changes regarding the role of the shrew, I have discovered encouraging messages: by no means set in stone, those representations are seen to have undergone transformations when examined within the literary tradition of writing the shrew. Rather than merely engaging in disparagement and defamation of women, male writers and critics strategically planted their dissatisfaction with the early Republican political and gendered environment in their constructions of the shrew-suffragette characters. The evolution of the trope reveals the shifting of male voices and intentions, as well as the ways in which public attitudes forged new directions in treating (instead of taming) the Chinese shrew.

CHAPTER 2

Jealous Shrew, Judicious New Woman

May Fourth Disputes on Female Jealousy and Virtue

Women's liberation took on a new urgency during the New Culture movement. To the New Cultural intellectuals, who were mostly overseas-educated students, the gender order in traditional China was symptomatic of the inhumanity of Confucian values and the inability of the state to develop into a modern democracy. They criticized female subordination as both a social reality of Confucian culture and a metaphor pointing to China's submission to foreign domination. The concern over women's status, therefore, was closely intertwined with the desire of the intellectuals to redefine China, and by extension themselves. Debates raged in the pages of progressive publications on aspects of the "woman question" from female chastity to women's rights.

The women's suffrage movement regained morale in this contemporary milieu and made significant advances. Negative voices "were thoroughly discredited during the early and mid-twenties," because any arguments against women's suffrage could be linked to the Confucian traditions that were under attack at the time. The public came to view the threatening women activists with more sympathy and enthusiasm. In the press, radical figures such as Tang Qunying were transformed from troublesome shrews to exemplars for young women to emulate.

Their violent actions were credited as cases of "radical Chinese feminism" with their past call for a social revolution transvalued as "words of prophecy."[1] Besides violence, other forms of traditionally censured female behavior were also moderated by the standards of the New Culture circles centering on female subjectivity and gender equality. The issue of female jealousy, a staple marker of the shrew, stimulated prolonged discussion on the credentials of the May Fourth new woman.

Late Imperial Changes: Female Jealousy, *Qing*, and Order

Jealousy is not exclusively a women's issue. In Western cultures, male jealousy constitutes a motif in history, literature, philosophy, religion, psychology, and other areas; jealous women, on the contrary, seldom "appear not only in popular literature but also in the literature of the high culture."[2] In the context of Confucian ideology, however, jealousy is coded as an inborn attribute of women. While male jealousy is acknowledged to exist, it is treated allegorically and sympathetically; it was predominantly ascribed to the configuration of the loyalty of ministers to their rulers or was justified as related to men's desire for sex and power. Male jealousy never was a problematic as simultaneously tantalizing and threatening as female jealousy.

In traditional China jealousy is considered "the foremost of women's evils" (*nüdu wei e zhi you* 女妒為惡之尤), one that carries catastrophic effects for family and society.[3] The idea of linking female jealousy with danger can be traced back to the Chinese philologist Xu Shen (58–147), who explained that *du*, signifying jealousy, follows the female radical and means harm (*hai* 害). In Chinese history and literature there are frequent accounts of jealous wives causing disorder in the house, seriously disrupting familial and social stability.[4] Female jealousy looms so large in shrew stories that it is often treated as the root of women's bad practices. A jealous wife is normally violent, sharp-tongued, or wanton, or sometimes all of these at the same time.

Starting from the late imperial era, with the rise of the cult of *qing* 情 (emotion, passion, sentiment, love) and prospects for gender transformation, discourses surfaced in Chinese literature and intellectual essays shedding light on female jealousy. In late imperial women's prosimetric *tanci* 彈詞 ("plucking lyrics") fiction, an idea emerged that a wife's jealousy is necessary and even conducive to a pleasant domestic life. For example, the text *A Pair of Male Phoenixes Flying Together* (*Feng shuang fei* 鳳雙飛; 1898) positively describes how a shrew spices up her polygamous marriage. Her jealousy, rather than being the scourge of the household, functions to maintain a stable family order.[5]

Some male intellectuals of the Ming and Qing dynasties made similar observations on the upside of having a jealous wife. The Ming scholar Zhang Xuan (1553–1636) wrote "Jealous Women Are Indispensable" (*Dufu buke shao* 妒婦不可少), acknowledging how jealous women can help nourish men's minds (*yangxin zhi zi* 養心之資).[6] The Qing Hanlin academician Hong Liangji (1746–1809) took the case of the jealous Empress Dugu Jialuo (544–602) in the Sui dynasty to validate the point that "only upon reaching a healthy old age can a man understand the virtue of a jealous wife" (*laojian fangzhi dufu xian* 老健方知妒婦賢).[7] These remarks largely use female jealousy to gloss over men's failures in regulating their desires and maintaining their health. Practically oriented and patriarchy-inflected, this style of reasoning underpins the majority of late imperial male voices championing female jealousy, including celebrated male feminists.

Yu Zhengxie (1775–1840), acclaimed as one of the foremost feminist thinkers of the Ming and Qing periods, penned a famous essay titled "Jealousy Is Not Women's Vice" (*Du fei nüren ede lun* 妒非女人惡德論). In this essay, Yu took the side of jealous wives, claiming that jealousy is not women's nature or fault but a result of the unjust polygamous system. He contended that jealousy is a woman's normal response to her husband's practice of taking concubines. If a wife does not become jealous when her husband buys a concubine, he argued, the wife must be indifferent, and indifference leads to the breaking of the family order (*maiqie er qi budu, zeshi jia ye, jia ze jiadao huai yi* 買妾而妻不妒, 則是忽也, 忽則家道壞矣). Yu called for greater freedom for women, as well as less guilt and blame. He differentiated between "jealousy as a natural emotion or response" (*du* 妒) and "jealousy involving malicious behavior" (*ji* 忌), adding nuance to the negotiation. *Du* without *ji* is a superior virtue (*du er buji, si shangde yi* 妒而不忌，斯上德矣), thus a new paradigm for gauging female (im)morality.[8] Although pioneering in his time, Yu Zhengxie still constructed his opinion within the conventional utilitarian framework of women's role and duty in the family.

Some positive voices viewed female jealousy as a representation of equality across sexes. The late Ming scholar Xu Shupi (1596–1683) argued that women who are not jealous are barbaric: "Judged by the rule of equality, unjealous women precisely mirror animals [*budu furen, zheng yu wangba duijing* 不妒婦人，正與亡八對鏡]. . . . Men and women are not so different in their thoughts, desire, love, and hatred, why on earth are there contrasting standards treating one sex so loosely and the other so harshly?"[9] Xu deemed jealousy to be a normal human emotion for both sexes. Policing female jealousy, in his view, is suppressive of human nature. Since *wangba* is also a swear word in Chinese referring to shameless bastards, besides blaming the sexual double standard for making women unhuman and inhuman, Xu's use of this term also suggests that unjealous women are unethical.

Another male feminist writer, Li Ruzhen (1763–1830), explored the issue of gender equality in his novel *Flowers in the Mirror* through the character of a jealous wife. In chapter 51, the wife of a bandit chief beats her husband when he attempts to take a concubine. She scolds him for ignoring her feelings and questions whether he would be happy if she were to take a male concubine. This jealous and violent wife figure was praised by modern new-style intellectuals for her ability to expose the double standard of chastity. Hu Shi lionized the novel as the earliest Chinese book to cast light on the women's question, recognizing it for not following abusive naming conventions to vilify the shrew.[10]

Others reevaluated female jealousy through *qing*. While in English *qing* could be translated in multiple ways, when associated with jealousy in affirmative texts of late imperial China, it designates love—the intense feeling of affection for one's partner or spouse. In declaring jealousy as an expression of *qing*, proponents purged negative connotations to focus on the root or innate properties of jealousy. Gong Wei (1704–1769) in "The Source of Jealousy" (*Yuan du* 原妒) attributed jealousy to *qing* and argued that "if it were from *qing*, jealousy could especially be excused" (*yi qing er du shu keyuan* 以情而妒殊可原).[11] He thought past cautionary stories, including "Warnings against the Black-Hearted" (*Heixin fu* 黑心符) of the Tang dynasty, all lose sight of the positive root of jealousy.[12] He embraced the shrew for possessing *qing* toward her husband, whose dissipation he believed to be the ultimate reason for family conflict. Much like Yu Zhengxie, Gong Wei categorized jealousy into different types and stages (*du you chadeng* 妒有差等). Whether an instance of jealousy is redeemable depends on its relation to *qing*: jealousies that are despotic cannot be excused because they are outside of *qing*; jealousies that are less violent, even though still featuring harsh words and emotions, can be justified if stimulated by *qing* (*zhi you qing zhi suoji gu keyuan* 祗由情之所激故可原).[13] As female jealousies are mostly *qing*-based, Gong contended that there are morally legitimate grounds for women to be jealous.

The *qing*-inflected female jealousy found powerful expression in the Ming-Qing cult of *qing* literature. Exemplified by the stories of Lin

Daiyu in *Dream of the Red Chamber* and Yang Yuhuan in *The Palace of Eternal Youth* (*Changsheng dian* 長生殿), the jealousy of these heroines is tied to female fidelity. The male protagonists in the two works enjoy, rather than being disturbed by, their women's jealousy-induced words, mood swings, and dramas. Emperor Tang Ming endorses Lady Yang's jealousy as the very incarnation of *qing*: "When she appears coy she is charming; it is deep love that makes her jealousy authentic" (*meichu jiao he xian, qingshen du yi zhen* 媚處嬌何限, 情深妒亦真).[14] Jia Baoyu tolerates Daiyu's fits of jealousy, willingly subjecting himself to her love-generated suspicion and grievance.[15]

Lin Daiyu embodies the sort of ideal jealous woman described by Yu Zhengxie and Gong Wei. Her jealousy derives from *qing* and does not involve violent assaults. In the meantime, she also transcends Yu and Gong's standards. Instead of aiming to maintain the traditional family order, Daiyu's jealousy has to do with her personal desires, which are often at odds with conventional rules and rituals. This kind of individualistic, rather than ethical, jealousy foreshadows the May Fourth period, when jealousy would become more emblematic of women's agency.

Ouyang Yuqian: Dramatizing Jealousy in the Chinese Nora

There was a heightened discursive focus in the May Fourth period on rewriting standards of female morality. On the issue of female jealousy, familiar clichés claim that jealousy is a major female vice that should have nothing to do with the new woman. These writings emphasize the linkage of jealousy with the old cultural system by labeling jealous women either "old-style" (*jiushi* 舊式) or "artificially new" (*shishi* 時式: literally, new only in form). In 1917 the *Ladies' Journal* published Wang Jiting's article "The Artificial New Woman and the Authentic New Woman" (*Shishi nüzi yu shishi nüzi* 時式女子與時實女子). Using the term *shishi* (fashionable to the core) in opposition to *shishi* (fashionable in form), the article warns women not to be the wrong kind of new woman. Jealousy is listed as one of the four residual qualities of old-style womanhood that prevent one from becoming a real new woman, fashionable on the outside and progressive on the inside.[16] Two years later, in 1919, unexpectedly, the same author would come to connect jealousy with romantic love and perceive social bias against jealousy as indicative of gender oppression.

Others addressed admonitions to Chinese readers, presenting jealousy as a defect and hence a hindrance to women's modern identity-building.[17] Some writings pathologize jealousy as the worst incurable disease in the world, an illness that inflicts infinite pain.[18] Authors of the 1941 guidebook *Manners of the New Woman* (*Xin nüxing de dairenjiewu* 新女性的待人接物) identified Wang Xifeng as a failed jealous wife and asked their new woman readers to suppress feelings of jealousy.[19] Repudiations of female jealousy also extended to account for emerging social problems. For example, in line with the growing interest of modern Chinese scholarship in psychological studies, jealousy was referenced in pathological terms as the cause for and the symptom of psychopathic disorders of female same-sex lovers. One influential example was the interpretation by Pan Guangdan (1898–1967), a distinguished sociologist in Republican China, of the sensational 1932 murder case featuring two romantically involved female students, which highlighted the power of jealousy.[20] When it came to the criticism of female celibacy—another increasing social phenomenon that was likely an outgrowth of the women's liberation campaign—jealousy was deemed harmful to women's physical and psychological health.[21] These discourses still associate female jealousy with notions of disease and destruction; but compared to premodern critiques, they have less relevance to familial or marital structure than to the lives of individuals.

Favorable voices on female jealousy had scarcely begun to emerge prior to the May Fourth era. In 1911 the *Women's Eastern Times* published an article praising jealous wives for being able to prevent men's moral decadence (*daode shang zhi fangzhi ji* 道德上之防止劑) and stimulate true love between the sexes (*aiqing zhi ciji ji* 愛情之刺激劑).[22] More enthusiastic celebrations came out shortly after, along with the New Cultural tide, treating jealousy as a natural and humane quality. Published as a volume of the "New Culture series" (*xin wenhua congshu* 新文化叢書), the 1919 book *Discussions on Women* (*Nüxing lun* 女性論) offers an encyclopedic overview of women's condition worldwide, attributing masculine traits to women's jealousy, which propels men to compete and develop strong bodies and minds.[23] In the same year, pieces in the *Republic Daily* and the *Ladies' Journal* (including one article by the previously noted author Wang Jiting) verify jealousy as a virtue (*du de* 妒德) in love relationships and expose how the sexual double standard grants liberty to men yet contains women by attacking female jealousy.[24] The catalytic role of jealousy in the development and preservation of love was also introduced to girl student readers who aspired to understand affection. Only love with jealousy was recognized as "the stalwart passion of a hero"; otherwise, it is "the frail sentiment of a weakling."[25]

Even some old-style fiction written in literary Chinese approaches jealousy as a factor for cultivating love and countering concubinage. In 1922 the *Fiction Daily* published a story titled "Jealousy" (*Du*) by Butterfly writer Xu Qinfu (1891–1953). With its concentration on the life of a *dufu*/jealous woman and its dramatic plotline, it seems like a shrew story in the traditional sense. The author, however, did not impose any karmic retribution or moralistic lessons. He defended the woman's jealousy in the popular language of romantic love (*aiqing* 愛情). It is because of the wife's talent (*cai* 才) for jealousy, the author commented, that her husband's family is able to survive.[26] Though barren, she has means to expel unwanted or non-beneficial women and keep those who can bear sons, whom she soon claims as her own. The story values familial order but goes so far as to hint at a woman's genius in performing jealousy to get her way.

Also written in 1922, the dramatist Ouyang Yuqian's plays *The Shrew* and *After Returning Home* (*Huijia yihou* 回家以後; first published in 1924) provide additional instances of women's strategic wielding of the power of jealousy in their protests against concubinage. Both plays fall under the Chinese Nora category, so I will first introduce this genre before analyzing Ouyang's contributions.[27] Known as "new woman plays" or "Nora plays" (*Nala ju* 娜拉劇), theatrical productions like these were influenced by Western literature for the sake of exploring unconventional roles for Chinese women. The May Fourth generation lauded Ibsen's Nora as a model for independent personhood, which was central to the struggle of the new intellectuals against familial oppression. Nora was therefore introduced to Republican China more as an icon for youth rebelling against traditional families than for awakened women protesting marriage and patriarchy. The feminist streak in Ibsen's play *A Doll's House* was largely subsumed under anti-parent tendencies, transformed into the actions of unruly Chinese daughters who ran away from oppressive parents in search of freedom in love.

The first localization of *A Doll's House* into a Chinese story was Hu Shi's play *The Greatest Event in Life* (*Zhongshen dashi* 終身大事; 1919). The Nora-like heroine Tian Yamei slams the door of her parents' house and gets into the car of her lover Mr. Chen, who is socially privileged and dominant in their relationship. It can be inferred that, were it not for Chen's status and instruction, Yamei would not have mustered the courage to leave her parents so suddenly. She does not challenge male-centrism. Her final note to her parents upon her departure shows that she has chosen to leave her parents' protection (temporarily) to enter

Mr. Chen's: "Now I have gone along with Mr. Chen by his motor car, and I must bid you, my dear parents, good-bye for the present or time being."[28] Yamei's words bespeak her childish blindness in love and her ignorance of Chen's manipulation. Inspired by *The Greatest Event in Life*, the emergent Chinese Nora plays normally construct rebellious daughters instead of wives.[29] The opposition of Ibsen's Nora to male hypocrisy and hegemony was taken less as a gender issue than a general concern of the youthful heroines. Real tragic cases of young women running away or killing themselves to break up arranged marriages reflected this movement against parental control.[30]

Ouyang Yuqian was one of the few local dramatists whose new woman characters come closer to the feminist profile of Ibsen's original construction. As a founder of modern Chinese new theater, Ouyang had studied and performed in dramas in Japan from 1904 to 1910. After returning to China, his drama troupe Spring Willow Society (*Chunliu she* 春柳社) staged over eighty plays, mostly foreign or contemporary stories, between 1912 and 1915 in Shanghai.[31] Ouyang and his colleagues had been expecting to stage *A Doll's House*, yet Chinese society at the time was not ready for a tale of a wife's feminist rebellion.[32] It was not until a decade later, in the mid-1920s, that the Chinese audience got to see awakened, fierce wives onstage.

In addition to *The Shrew* and *After Returning Home*, Ouyang's major Nora plays also include *Pan Jinlian* (*Pan Jinlian* 潘金蓮; 1928). Guo Moruo once called the character Pan Jinlian "the predecessor" of Nora (*Nala xianbei bin Jinlian* 娜拉先輩繽金蓮) in his eulogy of Ouyang Yuqian.[33] These plays place the Nora theme in man–woman relationships rather than (only) generational conflicts. Ouyang went beyond the Chinese paradigm to instill in his Nora(s) more awareness of and resistance to the gender inequality that was often glossed over in Chinese Nora plays. His creation of righteous female unruliness revives despised qualities such as female jealousy and promiscuity. While *Pan Jinlian* will be the focus of the next chapter on promiscuity, the remainder of this chapter analyzes how *The Shrew* and *After Returning Home* reinterpret jealousy in relation to new womanhood.

Both are one-act dramas written in the same year; *The Shrew*, however, is commonly considered the earlier text, which lays the groundwork for Ouyang's exploration of the association between the shrew image and the Nora ideal.[34] The play revolves around the divorce of Yu Suxin and her husband, Chen Shenzhi. The two characters meet in school and find they share beliefs about women's emancipation.

After getting married, Shenzhi works at a bank, while Suxin remains in school, trying hard to balance her studies with her roles as a mother, wife, and daughter-in-law. As an educated new woman, Suxin longs for nuclear family life. Her upper-class conservative in-laws are offended by her independence. Behind Suxin's back, the Chen elders arrange a concubine for Shenzhi, who willingly accepts the arrangement in the name of filial piety.

The action of the play takes place on the day when the concubine arrives. Everybody is nervous about the upcoming encounter because Suxin is known for opposing concubinage, which is unfortunately practiced in the family, with concubines in the possession of the Chen elders and Shenzhi's younger brother-in-law. It is a tacit understanding among the Chens that women should tolerate polygamy, as "a wife meddling in her husband's business of taking concubines is time-wasting and conflict-causing." Jealousy is discouraged: "An upper-class woman should care about the reputation of herself and the family and not become jealous" (*zhengfeng chicu* 爭風吃醋).[35]

Upon learning that the concubine has arrived, Suxin strives to suppress her indignation and assume a generous manner, acting oblivious to the scheme. When the Chens praise her virtue (*xianhui* 賢惠), she calmly calls in the woman. In front of Shenzhi, who is shaking, Suxin criticizes his dishonesty (*zhawei* 詐偽) and falseness (*jiamian* 假面), requesting that he free the concubine and give the woman two thousand dollars for her to start a new life. Suxin's defense of women's rights is taken as the classic jealousy of a main wife. Her father-in-law yells in a rage over her breach of her wifely duty: "How can a wife force her husband to return his concubine? Even if this is a nasty act of jealousy, you simply can't do it in front of everyone!" He labels Suxin a jealous wife and points at jealousy as women's sordid means of asserting their dominance. Unintimidated, Suxin retorts that she has made up her mind and "will not be afraid no matter what foul labels [*wochuo zuiming* 齷齪罪名] are being attached [*jia* 加]."[36] Her declaration exposes the way in which patriarchal power works to criminalize unruly women. The word *jia* captures the arbitrariness of the oppressive process of inventing sins—be they jealousy, promiscuity, violence, or others—for women.

Suxin threatens that if her request is not fulfilled, she will murder her child. She then puts a knife against her son's throat. When the crowd tries to seize the knife, she warns that she may cut him down on the spot. Shenzhi has no recourse but to surrender. He delivers the contract for purchasing the concubine, the check, and a divorce letter in accordance with Suxin's demands. Suxin claims responsibility for taking care of the concubine and arranges for her to receive an education to "make her a useful person." She also swears to free her son of this "deceiving patriarchy" (*qipian de fuquan* 欺騙的父權), to raise him to be a "capable citizen": "It would be a mother's sin to leave an innocent child to such a problematic family." Against everyone's objection, and despite even the concubine's hesitation, Suxin grabs the woman and the boy and storms out. The Chen family exclaims in awe, "What a shrew!" (*zhen hao pofu a* 真好潑婦啊).[37]

The concluding scene dramatizes marital conflict as a clash between conservative patriarchal forces and new progressive values. Suxin stands not only as a new woman, but also as a New Cultural enlightener in a broad sense, one who cares about the freedom and education of children as much as the emancipation of oppressed women. Her claim regarding her motherly duty adds a twist to the modern discourse of new motherhood, with an orientation toward rearing good citizens. She bitingly questions men's role in such discourse, challenges failed fatherhood, and replaces a blighted family structure with the prospect of single motherhood for the sake of good citizenship.

In the eyes of the Chen family, Suxin's modern spirit makes sense when understood as akin to the propensities of the traditional shrew. Her undaunted defense of women's rights is interpreted as jealousy of the worst kind, for it involves violence. The shrew and the new woman exude a similar air of relentlessness and intimidation. The Chen family may not understand the new era and its expectations for women, but they recognize the threat from a woman who is stubborn enough to pursue her goals without caring about offending others. The "shrew" insult, in their final indictment, represents their last attempt to suppress a woman's autonomy. Calling Suxin a shrew gives them at least an illusion of verbal privilege over the assertive woman whose rejection of shame effects her empowerment.[38]

Structurally, *The Shrew* combines elements of traditional shrew stories and the imported Nora plot. The outline of the play, with some deliberate twists, evokes events commonly found in a shrew story: the principal wife deals with her husband and in-laws; her jealousy and ferocity toward concubinage turn the family upside down. Although the educated and restrained Suxin does not throw tantrums in the way the traditional shrew does, it is still her fury and presumed jealousy that propel the plot forward, which culminates in the final Nora-style departure and the shrew's revenge (in causing the family's loss of the heir)—even if it means that this Chinese Nora must shoulder an additional burden by dragging the child along with her whereas Ibsen's Nora does not.

In setting the Nora story in a multigenerational and polygamous family, Ouyang Yuqian welded together the modern/Western idea of independent womanhood and the reality of Chinese society. He couched the theme of male duplicity in polygamous relationships as a localization of the original focus in *A Doll's House* on bourgeois monogamy. By positioning Suxin's alleged jealousy on the front line against polygamy, Ouyang configured a situation in which female jealousy functions to reject polygyny in a time of social and political unrest. Whether a real aspect of Suxin's character or a camouflage for her agency, jealousy is represented with good motivations, as an extension of a wife's awareness of her capacity to dispute social institutions and regulations.

Such a reconfiguration of the shrew as an ally and defender of modern values was so novel that it caused confusion for the Chinese audience. When the play was staged, the viewers thought "the shrew in the play is not like a shrew" (*pofu bu po* 潑婦不潑).[39] For those who had been accustomed to a conventional shrew plot, *The Shrew* was shocking in that Suxin's fierceness is so laden with progressive principles, not to mention that the shrew is never punished or tamed. Rather than issuing jeers and scorn, the audience was reported to have appeared solemn throughout the play. When Xu Gongmei performed as Chen Shenzhi at a school, he noted that "the audience was very quiet. There was not even a single cough. It was to everyone's surprise that the normally noisy theater suddenly became an awe-inspiring church [*zhuangyan de libaitang* 莊嚴的禮拜堂]. What a great comfort!"[40] The shrew's role now demands attention and respect. This transformation posed challenges to the actors, audience, and critics about how to understand her appropriately. Even recent scholarship sometimes misreads Suxin as "a fake shrew," which neglects the evolving definition of the shrew in modern China.[41] Misreading like this does not do justice to her shrewish spirit and deeds, such as her confronting her husband and in-laws, her use of violent threats, and her steadfast resistance to polygamy. Instead of faking shrewishness, Suxin redefines what a shrew should be like in the reformist context. The idea that the shrew was a static, exclusively premodern concept loses sight of this character type's exciting convergence with the modern new woman.

Written after *The Shrew*, Ouyang's *After Returning Home* complicates his depiction of the shrew-like new woman. Often taken as Ouyang's return to tradition or anti-modern ideology, *After Returning Home* reduces the new woman character to a supporting and villainized role while seeming to applaud the demeanor of the traditional woman. The play involves uneasy authorial struggle with changing female qualities. Female jealousy again comes across as a theme pertaining either to women's loss of virtue or to their attainment of personal autonomy.

Liu Mali and Wu Zifang constitute two polar female opposites in the play. Mali's name (with its similarity to Mary) suggests her Westernized background as a foreign-educated city girl. Zifang's name, meaning "fragrant or virtuous on one's own," serves to identify her as a pleasant country girl. She is filial, self-taught, and impressively sensible and collected. Her husband, Lu Zhiping, leaves her behind in the countryside to take care of his family while he studies in America. He then meets and marries Mali without disclosing anything about Zifang. The play starts with Zhiping's return to his hometown to divorce Zifang. He soon realizes, however, that she has many good qualities that "the new woman does not have" (*shi xinshi nüzi suo meiyou de haochu* 是新式女子所沒有的好處).[42] He hesitates and keeps denying his affair even though Zifang has heard rumors and found a love note in his pocket. Later, when Mali suddenly arrives (resonating with the gesture of a runaway Chinese Nora pursuing freedom in love) and requests that Zhiping leave Zifang, the man becomes even more cowardly. Eventually it is Zifang who calmly resolves the crisis by sending Zhiping away with Mali and declaring that she does not object to a divorce and will continue to take care of Zhiping's family.

Mali is portrayed as peremptory, impatient, and loud. Although seemingly less pleasant than Zifang, she facilitates the unfolding of the story. Her sharp tongue unmasks male deception. Her open denunciation of Zhiping for being "base and rascally" (*beilie wulai* 卑劣無賴) lets his secret out of the bag, causing him to lose face in his family. Mali is the foil to the virtuous Zifang, yet the two women are not fundamentally oppositional. While Zifang behaves thoughtfully and tolerantly in front of others, when in private with Zhiping, she acts in the manner of a jealous wife. Whenever there is a chance, she mocks him to his face for his dishonesty, irresponsibility, and cowardice. She makes it sound like she is speaking for the wronged second wife, Mali, but her words describing her own misfortune are drenched in jealousy and grievance. She speaks intelligently, which subverts Zhiping's impression of his country wife. Some of Zifang's remarks are as bitter and biting as can be. She ridicules Zhiping when he says that he and Mali are only friends: "You use marriage to repay her for friendship. Is marriage the only thing with which you can reward your friend?" Later, when Zhiping says that his affair with Mali has increased his experience and his love for Zifang, she says with a sneer: "So, you are telling me that one's love will flourish upon having many affairs. One's conscience will be strong after getting married many times. I did not know until now that people who fool around are simply gathering experience."[43]

Zifang is far more complicated than a proper traditional wife. She protects her husband's dignity in public while exhibiting her aggression in private. She fulfills her duties as a daughter and daughter-in-law without complaint but dares to speak up against her father and father-in-law when confronting the outsider Liu Mali. Her life falls into the ordinary rut of a conventional wife, but her ability to assert herself and her insubordination to men distinguish her from Confucian norms.

The ambiguity in Zifang's characterization stimulated wide public discussion. After the play's publication in the *Eastern Miscellany* (which was the most widely circulated Chinese magazine of the time) in October 1924 and its staging in December, a debate occurred between the liberals and the conservatives for over two months, focusing on how to define Zifang and where to place her within modern and/or traditional womanhood.[44] Led by Zhang Xichen (1889–1969) and Zhou Jianren (1888–1984), members of the liberal camp accused the play of "restoring old ways in a new drama."[45] They condemned Zifang for suppressing her emotions and sacrificing her life for Zhiping's family. Zhou Jianren singled out Zifang's "lack of jealousy" (*budu*) as evidence of her conformity to patriarchal expectations.[46] He then laid out his standards for the new woman (*xin nüzi*): "Although there is no need to pound the table or attempt suicide to prove her fierceness, she should definitely be able to express her distinctive personality" (*xianming de gexing de biaoshi* 鮮明的個性的表示).[47] To the liberals, Zifang's private shrewishness and incipient insubordination are unsatisfactory. They wanted a heroine who is more open and at ease with her jealousy, anger, and distress, even if that means she would be like Mali. "We'd rather our modern women acted like the disparaged new woman Liu Mali instead of the sacrificing, old-style Wu Zifang," commented Zhang Xichen.[48]

To the conservatives, by contrast, Zifang is not at all virtuous. The conservative camp was shocked by her witty ridicule of her husband and her rebellious speech. If she were traditionally ethical, they argued, she would not have "used caustic language to deride her husband"; she would not have "disobeyed her father and father-in-law to speak her mind"; and she would not have "dared to ask for a divorce despite the elders' opposition."[49] As a peculiar type who holds seemingly contradictory codes of conduct, Zifang represents a sort of ideal Chinese woman that Ouyang envisioned when he wrote *After Returning Home*: "[She] is not necessarily one indoctrinated with foreign education and manners, but she is also not so bound by tradition that she cannot assert her own capacity to determine her fate."[50]

The question is, why did Ouyang Yuqian, after celebrating the shrewish new woman Yu Suxin in *The Shrew*, make this unexpected turn to write the hybrid and complex Wu Zifang? Why did Ouyang suddenly shift to smearing the reputation of the new woman and expressing favor for conventional female qualities such as self-restraint, sacrifice, and tolerance? The answer might have to do with a family tragedy that happened the same year he wrote the play. On August 17, 1922, the famous supplement *Enlightenment* of the *Republic Daily* published a reader's letter titled "The New Ghost under 'Free Divorce'" ("*Ziyou lihun" xiamian de xingui* "自由離婚"下面的新鬼). The letter narrates the tragic death of Ouyang Yuqian's younger sister Ouyang Liying (?–1922), who received a new-style women's education but died after suffering a nervous breakdown when her husband filed for divorce while he was studying in Japan.

Enlightenment was known for espousing freedom in love, marriage, and divorce. The author of the letter used Liying's case to ask the editors: "Since you advocate free marriage and free divorce, please now give your judgment on this tragic event. Should social ethics allow this kind of divorce to happen freely?"[51] By writing *After Returning Home*, Ouyang Yuqian seems to have provided his answer to this reader's concerns. First, within the play, new-style education is depicted as less useful than a woman's personal spirit of self-reliance and assurance. The self-taught Zifang embodies Ouyang's regrets over the failure of women's education to cultivate a basic sense of independence in young Chinese women. He implied that women, instead of placing their hope in men, could at least avoid falling victim to new-style marriage and divorce by conducting themselves with poise like Zifang.

Second, by not fully going against the social movement of the time, Ouyang in *After Returning Home* called into question only some aspects of the new (wo)man. He seems torn between his ambition to assert himself as a public New Culture intellectual and the personal sympathy he felt for his sister and other women who were victimized by free divorce. His unusual construction of Mali and Zifang reflects this struggle and demonstrates that no matter how ambivalent the text is, Ouyang never turned away from modern tenets to embrace traditional principles. His Mali is flamboyantly aggressive but not substantially negative; the liberals even understood her as symbolic of women's agency and independence. Zifang, not immune to new woman predilections, is not a one-dimensional figure either. She resembles the positive new woman/shrew Yu Suxin in *The Shrew*: both possess insight, courage, free will, and the ability to turn their jealousy and frustration into a disruptive force against patriarchy. Zifang's character helps her (female) readers realize that when facing betrayal, the original wife can at least act wisely and firmly to resist pitiful victimhood; and to be self-affirming, she must disregard some traditional creeds and behave somewhat disobediently. Zifang blends both appropriate and offensive properties. She holds her jealousy before her like a shield but can also brandish it as a weapon when needed.

More on Female Jealousy: Voices, Vagaries, Virtues

Around the same time when Zhang Xichen and Zhou Jianren commented on the characterization of Zifang, the two liberal feminists were also writing about female jealousy on other occasions. In 1924 Zhang published his translation of Honma Hisao's (1886–1981) book *Ten Lectures on the Women's Question* (*Funü wenti shijiang* 婦女問題十講). He shortened the tenth lecture on Japanese thoughts on women into the appendix and replaced that chapter with his own article on Chinese thoughts on women. Zhang denounced the "seven reasons" (*qichu* 七出) in premodern China for expelling a wife: barrenness, promiscuity, neglect of in-laws, loquacity, theft, jealousy, and incurable illness. Aligning them with women's "slavery and machine-like" (*nuli he jiqi* 奴隸和機器) status in traditional households, he saw potential for women to subvert patriarchal constraints. He explained that "barrenness" and "incurable illness" indicate malfunction of the "machine," and "promiscuity" precludes the master's exclusive ownership of the "slave." The other four reasons, including jealousy, all serve to shape a woman into an "unsubmissive slave" (*bu xunshun de nuli* 不驯顺的奴隶).[52]

Zhang Xichen thus reformulated the conventional sins of women into signs of insubordination. He pointed out that promiscuity and jealousy are not women's problems but are apparent in both sexes. The reason men demand female chastity and generosity is that if women were wanton and jealous, men could no longer indulge themselves. In making this claim, Zhang seeks to liberate jealous women from deep-seated cultural prejudices and aversions. According to him, common metaphors regarding jealous wives (such as "eating vinegar" *chi cu* 吃醋 and "the East-of-the-River lioness roaring" *hedong shihou* 河東獅吼) dehumanize women as affectless things (*wu ganqing de dongxi* 無感情的東西). He also expressed admiration for Yu Zhengxie's article (while considering Yu somewhat condescending), lauding it as the "boldest and most outstanding" contribution.[53]

In early 1925 Zhou Jianren published two articles successively in the *Ladies' Journal* examining traditional codes of ideal womanhood: "The Ideal Woman" (*Lixiang de nüxing* 理想的女性) and "The Anatomy of Chaste Martyrdom" (*Jielie de jiepou* 節烈的解剖). The former attacks gender norms for "idealizing" women and thereby depriving them of their individual character. Zhou noted that women in traditional China were expected to be beautiful, unjealous (*budu*), and chaste, subject to the patriarchal order. In calling these codes "false ideals" (*cuowu de lixiang* 錯誤的理想), he took jealousy as a fair expression of a woman's personhood.[54] To him, daring to be jealous, and being able to do so, signify a woman's agency, which is sorely needed to disrupt long-standing injustice.

Enthusiastic in their remarks in recognizing jealousy as women's resistance to oppression, Zhang and Zhou, however, adopted an admonitory stance in the contemporaneous debate on the new sexual morality (*xin xingdaode lunzheng* 新性道德論爭) when someone promoted jealousy to the rank of virtue. The debate was launched by the two in early 1925 to discuss the prospect of replacing chastity with free love as the underpinning sexual standard for new women. The liberals maintained that unchastity or marital infidelity should not be labeled immoral if they were based on the will of individuals and caused no harm to others. While scholarship to date has acknowledged the humanistic core of this debate and its feminist attempt to enhance Chinese women's status, the spin-off discussions about female jealousy have not received independent attention.[55]

In January 1925, utilizing the platform of the *Ladies' Journal*, Zhang and Zhou raised ideas about polyamory which immediately provoked protests. Chen Bainian (1886–1983), also called Chen Daqi, an established psychology professor at Peking University, wrote a response in an alarmed tone denouncing the two for defending polygamy. Chen stated that the liberals were encouraging sexual indulgence; and since love and possessiveness are interconnected, multiple love relationships would give rise to jealousy and cause hurt in individual lives.[56] In response, Zhang Xichen questioned the legitimacy of jealousy in love. Invoking Western thinkers including Ellen Key (1849–1926) and Havelock Ellis (1859–1939), he argued that Chen equated love with jealousy and mistook love for possessing rather than giving. Zhang sounds essentialist and dogmatic in saying that jealousy is an animal instinct that should never exist in modern citizens.[57] Zhou Jianren provided additional evidence by quoting Key, Ellis, Edward Westermarck (1862–1939), Edward Carpenter (1844–1929), and others.

Chen Bainian refuted Ellen Key's love discourse, arguing that love is about giving as well as possessing. He ascribed positive value to jealousy: far from being immoral or animalistic, "jealousy is in fact quite moral" (*jidu shi hen daode de* 嫉妒是很道德的).[58] This claim took the debate to a new level. Zhang and Zhou, upon receiving Chen's challenge, remained opposed to the conception of virtuous jealousy in modern love relationships, even though they admitted the necessity of jealousy in premodern society. Zhang ridiculed Chen for placing hope in jealousy to protect one's property: "Identifying jealousy as moral is no different than taking thieves as children; peace will never come if it is jealousy, the robber, that guards the door of love."[59]

Much to Zhang's chagrin, public responses echoing Chen's valorization of jealousy quickly appeared. In July 1925 someone writing under the pseudonym Tian You published an article titled "Jealousy" (*Du*) in the *Eastern Miscellany*. Self-identifying as a modern disciple of Yu Zhengxie, Tian legitimized female jealousy through a poem he once composed to console a friend who had given up a newly bought concubine out of fear of his jealous wife. In the poem, quoted in part here, Tian admonishes his friend to treasure his wife's jealousy:

> Husband and wife are devotedly attached, day and night.
> Having only each other, how can the heart open to someone else!
> Out of sincerity, who has drunk that much vinegar [been so jealous]?
> It was a fallacy of old pedants: no female jealousy, no family strife.
> Jealousy is not a wicked trait, refuted recent scholars.
> No more arguing! Clothes should be new but not wives.
> What a great nightmare, if immersed in a pool of women.[60]

Tian You believed that jealousy grows out of conjugal affection and fidelity. Unlike Zhang Xichen, who reasoned jealousy had or should become obsolete in egalitarian modern monogamy, Tian explained how jealous women are important in a society that had yet to modernize. He upheld female jealousy as necessary compensation for the lack of equality in reality: "Based on the fact that China's economics and education are now developing abnormally, it will take quite some time to realize gender equality. Under this status quo, if wives could be equipped with 'the virtue of jealousy' [*du de*]—the rebellious attitude against husbands' indulgence in prostitution and concubinage—polygamy can be successfully resisted!"[61]

At the time when Tian You's article was published, Zhang Xichen was about to be discharged as editor in chief of the *Ladies' Journal* under pressure from the conservative camp. Even at this intense moment, Zhang remained alert to the shift of discursive direction. As soon as his own journal *The New Woman* was established half a year later, he promptly responded to Tian. Zhang published an article modeled on Yu Zhengxie's piece, titled "Jealousy Is Not Women's Virtue" (*Du fei nüren meide lun* 妒非女人美德論), which emphasized the incompatibility of jealousy with modern womanhood. Considering jealous women "the most despicable and debased" (*zui beibi loulie* 最卑鄙陋劣), who either seek happiness in men or throw temper tantrums over them, he asserted that a modern new woman should first and foremost get rid of that characteristic.[62] "Jealousy is always the method used by low-status women to secure their husbands' favor. Women who are on par with men today should maintain healthy relationships through noble and equal love, instead of the obnoxious and merciless emotion of jealousy."[63]

These discourses that I have just discussed seem firm on removing jealousy from the package of the new woman. But textual details convey a different message. The liberals were concerned more about the incompatibility of the base appearance of jealousy with the progressive profile of modernity than about the functions of jealousy. Given that the disputation on sexual morality was arguably "the first official debate" initiated by Zhang Xichen and Zhou Jianren, their opposition might be seen as purposeful and strategic, an attempt to quickly establish their difference as the new liberal social reformists.[64] Like the way chastity and love are polarized against each other in reconstructing sexual morality, and like the boundaries drawn between old and new, traditional and modern, backward and progressive, jealousy had to be made to occupy the end of the old and obsolete so that the modern relationship based on equal respect could stand out as revolutionary. As analyzed earlier, the other remarks Zhang and Zhou made around late 1924 and early 1925 on women's jealousy present a contrasting picture, therefore leaving one to wonder whether they set out to refute female jealousy because of the practical need to defend and declare themselves in the debate. When they were not involved in an outright dispute, after all, their tone regarding the same issue is less harsh, which confuses their positions in such venues.

Public interest in jealousy did not diminish even after Zhang Xichen concluded the debate. A certain young Marxist named Fan Xianggu (dates unknown) wrote to Zhang's new journal, trying to carry on with the discussion.[65] In its sixth issue in 1926, *The New Woman* published Fan's letter to Zhang. Titled "Is Jealousy a Vice?" (*Jidu shi ede ma* 嫉妒是惡德嗎？), the letter casts doubt on Zhang's previous writings for failing to understand jealousy as a natural, common emotion inevitable in love relationships. Fan stressed a mutual reliance between jealousy and love: "Only true love generates genuine jealousy."[66] In converting jealousy from the contaminator of love to the touchstone that tests the purity of it, he situated love and jealousy in a complementary rather than an antagonistic relation. If a woman's jealousy derives from her love, it is "not immoral but quite respectable" (*bingfei bu daode, fanshi hen ke chongjing de* 並非不道德, 反是很可崇敬的).[67] Later, in a short reply to Fan's letter, Zhang Xichen referred to two translated Western sources: "Ellis on Jealousy" (*Ailisi jidu lun* 靄理斯嫉妒論) and "Carpenter on Jealousy" (*Jiabende lun jidu* 賈本德論嫉妒). Both translations and Zhang's way of using them are reductive and problematic, which again undermines the credibility of his opposition.[68]

It cannot be denied that female jealousy had taken a long stride beyond the limits of Confucian ethics toward new recognition. This trend carried through the waves of discourses of the 1920s. The *Ladies' Journal*—the very same venue where many discussions about jealousy had taken place—sent out a "Call for Contributions" in October 1929 on the theme titled "Occasional Jealousy Can Be a Talent" (*Youshi neng du yi cheng cai* 有時能妒亦稱才). The word *neng* in the title indicates that jealousy should not be deemed a default capability for everyone; only those who are able and dare to be jealous under certain circumstances are talented or virtuous. The journal then selected eight submissions and published them in 1930. Including fiction and analytical essays, these writings acclaim aspects of jealousy as valuable. Across both sexes, jealousy is described as conducive to desirable competition, family stability, and personal growth. The jealousy of women is highlighted as a channel through which they can secure intimate relationships and actualize self-protection.

The first publication, "The Guard of Love" (*Ai de fangyu wu* 愛的防禦物), coins the term "love-jealousy" (*ai du* 愛妒) to refer to a wife's ability to be jealous out of her affection for her husband and family. "A jealous wife is not blamable," the essay argues. "On the contrary, she is being very appropriate because she shows her sense of responsibility." In its conclusion, the essay denounces women who do not feel jealous and designates jealousy as the basis for multiple virtues.[69] Two other stories, "Observation Based on Personal Experience" (*Jingyan zhi tan* 經驗之談) and "The Return of Older Brother" (*Gege de guilai* 哥哥的歸來), emphasize wifely jealousy for the sake of combating concubinage and extramarital sex. The former is a letter written by a first-person narrator to a perplexed younger wife, intending to instruct her in how to win her husband back against the seduction of other women. The narrator claims to be a successful wife experienced in deploying her jealousy to save her marriage. Using her own story and a counterexample of her sister-in-law, who laughs at her jealousy but loses to prostitutes and concubines, she identifies jealousy as a new woman's characteristic, since the "old-style women only know to obey and indulge" (*jiushi de nüzi zhi yiyi de fucong he fangren* 舊式的女子只一意的服從和放任). The narrator refuses to link jealousy with women's morally lacking (*quede* 缺德) or wicked (*ede* 惡德) status, persuading the recipient of the letter to master jealousy as a means for seizing control of life.[70]

Another publication, "Who Is the Unfaithful One" (*Shei shi fuxin zhe* 誰是負心者), represents jealousy in relation to a woman's astuteness in testing the truthfulness of a relationship and thus her means to protect herself. In the story, it is the heroine's lurking jealousy toward potential competitors in her love relationship with a man that prompts her to set up a trap which exposes the man's unfaithfulness.[71] The plot begins with the man arriving for a date with the woman at a park as she has requested and ends with his appointment at the same park with his supposed would-be lover, who turns out to be the woman herself. She soon suggests her disappointment and her intention to leave him. Coming full circle, the plotline foregrounds her dominance, showcasing that even an occasional flicker of jealousy adds to a woman's advantage.

Discursive vagaries on female jealousy persisted, vacillating between traditional mores and new morals. The voices examined in this chapter explored how the shrew's jealousy could make a new woman more judicious, as well as how conventional ideas on women's virtue could be camouflaged and repackaged in a changing environment within the jealousy debate. Despite doubts and uncertainties, reservations and reversals, modern cultural figures kept visiting female jealousy as a productive source for discussing progressive or promising womanhood. For Ouyang Yuqian in particular, the shrew archetype maintained a strong hold upon his constructions of the Chinese Nora. After the struggle in writing *After Returning Home*, he finally let go of his hesitations and revived Pan Jinlian, the ultimate *yinfu* in traditional Chinese literature, to accomplish his theatrical redemption of promiscuous women.

CHAPTER 3

Reconfiguring Female Promiscuity in Love and Independence

Pan Jinlian, Nora, and Jiang Qing

Ouyang Yuqian's *Pan Jinlian* excited the public for its unprecedented creation of a Nora figure based on the notorious traditional shrew Pan Jinlian. While sharing with other shrew types a jealous and violent nature, Jinlian is fundamentally recognized as a *yinfu* infamous for her unruly sexual desire. As the prefix character *yin* (originally referring to excess water) indicates, the *yinfu* is the type of woman whose pursuit of sexual fulfillment exceeds normative standards of virtuous womanhood and whose overflowing sexuality denotes social and moral decay.

Unbridled female promiscuity is a marker of crisis across time and cultures, but the issue of female sexual agency had particular importance within the Chinese writing tradition. The *yinfu* frequently appeared in late imperial Chinese literature as "a byproduct of the chastity cult" or a "mirror image of the chaste martyr," carrying the most misogynistic depictions.[1] Defying the doctrinal ideal of female chastity, modesty, and fidelity, the hypersexualized *yinfu* kills men with her lust. Although possessing excessive sexual energy, the classic *yinfu* is barren, resistant to channeling her sexuality into reproduction for the patrilineal system. She is comfortable asserting her sexual agency publicly; neither hiding away her desires nor internalizing a sense of shame, the *yinfu* shakes off the social stigma integral to Confucian regulation of women.

Pan Jinlian is the arch-*yinfu* who is without rival in late imperial Chinese literature. Originating in the fourteenth-century story *The Water Margin* (*Shuihu zhuan* 水滸傳), Jinlian, together with other lascivious women in the novel, serves to heighten the tough, asexual masculinity of the heroes. The hero who kills Jinlian is the "tiger slayer" Wu Song, her manly younger brother-in-law. With the help of a local peddler-matchmaker, Wang Po, Jinlian has committed adultery with a playboy named Ximen Qing and poisoned her husband, Wu Da, Wu Song's lowly and unattractive older sibling. Later, in the sixteenth-century pornographic novel *Plum in the Golden Vase*, Jinlian and her sexual fervor assume the central place. Becoming Ximen's concubine after the death of her husband, she indulges her desires by dominating Ximen and many other men in bed. Even though Wu Song still executes justice toward the end of the story, his heroism appears out of place in *Plum* for its incompatibility with the novel's dense sexual scenes. Wu is not even given the chance to kill Ximen as he does in *The Water Margin*; Jinlian has taken Ximen's life ahead of time with her grueling sexual demands.

The two mother texts established the misogynist paradigm for writing Pan Jinlian and every *yinfu* that followed. The name Pan Jinlian became a synonym for *yinfu*, typifying the promiscuous villainess, the most debased of women, and hence the last character with which a woman would ever want to associate herself.[2] Many critics have nevertheless been enthusiastic about reversing the verdict for Pan Jinlian, either legitimating her lust through the freedom of love, identifying her sexuality with rebellion against patriarchal panopticism, or applauding her autonomy as expressed in her defiant badness.[3] As Martin Huang points out, what makes Jinlian particularly *yin* is not necessarily her sexual desire but the fact that "she is a woman of strong *qi*": she "is not ready to accept Ximen Qing's dominance" and "is also trying to seek dominance—over Ximen Qing as well as over other women."[4] It is her spirited, headstrong resistance to (male) control and sexual double standards that makes her forever fearsome and awesome.

Ouyang's play *Pan Jinlian* was arguably the earliest modern attempt to rewrite Jinlian into a respectable woman. He reframed her as a Chinese Nora by integrating the love discourse and shedding light on issues of sex and the body. Corresponding to the modern scientific perspective, the sexual body in this text becomes a positive material truth that stands in contrast to the moralistic hypocrisy of Confucian ideology. Ouyang shifted Pan Jinlian's sexuality from a site of misogyny to the stage for female power. Her transformation is enacted through her defense of *yinfu*, her refusal to internalize the custom of shame, and her controlled use of her sexuality to shatter the aura of male heroism.

In addition to Ouyang's *Pan Jinlian*, this chapter also discusses an incident involving Lan Ping, later known as Jiang Qing or Madame Mao, whose association with the Nora icon adds new twists to the revaluing process on *yinfu*. The conflict between Lan Ping's stage achievement as a forceful Nora and her failure to receive endorsement for her personal Nora moments off the stage speaks to patriarchal surveillance of women across representational and realistic spheres. The critics, at their will and pleasure, could destroy a Nora in real life as easily as they could build one in the symbolic space of the theater. Lan Ping, who portrayed the extolled Nora model onstage, had to face slut-shaming, or Pan Jinlian–shaming, when acting in the style of a Nora in her own love life. Whether a Nora or a Pan Jinlian, unruly women like Lan Ping seemed to care less about labels than about the power they could claim by turning insults into demonstrations of their convention-defying ambitions and competencies. Female promiscuity, seen from these intertwined strands, served as both the target of, and a weapon against, social forces that categorized and contained women on the basis of their sexual choices.

Elevating the *Yinfu* to the Role of a Nora

While in *The Shrew* and *After Returning Home* the new woman characters are called or presented as shrews, *Pan Jinlian* is a direct rehabilitation of an established shrew in the history of Chinese literature. This is a bold approach considering how familiar the Chinese reading public was with the story and evaluation of Pan Jinlian. Ouyang Yuqian made her, the originally "licentious shrew and bloodthirsty villainess," a champion of women's rights.[5] Identified as a Nora, Jinlian came to speak for the May Fourth ethos in promoting romantic free love and protesting Confucian traditions.[6] *Pan Jinlian* has so far been recognized as "one of the earliest modern efforts to rewrite the 'bad woman'" and a most "daring" and "innovative" play that overturns paradigms through the *yinfu* theme.[7]

Published in 1928 as a spoken drama, *Pan Jinlian* was said to have been adapted from the script of its 1926 opera version.[8] It was then

revised and staged as a Chinese opera in 1927 by the Southern Society
(*Nanguo she* 南國社) at the Shanghai University of Arts.[9] In the 1928
publication, which is the only surviving text of the play, *Pan Jinlian* consists of five acts. In the first act, Jinlian's former master Zhang Dahu
pressures Wang Po to return her to him after Wu Da's death. Act two
goes on to portray how Zhang's servant Gao Sheng, while trying to
persuade Jinlian into remarriage, is coldly confronted and beaten by
her and Ximen. In the next two acts, the vengeful Wu Song interrogates
Jinlian and the neighbors to determine the truth about his brother's
death. Act five turns the *yinfu*'s passive execution into all-out rebellion when she levels accusations against Wu Song, Wu Da, and male-
dominated society.

Pan Jinlian is radical primarily in three respects. First, the play highlights the spirit of strong individuality as that which underpins the
wantonness of Jinlian, attempting a feminist reading of her transgressive desire, speech, and action. Second, its heroine resists the *yinfu* epithet applied by Wu Song and other men. Her redefinition of *yin* and
yinfu frees female promiscuity from the catastrophic stigma imposed by
patriarchal double standards. Third, the final scene of the play enables
Jinlian to be not only vocally resistant but also physically defiant in her
solicitation and complication of her execution.

Sharp Tongue, Strong Spirit

Unlike the two sprawling mother texts, which feature multilayered descriptions of characters and relationships, *Pan Jinlian* is simple, short, to
the point. The whole play is a projection of new ideas onto the existing
plot. Leaving out a large chunk of events (including details of Jinlian's
affair and her poisoning of Wu Da), the play situates her in the central
role to focus on her subjective reactions. She is introduced in the cast
of characters as "an intelligent young woman with a strong personality" (*yige gexing henqiang congming lingli de nüzi* 一個個性狠強聰明伶俐
的女子), free of negative attributes.[10] She speaks openly, as a character
and a feminist voice-over, against the sense of superiority of the male
characters.

The play increases the role of Zhang Dahu, Jinlian's original master
and a minor figure in the two novels, to intensify the patriarchal perse-
cution that she faces. In *The Water Margin*, Zhang marries her off after
she resists his advances and reports him to the principal wife. In *Plum*,
although Jinlian submits to Zhang, their encounter quickly causes his

death, underlining the threat of the *yinfu*'s lethal sexuality. "Thus, even before the story proper begins, Pan Jinlian has already sent a man to his death, an event that foreshadows the other men who will suffer the same fate at her hands because of her insatiable, murderous sexual desire."[11] No previous texts ever gave Zhang Dahu a voice until Ouyang's rewriting. The play starts by showing Zhang's despotic behavior upon hearing about Jinlian's acts of adultery and murder. In front of his concubines and maidservants, he threatens to take this mischievous woman back for "discipline" (*guanjiao* 管教). Once his bondmaid, Pan Jinlian, in Zhang's understanding, will always be subject to his control. His beliefs typify the patriarchy's manipulation of women and their sexuality as men's products of exchange. Almost all male characters in the play hold similar opinions and assume a sense of entitlement to ridicule, insult, and censure Jinlian.

The play uses its initial male-female confrontation to foreshow one woman's battle with multifaceted male oppression. All men in *Pan Jinlian* are either negative or weak (verbally, physically, emotionally, morally), leaving room for the enactment of female subjectivity. Even though Wang Po and Zhang Dahu's concubines do not officially join Pan Jinlian in her battle, they refuse to conform to the gender norm of obedience and silence. With their sharp tongues, they gain (poetic) advantage over the male characters.

As established in the mother texts, Wang Po represents the source of trouble that an aged, worldly woman can bring to social and familial order. Her words are cunning, sophisticated, sometimes subtle yet damaging. In *Pan Jinlian*, she speaks more intelligently, with acute consciousness of the absurdity of patriarchal thinking. If she is the old and wicked outcast in the original texts, her character is brightened up with feminist hues in the modern play. She confronts Zhang Dahu (while in previous works she never crosses paths with him) to deliver the intended authorial message against male dominance. Zhang says to Wang Po:

> Jinlian was a maidservant in my household. She didn't know her place and wouldn't accept favors from me. All I could do was marry her off. Even then her refusal to do her duty as a wife caused some ugly talk. My idea is to take her back and straighten her out. Go tell her that if she's willing to turn over a new leaf, I'll take care of everything for her. If not, then one of these days the whole affair will get out and her number will be up. If she has any

sense, you'll come with her reply and I'll send someone to fetch her. Understand?[12]

Zhang is wrapping his desire for Jinlian in a cloak of moral duty based on his role as a leading member of the local gentry. Wang Po's response, rather than a mere rejection, criticizes the patriarchal obliteration of women's autonomy:

> Your Honor would like to take her back. But, as they say, "A daughter married is like water thrown out the door." Is it any less true of the maidservant that's been sold? Miss Jinlian has already been Wu Da's wife. Now that her husband is dead, do you really think that if you let her come back and be your maidservant she'll be willing? Forget about straightening her out; when a person is grown her mind is made up—who can change it? Be forgiving, Your Honor—let her go and be done with it.[13]

Wang Po's answer saves face for the patriarch by avoiding directly challenging his privilege. But instead of devaluing widowed women, she suggests that widowhood signals a rebirth and an increase in self-worth for a woman. In contrast to Zhang Dahu's degradation of women as sex objects and vulnerable dependents, Wang Po sees women as human beings who feel, think, and act. The use of the term "willing" says much about a woman's consciousness and growth in a torturous marriage. The death of a husband (especially an unwanted one) does not bring a woman misery as the patriarchal imagination would have us believe; it instead leads to an abundance of opportunities. Jinlian's being sold/married off and the subsequent loss of her husband facilitate her march toward freedom and independence. By defending the will of Pan Jinlian, Wang Po is instructing Zhang to come to terms with aspects of women that are normally dismissed or denied. Her last admonition about forgiving and forgetting plays down the seriousness of Zhang's request and dilutes his authority.

Likewise, younger female characters in *Pan Jinlian* also seize opportunities to exert their limited agency. Zhang Dahu's concubines and scenes of his family life never appear in the original novels. The way Ouyang Yuqian opens his play with amusing conversations between Zhang and his concubines changes the focal point of the story from patriarchal forces to women's spontaneous verbal genius in intruding into the realm of male supremacy. At the beginning of the play, Zhang complains about the appearance of his women: "What I can't

understand is how other men's women get prettier and younger looking all the time. Look at you dumbheads—the older you get the worse
you look." Not tolerating or internalizing the abuse, the concubines
talk back, mocking Zhang's looks and age. He in turn likens women
to fish: "Keeping women is like raising goldfish: you want the fish to
be pretty but what's the use of a pretty fish keeper? It's only for fun."
This comparison objectifies women by laying stress on domesticated
beauty required of women for men's pleasure, as well as women's
inherent dependence. Swiftly, one woman calls her sisters' attention
to the disparagement: "Listen to him—treating us as if we're goldfish!" Zhang's subsequent line further effaces women's subjectivity:
"A woman without a man to love her is finished, so if I take care of
you it's like doing a good deed."[14] The meaning of men to women is
compared to that of water to fish.

Zhang Dahu's fish bite. One concubine asks him straightaway to
stop blowing his horn, while others join in to laugh at his inability to
control one fish: Pan Jinlian. "It wasn't for lack of money or power—you
just weren't cute enough. [*Laughs*]."[15] Appearance and age are again used
to destroy the patriarch's feeling of superiority in a play about how the
patriarchy uses the same factors to restrain women. The concubines,
with their sharp tongues, quick wit, and uncontrolled laughter, shake
the gendered hierarchy and set a defiant tone for the rest of the text.
Their collaborative teasing of Zhang interrupts his self-articulation as a
master. His boasting only offers them the chance to create a spontaneous, intimate feminine carnival.

Besides these minor characters, *Pan Jinlian* also features a beggar, a
completely invented figure, for the sake of portraying Jinlian's spirit.
If the opening sequence outlines her headstrong stubbornness in resisting nasty men, her later encounter with the beggar is a fuller display of her worship of strength, autonomy, and ability. When the blind
and crippled beggar first appears, Jinlian and Wang Po are complaining about the decrease in a woman's value as she ages. They joke that
women should just die off so that men can suffer. In her moment of anger at men, Jinlian finds the soliciting beggar unbearable. She thwarts
Wang Po's attempt to give him money because she believes a useless
and hopeless person like him should simply die. This scenario parallels
how she refuses to be at someone's mercy: "Before I half resemble you
I'll be dead. You won't catch me eating other people's scraps." Later,
upon discovering that the beggar is a fake, she cracks up and surprisingly gives him money as a reward for his ability to trick people. Wang

Po is puzzled, saying, "It's horrid to lie and cheat," yet Jinlian retorts, "I'd rather be hated than pitied."[16]

Ouyang Yuqian employed the strong *qi* that the archetypical Pan Jinlian possesses to represent the self-assured personhood considered desirable by the May Fourth ideology. Jinlian is suggestively linked to the "strong man" image or philosophy (*qiangzhe zhexue* 強者哲學) that modern Chinese reformists had been advocating.[17] Fending off the stereotype of the "sick man of East Asia," advocates sought to build a new national character that was strong in body, mind, and spirit. This new version of Pan Jinlian, with her verbal and physical aggression revived for the purpose of denouncing weakness, shows how nationalist and feminist aspirations can intertwine and be fulfilled simultaneously through the ready-made fierceness of the shrew. The shrew's tongue and temper are so versatile that they are mobilized to challenge gender, geographical, and more general biases.

The *Yinfu*

In the Pan Jinlian character Ouyang invested his New Cultural visions of gender, modernity, and national identity. His foremost task, however, was to remove the *yinfu* label from his heroine. No longer portraying *yin* as women's sin that erodes masculine integrity, *Pan Jinlian* attributes the origin of the *yinfu* to male oppression. Every time the *yinfu* insult appears, the play contextualizes it by holding patriarchal abuse responsible for female misbehavior. Promiscuity constitutes a lawful expression of female resistance to gender biases related to sex, the body, pleasure, and ethics.

The earliest example in which the heroine of the title is referred to as a *yinfu* occurs in the first scene. Zhang Dahu's servant Gao Sheng discloses that the real reason Zhang married Jinlian off was that she dared to agitate him by scheming to choose her own lover. "She wouldn't go along, then on top of that she willfully fell for one of the servants" (*Ta buken, pian qu aishang women de yige tongshi de* 她不肯, 偏去愛上我們的一個同事的).[18] The word *pian* signifies willfulness, deliberation, and obstinacy, implying that Jinlian probably pretended to fall for someone to humiliate Zhang Dahu and push him to send her away. She may or may not have a lover but develops scenarios to prove to her master that she seizes every opportunity to assert her right to subjectivity. This disobedience earns her the name *yinfu*, which gives Zhang and his servants moral entitlement.

To Pan Jinlian herself, the *yinfu* stigma frees and empowers her rather than oppressing her. By giving in to (or deliberately inviting) the stigma, she successfully plans her escape from Zhang Dahu. *Yin* is her key to the door of liberation, her means to upset the patriarch, and her personal strategy for getting her way. Soon after being married, she performs her second *yinfu* act: committing adultery with Ximen Qing. Unlike the mother texts, which treat her infidelity as ironclad evidence of her sinful nature, the play exhibits the inhumane aspects of Jinlian's marriage to account for her betrayal. She charges: "He [Zhang Dahu] used his position as a rich and powerful member of the local gentry to marry me, without my consent, to that ugly, short, dirty, good-for-nothing and revolting Wu Da—the number one freak of Yang-ku County. I'm made of flesh and blood; how could I take that kind of injustice?"[19] Although Pan Jinlian never hesitates to curse her mismatched marriage in the earlier works, the tone and the essence of her accusation have greatly changed in the rewrite, which can be observed through the contrast between beauty and ugliness.

In premodern texts, women's—and men's—physical appearance was not to be taken at face value. Pretty women are often aligned with beasts to denote their seductive danger.[20] Men's ugliness, however, can be an indicator of their moral decency. The ugly Wu Da, for example, is described as a decent man on the inside: plain, honest, and well-behaved (*benfen* 本分, *pushi* 樸實, *laoshi* 老實).[21] Pan Jinlian's complaints about his appearance thus mark the arrogance and immorality that presage her doom in the mother texts. "*Yinfu* and *yinhua* [obscene speech, bestial language] are not what they seem, they cannot be taken at face value, their beauty hides filth—in short, theirs is a moral depravity."[22] Here Ouyang Yuqian's take on a person's looks speaks to a more straightforward perception of beauty and ugliness. His play rejects the old formula and instead presents a true mismatch, an injustice that is not only "skin" deep but also down to the bone: Jinlian is a true beauty in appearance and spirit; Wu Da, the despot, is as repulsive on the inside as he is ugly on the outside.

In the play, Wu Da joins other men in embodying patriarchal abuse. He and Zhang Dahu are repeatedly described as being ugly to dramatize their negative role. Wu's tyranny overturns his pitiful wronged husband persona, providing grounds for the wife's rebellion. As exposed by Jinlian, Wu "took the tack of playing the master-husband [*bai ta zhangfu de jiazi* 擺他丈夫的架子], which added to my troubles a thousand times over." Driven by despair, she accepts Ximen's tenderness: "Just when

I was thinking of killing myself I met Ximen Qing by accident. On the whole, he was gentle with me so I took him as my lover. Yes—I committed adultery."[23] Pan Jinlian's moral degeneration is attributed to Wu Da's abuse of power and his failure to be a worthy husband.

The play grounds *yin* in rational and commendable affection. Culminating in Jinlian's confession of love to Wu Song, the plot transforms the story of a depraved nymphomaniac into a melancholy tale of an awakened woman. Even her adultery is justified as a form of faithful love: for the first time Ximen Qing is rendered as an analogue to Wu Song in masculine valor; her affair with him is made an extension of her affection for her brother-in-law. In the last scene, Jinlian defends her infidelity: "After you [Wu Song] got angry and left, it was as if I had lost my soul. . . . Besides, he [Ximen Qing] was like you in some ways. [*With emotion*] I willingly became his plaything."[24] Ouyang Yuqian twisted the conventional characterization of Pan Jinlian as a sexual predator. He created a sympathetic woman who bravely pursues lovers who fit her own ideal of masculine strength. This adjustment vindicates her adultery and returns, once again, the responsibility for a woman's decadence to men. According to a critic in the 1930s: "Pan Jinlian is not really a *yinfu*. If she had not married Wu Da but instead were Wu Song's wife, it is quite likely that she would then have been a virtuous wife and mother adored by the old ethics."[25]

In the face of the new *yinfu*, even the image of the supreme hero Wu Song collapses. He comes to epitomize the Confucian hypocrite who possesses a strong body but not a steady mind. In order not to lose his aura of "some kind of hero, sage, and superior man," Wu hides behind standards of propriety and has pitifully "cut off [his] youth in its prime."[26] He conspires with Wu Da on his acts of tyranny. As Ouyang commented, although Wu Song is manly, he "unluckily holds strongly to the old ideas and this compels him to incite Wu Da to confine Pan Jinlian with his authority as husband [*ying jiao Wu Da na fuquan ba ta bi qilai* 硬教武大拿夫權把她闭起来]. How can she be willing to submit to that?"[27] The choice of the word *ying*, hard and harsh, reveals authorial discontent over the imposition of patriarchal intentions.

Another example can be seen in the following passage, which has been widely used to eulogize Wu Song's brotherly integrity while rarely being critiqued from a gendered perspective. "You've always been weak and timid," Wu Song tells his brother, "and people may try to take advantage when I'm not around. If you sell ten trays of buns a day usually, from tomorrow on don't sell more than five. Leave the house late and come back early. Don't drink with anybody. And when you get home, lower the curtain and bolt the door. In that way you'll avoid arguments."[28] In both *The Water Margin* and *Plum*, Wu Song gives this brief speech exhorting Wu Da to work less every day following his departure. Pan Jinlian is not mentioned, but every line in the passage registers Wu Song's concerns over the potential danger posed by his sister-in-law. Rather than going on to develop Wu Da into an oppressive husband, the mother texts, on the contrary, focus on making Jinlian an unreasonable wife who shrieks abuse at her husband for being so obedient to his younger brother. These original characterizations are reversed in *Pan Jinlian* as the brothers collude in oppressing the woman. Wu Song is reevaluated on the basis of feminist paradigms instead of his ability to adhere to familial relationships and moral duties. With his saint mask smashed by the *yinfu*, he is rendered a coward who shuns his desires and abets abuse.

Wu Song is the only male character in the play who shouts the insult *yinfu* directly into Jinlian's face. When questioning her about his brother's death, he equates "the whore who ruins a man" with "the thief who kills a man" to express his distrust. In a calm and rational tone, Jinlian refutes the *yinfu* label: "Whenever a man wants to abuse a woman there are lots of men to back him up. Only women who meekly allow men to torture them to death are 'chaste and exemplary' [*zhenjie lienü* 貞節烈女]. Anyone who survives the ordeal is a whore [*yinfu*]. A woman who isn't willing to put up with a man's abuse is a criminal [*zuiren* 罪人]. . . . You only preach one-sided truths."[29] Her words bring to light that the true sources of social malaise are the patriarchal mindset and the containment of women in the name of righteousness. She exposes the collusive tricks men have long been playing to keep women under control. By targeting patriarchal means of categorizing good and bad women, codifying female virtue and vice, and enforcing unjustified epithets to reinforce social discipline, Pan Jinlian discloses a problem of deception that is much larger than her infidelity.

The term *yinfu* arises from its derisive origin to acquire a combative edge marking women's revolt. In Jinlian's indictment, there is a quality of resistance, resilience, and rejuvenation inherent in the figure of the *yinfu*—the only female type that can live through abuse and remain vital. The denigratory *yin* now symbolizes an ability and ambition that combat adversity. There is this "symbolic potential of *yin*" that can "challenge the naturalized moral hierarchy of *yang* dominance and *yin* subordination."[30] While Pan Jinlian never shies away from the *yin* label, she acts more knowingly in the modern construction against the stigma of shame. She frees herself from moral guilt because she understands that the shame should be on the men. She is proud to carry the label of shrew or whore or criminal to display the extent to which she denies the force of phallic ethics to define women and their lives.

Facing Jinlian, Wu Song is unsettled and protests feebly, "What a mouthful of nonsense" (*yipai de fenghua* 一派的瘋話).[31] As *feng* means mad, crazy, and insane, Wu uses the age-old strategy of pathologization to police a woman's words and thoughts. When he says, "I fail utterly to comprehend your ravings," Jinlian returns the blow: "You're better off a little confused. If you were in less of a muddle you couldn't be such a good follower of Confucius."[32] Inverting power and moral hierarchies, she makes him the victim of ignorance—shattered, dull-witted, and deranged. He appears to be the truly *feng* party, a man who can't even keep a clear head and normal spirits. He gazes at the *yinfu* "in stunned silence" (*daizhe* 呆著) while ruminating, "I didn't think such women existed," drastically contrasting with his known image as the unshakable, iron-willed superhero (*zhengzheng tiehan* 錚錚鐵漢).[33]

Upon taking his leave, Wu stutters when he asks Jinlian to shut the door. His reminder seems less casual (while it corresponds to his virtuous character) than intentional in commanding the attention of his widowed sister-in-law. As he shakes and comes closer to a flesh-and-blood man, he is further subject to her influence. In the final scene of the hero's execution of the *yinfu*, Pan Jinlian manipulates the killing to the extent that she mesmerizes her killer with her daring words and actions. She solicits and facilitates her own death to seize the last residue of her autonomy.

The Killing

The final scene puts Pan Jinlian's bravery on full display. With her ceaseless mouth, even in the face of death, she articulates her contempt for the male characters. From Zhang Dahu and Wu Da's tyranny, to Ximen Qing's lust, to Wu Song's vulnerability, the scene delivers a conclusive rejection of patriarchal suppression by projecting forms of perversion, predation, and promiscuity back onto the men. The scene reverses many established accounts of Wu Song. The hero known for his cold, unbenevolent attitude toward women is shown to be preoccupied and overwhelmed by Pan Jinlian. His "extraordinary moral prowess" and "asexual virility" are demythified.[34] His will weakens when encountering her love confession and bodily seduction.

At the beginning of the scene, Wu Song invites the neighbors to a banquet, which is to be Jinlian's trial. She soon turns the court-like situation for judging her into a tirade against men. Wielding her revelatory tongue, she lets out a stream of invective with herself being the judge.[35] She testifies that Zhang Dahu and Wu Song are the real murderers: Zhang murdered her desire to marry someone she loves, and Wu murdered her last hope to fall in love and be a good woman. Her condemnation reflects the authorial disappointment in men that Ouyang disclosed in the preface:

> Men often step by step push women into crime or depravity. In the end, men shun responsibility as well as deride and curse women as if they were innocent. How come no one in the world has ever questioned it? There are also men who simply fear that women do not become depraved or brazen, because otherwise, how can they be noble and dignified? How can they find playthings for their entertainment? Confucian principles were made with supreme skill. For thousands of years, women could not jump out of the trap. My play is really asking for trouble.[36]

As Wu Song is about to disembowel Jinlian with his sword, she refuses to confess any of her crimes, and instead indicts her male oppressors. This scene, rife with passion and tension, is acclaimed for echoing Nora: "Ouyang's twist was to provide Pan Jinlian with the opportunity, before being killed, to tell her side of the story. She does so through an eloquent speech condemning traditional society's oppression of women, reminiscent in some ways of Nora's speech at the end of Ibsen's *A Doll's House*."[37] In the original texts, her confession was rendered in indirect speech from a male perspective. Here she enjoys full rights to speak her mind.[38] The freedom of speech enables the parallel with Nora's indictment against her father and her husband, facilitating the utterance of Jinlian's affection for Wu, which then turns into an appeal to him to kill her. She still must die, but she now dies in an active manner.

When Wu Song demands her death, Jinlian—rather than being petrified and throwing herself on the mercy of her executioner (which is what happens in earlier texts)—adopts the pose of a martyr and faces death with defiance. She addresses him: "Everyone has to die. Better to commit the crime, face disaster, and die forthright than be tortured to death bit by bit. To be able to die at the hands of the man I love—even to die—is something I'll do gladly. Brother—is it my head you want, or my heart?" He wants her heart: "Ah, you want my heart. That's very good. I've already given you my heart. It was here, but you didn't take it. Come and see—[*She tears open her clothing*] inside this snow white breast is a very red, very warm, very true heart. Take it! [*As the neighbors, nerves drawn taut, watch with amazement, Wu Song drags Jinlian to him with one arm; she half reclines on the ground.*]"[39]

In *The Water Margin*, Wu Song rips open Jinlian's bodice, plunges his knife into her breast, and cuts her open. In *Plum*, Wu first strips Jinlian of her clothes, makes her confess naked before her husband's spirit tablet, and then takes "the dagger and cut[s] open her pale and fragrant breast with a single slash."[40] Ouyang's Pan Jinlian, rather than passively having her clothes torn open, takes the initiative in exposing her body to Wu Song. While her personal revelations would have been deemed licentious or improper in the traditional sense, they are revalued here as a manifestation of a deeper truth—of her conscious and effective exertion of her sexual power over men. Even if female sexuality is not as dominant in *Pan Jinlian* as in the early literature, the moment of her spontaneous exposure of her chest to every male viewer shows Ouyang's creative labor in refashioning the *yinfu* qualities into a new woman.[41]

Oscar Wilde's (1854–1900) *Salome* (1891) had been recognized for likely influencing the final scene of *Pan Jinlian*. The scenario of Jinlian taking advantage of her sexual attractiveness is an example of one reminiscent element among other similarities, including the fact that the heroines in both plays are presented with the heads of their men.[42] Salome and Pan Jinlian are aware of their sexuality, and their controlled use of it undermines the sexual privilege attached to the male gaze.[43] With her exposure of her chest, Jinlian reveals a sexual truth that Wu Song famously denies. The performance photo (fig. 6) demonstrates the shocking effect when the condemned woman unexpectedly rips open her clothes for the male killer and the audience. A more explicit case of sexualization of this scene and dramatization of Wu's lust can be seen in a contemporary work of art by Li Zhanyang (1969–). In Li's 2004 bronze sculpture *Wu Song Kills His Sister-in-Law*, Wu is single-handedly holding Jinlian, who exposes her breasts and one leg, while tonguing her body.

Jinlian seizes control of what should be the ultimate act of patriarchal discipline by tantalizing, mesmerizing, and paralyzing the men onstage. As Wu Song raises his knife, the bare-chested woman raises

FIGURE 6.   Ouyang Yuqian performing as Pan Jinlian, and Zhou Xinfang (1895–1975), a renowned actor in the Southern School of Beijing opera, performing as Wu Song in the 1920s. *Tientsin Shanpao Illustrated Review* 6, no. 37 (1932). In traditional Beijing opera, all female roles were played by men.

her voice: "I can't be together with you in this life; in my next life I'll be reborn as an ox and flay my hide to make boots for you. I'll be reborn as a silkworm and spin silk to make clothes for you. Even if you kill me, I will still love you."[44] Criticism has been concentrated on the reiteration of women's servitude and sacrifice in Pan Jinlian's statement in such a rebellious moment. Some critics at the time went so far as to denounce its masochistic tinge.[45] Yet alternatively, this statement can also be read as reformulating traditional misogynist scripts into vows of feminist vengeance.

Because of her identity as a bondmaid-concubine, Pan Jinlian is morally base in earlier texts. "She is topologically close to domestic animals such as cats and dogs. These can be trained and groomed, and can give pride in ownership; at the other extreme, they can be punished and killed, or given away or sold."[46] Aware of this valuation, Jinlian likens herself to cows and silkworms, both known for easy domestication, labor, and sacrifice. She does not choose to counter the script, or she knows there is no way to counter it. She co-opts the bestial historical analogies: previous texts belittle the base women as symbolic "domestic and sexual appendages of the master of the household," but this modern Jinlian asks to become an appendage to the master's body to fulfill her revenge.[47] By serving as boots and clothing, she claims a perpetual attachment to the man, for she will forever bind his feet and constrain his body. This renders her co-optation as a wish and a curse, a reward and a reprisal.

Dumbfounded, Wu Song completes the killing in a trance. His eyes open wide (*dengzhe yan* 瞪著眼) as he repeats her words to himself: "You love me? I . . . I. . ."[48] Without finishing the sentence, he unconsciously plunges his knife into her chest.[49] He then stares at (*dengzhu* 瞪住) the corpse and lets the knife fall. Everyone in the scene is struck dumb (*dou dai le* 都呆了). In previous versions, Wu never hesitates before stabbing Jinlian. Neither he nor the witnesses are described as fixing their eyes on the partially nude dead body of the woman. This Wu Song, by contrast, is shaken and distracted. Even if figured as a piece of iron, he is now dissolving in the heat of her boldness. With altered details, Ouyang Yuqian unmasked the weakness of the hero and the not-so-righteous nature of the execution. Wu Song is no longer the unwavering superhero of *The Water Margin* who kills quickly and takes the woman's head with him to fetch Ximen Qing. Nor is he able to move on to the next killings as swiftly as he does in *Plum*. Ouyang reversed the established pattern, letting Wu present Jinlian with the head of Ximen, which makes the killing of the woman the definitive test of Wu's heroism.

How successful or rebellious is Ouyang's (new) ending of the Pan Jinlian story after all? To what extent does Pan Jinlian's provocation challenge the nature of the execution? Does her death, seemingly unavoidable and unchangeable, make the point that she is doomed to failure instead of Wu Song? Did Ouyang fail to write a fresh finale? Some scholarship uses Jinlian's death to designate the failure of the play as a modern attempt to reconstruct history: the death "symbolizes the power not only of male domination but also of the premodern text. . . . Pan Jinlian fails to change her fate, first and foremost because she cannot modify the narrative dynamics of the original plot."[50] Literature repeats itself in theme and pattern; the death of Pan Jinlian alone should not indicate the limits of textual reconstruction. Instead, Ouyang's ending showcases how a modern subject can play with bits and pieces of an existing script and put together a revision that both conforms to and alters the original design significantly. Rather than a defeat denoting the heavy hand of history, Jinlian's death signals the will of the heroine to die for her own ideals of love, desire, and freedom. Jinlian is an active participant in her destiny, willing to pay whatever price it entails. Her death therefore initiates instead of terminates the possibility of intervening in norms regarding law and justice.[51] A woman, facing her male executioner and assenting witnesses, is left alone to speak truth to power. With her *yinfu*'s utterances and sexuality, she manages to disrupt forms of male dominance and exposes how society hypocritically denies the knowledge of her desirability.

Ouyang Yuqian dazzled the audience with his own impersonation of the heroine in the 1920s. He transformed the *yinfu* into a "rebellious woman" (*panni de nüxing* 叛逆的女性) and received wide acclaim (*poshou huanying* 頗受歡迎).[52] The audience grasped a positive image of Pan Jinlian from Ouyang's performance. One reviewer stated, "With this play, I don't believe someone would still call her a 'vicious wanton whore' [*wan'e de yinfu* 萬惡的淫婦] or a 'shameless bitch' [*wuchi de jianren* 無恥的賤人]."[53] Another claimed, "Ouyang displayed the noble passions [*chunjie de reqing* 純潔的熱情] of the long-disparaged woman."[54] Another said, "[His enactment] was so different from other stage performances of Pan Jinlian which only depict her licentiousness [*zhuan miaoxie yindang* 專描寫淫蕩] and have no meaning."[55] One critic wrote, "[Ouyang] completely subverted [*wanquan tuifan* 完全推翻] the *yinfu* role of Jinlian established in previous Beijing operas, making her a martyr of love" (*wei ai er xisheng zhe* 為愛而犧牲者).[56]

Besides Ouyang's, other supportive treatment in the late 1920s and 1930s of the *yinfu* identity of Pan Jinlian include Wu Cun's (1904–1972) film *Wu Song and Pan Jinlian* (*Wu Song yu Pan Jinlian* 武松與潘金蓮; 1938), Xu Zhuodai's *The Exemplary Pan Jinlian* (*Lienü Pan Jinlian* 烈女潘金蓮; 1933), and Xu Xiaotian's (1886–1946) *Pan Jinlian: The Love Reactionary* (*Pan Jinlian: Ai de fandong* 潘金蓮：愛的反動; 1932). Xu Xiaotian disputed Jinlian's notoriety as a *yinfu*, making her the exemplar who resists Zhang Dahu's authority (*yinwei* 淫威), eludes the rape-like marriage with Wu Da (*qiangjian shi de fuqi shenghuo* 強姦式的夫妻生活), and dallies with Ximen Qing to free her repressed sexuality.[57]

Reducing Nora to *Yinfu*

Beyond the representational space, were there *yinfu*-Nora models? Would a free or "loose" woman in 1920s and 1930s China be lionized as a Nora or lambasted as a modern version of Pan Jinlian? Would her desire and search for sexual fulfillment be coded as Nora's autonomy or Jinlian's amorality? Would the image of a redeemable and admirable Pan Jinlian ever be tenable in the public perception? As an extension of the analysis on *Pan Jinlian* and an attempted response to these inquiries, this section examines Jiang Qing's onstage and offstage performances of Nora several years later, in the mid-1930s. Jiang's case went beyond the literary dimension to engage in the interplay between theater and reality, adding further evidence to the vision that connects the new woman with the *yinfu* and vice versa. The young Jiang Qing concretized the Nora–Pan Jinlian nexus through her public acting and personal life experiences. The sensation surrounding her expanded the textual scope presented in Ouyang's experimental play and once again highlighted how (un)favorably women's sexuality and agency were used.

Jiang Qing was known as Lan Ping (literally, "blue apple") in Republican Shanghai before her journey to Yan'an. The name was widely ridiculed and was said to align with her loose nature. According to Zhao Dan (1915–1980), Lan's colleague who played Nora's husband, the nickname she gained back then punned on Lan Ping: Lan Pingguo (literally, "rotten apple"). Zhao described her as being "stubborn and calculating" (*gexing juejiang bing gongyu xinji* 個性倔強并工於心計), using vulgar language, often uttering the curse words "damn" and "motherfucker." Therefore, "no men dared to touch her."[58]

Lan Ping brought her vulgarity to the stage and screen. In the 1930s the dominant female image was still of the "soft and lovely" (*roumei wumei* 柔美嫵媚) variety. Lan was fresh at the time, "performing female characters who had distinctive and fiery personalities" (*ta biaoyan xingge xianming pola de nüxing* 她表演性格鮮明潑辣的女性).[59] This feisty style made her a hit when she played Nora onstage. Audiences found her rebellious version of Nora exhilarating. Jiang Qing later on never stopped gloating over the ovations she won for her portrayal of Nora as a "woman rebel," the likes of which "were rare in those days."[60]

Lan Ping's Nora

Nora had begun to lose her popular appeal as an ideal woman by 1925, becoming the antithesis of the "woman hero" (*nü yingxiong* 女英雄) promoted by the leftists on account of her bourgeois background and pursuit of personal happiness.[61] During the mid-1930s, however, specifically from 1933 to 1937, she made a strong comeback. At that time, people began calling for "women to return to the home" (*funü huijia* 婦女回家) in response to the economic crisis and growing disillusionment with women's liberation.[62] To counter such regression, the leftist artists reclaimed the image of Nora, the most recognizable icon of women's independence. There were so many performances of *A Doll's House* in 1935 that that year became known as "the Year of Nora" (*Nala nian* 娜拉年). Lan Ping's version, presented by the Shanghai Amateur Drama Association (*Shanghai yeyu juren xiehui* 上海業餘劇人協會), was the most successful.[63] Although *A Doll's House* had been introduced to China and staged since the early May Fourth period (around 1918), it was not until Lan's performance that the play reached a wide audience and was even circulated as a radio drama and an illustrated serial.[64]

Premiering on June 27 at the Golden City Theater, Lan Ping's version of the play was a big hit in Shanghai. It "ran for two months—unusually long for a left-wing production."[65] She received high acclamation in the press for her feisty Nora. Reviewers raved about her acting, extolling her "forceful actions with lively facial expressions," and lauding how she was "really living in her character."[66] They gave special praise to the final moment when Nora delivers her speech in front of her husband in preparation for leaving the house. Lan was recognized for her ability to act in such a way that "the forces on the stage all transfer to her body."[67] Female feistiness gained public favor; some critics even urged Lan Ping to be "fiercer" (*xiong* 兇) when resisting the male characters.[68] She did not take the advice because she thought she "had already been too fierce" (*yijing tai xiong le* 已經太兇了).[69]

The celebration of shrewish qualities did not go far. While the press lionized Lan for her spirited onstage performance, when it came to her real life, the praise degenerated into personal attacks. One year after her success as Nora, Lan Ping caused another sensation when she began an affair with Tang Na (original name: Ma Jiliang, 1914–1988), an arts critic, scriptwriter, director, and actor in Shanghai. Tang was completely drawn to Lan's Nora and her unconventional, "bold" character.[70] The two acted together in the film *Scenes of City Life* (*Dushi fengguang*

都市風光) in 1935 and quickly fell in love. The press soon reported that they were married in April 1936, but it seems that she never signed the marriage contract.[71]

At the end of that same month, Lan left Tang to tend to her sick mother in Ji'nan (which turned out to be her excuse for abandoning him). After her departure, Tang received a farewell letter she had left with their mutual friend Zheng Junli (1911-1969).[72] He immediately went to Ji'nan but failed to find her. At an inn, Tang attempted suicide by swallowing matches and drinking pure alcohol.[73] Lan Ping later picked him up and they returned to Shanghai together. In May 1937 she once again left him because she was in love with Zhang Min (1906-1975), the most prominent director in Shanghai (also the director of *A Doll's House*), who soon divorced his wife for her. Tang Na then made a second attempt on his life by leaping into the waters of the Huangpu in the middle of the day.[74]

Lan Ping as Nora?

Scandals lit up the Shanghai press, even making their way into prominent national papers in Beijing and Nanjing such as the *Central Daily News*. The press uniformly depicted Tang Na and Zhang Min as victims. Lan Ping was identified as having characteristics of the *yinfu*: feisty, sharp, sexually attractive and insatiable, and shameless in her willingness to be publicly transgressive. She was portrayed as using men as playthings and trading her beauty for fame: "In order to become famous, Lan Ping makes use of the tactics of beauties" (*meiren ji* 美人計).[75] She was painted as a loose woman who had no commitment to love or marriage; she "got married twice, but still wanders around."[76] Turned into a drama queen, she was said to have "treated Tang Na far worse after marriage. She makes a fuss [*nao* 鬧] almost every single day."[77] She was also linked to the bad karma a man would experience if he had done wrong in his previous life: "Lan Ping has an arrogant temper and imperious manner. Some say, 'Whoever gets this woman must have done evil in previous lives.'"[78] The karma trope was common in traditional shrew stories, designating shrewish wives as punishment for men's moral failures. Instead of digging into Tang Na's problems, the press depicted him as a sincere, sensitive, and wronged lover. The *Eastern Times* published Tang's letters to Lan, approving them as "coming directly from the heart," being "exceedingly sentimental and touching," and "passionately devoted."[79]

Lan Ping's letters appeared in less influential and more entertaining publications, and without supporting commentaries. In her farewell letter to Tang in 1936 and her letter to the public in 1937, she provided an alternative picture to that painted in the press. First, she countered Tang's image as a committed husband by revealing that it was his affairs with other women during their relationship that caused her distress and drove her to leave him. She did not agree with the ambitious and vain identity constructed for her in the press. Instead, she showed her contempt for the luxurious lifestyle of Shanghai: "Ever since entering the movie world, the contradictions between words and actions had increasingly aggravated my sense of frustration, hopelessness, and self-destructiveness."[80] It was Tang Na, according to her, who had been persuading her to stay and keep acting in films. This divergence accounted for most of their quarrels: "We fought innumerable times over the fact that I had always wanted to leave the movie world, but not once were we able to come to any agreement." While he enjoyed the Shanghai entertainment world and desired a "somewhat easier" life, she hoped her life could be "somewhat more meaningful." Lan eventually accepted a friend's invitation to teach at a school and left "that greatly tempting life of prominence, position, and relative comfort."[81]

The constructed voices of Lan Ping, Tang Na, and the press appealed to mixed audiences. Tang unmistakably identified with the stock type of the male victim of a domineering and unscrupulous shrew. Lan aligned herself with the iconic Nora, who, in a similar manner, leaves a cheating husband and chooses a more meaningful life over domestic comfort. The press shifted its position to defend male privilege after initially adopting a progressive stance in celebrating the onstage Nora. The newspapers refused to look at Lan Ping as a positive Nora by acknowledging the similarities between her desires for herself and those of the modern-spirited woman they advocated in the arts pages. That which they celebrated onstage was framed negatively and labeled as shrewish offstage.

When press reports did mention Lan's connection to Nora in her personal life, it was used as criticism. In society any woman with any level of association with Nora was problematized.[82] Lan Ping was immediately subjected to insults. Her lifelike portrayal of Nora onstage was then taken as an indicator of her potential for disruptive behavior. As one writer mused, "Lan Ping, who once played Nora, must be rather confident about men" (*duiyu nanren, ta shi poyou bawo de* 對於男人，她是頗有把握的).[83] People whispered behind Tang's back:

"She'll do a real Nora. She'll play the role in Tang Na's apartment, just as she did at the Golden City Theater! When the time is ripe, she'll walk out on him just as Nora walked out on Helmer."[84] Tang's letter echoes this fear of abandonment. After his first suicide attempt, he wrote, "Ping, my dearest, I did not expect you would leave so suddenly, so hastily," implying that he had been harboring anxiety about being deserted all along.[85]

Even though Nora had been a cultural icon in China for decades, the mainstream press of 1930s Shanghai was still not ready to validate a real-life Nora. Journalists devalued the association between Lan Ping and Nora and glossed over forms of patriarchal abuse. The weak Tang Na depicted in the press was a torturing husband in Lan's letters. If in *A Doll's House* Torvald manipulates Nora through his sweet lies, Tang controlled Lan through his tears and suicide attempts. When she first found the love letters he wrote to other women, he wept and used suicide threats to force her to forgive him. He was "sobbing bitterly" such that she "shall never forget the pitiful way that he cried."[86] His suicidal behavior succeeded in luring her back after her initial attempt to leave. She recounted: "I primarily wanted to have a frank face-to-face talk with him, to urge him to respect himself and not to be like this again, after which we would again separate. But when I saw how miserable he was, how full of shame, my heart softened incredibly, to the point that I totally forgave his faithlessness. . . . Out of a sense of sympathy and pity, I did the most humiliating thing in my whole life—I returned with him to Shanghai."[87]

Soon after their return she found he had not changed, and his drama continued. Even his friends kept harassing her, trying to "hang 'the damaging blow'" on her. After Tang's second suicide attempt, his friends "were going to use force" in dealing with her. Lan portrayed herself as laughing in disgust at this pathetic patriarchal bluff: "Ha, ha! Good heavens! If they would be so brave in fighting against XX [referring to Japan], then, really, China would definitely not be defeated! Unfortunately, to use it against one young woman, ha, ha." The press focused on descriptions of her hysterics as evidence of her unstable state. Although Lan Ping claimed she "had already fallen into a very serious depression" and frequently shook her head and hit herself, the press only captured (or concocted) her insanity while belittling her explanations for her situation.[88] After the fall of the "Gang of Four," her letter was still held up as proof of her *pofu* nature: "The public letter of Lan Ping vividly presents her as a shrew shouting abuse in the street" (*pofu majie* 潑婦罵街).[89]

Lan Ping had considered silence and suicide as means of meeting the social expectations of a good woman.[90] Facing aggravated abuse from Tang Na, his friends, and society, she eventually refused to conform to the idea of the sympathetic female suicide. "I'm certainly not going to be like Ruan Lingyu and kill myself because I'm 'afraid of what people might say.' Nor will I retreat. I'll just wait without moving a muscle, wait for them to curse me in large bold type." Lan Ping rejected the traditional gender criterion that prescribes suicide as a woman's best method of being virtuous. She made Tang play the passive, subordinate role in their relationship and had him act out the conventional attributes of a woman—sentimental, jealous, and fragile.

"Why should I be just a pitiful little bug and let others walk over me? No! Lan Ping is a human being and will never retreat, especially in the face of such shameless tactics."[91] Lan decided to be vocal and stubbornly live on (*juejiang de huo xiaqu* 倔強的活下去). Her spirit recalls Nora's declaration—"I'm a human being"—and resonates with the bitter assertion in Ouyang Yuqian's *Pan Jinlian* that "anyone who survives the ordeal is a whore."[92] The *yinfu* label did not scare her. Her embrace of its interconnection with the Nora model actualized Ouyang's textual insight that a shrew could best fulfill the modern requirements for the new woman, and that a new woman should never fear what others think or say of her and should be willing to be labeled a shrew. Lan survived and thrived, as an unyielding shrew and a persistent Nora, both onstage and in society. As she stated in the closing words of her farewell letter to Tang, "You must remember me only as a fiery female [*wo shi yige pola de nüxing* 我是一個潑辣的女性], as a woman unwilling to appear weaker than a man."[93] She adhered to the new woman ideal even when the real world expected her to do otherwise.

In the Lan Ping incident, the heroine and her opponents were engaged in a battle of public opinion in which they manipulated two semantic fields for their own benefit. Tang Na and the press constructed Lan Ping as a selfish and sexually immoral shrew, while she constructed herself as a fearless Nora following the modern ideals of autonomy and happiness. Lan as Nora/*yinfu* constitutes a fitting coda to Ouyang's literary rendition of this hybrid identity resulting from mixed perceptions of female promiscuity. Their cases show that there was greater social tolerance for symbolic and ideological battles than for transformations in social practices that threatened the hegemony of husbands or male lovers. Chinese society was forced to come to terms with the overlapping set of properties exhibited by the negative shrew and the positive new woman in its effort to enact female empowerment. When the fiery Lan Ping later fled Shanghai to join the communists in Yan'an in the late 1930s, her trajectory prefigured an even more imposing wave of integrative and cooperative practices between the shrew and the Communist state, to be continued in chapter 5 and the epilogue.[94]

CHAPTER 4

Popular Views on the Shrewish Wife

Henpecking Humor, Female Rule,
and Family-State Metaphor

The rest of this book centers on new takes on the trope of the shrewish wife and the henpecked husband in modern Chinese media. While the shrew's violence, jealousy, and promiscuity never seem detached from her wifely positioning, the materials to be examined in the remaining chapters announce explicitly their interest in and employment of this marital motif. *Pa laopo*, or henpecking, was revisited in these texts on comical, entertaining levels, but also rendered in close connection to discussions of modern national character, state-building, and revolutionary initiatives. In both popular writings and Communist propagandist depictions, wife-fearing is repackaged and remarketed.

This chapter begins with the early 1920s popular tendency toward imagining the new woman in her role as the shrewish wife in Mandarin Ducks and Butterflies stories. It then continues into the 1930s and 1940s to analyze the celebration of strong wifehood in playful writings by some well-known New Cultural writers including Lin Yutang (1895–1976), Hu Shi, Xu Zhimo (1897–1931), Hong Shen (1894–1955), and others. These texts, though having fallen into oblivion, conjure up unconventional or otherwise previously unheard interpretations of the meaning of the shrewish wife, who, in addition to succeeding at poking fun within shifting cultural dynamics, inspires alternative enactment of the fates of transgressive females.

The Early Stroke: Popular Comic Stories and the New Fate of the Shrewish Wife

In the early 1920s the Butterfly writers pioneered the first corpus of literary representations of the new woman in her role as a domineering wife. Commonly labeled "traditional," "feudal," "conservative," and "reactionary" by May Fourth and then Communist critics, many of these popular writers nevertheless exhibited a bold or even radical grasp on women's changing status.[1] Written shortly after the inception of the May Fourth movement in 1919, the Butterfly stories preceded the works of the leading May Fourth writers on modern-day wives; and while May Fourth fiction is marked by ambivalence, the popular comedies configure the Westernized new women as shrews who embody political-social challenges. These writings present novel depictions of the shrew/new woman without regressing to old literary and moral values. The shrewish protagonists in the texts discipline their problematic husbands and are not subject to punishment and karmic retribution like their premodern sisters.

The Butterfly works that involve the theme of the shrewish wife can be divided into two groups. The first group follows the premodern pattern regarding characterization, plot, and language style. Its representative works are often categorized as strange or eccentric. For example, Liu Tieleng's (1881–1961) *Secret Account of Henpecking* (*Junei miji* 懼內秘記; 1920) and *The East-of-the-River Lioness* (*Hedong shi* 河東獅; 1922) were published under the category of "fiction of the unusual and strange" (*huiqi xiaoshuo* 恢奇小說). In response to the rise of feminine power (*nüquan* 女權), they disparagingly treat strong women as shrews.[2]

Produced during the same timeframe, the second group of shrew tales features revolutionized fates for the browbeating wives. The stories incorporate modern terms in adapting the shrew into the new-style Westernized female student. They are less admonitory compared to the first group and were usually published as comedies. *The Diary of a Henpecked Husband* (*Pa laopo riji* 怕老婆日記; 1920) was labeled *huaji* 滑稽 (funny, comical, ridiculous) when first published.[3] It was reprinted in 1923 as the first piece in the "Grand Collection of Comic Stories" (*huaji xiaoshuo daguan* 滑稽小說大觀).[4] "The Laughable History of Honeymoon Travel" (*Miyue lüxing xiaoshi* 蜜月旅行笑史; 1924) and *The Funny History of Henpecking* (*Junei qushi* 懼內趣史; 1925) were also defined as comedies, according to the wording of the titles.

Derived from the "*huaji* Shanghai" phenomenon, the second group of works signal the voracious appetite of modern Shanghai for pleasure by making gender fodder for the creation of topsy-turvy carnival laughter.[5] Wife-fearing, in addition to its presence in the literary world, also made a regular theme for cartoon columns across different magazines.[6] The husband-wife relationship was reconfigured from multiple ends to provide stimulation for the increasingly worldly urban audience. Marital strife constituted a working site for experimenting with the fun as well as the danger of marrying a new woman. Beyond the widely noted entertaining or comforting effects, popular fiction of the early twentieth century also demonstrates its radical edge in keeping up with or spurring developments in early Republican gender discourse.[7]

Caricaturing Modern Henpecking

Unlike traditional shrew comedies and satires, *huaji* Shanghai stories came out of "a new reality" that was "more upbeat" rather than "abusive" or "cynical and defeatist."[8] The difference can be observed by reading the new shrew stories of the 1920s against earlier renditions of the same topic. *Tiger with Rouge* (*Yanzhi hu* 胭脂虎; 1916) is arguably the earliest work that writes a new-style female student into a modern shrew. In the story, the wife is described as "quite knowledgeable in Chinese and Western studies."[9] But she is also a *yinfu* who commits adultery, lives through the shame of gang rape without killing herself, mutilates her husband by cutting off his penis, and is eventually betrayed by her lover and executed by hanging. The author lamented the imbalance that women's education had caused between instilling common knowledge and cultivating female virtue (*nü de* 女德).[10] As we enter the 1920s, similar stories express less anxiety about the behavior of female students while giving more prominence to the newness. Even though Western influences were still often deemed factors in domestic conflicts, the new woman/shrew's Westernisms in the texts function more as a site of kaleidoscopic performance than as a foundation for didacticism.

The Diary of a Henpecked Husband showcases a revised view of shrewish wifehood and the revival of shrew literature. It features a heroine named Wan Fuxiong (literally, "as masculine as ten thousand men"), who is also referred to as Wan Xingshi (note that Xingshi is a pun on the Chinese title of *Marriage Bonds to Awaken the World*) and aligned with the shrew from "East-of-the-River."[11] Her husband, Bi Liang, is known as Longqiu Sheng, a name that evokes the henpecked historical figure Chen Jichang (alias *Longqiu jushi*). The man had been hoping to marry his younger cousin Qiu Ping, his childhood sweetheart, but his mother insists that a modern, educated man like him should marry a new-style female student.[12] Xingshi is selected. Besides being a graduate of a girls' school, she also possesses credentials including member of the Women's Suffrage Alliance, instructor at the women's sports field, and interim teacher at a girls' school. She is aggressive and acts upon her educated values in a hilarious manner; in contrast, the illiterate Qiu Ping is humble and gentle, representing tradition and comfort. The reader is informed from the beginning of the story that, faced with the provocative new style embodied by Xingshi, the conservatism of Qiu assures one that "premodern values are still there, waiting in the wings."[13]

The formula of bipolarity between opposite types of women had a premodern counterpart: the triangular relationship in Ming–Qing shrew stories between the husband, concubine(s), and the shrewish main wife. In the 1910s the triangle was reformulated to illustrate the dilemma facing the leading man as he chooses between tradition and modernity. In sentimental love stories including the well-known *Jade Pear Spirit* (*Yu li hun* 玉梨魂; 1916), the plight is usually figured in the man's uneasy choice between a threatening new woman and an old-style female.[14] The Butterfly writers borrowed these triangular affairs as a device for ridiculing new women and reaffirming the reliability of traditional womanhood. Later May Fourth writers such as Mao Dun adopted the love triangle to discredit old-style femininity and make the revolutionary new women the desired model for male characters and readers.[15]

At the start of *The Diary*, the man has a dream after first hearing about his fiancée, immediately identifying Xingshi as a shrew with a beautiful exterior but a bestial essence. In his sensual dream, Xingshi has light eyebrows, a small mouth, delicate fingers and legs. When he fantasizes about bathing her in fragrant water, her appearance suddenly changes, revealing a red face with fiery eyes, green eyebrows, a huge bloody mouth, sharp claws, and hairy legs, a stark "female yaksha" (*wuyi mu yecha* 無異母夜叉). This Janus-faced monster invokes the visual duality of the image of Wang Xifeng reflected in the double-sided "Precious Mirror of Love" in *Dream of the Red Chamber*. Parallel to Xifeng's opposing reflections in the two sides of the mirror as an enchanting woman and a skull, Xingshi's dual appearances reinforce the shrew archetype in her satisfying and sickening, appeasing and appalling powers. In the same chapter in *Dream of the Red Chamber*, Jia Rui leaves a large pool of cold, wet semen after indulging in a sexual frenzy with the illusory beauty in the mirror. Longqiu Sheng likewise finds himself drenched in a cold sweat (*lenghan bianqu* 冷汗徧軀) upon awakening. The text employs excessive *yin* imagery and discloses that Longqiu Sheng's inability to resist his desires will precipitate his sufferings and family misfortunes.[16]

As a new woman, Xingshi constitutes an alien intrusion into the traditional community, generating a spectacle. On the wedding day, the bride's sedan approaches, accompanied by high wind and a heavy rainstorm. The cold deluge foreshadows the entrance of a disruptive shrew. She curses the ceremony for requiring her to kneel like a dog or a horse. Later at the banquet she wears her new woman clothes, which shock everyone for their sinister suggestion of a new widow.[17] As she runs and does calisthenics in the yard, her skirt flies up, leaving the guests all dazed. Longqiu Sheng, like Jia Rui, who is locked outside in the cold by Wang Xifeng in the precious mirror chapter in *Dream of the Red Chamber*, stays outside till dawn on the wedding night, only to receive a note squeezed out through the crack of the door, written in English in offensive red ink, laying out Xingshi's principles for marriage. The man takes his ridiculous wife as a novelty of marital life (*guifang zhong biekaishengmian zhi yunshi* 閨房中別開生面之韵事) and is willing to tolerate her shortcomings and abuse of everyone, even a little cat.[18]

As discussed in chapter 3, the presence of a cat or dog in a shrew story is not accidental.[19] In *The Diary*, in addition to direct analogies between Xingshi and lethal animals (tigers, leopards, lions, and elephants—*hu bao shi xiang yuanshi tonglei* 虎豹獅象原是同類), the cat episode employs the ready-made trope of killing a pet to depict the jealous and vicious nature of the shrew.[20] The cat first appears at the end of the fifth chapter, preceding and prefiguring the *yin* chapter, chapter 6, about how Xingshi disturbs the public order during the couple's honeymoon trip. The cat is killed in chapter 9, following a visit from Qiu Ping. During the visit, Xingshi accidentally hits and breaks a teacup that a servant is carrying, a plot detail evoking the shrew's classic troublemaking. Later, when Longqiu Sheng is holding the cat in bed, Xingshi mistakes it for an illicit lover. She picks up the cat by its neck and dashes it to the ground several times until it is dead.

The potential love rival or concubine Qiu Ping is symbolically linked with the cat, a simple, gentle creature that is close to the husband. Since imperial concubines and prostitutes are more likely than main wives to keep cats "as a substitute for the master('s penis-phallus)," the presence of the cat in the man's bed right after Qiu's visit clarifies the relevance of such an analogy. Cats "will come without the master's having called for them, and will not leave even upon being scolded. It is because of their intimate disposition [*qin*] that the master is close to them."[21] Qiu Ping too can always visit freely as a relative and an intimate. Unable to compete with this closeness, Xingshi can at least kill the cat as Qiu's stand-in. Similar scenarios are easy to locate in premodern shrew episodes. Ximen Qing in *Plum in the Golden Vase* cannot kill Pan Jinlian but can kill her cat, an accomplice who attacks and kills his child by another woman.[22] In placing the killing sequence in chapter 9, a *yang* chapter, *The Diary* alludes to an inversion of the couple's gender roles, rendering the wife the ruthless party and the husband the companion or extension of a mere cat.

Xingshi even asks to tattoo her husband, thus emulating the mother of Yue Fei (1103–1142) in the Song dynasty who tattooed four characters on her son's back to urge him to loyally serve the country. Xingshi tattoos the word "fear" (*pa*) on the back of Longqiu Sheng's hand to remind him to be submissive. In the commentator's words, the wife's action transforms the model of "virtuous mother and filial son" (*xianmu xiaozi* 賢母孝子) to that of "cruel wife and cowed husband" (*hanfu nuofu* 悍婦懦夫).[23] As a *pofu*, she hides her mother-in-law's Buddhist shrine in the chamber pot and dumps a bucket of nightsoil all over the room. In the end, order is restored when Xingshi files for divorce; Qiu Ping and her mother help to pay off debts, and they form a new family unit with Longqiu Sheng and his mother.

Radicalizing the Comical

The Diary conforms to the pattern of writing shrewish wives and henpecked husbands as "enduring comical types."[24] The comical element of the story lies in the wife's socially transgressive actions as well as the husband's failure to maintain marital hierarchy and family order. Just as premodern shrew stories indulge in hyperbole for comic or shocking effect, *The Diary* caricatures its absurd central couple. Meanwhile, the story is not a mere modern echo of old shrew literature. The subjects have adopted new identities, and the text has departed from its precedents in terms of how much tolerance and freedom it grants to the shrew. The shrew is placed in the story for her provocative potential; once the job is done, she is easily left out, her personal story left without resolution. It is not disclosed whether Xingshi remarries or remains single after the divorce. The text seems not to care about bringing the shrew to justice, a situation that would be unthinkable in premodern shrew literature, where a conclusion involving punishment or reform was the norm, even in relatively lighter comedies. The focus here is instead the stimulation of unconventional womanhood or wifehood in relation to Westernism.

The Diary exhibits leniency toward the much-debated Western-inspired "new-style divorce" (*xinshi lihun* 新式離婚).[25] Even though treated as positive in progressive discourses, in popular representations "stories about new-style divorce almost always show that the act is superficial and its results tragic."[26] *The Diary* implies, however, that it is because of new-style divorce, with its easy procedures and fast results, that it is possible for the plot to reach a turning point leading to a happy ending for the different parties. Xingshi brings up the idea of divorce several times in the story, but every time the man kneels and begs her to stay. Obsessed with her, he is unable to restore order to the family, even in the face of his mother's misfortune. The new-style divorce grants the trapped wife the possibility of bringing her request to court to avoid dealing with a weak-kneed husband. In court, the woman defends herself in an eloquent speech. Longqiu Sheng is drawn to her natural and confident demeanor when she talks about the sanctity of freedom (*haowu xiuse kankan tan ziyou shensheng* 毫無羞澀侃侃談自由神聖).[27] He fails to speak up for himself or to respond to her questioning.

Together with other outlandish practices, this new-style legal avenue gives Xingshi a chance to act. It is female resoluteness that compensates for the inability of a man to rebuild harmony. Xingshi is no doubt the source of affliction in the family, but she is simultaneously the terminator of these trials and tribulations, a role that neither the characters of the old world nor the half-new, half-old husband can play. With the aid of progressive rules and laws, she shows that a modern-day, well-equipped shrew could also help restore peace.

Other stories of the 1920s with new women as shrewish wives similarly play with gender role transformation. "I Wish to Transform Myself into a Woman" (*Danqiu huazuo nü'er shen* 但求化作女兒身; 1924) derides the undesirable consequences of modern female education. By narrating how the wife, originally a Confucian model of feminine virtue, becomes a shrew after going to a women's school and studying in Japan, the text makes fun of the reversal of gender hierarchy, joking that it is as if the female sex is now flying high into the sky while the male sex is falling to the ground (*qunci feitian zhuxiong saodi* 群雌飛天諸雄掃地).[28] Likewise, "The Laughable History of Honeymoon Travel" reverses gender roles by giving the husband a feminine name and having the wife adopt a male name and assume characteristics of a despotic warlord (*junfa laopo* 軍閥老婆).[29] Another text, *The Funny History of Henpecking*, consists of ninety anecdotes about all kinds of laughable behavior of shrewish wives. Though called a "history," the collection is not about the diachronic development of the henpecking concept or a compilation of past writings on wife-fearing. Rather, it is a miscellany of modern stories concentrating on comic instances of new-women-turned-shrews, including female students, teachers, athletes, and others. Mimicking contemporary how-to books, the collection provides its (predominantly male)[30] readers with access to numerous conceivable aspects of the new woman, especially what it would be like to marry one.[31] In these stories, the men are spineless and emasculated; the wives are bold, spirited, and manipulative. The plots poke fun at various aspects of the arrival of the new women: upheaval in gender relations, unease with new terms, and artificial or superficial modern minds and appearances. For instance, a self-proclaimed new woman would give up the modern habit of kissing because her husband likes eating garlic.[32]

As in *The Diary*, none of these texts has a moralistic ending. Engaging readers with the kaleidoscope of new female unconventionality, the stories are divorced from the ingrained cautionary tone found in traditional shrew literature and instead invent a carnivalistic play on gender and norms of decency.[33] Figuring gender as a playground in "the fantasy world of play" of *huaji* Shanghai, such constructions make the idea of play and display seem all the more important than conversions of the shrew.[34] While it is widely believed that the temptation of popular fiction lies in its remedying function for urban readers, the texts so far analyzed provide no solutions to the problems wrought by social upheaval and unruly women. Both Westernism and new women are narrated with considerable curiosity and tolerance.

This narrating mode marks the textual difference between the fate of Chinese shrews in the 1920s and that of comparable, corresponding character types in other cultures around the same period. Among them, the category of "the castrating bitch" in American literature "reached full bloom during the male angst–ridden 1920s."[35] Compared to the

American bitch who "will find no victory in male-authored literature; her rewards will be at best an unrelenting existential loneliness and at worst death," the Chinese shrews walk away after wreaking havoc without being tamed, reformed, or subjected to retributive justice.[36] They remain intact in the texts, and the newness associated with them is caricatured rather than compromised, punished, or rejected. The threats are there but are not treated as urgent. Rather than being comfort food, popular fiction in modern China stirs together unusual flavors for the readers to sample. In its unusualness and unconformity, it radically rewrites both gender and genre.

The 1930s and 1940s: Shrewish Wives and Post–May Fourth Polyvocality

In mid- to late Republican China, popular discourses on strong wifehood were more polyvocal and multivalent, and included productions by some well-known New Cultural intellectuals. These materials have been overlooked, repressed, or relegated to positions of relative insignificance because of their seeming frivolity. In making them visible, this section of the chapter examines how they extended May Fourth discussions on women and intersected with the leftist and Communist integration of wifely unruliness.

While some scholarship accounts for the transition from the New Cultural era to the mid- to late Republican period with the notion of "national salvation overriding enlightenment," when it comes to women's liberation, this popular framework is reductive.[37] Rather than being erased by national crisis, the "woman question," covering discussions on female empowerment and repurposed feminine qualities, continued to draw attention, even in the wartime atmosphere. Writings of the 1930s and 1940s update the theme of shrewish wifehood and bring it to a new level of relevance in debates on women, family, and nation. Unlike the leftists (see the next chapter), who incorporated wifely leadership into ideological propaganda, the writers examined in this section showed a diverse approach to the concept of domineering femininity and its relation to state-building.

Tentative, hypothetical, and fanciful, these writings stand in contrast to the serious and strident revolutionary pieces. Although not lacking in incisiveness, they were often sidetracked or diminished on account of their non-canonical, nonpartisan, experimental, and indefinable qualities. Their tone poses a difficulty for scholarly interpretation since textual jokes and facetiousness can be taken in many ways, and the extent to which the authors were being sincere and trustworthy is in question. While there can be no clear answers, this section provides insights into the following issues: Why did the theme of strong wife-hood gain traction in male-dominated discourses in the later phases of the Republic? Why did these male intellectuals, coming from different backgrounds, happen to adopt a similar jocular tone in their treatment of this subject matter? What did the miscellaneous discourses reveal about the shrew's position in the wartime context and her stimulation of men's thoughts on women?

Given the polyvocality of the post–May Fourth era in reshaping cultural, political, and sexual conditions, several factors might have been at play in bringing about the phenomenon of rewriting Chinese wife-hood. First, the escalating national crisis starting from the mid-1920s had impacted elite and popular visions of sexual relationships. On the one hand, along with the global wartime tendency toward an increasing social emphasis on family roles and childbirth (for instance, consider the influence of the world wars on familial status and baby booms in the West), military catastrophes in Republican China gave rise to efforts in law, policy, and public opinion to reaffirm the value of family and women's conventional duties as wives and mothers. Both the Nationalist regime during the Nanjing decade and the leftists and Marxist followers held onto conservative ideas about women's domestic identities. This conservatism constituted the basis for some pro-women discussions. The 1930s and 1940s witnessed debates on the "virtuous wife and wise mother" (xianqi langmu lun 賢妻良母論) and "women going back into the home" (funü huijia lun 婦女回家論).[38] Mounting social tensions resulting from the war stoked public anxieties over abandoned households and neglected child care attributed to women's liberation. On the work front, women launched strenuous objections to the idea of returning to the home for the sake of motherhood.[39] As some contemporaries had observed in 1930s China, the feminist issue was "a subject which seems to have become more and more controversial since the great war," and people had grown to "much prefer the continental type [of feminism] which has always made the home and motherhood the main objectives of its solicitations."[40]

On the other hand, the political turbulence and discursive vacillation also facilitated the public presence of women and opened up opportunities for female transgression in personal and political affairs.[41] The clash between thriving new womanhood and the conventional understanding of women resulted in controversial writings that are uncertain or evasive about women's roles. Focusing on forceful wives at home, these works seem to have adopted an expedient solution for simultaneously saluting the growing profile of Chinese women and sustaining common opinions about domesticity.

"The vogue for humor literature" in the 1930s was another factor likely contributing to the authors' tacit interest in approaching the theme of strong wifehood through comedy.[42] The return of the traditional shrew figure in these writings signals a practice of cultural reconciliation by which both the authors and the audience were able to process the current feminist wave more smoothly. The comical dimension inherited from premodern shrew stories also provides a shield for the writings against castigation and suppression. Yet in the meantime, neither the didactic standpoint in old shrew literature nor the diehard misogyny in popular jokes can fully address the ambivalent stance of these writers. Like the popular comic fiction analyzed in the earlier section, the post–May Fourth renditions are dynamic works that feature creative play with the legacy of the shrew. Rather than grappling with the intent and sincerity of the players, my interpretations pay attention to textual performances, nuances, and any new elements of the shrew–new woman connection.

Lin Yutang: Humor and Beyond

In August 1933 China's "master of humor" Lin Yutang, whose trademark gimmick involved writing about serious topics in a frivolous manner, published an article calling for women to take over the world. Titled "Let Women Do It!" (*Rang niang'er men gan yixia ba* 讓娘兒們幹一下吧), the article appeared in the *Shanghai Daily*'s influential literary column "Free Talk" (*Ziyou tan* 自由談). It follows the American feminist Inez Haynes Irwin (1873–1970) in claiming that men should pass the world to women to rule, as men should feel ashamed of their lack of achievement in governing it.[43] As lighthearted as most of Lin's writings, the article reinforces the notion of unconventional womanhood as a source for resolving thorny issues. The term *niang'er men*, though translated as "women" in English, in no way refers to normal, proper women. This sexist term, together with the male counterpart, *ye'er men* 爺兒們, highlights sex difference and regulation. *Ye'er men* refers to manly men, and *niang'er men* is often derisive (though sometimes mixed with admiration), describing the kind of women who are too strong-willed to be subjected to men's standards and control. Women who are called *niang'er men* are rarely conventionally virtuous types or Confucian ideal ladies but rather the difficult ones whose uncompromising spirits agitate men. In his article Lin listed high-class prostitutes, female intellectuals, and revolutionaries as his candidates for the proposed female leadership position. His choices may seem mischievous and snide, but they attest to the textual espousal of the unrestrained *niang'er men* category; not to mention that the three groups of candidates were indeed at the pioneering forefront of challenging normative stereotyping of Chinese women during the Republican years.

Lin Yutang's proposal about female rule never received its due attention. Critics, including Lu Xun (1881–1936), either took it too literally, denying its probability, or considered it too lightly as lacking substance.[44] Given Lin's flippant style and his pronounced support of wifehood and motherhood, his discourses engaging strong womanhood were largely passed over as nonsense. His other writings in the 1930s criticizing men while glorifying women elicited disgust from some female readers, who interpreted his attitude as deceptive.[45] Likely stemming from his Christian family background and his less radical approach to traditions than those of "almost all the leading proponents of the new culture," Lin's conservative feminism is an eyesore to his contemporaries and some recent researchers.[46] The discrepancy lies in his beliefs about whether traditional Chinese culture should be "uprooted and discarded completely," which also underlie his approach toward new womanhood.[47]

While Lin Yutang is considered a leading exponent of the ideal of the "good wife and virtuous mother" and is linked with the conservative countercurrent of the 1930s and 1940s, particularly in relation to the New Life movement of the Kuomintang Party, we should be aware of the following facts before denouncing him as a hypocrite.[48] First, rather than advocating the New Life movement, he signed a petition against it and the whole KMT idea of resurrecting Confucian ideology.[49] He referred to the movement as "futile," "comic," like "a bad joke, a sick joke."[50] Second, in addition to eulogizing motherhood and wifehood, Lin also constantly promoted the importance of education, independence, and social occupation for Chinese women. He lamented over women who disappear from society after marriage, turning themselves into "breeding machines" (*shengyu jiqi* 生育機器).[51] Third, Lin was one of the few male intellectuals who provided lifelong support for aspiring young Chinese women, including the female soldier Xie Bingying

(1906–2000) and the writer Su Qing (1914–1982).[52] Many of these women's now famous writings were originally encouraged or initiated by Lin. He facilitated modern Chinese literary feminism and even radical feminism instead of thwarting them. When first meeting Xie Bingying, he was drawn to her new woman look and demeanor: "Her hair bobbed, talking and laughing in a hoarse voice. . . . Very soon she was talking so familiarly that we felt as if we had known each other for years, and was telling us stories of the front until I thought the roof was going to fall down on our heads."[53] Although holding dear traditional womanhood, Lin felt no scruples about celebrating Xie's new femininity.

Recognizing this paradox in Lin Yutang's feminist thoughts provides a fuller picture concerning the author and his writings. As Lin himself confessed: "The moment I write about women, my head gets confused. I have thought my way through most of the problems of the universe, but in the matter of women, I find myself continuously landing in contradictions."[54] Not a confirmed believer in the feminism of the day, he vacillated between the ideal of the traditional woman and the idea of unconventional womanhood. His hesitancy in letting go of women's domestic identities could be interpreted as a display of honesty or rigor upon wrestling with women's dilemma. Seen in this light, his points about female rule should be treated more as a case of an ignored strand of thought on female empowerment and the shrew types which goes beyond the widely noted virtuous wife-mother models. Instead of a whim or caprice, "Let Women Do It!" can be viewed differently as it pertains to Lin's corpus of works on powerful women.

The most rebellious of Lin's texts prior to his writing on *niang'er men* was the play *Confucius Saw Nancy* (*Zi jian Nanzi* 子見南子; 1928). Even though the play came out in the late 1920s, it is more in line with the 1930s and 1940s experiments with strong wifehood and state-building. This "one-act tragicomedy" is derived from an enigmatic passage in *The Analects of Confucius* (*Lunyu* 論語) on Confucius's visit to Nanzi, Queen of Wei. Because of the queen's notoriety, the disciple Zi Lu remonstrated with Confucius, making him swear that if he had any improper thoughts, may Heaven strike him. "The oath was so energetically made that it was repeated twice, as it is now recorded in the *Analects* and the *Shiji* [*Records of the Grand Historian*]."[55] As the sole incident in *Analects* involving man–woman interaction with Nanzi being "the only woman mentioned by name," for centuries the meeting had been used as fodder for enactments of what Confucius was truly like.[56] It sparked as many efforts to defend him as intentions to rethink him. When writing the play, Lin went through early sources and legends in hopes that he could re-create a Confucius who has an "extremely human side," beyond being "a sage of immaculate character and divine wisdom."[57]

The emphasis on bringing out "intense humanity" in Confucius, reflecting the May Fourth humanitarian goal, gained support from the New Cultural leaders. Lu Xun commented: "A sage is only human after all and human frailty is excusable. But when the sage's disciples come out and rant, claiming this and that perfection for their Master and insisting that others do likewise, the men cannot help roaring with laughter. . . . Confucius in that play may seem irresponsible and stupid for a sage, but considered as a man he is quite a sympathetic character."[58] The humanitarian light, regrettably, did not shine equally on the characterization of Nanzi in the critique of the play. Lin's contemporary supporters had no comments on the re-creation of the queen. Researchers in China and overseas have likewise paid the most attention to how this play updates the image of Confucius and Confucian ethics. Very few scholars have written on the play's humanization of the lady in question and the feminist tendency in her character.[59] No studies have noted the perspective of the shrew for (re)evaluating the play. I argue that *Confucius Saw Nancy* resembles Ouyang Yuqian's *Pan Jinlian* (which came out a bit earlier the same year) for engaging with the same "shrew versus sage" conflict in its structure.[60] In other words, the play not only scandalizes the sage but also sanitizes the shrew.

Is Nanzi a shrew? She may be more of one than Pan Jinlian, at least at the discursive or imaginative level. She is a lewd *yinfu* according to the Confucians, who portrayed her as "an adulterous, incestuous would-be murderess."[61] She did not really murder her husband like Pan Jinlian, but she is adequately murderous because of her political ambitions and machinations. Symbolically, she had long ago killed her husband, the King of Wei, as she was "more powerful than the king himself, being the real ruler of the kingdom."[62] Nanzi intervened in politics and even had her own partisans.[63] In turn, the king had been criticized in history as "an ineffectual ruler," "a weak monarch dominated by his capable wife," and "an alcoholic lecher," much like a heightened version of a henpecked husband in the shrew narratives.[64] It was also due to Nanzi's (supposed) luridness that she suffered a fate similar to that of Pan Jinlian, threatened by the king's son and nearly killed.

Described as witty in at least *Records of Exemplary Women* (*Lienü zhuan* 列女傳), Nanzi nonetheless remains voiceless in *Analects*.[65] In his comedy Lin Yutang made her a full-blown shrew who engages in sharp repartee that skewers the belief system of Confucius. The sage's glory, in the role of an eloquent educator, dims as he is now educated by the loquacious Nanzi. Confucius sings in the play, "Beware of a woman's tongue, sooner or later you'll get stung" (*furen zhi kou, keyi chuzou* 婦人之口，可以出走).[66] Her words shatter his confidence. Imbued with the mindset of a new woman seeking power and pleasure, her speech escalates in force from attacking patriarchy to denouncing the doctrinal repression of human nature, from speaking for women to expressing her own longing, mirroring the steps that Pan Jinlian takes in occupying Wu Song's mind in *Pan Jinlian*. Nanzi titillates Confucius with ideas about a co-ed literary salon, sexual mingling, and human desire. She also flirts with him through the handling, examining, and (accidental) shattering of a piece of jade—an object that carries a cultural undertone pointing to lust and is suggestive of the destruction of the shrew.

Eventually Nanzi, "taking off her gown, revealing beautiful vests and undergown, joins in the dance, flirting all the while with Confucius."[67] The overwhelmed sage murmurs, "If I were not a believer in the Duke of Chou, I should be a believer in Nancia."[68] Paralleling the trance and stammering in *Pan Jinlian* of Wu Song after being seduced, Confucius at the end of the play hastily chooses to flee, as if in a dream state, to save himself from the influence of Nanzi: "I do not know . . . I have to think . . . [meditating] Nancia's ceremony . . . Nancia's music . . . Life . . . Rhythm . . . Simplicity . . . Naturalness . . . no seclusion of women . . . all freedom . . . emancipation . . ."[69]

When staged, the play received responses similar to those for the other shrew–new woman plays examined in the earlier chapters. The audience mistook Confucius for a laughable negative character, thinking that the sage was being turned into a "clown" (*choumo jiaose* 丑末腳色). The performance and its reception even led to a national political uproar.[70] Nanzi's characterization was not at the center of the dispute since people were busy arguing over Confucius's image. From one instance of criticism recorded by Lu Xun, however, it can be observed that the public was much troubled by her identity. That entry criticized the female teacher who played Nanzi onstage for dressing flamboyantly (*yeyan chushen* 冶艷出神), like a "whore."[71] Even if the definition of the shrew had shifted to place more stress on a woman's feisty spirit and feminist consciousness, to the conservative public, a provocative appearance still marked their assumptions about female transgression. It was Nanzi's look and manner that fired the audience's imagination, not her opinions. Like the controversies stirred by the staging of

Ouyang Yuqian's *The Shrew* and Lan Ping's *Nora*, the criticism targeting the performance of Nanzi reminds one that it was easy for the current public perception of the new woman to slide into the shrew trope for negation and insult. The public was so used to falling back upon misogynistic rhetoric that the interplay between views on the new woman and views on the shrew was always dramatic.

Although it was common for the reception of onstage performances of the new woman to get mixed up with opprobrium toward the shrew, *Confucius Saw Nancy* still conveys something uncommon: the shrew, besides asserting herself and combating gender inequality, could achieve something bigger—she could rule. Nanzi assumes a self-bestowed subjectivity as the female ruler, referring to herself as *gua xiaojun* 寡小君 (which can be translated as "I, the humble lady with sovereign power"). This term of self-reference is mentioned in *Shiji* in connection with Nanzi's summoning of Confucius. It indicates that "Lady Nanzi seems to have been the only woman in the pre-unification era whose public life required her to use this honorific."[72] Given that *guaren* 寡人 and *jun* 君 are both established honorifics culturally and hierarchically reserved for male rulers, the term suggests her high-ranking position in history as well as an innovative and potentially subversive fashioning of her own identity through a play on pronouns, personas, and power.

The myth surrounding Nanzi's notoriety is never clear as to whether it was actual promiscuity that made her scandalous or whether it was general hostility toward capable aristocratic women that caused opponents to smear her through the charge of sexual immorality. Nanzi's situation seems like the article "A Wanton Woman Joins the Reform," analyzed in chapter 1, in which a woman is vilified as a *yinfu* because of her enthusiasm in participating in the reform movement. Lin Yutang added his understanding to this puzzle, which is revealed by some textual particularities. Since the play was based on limited material in ancient documents, where to place and how to ground Confucius's most confusing oath is significant. Instead of having Confucius swear after hearing from other characters about the spreading of "filthy language and obscene conduct" (*yinyan huixing* 淫言穢行) in the kingdom of Wei (although he must have had heard about the queen's infamy), the play situates the oath almost halfway through, when the sage has heard an abundance of information about Nanzi's political dominance.[73] The oath appears right after the disciple Zi Lu quotes the queen's statement about her role as the *gua xiaojun*: "She says that all scholars who visit her country and wish to remain as guests of the court must see her about it" (*dou fei jian gua xiaojun buke* 都非見寡小君不可).[74]

Lin Yutang did not offer a direct explanation of Confucius's oath, yet by introducing Nanzi as both a seductive beauty and the de facto ruler, he seemed to refute the suspicion that the sage might be lustful. He showed that Confucius's anxiety as articulated by the oath may be related more to the fact that he is meeting someone in power (despite the sex of that person) than to the assumption that he is lowering himself by visiting a woman of ill repute.[75] There is a constant tug-of-war in the text between Zi Lu's emphasis on Nanzi's moral decadence and Confucius's insistence on hearing about governance from women ("*zheng*" *buyou furen tinglai, you nali tinglai?* "政" 不由婦人聽來，由那裏聽來?).[76] Lin never diminished Nanzi's political excellence to foreground her sexual attraction. Therefore both desire and hierarchy are responsible for Confucius's unsettled state. An adjustment made in the translation of the play further demonstrates authorial approval of female power in politics. When Nanzi is first mentioned by the male characters, Lin replaced a plain and irrelevant line in the Chinese script with this punch line in the English version: "You know women always rule the world, don't they?"[77] It comes as a surprise since the message on female rule appears much later in the original script. The author-translator seems to have been eager to spotlight this topic early and explicitly for English-language readers.

Nanzi is a *yinfu* and/or a ruler. The image of the shrew here is versatile, engaging with not only unruly femininity but also feminine rule. Lin's approach, compared to the visions of other Nora plays, goes a step further in celebrating shrews as rulers and vice versa. The benefits of the shrew figure extend beyond personal subjectivity and family welfare to public governance. From Nanzi and from the 1930s onwards, Lin Yutang then made a series of efforts to explore themes of wifely mastery and women's management. His later "Let Women Do It!" hence signifies a breakthrough in his line of writing on strong women. As a straightforward shout-out to capable women, "Let Women Do It!" no longer wraps the motif of female force in the clothing of a man's story, as in *Confucius Saw Nancy*—in which, as indicated by the title itself, Confucius is the subject who drives the plot and makes Nanzi seeable through his "seeing" initiative. The Chinese word *jian* for "saw" also carries the meanings of "to reveal" or "to make seen" (*xian*), which hints at the woman's secondary, derivative existence.

Two years after publishing "Let Women Do It!" in 1935, Lin impressed the public with two of his English works: the book *My Country and My People* and the article "Feminist Thought in Ancient China" published in *T'ien Hsia Monthly*.[78] The former devotes a chapter to women's lives in China, which, in addition to clichés about women's innate position in the home, passionately embraces female power. It attributes the idea of "suppression of women" to superficial Occidental criticism that dismisses how Chinese women "rule the household and their husbands." Lin asks: "Have women really been suppressed in China, I often wonder? The powerful figure of the Empress Dowager immediately comes to my mind. Chinese women are not the type to be easily suppressed. Women have suffered many disadvantages, have been prevented from holding stenographic positions or judicial posts, but women have ruled nevertheless in the home, apart from those debauchee households where women have become toys. Even in these homes, some of the concubines manage to rule their lords."[79]

Promoting the right to be "wife and mother" as the "best weapon for power" for women, Lin Yutang's exhortation alongside the "good wife, wise mother" discourse of the time might seem like two faces of the same coin. Yet textual details suggest an ambivalence. The forceful females he listed, from the Empress Dowager to Cleopatra and King Lear's daughters in Shakespeare's play, are obvious counterexamples to the ideal of Confucian virtuous women. While claiming that "woman rules in the family, while man rules outside it," he also encouraged women to rule the world through their wifely and motherly talents. "There are many Empress Dowagers in China still, politically or in common households. The home is the throne from which she makes appointments for mayors or decides the professions of her grandsons." More critically, Lin interpreted Chinese women's nonconforming behavior at home as their conscious resistance: "Man has undoubtedly been unfair to woman, yet it is interesting to see how sometimes woman has her revenge."[80] He took delight in the references to the shrew as indications of women's ability, rather than using the shrew examples to reinforce the demeaning custom.

In writing "Feminist Thought in Ancient China," Lin was "the first to outline the dissent 'feminist' voices within the tradition."[81] In this long essay, he disclosed aspects of masculine ethics underpinning Chinese history and culture. By identifying three writers "whose views on the woman problem entitle them to be called Chinese feminists," Lin lashed out at unfair codes imposed upon women. He praised the reversal of the sexes and women's rule in the Qing novel *Flowers in the Mirror*. Like Hu Shi, he paid tribute to the jealous wife of the bandit chief (also see chapter 2), linking her shrewish attributes to the prospects of the feminist movement: "My feeling about the whole affair is that it always requires some measure of feminine ferocity to put a feminist programme through. This robber's wife could have smashed shop-windows in Piccadilly, true to western feminist style. Women who are sweet-natured always marry off and shut up, and that is the secret of the defeat or lull in the feminist movement to-day."[82] Lin's statement on feminine ferocity resonates with other thoughts and representations examined in this book, stressing again the uncomfortable truth that women had and will have to revert to the shrew's means to be heard, seen, and taken seriously in a frustrating environment.

In 1936 some publications about Lin Yutang again attracted public attention to his evasive standpoint on the status of Chinese women. In an interview with Lin and his wife that was published in the *Shanghai Daily*, this master of humor "denounced" contemporary new women, especially those engaging in politics, for "holding the limelight" (*chu fengtou* 出風頭). His remarks as well as the idea of women's inherent duties as wives and mothers have been used as proof of his regressive conservatism.[83] Criticism like this nonetheless ignores the fact that Lin, in that same interview, also urged men to be "good husbands and virtuous fathers" and openly condemned the dependent status of Chinese women, the repressive sexual morality, and the double standard that obstructed women's emancipation in society.[84]

In subsequent years, after relocating to the West, Lin continued to bring strong Chinese femininity to the fore and to the world. In his most popular novel, *Moment in Peking* (*Jinghua yanyun* 京華煙雲; 1939), the character Yao Mulan represents a pleasant fusion of traditional feminine virtues and modern womanhood. Lin also translated and retold stories of marginalized women from Chinese literature (as reflected in his *Widow, Nun, and Courtesan* in 1951 and *Famous Chinese Short Stories* in 1952), highlighting outspoken, resilient, and bold female characters.[85] His *Lady Wu: A True Story* in 1957, intended as a "strictly historical biography" of Empress Wu, adds more strands to the issue of female rule. "This is the last novel Lin wrote. It forms an interesting contrast to the first female image Lin created in 1928, the queen Nanzi, and reflects his lasting effort to reconstruct demonized women in Chinese history."[86] The political atmosphere of the late 1950s might have

affected his analogizing of Wu Zetian to Stalin. But his textual indictment is directed against the sweeping concept of despotic rule and "the
wicked" in general, which can pertain to either sex. When seeing Wu
as a woman, he recognized her "fabulous" and "unique" character, her
"high, keen, cool intelligence," "sanity," "astuteness," and "boundless
ambition and audacity."[87]

Hu Shi and Xu Zhimo: The Nation of Henpecking

To Lin Yutang and other New Cultural thinkers, the ruling shrew is a
haunting theme. Among them, Hu Shi was particularly vocal on this
matter. In December 1931 Hu finished the overdue work "A Textual
Study of *Marriage Bonds to Awaken the World*" (*Xingshi yinyuan zhuan
kaozheng* 醒世姻緣傳考證), a solicited preface to Yadong Press's punc-
tuated edition of the novel. Hu's commitment to this outrageous shrew
story might have intertwined with elements of his personal life.

He got the invitation to start working on the preface in 1924 or 1925,
around the time when he made failed attempts to divorce his wife from
an arranged marriage, Jiang Dongxiu (1890–1975). It was widely spread
that Jiang, though having bound feet, was quite fierce. She once threw a
kitchen knife at Hu when he tried to leave her for his young lover (and
non-blood-related cousin) Cao Chengying (1902–1973).[88] According to
the account of the historian Tang Degang, Jiang's feistiness even scared
away a burly burglar when the couple was staying in New York in the
1950s.[89] Other anecdotes surrounding her are plentiful.[90] Unlike most
wives of arranged marriages to contemporary male intellectuals, who
usually remained voiceless and insignificant, Jiang played a sizable role
in her husband's life. She seemed to understand how best to manipu-
late him. Knowing that Hu Shi cared about his "face," or reputation,
she was said to have consciously chosen to behave loudly and hysteri-
cally in public to make him less likely to argue with her.[91]

Although the real-life incidents provide additional dimensions for
explaining Hu Shi's interest in the shrew, the more verifiable sources
are the author's speeches and writings on this theme.[92] In July 1933 Hu
spoke in the Haskell Lecture Series of the Department of Comparative
Religion at the University of Chicago on Chinese cultural transformation. One of the lectures he delivered was titled "Social Disintegration
and Readjustment," in which Hu, like Lin Yutang later in *My Country
and My People*, presented to the Western audience a non-stereotyped
image of Chinese women: "The position of women in the old family

was never so low as many superficial observers have led us to believe. On the contrary, woman has always been the despot of the family. The authority of the mother and the mother-in-law is very well known. Even the wife is always the terror of the husband; no other country in the world can compete with China for the distinction of being the nation of hen-pecked husbands."[93] He went on to label henpecking a national hallmark for which China should be respected. The prevalence of strong wives, he claimed, indicates superiority and democracy for the nation. He listed exemplary females from Sujie in *Marriage Bonds to Awaken the World* to some historical figures, using the shrew imagery to enable a refreshing look at China for the Westerners. It was through the rhetoric of the shrewish wife and the henpecked husband that Hu found a shortcut to political wisdom, humor, and ways of international communication.

Between 1938 and 1942 Hu Shi served as Chinese ambassador to the United States. The Republican scholar Luo Jialun (1897–1969) recalled a joke that Hu used to tell him:

> People all know that I [Hu Shi] collect honorary degrees, and they also know I collect matchboxes. (He liked to collect the various kinds of exquisite U.S. matchboxes, and had thousands of them.) But they don't know that I also collect stories of henpecked husbands. I have collected stories of henpecked husbands of various countries and done an analysis of them. I found that Germany and Japan have the fewest stories of henpecked husbands, and often their limited number of such stories are imported from foreign countries, too. So my conclusion is: Only in democratic countries do you have the phenomenon of henpecked husbands; in totalitarian countries you do not.[94]

Hu's hobby was more than a "light and humorous" joke, as Luo put it.[95] According to Hu himself, he "began as early as 1942 to collect henpecked husband stories, jokes, and cartoons in all language."[96] The Indian diplomat K. P. S. Menon also referred in his memoir to Hu Shi's idea about the relationship between the number of henpecking stories in a country and its degree of democracy.[97] Hu had been giving speeches on henpecking and politics at clubs and universities, being rather open about his penchant for collecting anything relevant to wife-fearing.[98] He explained his politicization of the shrew theme as follows:

> In this collection you may find the key to the understanding of great international problems, even the problems of war and peace. Look

here: I have many hundreds of Chinese stories of hen-pecked husbands, but none from the Japanese. I have hundreds of American,
English, French and Scandinavian stories (and I have only included
a few out of McManus' *Bringing Up Father*), but there is none from
Germany. Shall we be justified to conclude that the sub-species
of mankind—the hen-pecked husband—is the product of only the
democratic countries, and does not grow on totalitarian soil?[99]

When his collection expanded in 1943, Hu Shi found that his conclusion was verified by the case of Italy: with many henpecking stories in
its culture, it surrendered to the Allies.[100]

In 1948 someone pen-named Yin published an article titled "Long
Live the Missus" (*Taitai wansui* 太太萬歲) in *Peking Daily*, which might
have intersected with the public sensation (to be discussed in a later
section of this chapter) stirred up by the screening of Zhang Ailing's
(1920–1995) film of the same title in 1947. The article recounts a
speech Hu Shi had recently delivered at Peking University on the political reading of wife-fearing. Hu had stated again, "China has lots of
these stories, so China is sure to be democratic."[101] Yin's writing exhibits sensitivity to popular cultural trends and a grasp of the change of
terminology designating women's (political) power.

Acknowledging that henpecking had achieved rising visibility and
value in public discussion, Yin commented on a linguistic transformation engendered by this trend: "The long-standing colloquial term
'*pa laopo*' has recently been replaced with a new popular phrase: '*taitai
wansui*.'"[102] Different from the misogynistic connotation carried by the
verb *pa* (to fear) in *pa laopo*, the neologism *taitai wansui* communicates,
at least linguistically, a celebratory attitude toward forceful wives. The
once passive husband who was "scared and henpecked" now wishes for
the longevity of his wife. Instead of a fearsome being making men nervous, the wife is transformed into an admirable ruler who receives worship. By shifting from the object of criticism in *pa laopo* to the superior
subject in *taitai wansui*, the wife takes on increased authority. As *wansui*
(ten thousand years of living) is a blessing dedicated to male rulers,
the new catchphrase evokes the notion of female leadership along with
the heightened social recognition of wifely supremacy. As supporting
evidence, Yin mentioned the central position that female delegates had
assumed at recent National Assembly and argued that women's abili-
ties are the exact reason why they are vulnerable to men's manipulation,
a point that asserts the extension of female power into politics and the
desirability of having a ruling wife at home.

Stimulated by Hu Shi's speech, the leftist writer and critic Nie Gannu launched an accusation against patriarchy. Nie suggested that wife-fearing would be more meaningful if approached as a social phenomenon rather than a story genre. He found fault with the fact that there never were any terms for husband-fearing in a patriarchal culture. Chinese women were taken for granted as "sex objects of the husbands" (*laogong de xing de duixiang* 老公的性的對象) and "non-human beings" (*nüren bushi ren* 女人不是人) who "existed secondarily in addition to dependently" (*bushi yicong zhi cong, dao jingshi zhucong zhi cong* 不是依從之從, 倒逕是主從之從).[103] Nie questioned wifely vices such as jealousy and resistance to concubinage, and characterized the literary convention on women's situation as problematic: "The female characters that great writers are happy to write about are often the victims [*xisheng zhe* 犧牲者] like Lin Daiyu and Anna Karenina."[104] He instead supported Pan Jinlian, who he thought does nothing wrong in a mismatched relationship. Other contemporaneous reflections on Hu Shi's remarks either carried on with the comical tone or similarly took it as a chance to attack male-centrism.[105]

Hu Shi and his contemporaries felt the need for underlying banter in addressing women's expanding role. They showed that the current promotion of renewed ideas on the good wife and mother as well as women returning to the home was inadequate for describing the status of Chinese women. No matter whether discussing sexual equality, democratic prospects, or colloquial vogue, their uses of the shrew point out that there is more to this female type than how tradition had handled her. In her existence and endurance lies her value; like a treasure house not yet drained of its contents, she always seems to have things to offer to explorers.

Xu Zhimo, a close friend of Hu Shi, also joined in the exploration. In his preface to *Marriage Bonds to Awaken the World*, Xu expressed practical views on the positives of wife-fearing. Invited by Hu to write an article on the literary greatness of the novel for its republication, Xu later laughed about the fact that he had ended up commenting too much on marital relationships. He thought the kind of strife depicted in this premodern piece was quite common in modern marriages. In his opinion, the shrew Sujie is defensible on two grounds: her "open" temper and her fair disciplining of her husband. Xu excused the shrew's violence on the grounds that the husband is not worthy of pity in either emotion or reason. Sujie's vehement tongue is appreciated for producing "superb speeches" (*juemiao de ciling* 絕妙的詞令) filled with "pure rationality" (*chuncui lixing* 純粹理性). "Her sharp tongue points to the fact that she is at least a frank lady. Yes, Sujie beats and curses, but hers are all open and positive deeds. With her assurance and eloquence alone, you simply cannot take her as a bad woman. Some friends of mine only wish that their wives could have Sujie's openness and fairness!"[106]

Xu used polite, modern wording (such as *yiwei* 一位 and *nüxing* 女性) to describe the shrew. As a Westernized neologism for "women," *nüxing* especially designates the new women, since it rarely appears with prefixes like "old," "old-style," or "traditional." The choice of diction indicates that Xu Zhimo was purposeful in employing Sujie's image to concretize expected qualities for favorable modern wifehood. Calling the new women "modern Sujies" (*xiandai de Sujie* 現代的素姐), he stressed wifely discipline of problematic husbands and urged modern Chinese wives to emulate Sujie by being "completely objective and clearheaded" so that they could wield their feminine advantages with dignity.[107]

There exists a thin line in Xu's writing between pleasant wifely maneuvering and the preposterous kind. Unruly womanhood is handled with authorial caution. While it is not hard to perceive overtones of superiority, of the author positioning himself as the supervisor surveilling and instructing women in their performance of femininity and wifehood, Xu's article articulates more frustrations and compromises in comparison with earlier discourses on the molding of new womanhood. As women themselves grew more self-aware as modern subjects holding power over men, they constituted an independent source of distress, instead of being the result or projection of "an aesthetics of despair" of "the intellectual (male-centered) self."[108] The textual excitement about wifely regulation overshadows Xu's light sarcasm targeting the threat of the modern wives. Both Xu Zhimo and Hu Shi recognized the challenge of shrewish wifehood, but they were more willing to reckon with its pervasiveness, considering it so commonplace nationally that it formed the basis of their alternative expressions on the intersection of femininity, family, and the fashioning of modern democracy.

Li Zongwu: Redefining Virtuous Wifehood

Women remained easy targets of critique in the 1940s when overall political conditions deteriorated. Debates on the role of wives in building mature manhood continued in this war-ravaged era. Li Zongwu (1879–1943), a politician and scholar, wrote a short pamphlet titled *The*

Philosophy of Wife-Fearing (*Pa laopo de zhexue* 怕老婆的哲學), which was published in 1946. The text bears a resemblance to Hu Shi's discourse on henpecking but has been much neglected. Given the name Zongru (宗儒: literally, "following Confucianism") at birth, Li underwent an iconoclastic transition in his mid-twenties and decided to rename himself Zongwu (literally, "following myself"). He was one of the pre–May Fourth iconoclasts who launched scathing attacks on Confucian principles. Even before Lu Xun's awakening cry in 1918 in writing his madman character against the cannibalistic ideology of Confucianism, Li had published several widely recognized writings, including *Thick Black Theory* (*Houhei xue* 厚黑學), exposing the dark side of Confucian strictures. During wartime, many of Li's writings were converted into humorous self-help handbooks on survival strategies.[109] Today, some of his works are still shunned by researchers for his penchant for using popular formulae and cheap humor.

The Philosophy has received little to no scholarly attention. The text, written during the Second Sino-Japanese War, contends that the way to revive the Chinese nation is to replace the central child-parent relationship with the husband-wife relationship. It foregrounds wife-fearing as the force that can strengthen men, fortify families, and eventually save China from the war.[110] If a man fears his wife, Li Zongwu reasoned, he will become a better climber of the social ladder, as proved by high-achieving and heavily henpecked men in history. He proposed that there should be a new set of ethics on henpecking: there would be "biographies of henpecked husbands" instead of "biographies of loyal ministers" and "biographies of filial sons"; there would be a specific discipline of wife-fearing; men would attend "The Research Society of Fear-ology," and women would go to "The Practice Seminar of Roaring Lionesses."[111] He created a *Classic of Wife-Fearing* (*Pa Jing* 怕經), which is modeled on, alters, and pieces together traditional classics including the *Classic of Filial Piety*, *Analects*, and *Book of Rites*. In replacing filial piety with wife-fearing and inverting the marital hierarchy to privilege wives, the treatise exceeds the limits of bantering fun and swerves into radicalness. One passage in the text reads: "There are few who, while fearing one's wife, dare to do evil outside. There have been no countries, where nobody dares to do evil, that cannot prosper. The gentleman bends his attention to what is radical. That being established, all practical courses naturally grow up. The ones who fear their wives are the foundation for reviving China!"[112]

Li's satires have been treated as forms of cultural cynicism. Zhang Mosheng (1895–1979), a reader-turned-friend to Li and his self-proclaimed soulmate, maintained that *The Philosophy* should be read in a similar vein as *Thick Black Theory* for ridiculing social ills and moral decline. Others took Li's points on wife-fearing as a political metaphor directed at the Nationalist government in the "Great Rear Region" (*da houfang* 大後方).[113] In 2009 a scholar named Chen Yuan challenged the mainstream approaches to Li Zongwu's works. Chen argued that Zhang Mosheng's interpretations are based on his speculation instead of Li's "original intent." On *The Philosophy*, Chen claimed, "Other than as another satire, it should be understood as an echo of Hu Shi."[114] It is unknown whether Hu and Li had any interactions, but Chen Yuan made a sound point by approaching Li Zongwu's wife-fearing discourse on its own terms and in association with comparable articulations of the time. Li did share with Hu the habit of linking henpecking to larger issues of patriotism, democracy, and diplomacy. They both reversed the neo-Confucian gender code and assigned the prescribed morality of "three followings and four virtues" (*sancong side* 三從四德), originally required of women, to men.[115] While Li asked for societies and seminars, Hu intended to establish a "PTT Club" (*pa taitai julebu* 怕太太俱樂部), which was said to have existed in Chinese circles in the United States.[116]

More than being simply a facetious play on traditional concepts, *The Philosophy* updates the definition of the "good wife and wise mother" ideal. At the end of his pamphlet, Li wrote:

> These days people are singing the praises of the old idea of "virtuous wife and good mother," making our women unhappy. It is a misunderstanding. The four words—virtuous, wife, good, mother—follow along, forming a natural flow, rather than two parallel concepts. The virtuous wife is the good mother. The way of being a wife is the way of being a mother. . . . Therefore, a wife bears in herself the responsibilities of a parent, a teacher, and a guardian to her husband. How can she act casually and carelessly? Wives guide husbands. Can our women shun this duty?[117]

When read against the current social backdrop, this remark comes across as less surprising or preposterous. Like many others, Li Zongwu seems to have been negotiating the conflict for women between returning to the home and reaching for greater goals. As he described it, wifehood is, or should be, no longer secondary to motherhood; in this fused model he proposed, being a newly defined virtuous wife automatically fulfills the duty of being a mother. Wives can be moral and patriotic because their mothering of their husbands would prepare the men for the state. It is men who require mothering, monitoring, and molding from women.

In closing his treatise, Li emphasized that the ability to mother and rule (husbands) marks the new virtue of modern Chinese wives. The social call for "women going back home," according to him, should be understood as publicizing women's power in an alternative manner. The call, instead of repeating doctrines, was in fact encouraging women to explore the "home front" as their battleground; their ambitions in career, life, and nationalism could all meet in the act of exerting control over their husbands. In line with Lin Yutang and other pro-women writers during the unrest of the mid- to late Republican period, Li Zongwu blended absurdity and compromises into his language when commenting on Chinese new womanhood. His redefinition of the virtuous wife, toying with the idea of women's rule at home, underscores the choiceless choice facing liberation-minded women. "Since the society was not yet ready to provide women sufficient opportunities, both economically and politically, for their independence," Li and other male thinkers might "have thought it best to remind them not to ignore their power at home."[118] Such an approach is not unlike the *kunwei* idea mentioned in chapter 1, which, on the eve of the new era, had attempted to regulate women's influence by persuading them to exercise power at home. Now, registered in the closing stage of Republican China, the same rhetoric reads more like a desperate expedient derived from three decades of struggle over the position(ing) of women.

One year after the publication of *The Philosophy*, resonances of Li Zongwu's points on wifely mentorship fired up Shanghai popular opinion columns in response to the screening of the film *Long Live the Missus* (*Taitai wansui*; 1947). Written by Zhang Ailing and directed by Sang Hu (1916–2004), the film follows the story of Chen Sizhen, a petty-bourgeois housewife who compromises her happiness for the sake of family, and her cheating husband. This family melodrama was a big box office success in postwar Shanghai but received few positive reviews in the media. Critics including the famous leftist dramatist Hong Shen published articles in leading Shanghai newspapers for more than a month denouncing the wifely submission and sacrifice the movie embraces.[119] The intellectual circles had anticipated a strong female lead as advertised by the movie title, only to find a mediocre bourgeois wife. Even though she is not a conventional type of woman, she uses her cunning in lying and preserving the marriage. The film presents elements of "matriarchal victory" and power-wielding wife-hood resembling the remedy that Lin Yutang, Hu Shi, and Li Zongwu prescribed for ambitious yet publicly thwarted new women; the audiences of the late 1940s, however (especially the leftists), found Sizhen too mild, even self-deprecating.[120]

A female viewer, Shen Xie, wrote a letter to a newspaper from the perspective of a *taitai*, expressing her frustration over the fact that this vision of submissive wifehood was from a woman writer. Shen identified herself as a movie lover in her twenties who often felt annoyed by the weak and tragic wife characters in films written by male scriptwriters. Having expected *Long Live the Missus* to be different, she was disappointed and offended. "A good wife is not a lapdog or stupid slave [*hao qizi bushi habagou ye bushi sha nucai* 好妻子不是哈叭狗也不是傻奴才] but someone with human dignity," she insisted, and went on to question how the female writer could wish longevity for a failed wife model (*mei chuxi de "taitai" haixiang rang ta huo "wansui"* 没出息的"太太"還想讓她活"萬歲").[121] In her letter, Shen referred to a character named Xie Dai'e in Tian Han's *Recalling the Southland* (*Yi Jiangnan* 憶江南; 1947) as the kind of capable wife she revered. She lauded Xie for being a "new type of virtuous wife and wise mother" (*xianqi liangmu de xin dianxing* 賢妻良母的新典型) who "resists a husband of no soul," "never takes off shoes or fetches cigarettes for her husband but always smilingly encourages him to improve himself."[122] To Shen, the ideal wife should lead, not follow, and be willing to regulate the problematic husband instead of lowering herself to suit him.

On the same page where Shen Xie's letter was published, Hong Shen wrote from a husband's point of view. Unsatisfied with the absence of discipline for the husband in the film, he had wanted immediate "punishment" (*chengfa* 懲罰) and "admonition" (*xunjie* 訓誡) from the wife, hoping that she could either transform him or leave him.[123] Given Hong's identity as a left-wing dramatist (like Tian Han), scholars have suggested that the whole campaign of criticizing *Long Live the Missus* was organized by the Shanghai underground Communist Party, with Hong's piece serving as the voice of the "organization" (*zuzhi* 組織).[124] Whether or not the criticisms were related to the CCP movement, Hong Shen's wish gives a snapshot of the more didactic and authoritative style of the leftist approach toward wifely duties and functions.

The works this chapter has examined represent the popular strand of discourses on new configurations of the shrewish wife. Although some writings were disregarded or derided for their seeming flippancy, there was clearly an active trend toward the popularization, prioritization, and politicization of feisty wifehood. The concept of wifely leadership and rulership, so dominant in popular constructions, goes beyond the jesting pattern even to secure a grip on revolutionary creations. In the leftist and Communist writings, transgressive (while ideologically conforming) rural wives are publicly upheld as models. The way that modern womanhood is woven into ideological fabrics foreshadows the shrewd Maoist in/exclusion of women in Communist state-building in the decades to come. In Maoist literature, the first step for the revolutionary new woman is to revolt against her backward husband, a plot point that would lead the connection between challenging forms of wifehood and national progress to political monotony but also further textual complexity.

CHAPTER 5

Revolutionary Views on the Shrewish Wife

From Husband-Disciplining to Early Communist State-Building

From Shanghai to Yan'an, from individualism to collectivism, Jiang Qing's life trajectory in the 1930s followed the recurring scenario in many post–May Fourth Nora stories by the leftist writers. Compared to illusionary ideals of freedom depicted in earlier Nora constructions, the leftist stories grounded the Nora dream in revolution. They aimed at transforming Nora from a bourgeoise to a revolutionary who joins the masses and serves the larger missions of the nation.[1] Public discussions in the 1930s centered on Nora's social interactions after leaving home, mostly concluding that for a Chinese woman to become a real Nora, she should walk not simply out of her house but into the revolutionary crowds in the streets.[2] To the early Communists, the Nora-as-shrew imagery acquired new representations in policy and propaganda. From its initial years to the heyday of the Great Leap Forward (1958–1961), Communist state-building was intertwined with negotiations of gender, home, labor, power, and specifically the wife's role.

Mao Dun and Jiang Guangci: The Early Leftist Writings

Mao Dun wrote several new woman stories during the late 1920s and early 1930s. These works provide an example of the leftist path that reshapes the Chinese Nora into a revolutionary icon. Mao's heroines, though sexually alive and aware, treat their bodies lightly, aspiring to channel their libidos into the collective cause. On the one hand, these new Chinese Nora characters are recognized for their strong personalities as "shrewish, spicy, and wild" (*pola kuangfang* 潑辣狂放).[3] On the other hand, because of the overall uncertainty of the leftist revolution at the time, Mao's new woman characters also feel perplexed and stymied. They long for the heat of revolution but are unsure where to go or what to do.

Among Mao Dun's new woman stories, his first short story, "Creation" (*Chuangzao* 創造; 1928), establishes a new mode of narrative on the theme of women and revolution. Setting out to follow the Nora formula, the story sketches a brief fragment of the life of a middle-class couple which is a mix of enlightenment, discipline, and deception. The husband, Junshi, like many New Cultural male intellectuals, is obsessed with inventing a new-style wife, and his methods include coercion and manipulation. The awakened wife, Xianxian, soon finds herself increasingly intolerant of her husband's control and his petty foibles. As she absorbs more progressive ideas, she begins to feel that Junshi, rather than elevating her, is trapping her in domestic life, holding her back from embarking upon other meaningful paths. At the end of the story Xianxian leaves home. She asks the maidservant to tell Junshi that "she will go first, please catch up with her. Even if he won't, she is not going to wait." The man is left in a speechless trance (*huanghu* 恍惚).[4]

"Creation" introduces changes to the standard Nora narrative. Instead of slamming the door in the man's face, Xianxian chooses to sneak out, making the act of flight more urgent than a dramatic performance. The fact that she does not even bother to write a note to her husband points to her determination to leave. Unwilling to assert her independence in front of Junshi, or perhaps not expecting him to listen and follow, the resolute Xianxian turns a new page in the writing of the Chinese Nora. But where does she go?

Mao Dun once disclosed in an article that he had a clear vision when writing "Creation": the path Xianxian selects is "revolution" (*geming* 革命).[5] This statement has led scholars to celebrate the story for "representing the contemporary leftist ideology" and constituting the perfect leftist "Pygmalion myth."[6] Mao also explicated his perception of women and revolution, writing: "Xianxian is 'the created,' among many other Chinese women who are bound by Confucian ethics. However, once she is 'created' and liberated, her revolutionary ambitions go far beyond the imagination of Junshi. She fears nothing and proceeds with great courage. . . . I imply this idea in 'Creation': Once the revolution is started, it will go out of control and press forward with unstoppable force. Even if there will be many obstacles along the way, nothing can stop the advance. The awakening of the oppressed is like this too."[7]

Paralleling two agents of the same action (of proceeding and pressing forward), Mao Dun equated the fate of Chinese women with that of the social revolution. In his view, revolution is to be articulated and fulfilled through the vehicle of women. Xianxian hence carries more metaphorical value than a young woman fighting for her own good. Mao's use of the gender-specific pronoun "she" (*ta* 她) seems deliberate in referring to Xianxian and revolution at the same time. Since the Chinese state and causes in the service of the nation are often gendered female, the author here was allegorically envisioning a promising future for the Communist struggle. The irresistible craving of the creator for a blend of a flourishing nation and a vigorous woman gives shape to this ideal Xianxian, acclaimed as the "revolutionary goddess" (*geming de nüshen* 革命的女神), who is commendable in both sexual and political terms.[8] The story gives Xianxian a considerable degree of autonomy in terms of leaving her husband/creator, but she is still subject to the intention of the author. She is not so much a free woman as she is a doll manipulated to express the fantasies of Mao Dun—her ultimate creator.[9] It is universally disturbing to see women's identities tied up with revolution in the leftist works; yet we should note the textual particularity of "Creation." If Xianxian is used and exploited, what about men's identities? Do male characters enjoy (more) autonomy and power? In "Creation," the answer is no.

In May Fourth fiction, the wives, even if identified as new women, are subject to supervision and control by their husbands. The most noted works included Lu Xun's "Regret for the Past" (*Shang shi* 傷逝; 1925) and Ye Shengtao's (1894–1988) *Schoolmaster Ni Huanzhi* (*Ni Huanzhi* 倪煥之; 1928). In both works the wives are the objects of criticism and transformation, and their husbands sigh over the women's failure to meet their expectations. No room is provided for the wives to claim their way of living and confront or change the husbands according to their standards. Scholarship coins the term "wife-taming" (*xun qi* 馴妻) to describe this literary phenomenon in the May Fourth canon, where the husbands are "brutal and tyrannical" (*baonüe* 暴虐).[10] "Creation" nonetheless presents a shift in such a power paradigm. If Xianxian has a deprived form of subjectivity, her husband, Junshi, is further stripped of power. Gradually shifting away from wifely passivity, the textual characterization of the couple implies a changing hierarchy between husband and wife. When the wife comes to figure the revolutionary path, she gains the upper hand and starts to lead. The image of the husband, previously dynamic and dominant, now symbolizes backward and reactionary forces to be corrected or eliminated. As an element critical to the Communist reform, marital relationships would continue to undergo remodeling in the propagandist writings to come.

Mao Dun's experiment with wifely leadership soon found a resonance in Jiang Guangci's (1901–1931) novel *The Roaring Earth* (*Paoxiao le de tudi* 咆哮了的土地; 1932). Jiang was one of the most influential proletarian writers of revolutionary literature, known for his invention of the "revolution plus love" formula. *Roaring* was Jiang's last novel, which marks his transcendence of that formula to write about peasants, class struggle, and direct revolutionary activities. The novel is set against the failed Communist revolution in 1927, focusing on a young revolutionary intellectual named Li Jie. Although the son of a landlord, Li believes in Communism; after he completes his studies, he returns to the countryside to mobilize the peasants against the landlords. His ambition in class struggle is mixed with pain and sorrow stemming from an intergenerational clash that imbues the story with emotional tension. The groundbreaking depiction of Chinese peasants as awakened militants instead of benighted and weak-minded countrymen adds to the reputation of the novel.[11] Espousing "a 'spontaneous' uprising of the proletariat against the ruling class," the work is regarded as "one of the most important models for Chinese Communist fiction of the 1940s and 1950s."[12]

A less noted aspect of the novel lies in its advocacy of wifely rebellion against oppressive husbands. From *Roaring*, the most crucial form of patriarchal oppression in the leftist works started to switch from intellectual arrogance (with the urban husband in "Creation" as an example) to physical abuse of peasant women by their men. Women's liberation was accordingly recoded as first and foremost the right to live free from violence. The story of Hejie (or Sister He), the farmer Wu Changxing's wife in *Roaring*, expresses this idea. She is only a secondary character, but her growth from a victim of domestic violence to a spontaneous leader at home and in the community reflects the tactics that the early Communists employed for recruiting rural women.

Wu Changxing is a poor tenant peasant in his thirties. Unlike other exploited peasants who rely on superstition to relieve their suffering, Wu is conscious of social injustice and does not believe that the class distinction between peasants and landlords is predestined. He is often indignant and takes his anger out on his wife. At least at the outset of *Roaring*, women's oppression is taken as parallel, instead of complementary, to peasants' oppression. The two forms of oppression have not yet converged. The abused wives like Hejie are separated from the peasantry; their protests are directed at violent husbands instead of class enemies. Angry (male) peasants and raging wives coexist on this "roaring earth" with their respective targets. The peasant women in *Roaring* possess only the simple wish to be treated as people. In later Communist writings, notions of gender would be more clearly elucidated. Gender oppression would come to be subsumed under class oppression, with violence against women being formulated as a sin exclusive to the class enemy.[13]

The episode in which Wu Changxing beats his wife is realistically detailed to foreshow Hejie's awakening. The scene starts with a visit from Li Jie and Zhang Jinde (who is Hejie's younger cousin) to Wu's house to broadcast revolutionary objectives. As they reach the house, Li's zeal is almost quenched when he hears a woman's screams. He peeps through the door and sees the thin, dark-skinned Wu, against the dim gray-yellow light of an oil lamp, pressing down on Hejie while clenching his teeth. Her hair is disheveled as if she is about to lose her strength. When the visitors enter the home, they find her lying on the ground "half dead." At a later moment, when the men are eating and talking, she suddenly jumps up and shouts, "Okay, since Master Li is here, let us judge who is right!" Emboldened by the presence of the revolutionaries, Hejie raises her voice against her husband for the first time, a scene that is likened in the text to the outburst of a "female yaksha." She delivers an eloquent tirade (*taotao* 滔滔, recalling the popular depictions of the suffragettes in chapter 1 and Pan Jinlian's torrent of indictment in chapter 3) with tears flowing down her cheeks uncontrollably (note the watery imagery and the emphasis on unrestrained bodily fluids).[14] Unlike the repulsion usually felt by intradiegetic viewers when witnessing a shrew's hysteria, Li and Zhang express compassion, indicating Communist sympathy toward suffering and shrewish wives. The scene even previews the "speaking bitterness" (*suku* 訴苦) ritual, a rather theatrical mode of accusing oppressors which became prevalent in Communist practice during the 1940s land reform.[15] Traditional shrew-style performances were visible in the *suku* practices for acting out peasant women's autonomy through tears, tirades, and tantrums.

Hejie's verbal and emotional catharsis opens her to a fuller recognition of herself and the world around her. The next morning, she takes the initiative to ask Zhang Jinde about Li Jie and their revolution. Upon hearing that Li is leading a revolution against his father (*ge ta laozi de ming* 革他老子的命, which can also be understood literally as "to end his father's life"), she is puzzled: "Is it OK to undertake a revolution against one's father?" (*laozi de ming ye keyi ge de ma* 老子的命也可以革得嗎). Zhang assures her that with a legitimate reason there can be a revolution against anyone—sons against fathers and wives against husbands. Hejie lights up: "Can a wife start a revolution against her husband?" (*qi keyi ge zhangfu de ming ma* 妻可以革丈夫的命嗎). Tears well up in her eyes when she asks Zhang how to revolt. When told that there will be a Peasants' Association that polices domestic violence, she determinedly states: "I will for sure join your association! If not, I am not a human!"[16]

With Hejie's pledge, women's liberation seems to converge with peasants' liberation. Yet her emphasis on "*your* association" (instead of "*our* association") distances her from the revolution. It can be implied that she draws a boundary between herself and the revolutionary activists. She is willing to join and wield the power of revolution, but only to suppress her husband. Hejie lacks knowledge of the true meaning of the cause, though the individual benefits are enticing enough for her to be on board. In later periods including the Soviet Republic, the Yan'an era (1935–1948), and Maoist China, the promise of family intervention continued to be used as bait by the Party for mobilizing rural women. Reciprocally, the peasant wives took advantage of the campaigns to sweep obstacles from their personal paths to happiness and freedom.

Hejie's identification with the oppressed wife (though perhaps not yet with the oppressed peasant) is also telling in her self-positioning and relationship with other women in the story. She is described as one of the early awakened, and thus a self-appointed leader who works hard to persuade other oppressed wives to join the revolution. She declares, "If we women are not going to start a revolution, it simply will be unbearable!"[17] Her language, once again, singles women out as a separate revolutionary sector targeting abusive husbands rather than class enemies. The female characters in *Roaring* have not developed civil awareness beyond their will to "rise up" (*chutou* 出頭: literally, "head emerges") from abuse.[18] Hejie's choice of this term captures the difference between the head-down, subjugated situation of her past and her empowered present under the wing of the Party when she can hold her head high. She actively defends the Peasants' Association to secure her benefits, even if this means standing against other peasants.

In this mutual protection between women and revolution, the novel displays the degree to which the Communist cause works to mobilize the masses and wins their hearts. Compared to writings in later decades, *Roaring* eliminates conflict and confusion, providing a harmonious vision of revolution. First, it focuses on the domestic safety and rights of rural women, avoiding the thorny and premature issue of women's position in public political affairs. Maogu (or Aunt Mao) is the only peasant woman in the story who participates in decision making in the association. Other women, although eventually able to enjoy some "equal status" (*duideng qilai* 對等起來) with their husbands, see little change in their daily routines and social mobility.[19] Even Hejie does not join the revolution until the very end of the novel, when she is allowed to bring a weapon to the mountain where the revolutionaries have gathered to join them in battle. The final episode still holds back from giving her actual footing in the struggle. When on the mountain, the women are kept in a temple for safety while the men are out fighting the enemy. In this intense scene of revolution, women are confined to the symbolic *nei* space, their mobility and ability restricted.

Second, *Roaring* screens out protests from the husbands after their wives gain protection and privilege. Later in Yan'an and Great Leap stories, the complaints of the husbands would constitute a motif, but in *Roaring* this concern has not yet taken shape. The husband, Wu Changxing, soon quits his violence and even becomes obedient to Hejie after learning about her rights. When Wu is about to follow the defense team to the mountain, he asks her to stay at home. She refuses, and for the first time in the novel she questions her husband for confining her within the household. Surprisingly, Wu submits entirely. He "submissively follows [*hen fushun de genzhe* 很服順地跟著] while she walks ahead in an upright manner [*zai qianmian zhiting de zouzhe* 在前面直挺地走著]."[20]

The ending of *Roaring* gives concrete and conclusive form to the "wife-leading-husband" formula that is tentatively outlined in Mao Dun's "Creation." By applying the formula in a rural context to peasant couples, the novel reinforces the leftist direction to expand the potential of wives. The Communist *geming* is favorably constructed as an inclusive, adaptable, and secular practice that benefits all oppressed individuals regardless of gender, age, and education. In the ensuing Soviet Republican and Yan'an eras, this composed or intended path of the Communist revolution as flexible and credible on gender matters would undergo dips, twists, and turns.[21] The cooperation between the shrew and the state would be further complicated as it was adjusted to suit political expediencies.

Mao Zedong, Communist Feminism, and the Yan'an Way

Jiang Guangci's *The Roaring Earth* is acute in its revolutionary sensitivity. It correctly integrates the liberation of wives with the revolutionary theme, barely leaving room for failure and personal desperation—a scenario that was common in other contemporary leftist writings. For example, the novella *Star* (*Xing* 星; 1936) by Ye Zi (1910–1939) is pessimistic about the fate of oppressed rural wives. To free herself from her violent husband, the abused character Mei Chun has to have sex with a revolutionary cadre. Unlike in *Roaring*, revolution is not depicted as directly available for women who seek salvation. *Roaring* was therefore pioneering in its time, presenting the Communist revolution as tangible and reliable, and identifying the Party as the fundamental source of help for resolving domestic violence in peasant families. Hejie does not need to sacrifice her body to gain benefits. The idea of using sex as the fuel or compensation for revolution is denied in *Roaring*. It instead insists that revolution should be asexual, transcending bodily indulgence.

From its revolutionary scenes to its political notions, *Roaring* resonates with some of Mao Zedong's early writings of the 1920s. Jiang Guangci's vision of the role of the Peasants' Association and the force of the to-be-liberated wives in the Communist campaign is in line with Mao's points in the well-known "Report on an Investigation of the Peasant Movement in Hunan" (*Hunan nongmin yundong kaocha baogao* 湖南農民運動考察報告; 1926). Jiang was never in the countryside, but he went through a variety of Communist documents when writing his novel.[22] At the textual level *Roaring* reflects Jiang's familiarity with and faith in Mao's ideas.

Both *Roaring* and "Report" reject the authority of husbands. "Report" was the first Communist document singling out husbands' power over wives as a form of oppression.[23] As Mao commented, Chinese men are "usually subjected to the domination of three systems of authority: political authority, clan authority, and religious authority," while women are dominated by a fourth "thick rope"—"the masculine authority of husbands" (*fuquan* 夫權 or *zhangfu de nanquan* 丈夫的男權).[24] Mao's article prioritizes destroying the political and economic control of landlords before attacking clan, religious, and patriarchal authorities. Even though eliminating patriarchal oppression is considered of least importance, Mao's charge against husbands marks the beginning of a radical phase in the Communist movement.

The embracing of female rebellion connects the shrew model with the construction of the Communist heroine. Several scenarios referenced in "Report" are reminiscent of shrew narratives. Mao recorded that peasant women in Hunan were fighters against old rules that barred "women and poor people from the banquets in the ancestral temples." He observed that "the women of Paikuo [Baiguo] in Hengshan County gathered in force and swarmed into their ancestral temple, firmly planted their backsides in the seats and joined in the eating and drinking, while the venerable clan bigwigs had willy-nilly to let them do as they pleased."[25] Contrary to the historian Ono Kazuko's belief that "such an event would previously have been beyond anyone's imagination," the scene corresponds to how shrews in Ming–Qing literature were often depicted as violating gendered spatial regulations, forcing their way into temples and other public venues.[26] One example is found in Sujie's willful and catastrophic visits to temples in *Marriage Bonds to Awaken the World*. Her defiance of propriety provokes anger in her parents-in-law to the point where the father-in-law has a stroke. At the climax in chapter 73, Sujie is beaten up and stripped naked by some local youths when she visits a temple and refuses to veil herself.

Given the specificity of temples as a sensitive locus for testing women's virtue, the peasant women in Hunan who pushed their way into the forbidden territory were not only answering the call of revolution against religious constraints but also reenacting a deep-seated idea of unruly femininity in tearing down spatial and moral boundaries. Instead of being subject to humiliation and punishment like the tragic Sujie, the peasant women in "Report" transcended the fate of traditional shrews to assume heroic stances. Mao exuberantly envisioned that "the opportunity has come for them [women] to lift up their heads, and the authority of the husband is getting shakier every day."[27]

Radical Feminism and the Prevalence of Shrews

Mao Zedong's opinion was soon played out in policies and campaigns toward Communist radical feminism. Expedient as these campaigns might have been, the tactics used to suppress husbands do not seem to have been meticulously planned. As a result, the early Communist feminist movement stirred up controversy within rural communities, gave rise to shrews, and caused complications in gender relations.

Mao's emphasis on women's (especially wives') rights quickly emerged in the Party's legislation on marriage. In November 1931, soon after the establishment of the Chinese Soviet Republic in Jiangxi, the regime promulgated its Marriage Regulations (*Zhonghua Suweiai gongheguo hunyin tiaoli* 中華蘇維埃共和國婚姻條例), which provided the foundation for the Chinese Soviet Marriage Law in 1934 and the Marriage Law of the People's Republic of China in 1950. The regulations outlaw concubinage, grant wives the freedom to divorce, and stipulate the responsibilities that a divorced man should shoulder for his former wife and children.[28] The changes in the law helped to make marriage attainable for middle and poor peasants, whereas previously "almost a third of poor peasants and 99 percent of landless laborers were unable to muster the resources to acquire a wife."[29]

The advocacy for divorce rights and the regulation of polygamy and bride-buying functioned at the initial stage to clear barriers preventing poor men from getting married. The policy made women who had or would otherwise have been forced into an unhappy marital arrangement available to bachelors of lower social status. Mao Zedong in his "Xingguo Investigation" (*Xingguo diaocha* 興國調查; 1930) reported that within two months of the government's promulgating laws on the freedom of marriage, the majority of the middle and poor peasants in the area that was investigated found wives.[30] Yet since the policy exposed *all* men to the risk of divorce, it soon backfired on the government. Some peasants complained that the sweeping revolution was even sweeping away their wives (*laopo dou ge diao le* 老婆都革掉了).[31] Instances of "anarchist chaos" (*wu zhengfu zhuyi de hunluan zhuangtai* 無政府主義的混亂狀態) emerged, resulting from the promotion of the absolute liberty of marriage and divorce, with extreme cases involving sexual anarchy and dissemination of venereal diseases in areas of the Chinese Soviet Republic.[32]

Rural wives were the agents of early Communist radical feminism. They became easy targets for attacks from husbands and the community for perceived deterioration in family relations and feminine virtue. Some were attacked for abusing their freedom of marriage and divorce. Pu Anxiu (1918–1991), the wife of the Party leader Peng Dehuai (1898–1974), noted that a woman in Pingshan County divorced five times in three years; another woman in Zuoquan County divorced one month after getting married.[33] Some were denounced for taking advantage of the women's movement to frame their husbands. There was a famous case in the 1930s in the Chinese Soviet Republic: when their husbands demanded that they account for their daily outings, some wives reported the men to the government for controlling their movements, which resulted in the detention of the husbands for days.[34] In incidents like these, the Party played the facilitator and guardian of wifely privilege.

Things would take a drastic turn in the late 1940s, when the Party grew to be perceived as a destroyer rather than a savior of marriages, but in the 1930s and early 1940s, radical feminism was the leading ideology within the Communist women's movement in the countryside. Led by female intellectuals-turned-cadres who espoused ideal gender values, early Communist feminism emphasized "freedom of marriage" (*hunyin ziyou* 婚姻自由) and "economic independence" (*jingji duli* 經濟獨立). It "opposed the four forms of oppression" (*fandui sichong yapo* 反對四重壓迫), "favored the wives and castigated the husbands" (*piantan qizi, zhongze zhangfu* 偏袒妻子，重責丈夫), and "protected the daughters-in-law and chastised the parents-in-law" (*piantan xifu, zhongze gongpo* 偏袒媳婦，重責公婆).[35] Mao Zedong reported in late 1933, with a mixture of "satisfaction and amusement" toward social behavioral changes, that "husbands curse wives less frequently while, on the other hand, wives curse husbands more now."[36]

These patterns in resisting one's husband and in-laws recall the sins of the traditional shrew. In the new context, however, wifely transgression had started to receive the support of the CCP. The Party remained supportive until the movement turned into a threat to social order and government authority. Although the Party later distanced itself from radical feminism by labeling it biased (*pianmian de "funü zhuyi"* 片面的 "婦女主義"), bourgeois, and illegitimately independent (*xiang dang nao dulixing* 向黨鬧獨立性), this does not negate the fact that early Communist espousal of radical feminism pushed through some bold changes in the countryside, including the rise of shrews.

Communist documents of this period show approval for shrew-type women. In 1943 Pu Anxiu wrote a summary on the first stage (1938 to early 1940) of the women's movement in the northern anti-Japanese democratic base. She praised the dissolute (*fengliu* 風流) women in the villages for playing a key role in promulgating Communist gender reform. Conventionally labeled "tramps" (*poxie* 破鞋: literally, broken shoes, a common term in informal Chinese referring to debauched women or unlicensed prostitutes), she thought these women were actually brave revolutionaries: "They are the ones daring to speak and act [*ganyu shuohua xingshi* 敢於說話行事], and they easily open themselves to new ideas [*rongyi jieshou xin sixiang* 容易接受新思想]." Outspoken, mobile, spirited, and norm-defying—the adjectives formerly associated with the shrew now actualize the revolutionary requirements for women. Pu reported that she and her colleagues had been making special efforts (*zhengqu* 爭取) to recruit *poxie* women into the women's association. She was impressed to see these so-called "bad" women diligently disseminating new ideas on "gender equality" and "women's liberation," which even motivated ordinary women (*yingxiang le yiban funü* 影響了一般婦女).[37]

There was a change in the evaluation of the wanton woman or the *yinfu*. No longer a pariah, the *yinfu* was revolutionized by the Communists as a new role model, given currency over the normally favored docile and proper femininity. During times of political exigency, the shrew's spirit and energy came across as useful to the activists, though complications and compromises also surely existed. Pu once mentioned the risk of tarnishing the moral image of the Party because sometimes the masses got confused by the coexistence of the women's immodest behavior (*liumang zuofeng* 流氓作風) and their gestures as revolutionary pioneers. She then proposed that for the wanton women to better serve the campaign, they might need to undergo a transformation (*gaizao* 改造) in which they would discard their boldness but keep their bravery.[38]

Shrews were tricky to handle, while too tantalizing to be dismissed. Another case of the meticulous manipulation of the shrew's power was the issue of the illicit sex partner (*piban* 皮伴—originally *pipan* 皮袢, which is mainly used in the Wuhan dialect for illicit sexual relationships). In an article published in the *Qiqi Monthly* in 1941, *piban* is defined as unlawful sexual relationships occurring before, during, and after marriage or in widowhood. It was named as one of the two most urgent problems in the countryside, with the other being the need for women's united front in the anti-Japanese movement. In criticizing women who abused their freedom of divorce to pursue sexual license (*ziyou gao piban* 自由搞皮伴), the article adopts the phrase *piban funü* (皮伴婦女: wanton women), combining the use of *poxie* and *xingluan de funü* (性亂的婦女) in Pu Anxiu's article.[39] All the terms employ denigratory prefixes to denote the chaotic (*luan*), shabby (*po*), and physically raw (*pi*) nature of the women's disorderly sexuality.

Except for a few instances of negative wording, the article goes to great lengths to applaud the heroics of the loose women, even more fully elaborated than Pu Anxiu's approval. Centering on the benefits of the *piban* women, it compares them to the "well-behaved and dutiful" (*laoshi benfen* 老實本分) ladies, and concludes that wanton women have a greater ability to carry out revolutionary tasks. Like Pu, the authors of this article singled out the shrews' unrestrained mobility and undrained vitality for special celebration: "They are extremely mobile, running around everywhere to work [*daochu paozhe gongzuo* 到處跑著 工作]. They like to take initiative and take the lead [*xihuan da xianfeng, kai toupao* 喜歡打先鋒，開頭炮]. They are the indispensable trailblazers [*shaobuliao tamen kailu* 少不了她们开路] for women's liberation."[40]

The descriptions of the high-profile presence of shrews during the revolution may be accurate. An example provided in the article could be taken as proof: it was reported that at certain points in the campaign, the masses mistook the Women's Association for "the wanton women's club" (*piban funü de jituan* 皮伴婦女的集團).[41] Presumably these women must have enjoyed a high degree of visibility as well as superiority as the vanguards of rural Communist feminism, since otherwise their appearance would not have been so confusing and overwhelming to observers. This is why the contemporary propagandist term *fanshen* (翻身: literally, "body turning over") should be understood to mean, in addition to women's turnover from oppressed wives to rising revolutionaries, also a "turning over" or reshuffling of man-made female categories. The once repressed type of the shrew gathered positive momentum by serving the ideological demand.

Gold Flower: The Shrew's Way or "The Yan'an Way"

As Communist radical feminism continued to attract trouble, starting in 1941, the Party had to execute a series of new policies in the Shan'ganning Border Region, commonly known as "the Yan'an Way."[42] This reform was part of the Yan'an Rectification Movement (*Yan'an zhengfeng yundong* 延安整風運動) aiming to retreat from radical feminism to an emphasis on "family harmony" (*jiating hemu* 家庭和睦) and to encourage women to participate in social-economic production rather than indulge in their rights to divorce.[43] Several reasons accounted for this policy change. First, women in the northern countryside in China lived in a more closed society, and "unlike the 'formidable' women of South China," they usually "refused to accept" progressive ideas, including "freedom in marriage," "economic independence," and "opposing the four forms of oppression."[44] The spread of public dissent was another grave concern. Male peasants and cadres vehemently resisted their wives' empowerment. Ugly descriptions of women as cunning, cruel, and corrupt creatures were widely circulated as a means of opposing the Party's laws.[45]

The government quickly learned its lesson and shifted to emphasizing family prosperity.[46] Zhou Enlai (1898–1976) wrote an article in 1942 titled "On 'Good Wife Wise Mother' and Motherly Duties." Giving recognition to women's freedom in seeking social and political roles, Zhou's article nevertheless reiterates the late Qing and early Republican reformist discourse that prioritized women's maternal duties.[47] The Women's Committee of the Central Committee of the CCP drafted a new resolution the following year on the women's movement which was later revised by Mao Zedong. The resolution stresses economic production as the top task for women and stipulates that a well-functioning family life (*funü jiqi jiating de shenghuo dou guode hao* 婦女及其家庭的生活都過得好) should be the precondition for a woman's struggle against oppression.[48] If not intentionally blind to the logical error in the statement, the committee was at least deliberately excluding the possibility of husbands as the oppressors.

Despite the official call for a return to family unity, social and literary practices seem to have stuck to the path of radical feminism. During the transitional 1940s, defiant wives were still prominent in social life and literature, with the theme of family harmony arising occasionally. The story of Gold Flower (Jinhua), who is the "communist textbook heroine," illustrates this situation.[49] As a real incident, a retelling based on memory and fantasy, and reportage of a heavily mediated interview, the story cuts across the imagination and the lived experience of the Communist shrew, offering a venue for observing the tenacity of Communist radical feminism.

Included under the section "The Revolt of Women" in Jack Belden's *China Shakes the World*, the story was based on Belden's interview in what was probably the mid- to late 1940s of a northern Chinese village girl. In 1942, under family pressure, Gold Flower was forced to give up her lover and marry an ugly old man. She put up with her husband's violence and the abuse from her relatives-in-law until "in August 1945, [when] a small unit of the 8th Route Army entered Gold Flower's village." The Party cadres organized a Women's Association to encourage every woman in the village to strive for equality. Gold Flower was awakened by the *suku* ritual to men's unjust power over women. Upon her request, the association decided to "alleviate her of her sorry life."[50] The means they adopted were fierce.

They started with Gold Flower's father-in-law when her husband was away on business. Four women from the association showed up at the door and questioned the old man about his mistreatment of his daughter-in-law. In astonishment, he told them to leave. "One girl went away. The others fell into silence. In a moment the girl came back with fifteen more women. They were all carrying clubs and ropes. The old man was startled." He refused to admit his fault, so the women bound him up "like a fish in a net."[51]

The man was then "held a prisoner for two days" before a meeting was held to try him. At the meeting, a cadre had to calm down the furious women who were ready to beat him. Instead of making a confession, the father-in-law showed "deliberate roughness," forcing Gold Flower to tell his sins to his face. All the women were agitated:

> The crowd groaned. In the heavy swelling voices, the sound of shuffling feet could be heard. Gold Flower felt herself being pushed aside. A fat girl was at her elbow and others were crowding close. "Let us spit in his face," said the fat girl. She drew back her lips over her gums and spat between the old man's eyes. Others darted in, spat in his face, and darted away again. The roar of voices grew louder. The old man remained standing with his face red and his beard matted with saliva. His knees were trembling and he looked such a poor object that the women laughed and their grumbling and groaning grew quieter.

These roaring and spitting women were acting akin to the prototypical *pofu* and *hanfu*. They brought their anger out in ways that mixed justice and violence, discipline and pollution, high goals and low morals. While Gold Flower by herself was limited in her ability to rebel, the women together constituted an enhanced, collective version of the shrew. One of the female cadres remarked: "Alone, she cannot fight. But with us she can fight all bad husbands."[52] In the name of the Party, and in the way of the shrew, female bonding was politicized to maximize what rural women could procure from the movement.

With the triumph over the old man, the women were more aggressive when punishing the husband, who was later lured back home. Their face-slapping, name-calling, bodily abuse, roaring, and shrieking revitalized the shrew image under Communist radicalism. Especially when they hit the husband, the scene mirrors in detail familiar descriptions of the shrew:

> As if by a signal, all the women pushed forward at once. Gold Flower quickly went in back of her husband. The crowd fell on him, howling, knocked him to the ground, then jumped on him with their feet. Several women fell with him, their hands thrashing wildly. Those in the rear leaped in, tore at his clothing, then seized his bare flesh in their hands and began twisting and squeezing till his blood flowed from many scratches. Those who could not get close, dove under the rest and seized Chang's [the husband's] legs, sinking their teeth in his flesh.[53]

The passage is thorough in elaborating the violence. The tearing, pinching, and biting, sexually violent or violently sexual, are readily suggestive of the shrew's vulgarity in punishing, policing, and penetrating the male body. With this explicitly displayed cruelty, why, if the scene was narrated by Gold Flower, did she choose to dwell on the cruel specifics? What message did she intend by this manner of storytelling?

According to the scene itself, Gold Flower was not at all proactive among the women. She either got pushed aside or instinctively dodged during the chaotic moments. She was more of an observer than an executioner. As a newcomer to the Women's Association, Gold Flower was apparently appalled by the undisguised brutality of the revolutionary women. This whole film-like sequence of female violence functioned for her to revisit and digest in her mind what had happened so that she could come to terms with acts of radical feminism. It was this ferocity, intimidating but inviting, that assured her of the credibility of the Party. In Gold Flower's two eureka moments of articulated admiration for the CCP, her assurance was built upon the raw strength she witnessed. When her father-in-law was bound up and taken away, she felt suddenly enlightened: "So this is what happiness is! she thought. At last she believed in the 8th Route Army." The physical assault on him convinced her of the Communists' power and the prospect of finding satisfaction in the movement. Later, when her husband surrendered to the women's force and promised to reform himself, she sang their praises even louder: "How strong was her Women's Association, the Communist party, the 8th Route Army!"[54]

Men's violence at home was denounced as a form of oppression; women's violence in public was aligned with revolutionary rectitude. Behind this ambivalent account of violence was the Party's subtle (yet not very skillful) maneuvering of the husband-wife relationship to the advantage of its campaign. By criminalizing male domestic violence, the Party was able to recruit feisty shrews as a righteous counterforce. The husband in Gold Flower's story, as a result, is no different from many other backward husbands in leftist narratives—disempowered and unmistakably linked with counterrevolutionary elements. The husband turned out to be an anti-Communist who had been working in KMT-dominated areas, where he learned to identify disruptive women as a CCP product. He openly disparaged Mao Zedong and his turning-over movement for women: "You see in the 8th Route areas women have become crazy. They don't obey men."[55] The moment when the husband asserted that he would then live under the KMT regime and take another wife marked the high point of political rupture in the story. Instead of being abandoned by her man, Gold Flower took the initiative to divorce him, an act that symbolizes how Communism pronounced the verdict on its enemies. The spousal relationship was again (and would continue to be) used as a convenient formula for producing propaganda.

The Gold Flower story ended in another climax of shrewish performance. When the husband fled the next day, about "forty howling women" then "chased him for three miles through the fields," swearing that they would catch him and "bite him to death." Later, Gold Flower was publicly commended and asked to give a speech to the village women, in which she sent a clarion call: "Go home and make your husbands participate in the 8th Route Army!"[56] Husband-disciplining was made the top obligation of rural women. By exerting wifely volition, Gold Flower indicated, women would be automatically fulfilling revolutionary duties.

In the process of politicizing marriage as a site of both private triviality and public importance, mundane episodes of marital strife acquired a new veneer of progressiveness which accorded wives a greater vision of unity and integrity. It was arguably due to this sense of empowerment that many women chose to uphold radical feminism even when the Party had shifted to censure shrewish behavior.[57] As Belden's book summarizes, the illusion of power and the conception of justified violence accounted for the appeal of Communism: "It [the Gold Flower's story] reveals more clearly than a dozen speeches by Mao Zedong just what are some of the techniques of the Chinese Communist party and why they were able to win so many people to their cause."[58]

Mediating the Shrew Image in Yan'an Literature

With the intimidating shrews at the center, the Gold Flower story reflects the ineffectiveness of the Yan'an Way in intervening in social practices. In stories produced in Yan'an and the Shan'ganning Border Region, family harmony was similarly absent or represented reductively. A contrast to the ease of shifting policy, the production of Yan'an stories attests to difficulties that the authors grappled with to adjust to the sudden transition from radical feminism to a focus on family unity. The works struggle to find a way to resolve the dilemma created by the Party's political whims. How could a rebellious wife also be a contributor to marital harmony? How could a wife awakened by the Communist call against domestic oppression pursue her emancipation without hurting the feelings of her husband or threatening the old family order? How could the Party reconcile women's liberation at home with its grand goal of mobilizing the peasants, especially the men who had to experience the loss of their liberated wives?[59]

Even though sometimes a solution is provided, the majority of Yan'an texts take an approach like that of the Gold Flower story, dismissing the Yan'an Way while continuing to spotlight the wives' uprising against domestic violence. No substantive changes were taking place in literary writings on marital relationships before and after the appearance of the new policy in 1943. The wives are still more revolutionary and dominant, and the husbands embody the backward or reactionary ideology. The only noticeable difference is the means the wives employ in disciplining their husbands. Some wives in works written after 1943 use milder strategies, no longer relying on radical techniques. Instead of directly walking out on their men, they come to express their dissatisfaction through snubs. They abandon the husbands spiritually and symbolically as divorce was increasingly discouraged.

With these compromises, nevertheless, family harmony was still a lesser theme and was broached tentatively. In other words, the attempt to remedy the Party's image was largely wasted. In Yan'an texts after 1943 the Party still stands as an intruder, if not a destroyer, in the family lives of the peasants. A more mature literary solution to the conflict between empowered wives and complaining husbands would not appear until a decade later during the Great Leap Forward.

Except for a few conservative stories, the majority of Yan'an literature celebrates rebellious wives as models of the rural new woman and portrays husbands as violent, stubborn, and ideologically regressive.[60]

"The Wheat-Grinding Girl" (*Mo mai nü* 磨麥女; 1940), which won first place in the Yan'an May Fourth Youth Writing Competition (*Yan'an "wu si" qingnian wenyi zhengwen* 延安 "五四" 青年文藝徵文) in 1941, was successful in laying out the basic pattern of general Yan'an literary constructions. The story depicts the transformation of Guiying from an oppressed wife and daughter-in-law to a fighter for gender equality. She is enlightened by progressive ideas she overhears from the women cadres' gatherings next door about "freedom and liberation" (*ziyou jiefang* 自由解放), "pioneering" (*xianfeng* 先鋒), "women going to school" (*funü shangxue* 婦女上學), and "women participating in politics" (*funü canzheng* 婦女參政). Guiying then runs away from her family, a reformulation of the May Fourth Nora model yet toward a clearer, more cheerful destination: she cuts her hair and becomes a Communist cadre; her evil parents-in-law are brought to public trial.

This award-winning story builds a Communist revolutionary femininity that is different from and defiant toward ordinary femininity. The developing character Guiying, although favorably depicted in her journey to Communism, is pathologically weepy. She cries often because of fear or excitement, which differentiates her from other female cadres, who are calm, tough, and robust. In particular the images of the "manly" Comrade Zhang (*youdian nanzi qigai de Zhang* 有點男子氣概的章) and the "plump" Comrade Wu (*pangpang de Wu* 胖胖的伍) present a new face of femininity with which Guiying is unfamiliar. Their unusually healthy (and perhaps unwomanly) appearance keeps her awake at night, indulging in sensations aroused by the revolutionary vibe. When Guiying oversleeps the next morning, her mother-in-law shouts nastily, "Who did you sleep with so comfortably last night that you can't even get up in the morning?" The ridicule renders the Party—personified through the female cadres—an unexpected and unwelcome seducer who sneaks in to lure good women away. Equally symbolic and physical, the seduction is ambivalently indicative of both heterosexual and homosexual interest. "The shameless rotten bitches [*bu yaolian de lan biaozimen* 不要臉的爛婊子們] even come to our house to flirt [*sao qing* 騷情]!" complains the mother-in-law.[61] The "bitch" epithet has long been used as a colloquial reference to the shrew. The mother-in-law's vulgarism gives textual form to the current widespread anger toward the prevalence of shrews under radical feminism.

Published two years later, Liu Qing's (1916–1978) story "The Wedding" (*Xishi* 喜事; 1942) spells out the intrusive nature of the Party, particularly how the Communist advocacy of women's rights disturbs the marriages of ordinary peasants. It focuses on the second wedding of Zhao Cai'er. His first wife, Wei Lanying, cut her hair, divorced him, and joined the Red Army. Zhao's father derides his son's divorce as "the first disadvantage of the new society" (*xin shehui li, zhe pashi tou yiyang buhaochu* 新社會里，這怕是頭一樣不好處) and openly accuses the government of backing up women (*beihou haiyou gongjia de dianzi* 背後還有公家的點子).[62] Rumor has it that Wei was a shrew who used her new political power to counter Zhao's domestic violence. Whenever Zhao attempted to beat her, he ended up getting beaten by Wei.

The beginning of "The Wedding" tries to redeem the Party. It pushes all responsibility for the couple's marital problems onto Wei Lanying alone, denouncing her for rejecting the government's mediation. The text, however, still fails to reconcile women's gaining authority with the supposedly caring image of the government. Zhao's new wife also beats him and runs away. The villagers think she must have run to the government, where "even the bound-feet women know to go for protection" (*xianzai lian xiaojiao poyi yehui zhaodao shuoli de difang* 現在連小腳婆姨也會找到說理的地方).[63] The Party is identified as the destination for a runaway Nora or a potential eloper, the ultimate protector of shrewish wives.[64] Despite the initial promise, "The Wedding" ends similarly to "The Wheat-Grinding Girl," leaving unresolved the incompatibility between women's revolt and the Party's reputation.

Only a few pre-1943 stories address marital harmony. Their solutions were based on either abrupt changes in the husband or a flagging of the wife's rebellious spirit. "The Husband and Wife" (*Fufu* 夫婦; 1941), for example, depicts a couple's transformation from oppressor and slave to happy companions with the aid of the Party. Even if the husband resents the government for criticizing him for beating his wife, this resentment does not grow into a conflict. He soon comes to appreciate the changes in his wife after she attends a Yan'an university. In contrast to other awakened female characters who use their recently acquired literacy to write farewell notes to their husbands and in-laws, the wife in this story writes her husband a forgiving message: "I am not willing to divorce you."[65] The husband is moved and turns into a tender man. By precluding the wife's rebellion and downplaying the difficulty of altering an illiterate, violent husband, the text draws an ideal picture in which women's emancipation coexists with family harmony.

Another example is "The Story of a Woman's Turning Over/Transformation" (*Yige nüren fanshen de gushi* 一個女人翻身的故事; 1943), based on the biography of Zhe Juying (1919–2007), who was a model new woman during the Yan'an Rectification movement and a female senator in the border region. Without undermining Zhe's rebelliousness or embracing artificial harmony, the story resolves the dilemma through the simple tactic of class identification. It justifies Zhe's abandonment of her husband by categorizing him as a class enemy who deserves a divorce.[66]

Subsequent Yan'an productions of the late 1940s handle spousal relationships more subtly. As divorce became less and less favored as a means for settling marital strife, the resourceful wives in literature find symbolic ways to "leave" the husbands other than creating ruptures. The wife in "The Manzi Couple" (*Manzi fufu* 滿子夫婦; 1945) treats her unsatisfying husband with indifference. Every time he questions her, she replies with "nothing." Later, with the intervention of some Communist instructors, the wife gradually realizes her fault in "disliking and avoiding her husband" (*xianqi zhangfu de xinli he taidu* 嫌棄丈夫的心理和態度). She takes the initiative to reunite with him. Every night, in addition to sleeping together, the couple studies policy of the Yan'an Way regarding "the planning of housework and the maintenance of unity and harmony" (*moulü jiawu, tuanjie hemu* 謀慮家務, 團結和睦).[67] Slightly but critically different, the Party in this text intervenes at the decisive moment to keep the wife's dissatisfaction from developing into rebellion or divorce; it thus plays the role of a guardian instead of a destroyer of family order.

In the 1947 story "The New Rule" (*Xin guiju* 新規矩), the Party's intruder image was further whitewashed. Like the wife in "The Manzi Couple," the female protagonist Jiu'er grows dissatisfied soon after marriage. Her husband, Zou Zhusan, is a conservative businessman who believes that a woman's place is inside the home. He will not allow Jiu'er to join the women's school and production team. To him there is a clear line between the Party workers (*gongjia ren* 公家人) and the masses (*laobaixing* 老百姓); whoever works for the Party invites danger into his or her personal life: "What we ordinary people fear the most is becoming associated with the Party!" (*women laobaixing, zuipa de shi dang gongjia ren* 我們老百姓，最怕的是當公家人).[68] Zou even thinks that all male teachers at the Party school are bad people who, according to his friend Shopkeeper Wang, lure women away.

Jiu'er dismisses her husband's objections and goes to school every day. When at home, she gives him the cold shoulder, causing him to worry that she will run away with the Party cadres. Initially seeming to follow the common plotline in earlier Yan'an stories, the text soon exhibits its sophistication. Anti–domestic violence endeavors are more seamlessly integrated into this pro-Communist story. Zou pinches and beats Jiu'er in hopes of preventing her from seeking an education. Jiu'er brings the issue to the government. After a talk with the local leaders, he dares not beat his wife anymore. Such plot development marks textual creativity. Acts of domestic violence do not enter until the wife asserts herself to follow the call of the Party. Unlike in earlier texts in which abuse exists before the arrival of the Party, the alteration here renders domestic violence an intended provocation deliberately targeting the government. Since the husband resorts to violence for revenge, the Party naturally redeems itself as an intruder. This twist on writing abusive husbands provides legitimate grounds for the reach of governmental power over individuals and private homes. The Party is entitled to step in to regulate hostility and aggression.

"The New Rule" also rewrites the wife's absconding. Instead of presenting the Party as the destination or reason for women's escape (and thus the one to be blamed), the text pushes responsibility onto the husband. It restructures the whole escape scenario as merely the man's paranoid suspicion. One day, Zou Zhusan storms into the district government headquarters to report Jiu'er missing. He angrily implies that his wife must have run away with a male teacher. He fantasizes about his abandonment and directs his ungrounded indignation at the Party: "District Chief, you tell me whether our border region has this new rule!" (*kan bianqu youmei zhege xin guiju* 看邊區有沒這個新規矩).[69] The defiance he voices brings the touchy issue into the spotlight again: Do Communist rules encourage a wife's betrayal and desertion of her husband? Does the government aid and abet adultery?

The text then shifts to prove that Zou's claims are purely fanciful. On his way home Zou encounters a series of surprises. He sees the male teacher, the object of his suspicions, calmly sitting in the school office. He hears in shock that his friend Shopkeeper Wang is a spy for the Nationalist Party. What's more, Jiu'er has returned home after sending her girlfriend off to the Women's School in Suide. Shaken by his discoveries, Zou cannot help but hit himself repeatedly on the forehead, blaming his "old and wicked brain" (*jiu naojin* 舊腦筋; *gui naojin* 鬼腦筋).[70]

At this point, he comes to appreciate the Party and joins the struggle against Wang.

As a later Yan'an piece, "The New Rule" is a sophisticated and successful attempt at composing a positive image of the CCP. After conflicts, dramas, and dilemmas, things eventually fall into place, evoking order, peace, and political legitimacy. The story also handles female bonding elegantly to fend off problems. Textually it is the Party that convinces and converts the dissident Zou, but what makes him feel assured of his wife's fidelity is the fact that she has gone out with her female friends. In previous texts including the Gold Flower story and "The Wheat-Grinding Girl," female comradeship leads to political belligerence and sexual license. This story, however, in foregrounding the Communist education for women and the husband's sense of relief upon hearing about the women's day out, returns revolutionary sisterhood to a harmless, comforting place. Through Zou's character, it confirms that sisterhood is only sisterhood, carrying no political threats or likelihood of infidelity.

From the late 1920s to the late 1940s, leftist writings wrestled with the question of how best to shape the image of rebellious, revolutionary, and at the same time reasonable and relatable wives. The struggles paved the way for a more concentrated configuration of the strong wife during the socialist period, especially the late 1950s and early 1960s. Propagandist fiction and films would come to display more skillful means for contextualizing marital battles and warding off objections from (male) peasants. As fierce wives continued to assert their role in socialist movements, the shrew maintained her value to Chinese literature and society alike.

Epilogue
Shrews in the Great Leap Forward

The 1950 Marriage Law of the People's Republic of China accorded women freedom of marriage and divorce and supported their participation in socialist production. Derided as the "Women's Law," it was harshly opposed by peasants and some Party cadres. Bloody conflicts occurred when women struggled to free themselves from unwanted marriages and constraining familial ties.[1] New ideology dismissed women's traditional roles while placing emphasis on their position in the public sphere; policies and discourses defined the ideal socialist woman as one who actively joined in production and political events.[2] During the 1950s, the Party mobilized the mass media to circulate icons of female model workers typified by the *nüjie diyi* 女界第一 (literally, the first in the women's world, or the "first women"), who included China's "first female tractor driver, train conductor, streetcar driver, welder and so on."[3] The profile of the female proletarian was connected to machinery, labor skills, and political consciousness.

These efforts prefigured the apogee of women's empowerment during the Great Leap Forward (GLF), a short but intense period that witnessed the revaluation of *pola* womanhood. In the late 1950s, China faced external crisis in its relationship with the Soviet Union and continuous internal upheavals. In 1958 Chairman Mao launched the GLF, an all-out campaign to boost China's agricultural and industrial capacities to allow the country to "leap" into socialism in the shortest feasible time. It gave particular attention to rural women in hopes of enlisting the largest possible workforce. Women were expected and emboldened to "leap" out of their traditional constraints to the forefront of socialist movements. Celebrated heroines in the GLF literature are strong-willed workers in public and resourceful wives capable of smoothing out domestic tensions. The theme of marital conflict, now treated with increasing literary sophistication, is more likely to facilitate than impede desirable depictions of the socialist new woman and the ideology behind her.

The works extol the visibility of women by using the names of their heroines in story titles. *Hei Feng* (*Hei Feng* 黑鳳; 1963) by Wang Wenshi (1921–1999), "Xueying Learns to Cook" (*Xueying xuechui* 雪英學炊; 1959) by Duan Quanfa (1936–2010), and "A Brief Biography of Li Shuangshuang" (*Li Shuangshuang xiaozhuan* 李雙雙小傳; 1960) by Li Zhun (1928–2000) all highlight women's names and subjectivity. Other works embrace female friendship and comradeship. "The Newly Made Friends" (*Xin jieshi de huoban* 新結識的夥伴; 1958) by Wang Wenshi depicts competition and bonding between female leaders of two women's production teams.

The defiance of the traditional shrew against domestic order was appropriated in these texts to popularize the idea of the socialist public woman. The revival of the stock pairing of shrewish wives and henpecked husbands is one piece of textual evidence. Another is the use of *pola* as a positive term and quality denoting socialist new womanhood. Along with the message conveyed in Mao's maxim that "no revolution is without spiciness" (*bu la bu geming* 不辣不革命), linking one's penchant for strongly spiced food (especially red pepper) with one's valor, endurance, and ability to fight, *pola* women came to represent GLF model citizens.[4] The name of the title heroine in *Hei Feng* makes reference to Wang Xifeng in *Dream of the Red Chamber*. Hei Feng mirrors Xifeng's *pola* womanhood in her drive (*ganjin chongtian* 幹勁沖天) to insert herself into the masculine world.[5] Zhang Layue, one of the female leaders in "The Newly Made Friends," has similar qualities: she is feisty like a lion (*xiang shizi yiban pola* 象獅子一般潑辣), has a loud voice (*gao houlong da sangzi* 高喉嚨大嗓子) and a temper like a firecracker that goes off once lit (*huopao xingzi, yi dian jiu xiang* 火炮性子, 一點就響).[6] She has a dark complexion, brawny hands, and feels no qualms about revealing her arms in public. Her *pola* is associated with a woman's unconventional strength.

Except for the unmarried Hei Feng, other GLF heroines possess authority over their husbands, who are backward, weak, and incompetent. Wu Shulan's husband in "The Newly Made Friends" and Xueying's husband in "Xueying Learns to Cook" exemplify the harm that short-sighted men can do to their wives' public jobs, as captured in the recurrent phrase *la houtui* 拉後腿 (literally, pulling on the wives' legs to hold them back).[7] Wifely rule is in no way a new thing, yet the domination of the socialist women is nonetheless depicted with unprecedented delight and admiration in the GLF texts. When the wives embody the will of the state, their shrewishness contributes to the new gender order rather than interfering with it. The husbands, compared to their derided brothers in premodern literature, further lose ground in their battle against their wives, who now speak and act with political righteousness. As personal conflicts became emblematic of ideological clash, *pola* femininity and shrewish wifehood were elevated to badges of honor that progressive women are, and should be, eager to wear.

Writing Li Shuangshuang

A milestone of GLF fiction, "A Brief Biography of Li Shuangshuang" was the most widely read and raved-about literary text of the period.[8] Written in 1959 by Li Zhun, a "village fiction writer," the story was based on the author's experience in the Henan countryside in 1958. The earliest version of the story was written in March 1959 and appeared in the 1977 collection of Li's stories. A revised version was published in the premier national literary journal *People's Literature* under the same title in 1960. It was next adapted into a film in 1962 by the director Lu Ren (1912–2002) and an illustrated storybook in 1963.

The heroine, Shuangshuang, is an oppressed wife who has been suffering her husband, Sun Xiwang's, beatings ever since she married him. Much like the "first women" promoted in the media during the 1950s, Shuangshuang has ambitions to succeed in fields outside the home that were previously dominated by men. She is described as having a peppery temper (*huolala de xingzi* 火辣辣的性子), a quick tongue (*zui taikuai* 嘴太快), and a spirited energy (*you guzi chongjin* 有股子衝勁).[9] Feeling unhappy as a housewife raising children and serving an overbearing husband, Shuangshuang attends night classes during the GLF. Her newly acquired literacy skills give her the opportunity to express herself and emerge as a heroic model in the movement. When, seeking solutions to the labor shortage, the Party branch of the local commune calls on the masses to "Bloom and Contend" (*mingfang* 鳴放), she puts up a big-character poster proposing a collective canteen for freeing young wives from domestic servitude and assisting them in their participation in the public workforce. The idea is immediately supported by the local officials, and Shuangshuang starts to work outside her home. The couple then engages in a period of bickering and squabbling because Xiwang does not understand the campaign or his wife's desire to break from the confines of the home. Eventually he sees the light and begins to emulate her achievement.

The written versions of Shuangshuang's story underscore women's power and their homosocial bonding. Unlike the film adaptation and the comic book, in which Shuangshuang needs to direct part of her attention to some female adversaries, negative female characters are absent from the literary versions. The only obstacle that Shuangshuang and the other women have to overcome is dealing with backward men at home and at work. The second of the two literary versions altered Li Zhun's original text to fit the standards of *People's Literature*. The changes, which have not received due scholarly attention, reflect the ideological molding of a literary piece to accommodate the Great Leap ethos.[10]

The *People's Literature* version largely maintains the background story of the couple but grants more power to the women characters in configuring their great leap forward. In Shuangshuang's poster doggerel, the last line was changed from the slogan "women can hold up half the sky" (*funü neng ding ban'ge tian* 婦女能頂半個天) to the statement "we women dare to challenge the men" (*gan he tamen nanren lai tiaozhan* 敢和他們男人來挑戰).[11] With this change, Shuangshuang is making an individual claim (rather than repeating a propagandist catchphrase) that calls for competition instead of collaboration between the sexes in the style of the feminist callout. By rejecting or ignoring the position of women as "the other half," the revision sets the tone, lending women greater credibility and ability than their male counterparts.

In the core scene of the couple's confrontation, there were minor changes that indicate official endorsement of Shuangshuang's feistiness. The scene depicts the couple quarreling about Shuangshuang's domestic responsibilities after she participates in digging a village irrigation channel. Her life has become a lot busier as she works outside the home and still cooks for the family. One day she returns home a little late and is furious to find that the children are crying for food while Xiwang is lying on the bed smoking. She questions why he has not at least got the dough ready for the noodles. He responds with contempt: "*Ai*! I just couldn't start that. Cooking is a woman's job. If I cook for you now, before you know it you'll be getting me to wash diapers!"[12]

After several rounds of exchanges, the frustrated Shuangshuang throws down the kitchen knife with a clang, slumps down angrily on the doorstep, and starts to cry. Unperturbed, Xiwang gets off the bed and starts to cook the noodles she has sliced for himself. When the noodles are boiling, he minces some garlic and puts in a little vinegar. When her wailing gets more anguished, he pounds away at the garlic even more heavily. This detail of Xiwang adding garlic and vinegar (both known for their pungent smell) to his food symbolizes the man's sour jealousy toward his wife's selfless public service, as well as his patriarchal desire to confine her to the home. Shuangshuang grinds her teeth while watching him prepare his food. Then "she rushes over and delivers two vicious punches to Xiwang's spine." He yells that she is "overturning the cosmic order" (*fan tian* 反天) and turns around to hit her. She quickly "grabs hold of him and gives him a shove that pushes him out of the house and sends him sprawling on the ground in the courtyard." Seeing Xiwang in this state, Shuangshuang cannot help but burst into laughter. "She laughs so hard she shakes the tears off her face and onto the ground."[13]

The scene portrays Shuangshuang's unruly nature through her sharp tongue, irascibility, violence, and dramatic mood swings. Her "sudden braying laughter" after she sees him fall marks an unexpected sign of her subjectivity.[14] Her lack of empathy for her husband not only implies she has taken on the role of a shrewish wife but also shows that she has become a spokesperson, even an enforcer, for the socialist ideology in disciplining those who are less progressive or counterrevolutionary. If a woman's inappropriate and uncontrolled laughter suggests a challenge to male dominance, Shuangshuang's abrupt and loud laugh is a clear attack on the patriarchal mentality that Xiwang embodies.[15] The transgression of the shrew is employed by the new political order to symbolically laugh off the threat of opposing forces.

The primary changes in the altered version center on the plotline about the canteen work. After serving as the first cook at the commune canteen, Xiwang is misled by a kinsman and misuses public supplies for a private event. In the 1959 original text, the local officials decide to find someone to work with Xiwang and lead him to prevent future problems. Shuangshuang recommends herself and the couple starts to work together at the canteen. In the revision, Shuangshuang replaces

Xiwang as the canteen cook, pushing him off to the pig farm where she had been working. The couple, assigned different territories, shifts from collaborators to public competitors. By keeping Xiwang away, the revision erases any possibility of a man's contribution, making the canteen a stage for showcasing the hard work and creativity of the women alone. Even Xiwang's invention of a new pancake stove that reflects his progressive collaboration in the 1959 text is entirely attributed to Shuangshuang in the *People's Literature* version.

Female-only pronouns are used where there had previously been reference to both sexes. "Shuangshuang and others" (*Shuangshuang he dajia* 雙雙和大家) became "several women" (*jige funü* 幾個婦女); "Shuangshuang and Xiwang, Guiying" (*Shuangshuang he Xiwang, Guiying* 雙雙和喜旺，桂英) was reduced to "Shuangshuang and Guiying" (*Shuangshuang he Guiying* 雙雙和桂英); the gender-neutral pronoun "they" (*tamen* 他們) was changed to the specific "they, the women" (*tamen* 她們). Xiwang is relegated to the background and finally sings the praises of his wife.[16] Shuangshuang's displays of increasing affection toward her husband after she witnesses his improvement were completely omitted; instead, the new version ends with his serious vow: "I'll certainly try to keep up with you!"[17] Private conjugal romance was removed to make way for descriptions of competition and power struggles in the public realm. Political progressiveness replaced intimacy as the correct mode for attaining and maintaining marital satisfaction.

The Li Shuangshuang story positively engages with the type of the shrew. First, it is related to real-life models of feisty peasant women that inspired the characterization of Shuangshuang. According to Richard King's interviews of Li Zhun, one source of the author's inspiration came from a village woman he met in the late 1950s at an office of Nanyang County in Henan. The woman was "young," "very pretty," but also "straightforward and feisty." She came to the office to complain about her husband, who had been elected treasurer by the village but was too timid to do his job. During her tirade, she even shouted at the phone when it rang.[18] Voluble, loud, domineering, and good at subjecting her husband to public humiliation, this village woman conformed to the image of the shrewish wife whose *pola* now served the cause of the GLF. Li also described other peasant women he encountered in affirmative terms as "feisty, bold, and sharp" (*pola fengli* 潑辣鋒利; *pola dadan* 潑辣大膽), "frank and outspoken" (*xinzhi koukuai* 心直口快), revealing the socialist purification of disparaged female qualities for suiting political demands.[19]

Second, Shuangshuang's character can be traced to Chinese and Western literary sources relevant to the shrew theme. Li Zhun referenced the following literary works as influencing the creation of Shuangshuang: "Story of the Sharp-Tongued Li Cuilian" (*Kuaizui Li Cuilian ji* 快嘴李翠蓮記; Ming dynasty), "Yingning" (*Yingning* 嬰寧) in *Liaozhai's Records of the Strange*, *The Wild Girl Bara* (*Ye guniang Bala* 野姑娘芭拉, likely referring to the 1949 Czechoslovak film *Divá Bára*, also known as *The Wild Bára*), *Carmen* (*Ka'er man* 卡爾曼; it is unclear which version of *Carmen* Li Zhun saw or read), and Lu Xun's "Divorce" (*Lihun* 離婚; 1925).[20] Stemming from different time periods and cultures, these sources share one thing in common: their heroines are all unruly, transgressive, and carnivalesque.[21] While each of these texts in certain ways discredits its female protagonist, Li Zhun embraced them for constructing the ideal Shuangshuang. It is likely because these women in his identified sources "might not have been thought suitable as models for a new socialist woman" that Li was unwilling to admit to them until thirty years after he wrote the story.[22]

Performing Li Shuangshuang

Bringing Shuangshuang to the big screen was not easy. Much of the difficulty came from her spicy character. It was critical to visualize her feistiness, yet it was risky to evoke the image of the shrew on the screen. Scholarship has noticed the visibility of the traditional shrew in the film adaptation of the Li Shuangshuang story. One argument claims that Shuangshuang's image in the film is a combination of the *pofu* shrew and the *xianü* 俠女 (female knight-errant) of traditional literature.[23] Another source attributes the format of the film to the Chinese folk performance of the *erren* 二人 (literally, "two persons," known as "two-person play" or "double-role play"), where the female lead always has the advantage over the clownish and powerless male lead.[24] No one has addressed how the integration of the shrew archetype complicated the acting of the heroine and the production of cinematic sequences.

The director Lu Ren had high expectations for the scene of confrontation between the couple analyzed in the preceding section of this chapter. He thought the shove should signal Shuangshuang's attack on Xiwang's backward ideology in addition to her personal discontent: she is "knocking over both the man and his ideas" (*ba ta de ren he sixiang dou tui le ge yangmian chaotian* 把他的人和思想都推了個仰面朝天).[25] He wanted to see force in the performance. When the established actress

Zhang Ruifang (1918–2012) played Shuangshuang in the scene, she intentionally chose "a loud voice and infectious laughter as physical expressions for [Shuangshuang's] forthright character."[26]

Zhang, however, quickly found herself trapped in a dilemma, between the demands of the script and the anticipation of the audience. While she was proud of the confrontation scene and was applauded by the director for her fiery portrayal, the audience had a rather different opinion. Zhang said she received letters from audience members of various ages and social statuses denouncing her for being too inhumane (*tai bujin renqing* 太不近人情) and excessive (*guofen* 過分) in using a dramatic laugh and relentless push.[27] Some peasant viewers rejected Shuangshuang's image as a deviation from cherished norms of wifely virtue and suggested removing this scene of conflict from the movie. They argued that a woman beating a man should not be equated with a woman taking on a revolutionary identity.

The public was judging Shuangshuang on the basis of their cultural familiarity with a more traditional model of a good wife. Zhang Ruifang, when explaining the push and the laugh, had to invoke normative wifely behavior to appease her critics: she admitted that Shuangshuang's action "is indeed somehow illogical because normally her first reaction [as a conventional wife] upon seeing her husband's fall should be to pull him up and attend to his pains."[28] These debates and negotiations surrounding Zhang's acting proclaim the gap between the intention of the state and the mindset of the peasantry. The public failed to fully realize that the shrewish qualities they found unacceptable in Li Shuangshuang were what the state was promoting as desirable for the Great Leap model woman.

Another dilemma Zhang Ruifang encountered was between the performance and the perception of *pola* womanhood. The quality of *pola* is so central to Li Zhun's characterization of Shuangshuang that when he was considering Zhang for the role, his only concern was whether she could be *pola* enough (*zhishi danxin wo nengfou pola de chulai* 只是擔心我能否潑辣得出來). Zhang hence spent a lot of energy and pushed herself hard to prove her *pola* potential. She practiced her enunciation when speaking her lines so that she could sound like a sharp-tongued, fast-thinking (*zuikuai bujia sisuo* 嘴快不加思索) young woman. She was critical of herself for not being able to properly play a scene in which Shuangshuang is wiping the sweat off her face with a handkerchief. She reflected that, instead of gracefully fanning her face with the handkerchief, she should have used more strength in wiping off the sweat to make her action seem more *pola* (*dongzuo ruguo pola yixie* 動作如果潑辣一些).[29]

Zhang's enactment of *pola*, again, failed to please everyone. She reported how Li Zhun constantly urged her to be *pola*, but others reminded her to find the right balance to avoid making Shuangshuang a traditional-style *pofu*. The production crew were impatient with her intense focus on Shuangshuang's combativeness and *pola* character (*guang qiangdiao Shuangshuang douzhengxing qiang he xingge pola* 光強調雙雙鬥爭性強和性格潑辣). They asked her not to be too fierce (*dajia zong tixing wo bie tai xiong* 大家總提醒我別太凶).[30] The boundary between *pola* and *pofu*, between revolutionary spiritedness and repulsive shrewishness, was probably too subtle for any actress—even a professional like Zhang Ruifang—to grasp.

Why was the film crew trying to get Zhang to temper her fierceness, even at the expense of loyalty to the original story, the author's purpose, and the intended revolutionary message? This can be conveniently explained by the nature of the film. As one of the comedies produced after the GLF disaster, the film was meant to relax, entertain, and bring healing to the audience.[31] A heroine who is too feisty was obviously not appropriate for soothing the audience's nerves. Besides, the taming of (performed) female feistiness might also have reflected the changing reputation of the shrew within the political and cultural zeitgeist. The shrew was treated as alien and adverse to Confucian doctrines in the premodern context but was employed by some New Cultural intellectuals to motivate Chinese women to break from traditional strictures. The GLF campaign further appropriated her unruly spirit as an exemplar for the social progress of women in new China. Now aligned with the state ideology, *pola* womanhood was saluted as beneficial instead of being shamed as antagonistic to visions of the nation. It was also due to this affiliation that the *pola* quality had to be censored or sanitized before it could be staged and screened to emblematize socialist ideals.

As shrewish qualities became more integral to the socialist new woman, the shrew seemed to lose her radical edge. Co-opted into state imperatives, the socialist shrew was not free to act out in pursuit of her own ambitions. She needed to follow the lead of the Party in determining the limits of her transgression. Even the skilled Zhang Ruifang had to negotiate her interpretation painstakingly to make sure that her performance met the exact political standard without losing her audience. Zhang sometimes even had to awkwardly insert some tender femininity into her *pola* profile (*pola dadan zhong kandao ta nüxing de wencun* 潑辣大

膽中看到她女性的溫存) so that her Shuangshuang would not be perceived as a "wicked bitch" (*e poniang* 惡婆娘).[32] *Pola* womanhood was handled with care and concessions.[33]

Pola, to Be Continued

The socialist repurposing of the shrew trope exhibits the allure of female unruliness to ideological projects. As the case of writing and performing Li Shuangshuang has shown, Chinese Communist authorities have been keeping a strategic distance from *pola* womanhood—sometimes drawing near, coding *pola* as desired socialist femininity; sometimes pushing away to fend off public outrage at a state-sanctioned image that appears too radicalized. While it remains unclear how well the will of the state aligns with women's wishes in unleashing their rebellious energies, feisty womanhood has been the cultural shibboleth used to lead the push for reform and bear the brunt of backfires. Under Communist-style state-controlled feminism, wherein the Party has the final say on the rhetoric of femininity and feminine virtue, and wherein women are asked to both cultivate and curb their subversive temper, should we lament the fading threat of the shrew? Or should we laud the fact that she has been enjoying an extended and somehow upgraded life in socialist China, as the (un)willing ally of the state?[34]

The ups and downs of the shrew's fate in modern China have pointed to her tenacious hold on the state and society. Her intermittent yet persistent presence has shown the state's utilitarian attitude toward female expressions of power and influence. As this book comes to an end, the most recent revival of *pola* womanhood in the popular image of the *nü hanzi* 女漢子 (literally, "female man," referring to a "manly woman" or "a woman who is more like a real man than a man")[35] begs for more discussion. Behind this flexible new category of woman, what political, economic, and gender-based urgencies are calling on *pola* womanhood to again lead the attack against pro- and/or anti-state forces? What can *pola* women do for today's cultural tensions and for Chinese women themselves? When public discourses deliberately mix the image and language of the *nü hanzi* with that of the *pofu* in contemporary media, we must once again grapple with the polygenic nature of the archetype as both demeaning and empowering. Rooted in shame but rising to shine, the shrew's afterlife, to be continued.

NOTES

Introduction: The Shrew–New Woman Nexus

1. For a comprehensive study of the shrew in premodern Chinese literature, see Yenna Wu, *The Chinese Virago: A Literary Theme* (Cambridge: Harvard University Press, 1995). Wu groups traditional shrew literature into three categories: dark satire and condemnation, caution and reform, and comedy. Wu's book is likely the only scholarly publication to date that uses the term "virago" to refer to the Chinese shrew types. In an earlier article, however, Wu uses "shrewish wife" and "shrew" instead of "virago" to discuss the same literary theme and character type. See Yenna Wu, "The Inversion of Marital Hierarchy: Shrewish Wives and Henpecked Husbands in Seventeenth-Century Chinese Literature," *Harvard Journal of Asiatic Studies* 48, no. 2 (1988): 363–82.

2. For the use of the term "shrew" in current scholarship, see R. Keith McMahon, *Misers, Shrews, and Polygamists: Sexuality and Male-Female Relations in Eighteenth-Century Chinese Fiction* (Durham: Duke University Press, 1995); Paola Paderni, "Between Constraints and Opportunities: Widows, Witches, and Shrews in Eighteenth-Century China," in *Chinese Women in the Imperial Past: New Perspectives*, ed. Harriet Zurndorfer (Leiden: Brill, 1999), 258–85; Maram Epstein, *Competing Discourses: Orthodoxy, Authenticity, and Engendered Meanings in Late Imperial Chinese Fiction* (Cambridge: Harvard University Press, 2001), chap. 3; Janet Theiss, "Explaining the Shrew: Narratives of Spousal Violence and the Critique of Masculinity in Eighteenth-Century Criminal Cases," in *Writing and Law in Late Imperial China: Crime, Conflict, and Judgment*, ed. Robert E. Hegel and Katherine Carlitz (Seattle: University of Washington Press, 2007), 44–63 and briefly in Janet Theiss, *Disgraceful Matters: The Politics of Chastity in Eighteenth-Century China* (Berkeley: University of California Press, 2004); Mark Stevenson and Wu Cuncun, eds., *Wanton Women in Late-Imperial Chinese Literature: Models, Genres, Subversions and Traditions* (Leiden: Brill, 2017).

3. McMahon, *Misers, Shrews, and Polygamists*, 55.

4. JeeLoo Liu, *Neo-Confucianism: Metaphysics, Mind, and Morality* (Hoboken, NJ: Wiley, 2018), 3.

5. Ellen Widmer refers to "the demise of shrew literature" when reviewing *The Chinese Virago*. See Ellen Widmer, "Review of *The Chinese Virago: A Literary Theme*," by Yenna Wu, *Chinese Literature: Essays, Articles, Reviews* 20 (1998): 187. In her book, Wu mentions in passing that the theme of the virago "survives into the modern era in different forms" without providing any explanation. See Wu, *The Chinese Virago*, 18. Keith McMahon has made himself clear in refusing to see modernity as arising *ex nihilo* from tradition and has claimed that

"whatever was on the verge did not simply disappear afterwards." His exploration of continuity centers on idealized variations of "the remarkable woman," a stock character type in late Qing love stories. He does not discuss whether or how the shrew figure evolved after late imperial China. See McMahon, *Misers, Shrews, and Polygamists*, 26; "Love Martyrs and Love Cheaters at the End of the Chinese Empire," in *Performing "Nation": Gender Politics in Literature, Theater, and the Visual Arts of China and Japan, 1880–1940*, ed. Doris Croissant, Catherine Vance Yeh, and Joshua S. Mostow (Leiden: Brill, 2008), 136; *Polygamy and Sublime Passion: Sexuality in China on the Verge of Modernity* (Honolulu: University of Hawai'i Press, 2010), 3, 15, 150.

6. "Lun she nüfan xiyi suo" 論設女犯習藝所 (On building vocational training centers for women criminals), *Shuntian shibao*, June 12–13, 1906, in *Jindai Zhongguo nüquan yundong shiliao (1842–1911)* 近代中國女權運動史料 (Source materials on the women's rights movement in modern China, 1842-1911), ed. Li Youning 李又寧 and Zhang Yufa (Taipei: Zhuanji wenxueshe, 1975), 710–11.

7. For the "woman question" and a theorization of the category "women" in modern China, see Tani E. Barlow, *The Question of Women in Chinese Feminism* (Durham: Duke University Press, 2004), chap. 2.

8. Henrietta Harrison, *The Making of the Republican Citizen: Political Ceremonies and Symbols in China, 1911–1929* (New York: Oxford University Press, 2000), 77.

9. Catherine Yeh has written about a legendary Shanghai courtesan who took the name Lin Daiyu to attract customers. According to Yeh, in addition to Lin Daiyu, there were others called "Lu Daiyu, Li Daiyu, Su Daiyu," showcasing the popularity of Lin's character among Shanghai prostitutes. See Catherine Vance Yeh, *Shanghai Love: Courtesans, Intellectuals, and Entertainment Culture, 1850–1910* (Seattle: University of Washington Press, 2006), 142.

10. David Strand, *An Unfinished Republic: Leading by Word and Deed in Modern China* (Berkeley: University of California Press, 2011), 127.

11. Harrison, *The Making of the Republican Citizen*, 77–78.

12. Strand, *An Unfinished Republic*, 121. Strand associates cigarettes and cigarette smoking with the male gender. Carol Benedict, however, presents an established history of women's smoking in China. From the seventeenth century to at least the late nineteenth century, Chinese women, regardless of social rank, consumed tobacco, although not publicly. Women's smoking was officially stigmatized starting from the 1930s, but during the early decades of the Republican era, cigarettes were favorably associated with modernity, urban life, and Western-inspired fashion, and were openly enjoyed by women, including those from respectable families. It may be true that, as Strand has claimed, the new women were consciously styling themselves through smoking and might also have mimicked the ways that men smoked to demonstrate their boldness. Yet on the basis of Benedict's account, it would be risky to overstate Chinese women's gender-crossing intention, given that they had formed their own smoking habit long before. See Carol Benedict, *Golden-Silk Smoke: A History of Tobacco in China, 1550–2010* (Berkeley: University of California Press, 2011).

13. Cao Xueqin 曹雪芹 and Gao E 高鶚, *Honglou meng (sanjia pingben)* 紅樓夢 (三家評本), 2 vols. (The three commentaries edition of Dream of the Red Chamber) (Shanghai: Shanghai guji chubanshe, 1988), 1:41. For the translation, see David Hawkes and John Minford, trans., *The Story of the Stone*, 5 vols. (Harmondsworth: Penguin Books, 1973–1986), 1:91.

14. Cao and Gao, *Honglou meng*, 2:1491. For the translation, see Hawkes and Minford, trans., *The Story*, 4:224.

15. Lao She 老舍, "Liutun de" 柳屯的 (A woman from the Liu village), in *Lao She mingzuo xinshang* 老舍名作欣賞 (Appreciations of Lao She's masterpieces), ed. Fan Jun 樊駿 (Beijing: Zhongguo heping chubanshe, 1995), 467. Lao She also produced and ridiculed negative shrew characters such as Hu Niu in *Rickshaw: The Novel of Camel Xiangzi* (*Luotuo Xiangzi* 駱駝祥子; 1937) and Da Chibao in *Four Generations under One Roof* (*Si shi tong tang* 四世同堂; 1944).

16. Sha Ting 沙汀, "Shou dao" 獸道 (The way of the beast), in *Sha Ting xuanji* 沙汀選集 (Selected works of Sha Ting) (Hong Kong: Wenxue chubanshe, 1957), 120.

17. Mao Dun 茅盾, "Lu" 路 (The road), in vol. 2 of *Mao Dun wenji* 茅盾文集 (Collected works of Mao Dun) (Hong Kong: Jindai tushu gongsi, 1966), 319.

18. According to the historian Joan Judge, the concept of *liangqi xianmu* was "developed in Japan in the last decades of the nineteenth century and traveled to China in the early years of the twentieth." Judge also points out that while *liangqi xianmu* was most used in late Qing sources, *xianqi liangmu* (wise wife and good mother) and *xianmu liangqi* (wise mother and good wife) were both variants of the concept. See Joan Judge, *The Precious Raft of History: The Past, the West, and the Woman Question in China* (Stanford: Stanford University Press, 2008), 110–11. Wang Zheng, however, emphasizes the influence of Western examples in inspiring and molding Chinese women into virtuous mothers and good wives. See Wang Zheng, *Women in the Chinese Enlightenment: Oral and Textual Histories* (Berkeley: University of California Press, 1999), 68–73. For a review of the use of the concept in East Asia, see Chen Zhengyuan 陳姃湲, "Jianjie jindai Yazhou de 'xianqi liangmu' sixiang—Cong huigu Riben, Hanguo, Zhongguo de yanjiu chengguo tanqi" 簡介近代亞洲的"賢妻良母"思想——從回顧日本、韓國、中國的研究成果談起 (A brief introduction to the idea of "good wives and wise mothers" in modern Asia: Research findings from Japan, South Korea, and China), *Jindai Zhongguo funüshi yanjiu*, no. 10 (2002): 199–219.

19. Gail Hershatter, *Women and China's Revolutions* (Lanham, MD: Rowman & Littlefield, 2019), 57–58.

20. Paul J. Bailey, *Women and Gender in Twentieth-Century China* (New York: Palgrave Macmillan, 2012), 25.

21. Tze-lan D. Sang, "Failed Modern Girls in Early-Twentieth-Century China," in Croissant, Yeh, and Mostow, *Performing "Nation,"* 182.

22. Wang, *Women in the Chinese Enlightenment*; Amy D. Dooling, *Women's Literary Feminism in Twentieth-Century China* (New York: Palgrave Macmillan, 2005).

23. In addition to *xin funü*, terms such as *xin nüzi* 新女子 and *xin nüxing* 新女性 were also used to designate the new woman. By this time, Chinese terms in circulation for a new type of woman also included "new-style woman"

(*xinshi funü* 新式婦女, *xinshi nüzi* 新式女子, *xinpai funü* 新派婦女) and "modern woman" (*jindai nüzi* 近代女子, *jindai nüxing* 近代女性, *xiandai nüzi* 現代女子, *xiandai nüxing* 現代女性, *shidai nüzi* 時代女子).

24. Hu Shi 胡適, "Meiguo de furen: Zai Beijing nüzi shifan xuexiao jiang-yan" 美國的婦人：在北京女子師範學校講演 (Women in America: A speech at Beijing Women's Normal School), in vol. 4 of *Hu Shi wencun* 胡適文存 (Collection of Hu Shi's writings) (Shanghai: Yadong tushuguan, 1921), 58. Translation from Kristine Harris, "The New Woman: Image, Subject, and Dissent in 1930s Shanghai Film Culture," *Republican China* 20, no. 2 (1995): 64.

25. Dina Lowy, *The Japanese "New Woman": Images of Gender and Modernity* (New Brunswick: Rutgers University Press, 2007), 21.

26. Lowy, *The Japanese "New Woman,"* chap. 2, "Ibsen's Nora: The New Woman Debate Begins," 21–39.

27. Hu Ying in *Tales of Translation* has traced one of the genealogical roots of the late imperial composition of the new woman to the positive category of the talented woman (*cainü* 才女) in traditional society. Although the unacknowledged shrew type is left out of the "many antecedents" of the new woman, Hu's book refers to Pan Jinlian in interpreting the emerging new woman Fu Caiyun in the late imperial novel *A Flower in a Sinful Sea* (*Niehai hua* 孽海花; 1905). See Hu Ying, *Tales of Translation: Composing the New Woman in China, 1899–1918* (Stanford: Stanford University Press, 2000).

28. See, for example, Wang Dewei 王德威, "Pan Jinlian, Sai Jinhua, Yin Xueyan: Zhongguo xiaoshuo shijie zhong 'huoshui' zaoxing de yanbian" 潘金蓮、賽金花、尹雪豔：中國小說世界中"禍水"造型的演變 (Pan Jinlian, Sai Jinhua, Yin Xueyan: The transformation of "femme fatale" images in the world of Chinese fiction), in *Xiangxiang Zhongguo de fangfa: Lishi, xiaoshuo, xushi* 想像中國的方法：歷史，小說，敘事 (Ways to imagine China: History, fiction, and narration) (Beijing: Shenghuo dushu xinzhi sanlian shudian, 1998), 256–69; Yomi Braester, "Rewriting Tradition, Misreading History: Twentieth-Century (Sub)versions of Pan Jinlian's Story," in *Witness against History: Literature, Film, and Public Discourse in Twentieth-Century China* (Stanford: Stanford University Press, 2003), 56-80; Haiyan Lee, "The Shrew Rehabilitated," in *Revolution of the Heart: A Genealogy of Love in China, 1900–1950* (Stanford: Stanford University Press, 2007), 199-205.

1. The Shrew Is Back: Media Representations of the Early Radical Chinese Suffragettes

A longer version of this chapter was previously published. See Shu Yang, "Wrestling with Tradition: Early Chinese Suffragettes and the Modern Remodeling of the Shrew Trope," *Modern Chinese Literature and Culture* 34, no. 1 (2022): 128-69. The article version includes the suffragettes' responses to the shrew label and details about Shen Peizhen's trial.

1. "Nüquan pengzhang" 女權膨脹 (The expansion of women's rights), *Beijing nübao*, April 21, 1907.

2. Even though scribes were not high in the traditional Chinese social hierarchy, their elite status was mainly defined by their association with education and their sense of privilege.

3. Biographical details about Zhang Zhanyun are scarce. He was said to be quite sociable and active in Beijing newspaper circles. He founded the acclaimed *Beijing Pictorial News* during the late Qing, contributed to charity, and opened orphanages and factories to assist women from the lower social strata. For further information on Zhang Zhanyun and the *Beijing Women's News*, see Zhan Xiaobai 湛晓白, "Cong yulun dao xingdong: Qingmo Beijing Nübao jiqi shehui zitai" 從輿論到行動：清末《北京女報》及其社會姿態 (From public opinion to action: Beijing Women's News and its social attitude in the late Qing dynasty), *Shi lin*, no. 4 (2008): 37–48, see 38–40; "Beijing Nübao yu Qingmo Beijing nüzi jiaoyu chutan" 《北京女報》與清末北京女子教育初探 (Studies of Beijing Women's News and Beijing's female education in the late Qing), *Beijing shehui kexue*, no. 5 (2012): 96–101; Yun Zhang, *Engendering the Woman Question: Men, Women, and Writing in China's Early Periodical Press* (Leiden: Brill, 2020), 84.

4. Zhan, "Cong yulun," 41.

5. Epstein, *Competing Discourses*, 121.

6. For women's performance in (pre-)1911 revolutionary events, see Hershatter, *Women and China's Revolutions*, 86–87.

7. For a discussion of female students as embodiments of the new social category of "public women," see Judge, *The Precious Raft of History*, 72–81; Yuxin Ma, *Women Journalists and Feminism in China: 1898–1937* (Amherst, NY: Cambria Press, 2010), 132.

8. For cases and criticism of unseemly behavior of female students at the turn of the twentieth century, see Paul Bailey, " 'Women Behaving Badly': Crime, Transgressive Behaviour and Gender in Early Twentieth Century China," *Nan Nü: Men, Women, and Gender in China* 8, no. 1 (2006): 156–97, see 179–92.

9. Paul Bailey, *Gender and Education in China: Gender Discourses and Women's Schooling in the Early Twentieth Century* (London: Routledge, 2007), 74. For a study of women warriors throughout Chinese history, see Louise Edwards, *Women Warriors and Wartime Spies of China* (Cambridge: Cambridge University Press, 2016).

10. Louise Edwards, *Gender, Politics, and Democracy: Women's Suffrage in China* (Stanford: Stanford University Press, 2008), 66.

11. Louise Edwards, "Opposition to Women's Suffrage in China: Confronting Modernity in Governance," in *Women in China: The Republican Period in Historical Perspective*, ed. Mechthild Leutner and Nicola Spakowski (Berlin: Lit Verlag, 2005), 112–15.

12. In the second phase, gender equality was achieved in several provincial constitutions but had yet to receive recognition at the national level. From the mid-1920s, the women's suffrage movement became integrated into the public campaigns of the Communist and the Nationalist parties. Both parties granted gender equality and women's rights in their constitutions. The gains were maintained even after the establishment of the People's Republic of China.

13. In addition to the Chinese suffragettes' experience as militants, many studies have also pointed out their imitation of the activities of British and American suffragettes to account for their violent profile. See, for example, Ono Kazuko, *Chinese Women in a Century of Revolution, 1850–1950*, ed. Joshua

A. Fogel (Stanford: Stanford University Press, 1978), 85; Edwards, *Gender, Politics, and Democracy*, 71, 81–82; Strand, *An Unfinished Republic*, 116–17, 120; Jad Adams, *Women and the Vote: A World History* (Oxford: Oxford University Press, 2014), 357–59; Elisabeth Croll, *Feminism and Socialism in China* (London: Routledge & Kegan Paul, 1978), 70. Some studies call for a more meticulous representation of the violent or militant nature of the radical suffragettes. For example, Yuxin Ma questions the commonly used category of "militant suffragists." She contends that studies should distinguish "when and why" the suffragettes turned militant in their campaign, because even the most radical groups adopted legitimate institutional means in the beginning and during times when they considered militant methods unable to achieve desired results. See Ma, *Women Journalists*, 102, 110–17.

14. The idea of women participating in politics had been suggested in the Qing novel *Flowers in the Mirror* (*Jinghua yuan* 鏡花緣; 1828). The intellectual Jin Tianhe (1874–1947) had also promoted a violent method for fulfilling that goal. In 1903 he maintained in radical terms that it is necessary to resort to extreme means if written appeals cannot achieve women's suffrage, including shedding tears and blood, and wielding swords, bombs, and cannons. See Jin Tianhe 金天翮, *Nüjie zhong* 女界鐘 (The women's bell) (Shanghai: Shanghai guji chubanshe, 2003), 63–64.

15. Edwards, *Gender, Politics, and Democracy*, 80.

16. "Yaoqiu nüzi canzhengquan zhi wuli" 要求女子參政權之武力 (The force of those asking for women's suffrage), *Shi bao*, March 23, 1912; "Nüzi yaoqiu canzhengquan" 女子要求參政權 (Women ask for suffrage), *Minli bao*, March 23, 1912; "Nüzi yi wuli yaoqiu canzhengquan" 女子以武力要求參政權 (Women ask for suffrage by force), *Shen bao*, March 24, 1912; "Lun nüzi yaoqiu canzhengquan wenti" 論女子要求參政權問題 (On the issue of women's demand for suffrage), *Shen bao*, March 25, 1912; Meng Huan 夢幻, "Lun nüzi yaoqiu canzhengquan zhi guaixiang" 論女子要求參政權之怪象 (On the strange phenomenon of women demanding suffrage), *Dagong bao*, March 30, 1912; "Xianping er (Nanjing)" 閒評二（南京） (Random comments, no. 2, from Nanjing), *Dagong bao*, March 30, 1912.

17. "Yaoqiu."

18. "Nüshi da ma canyiyuan" 女士大罵參議員 (Ladies tongue-lashing the senators), *Aiguo bao*, December 11, 1912.

19. Strand, *An Unfinished Republic*, 2.

20. On the relationship between political situations and the possibility of women's transgression and transcendence, Wai-yee Li makes a similar observation: "Political disorder makes room for female agency." See Wai-yee Li, *Women and National Trauma in Late Imperial Chinese Literature* (Cambridge: Harvard University Press, 2014), 229.

21. Ma, *Women Journalists*, 102.

22. "Yaoqiu"; "Nüzi yi wuli"; "Xianping er"; Meng, "Lun nüzi"; "Nüzi da nao canyiyuan ji" 女子大鬧參議院記 (A report on the ruckus caused by the women at the senate), *Shengjing shibao*, March 31, 1912.

23. Lisa Raphals, *Sharing the Light: Representations of Women and Virtue in Early China* (Albany: State University of New York Press, 1998), 224.

24. Raphals, *Sharing the Light*, 7.

25. "Nüzi yaoqiu"; Meng, "Lun nüzi."

26. "Yingguo nüzi zhi baoheng" 英國女子之暴橫 (The cruelty of English women), *Minli bao*, April 23, 1912.

27. Australian senator Larissa Waters made history by becoming the first woman senator to breastfeed in Parliament when she nursed her three-month-old daughter while speaking before the legislature in May 2017. The news photo (see *The Guardian*, June 22, 2017) captures a similar situation facing Waters as that of the Chinese lady in figure 1 from about a hundred years earlier. Waters, like the early Chinese suffragette, nursed while addressing Parliament to visually demonstrate that women can be parliamentarians and mothers at the same time. Even the responses of the (mostly male) audience surrounding her bear a marked resemblance to those of the audience in figure 1. After a century, men still dominate the senate, and the facial expressions of most men still convey sternness, intensity, and uneasiness. Although it is almost certain that women breastfeeding in the chamber will continue to make news for quite some time and across cultural lines, it is important to acknowledge the big step achieved by a century of struggle. A nursing female politician in the early Republican Chinese cartoon was a fantasy for dampening women's political enthusiasm and tantalizing the voyeuristic public; now it is becoming women's lived experience, and an advance against both natural and man-made obstacles. For a study on public breastfeeding and the natural, excretory, and sexual implications, see Brett Lunceford, *Naked Politics: Nudity, Political Action, and the Rhetoric of the Body* (Lanham, MD: Lexington Books, 2012), chap. 3, "Weaponizing the Breast: Lactivism and Public Breastfeeding."

28. A chapter-linked novel of the seventeenth century, *Marriage Bonds to Awaken the World* depicts the lives of married couples in two incarnations. It features a shrew, Xue Sujie, notorious for her unruly tongue, extreme immorality, and violence. Her abused husband, Di Xichen, is one of the quintessential cowards among male characters in traditional Chinese literature, embodying weakness and failure.

29. Epstein, *Competing Discourses*, 130–31.

30. This cartoon has provoked various interpretations among scholars. I thank Maram Epstein for pointing to the resemblance of the woman's shoes to the black leather shoes worn by men during the French Revolution. I thank Christopher Rea for his suggestion of linking the visual of the sashes passing over the woman's crotch to oversized labia, which contributes to the entertaining effect of the cartoon. I agree that this cartoon was, or should be read as, presenting transgression rather than attacking it. The illustrator, Wang Dungen, had voiced opposition to conservative approaches to gender and promoted women's suffrage mere days before the publication of this image in the same newspaper. See [Wang 王] Dungen 鈍根, "Bo bo nüzi canzhengquan" 駁駁女子參政權 (Opposition to the opposition to women's suffrage), *Shen bao*, March 18, 1912. It is not very likely that his position had changed in a matter of days. The fact that violence was taken as a common political strategy at the time also persuades us to read this cartoon as is—as how the illustrator used forms of exaggeration to visualize women's "extraordinary valor" (which

might be mixed with aggression and sexuality) to impress and interest the audience.

31. She Zi 舍子, "Wuqi buyou" 無奇不有 (Nothing is too strange), *Shi bao*, March 23, 1912.

32. Shenjing bing 神經病, "Wuti" 無題 (No title), *Shi bao*, March 27, 1912.

33. [Zhou 周] Shoujuan 瘦鵑, trans., "Funü zhi yuanzhi" 婦女之原質 (The original qualities of women), *Funü shibao*, no. 8 (1912): 24.

34. "Wuhan nüjie qutan lu" 武漢女界趣談錄 (Interesting anecdotes about women in Wuhan), *Shen bao*, October 14, 1912; Xi Yinglu 息影廬, "Xinzhi kou-kuai" 心直口快 (Straight heart, fast mouth), *Shen bao*, October 16, 1912.

35. Gao Muzi 槁木子, "Nannü bu pingquan zhi biejie" 男女不平權之別解 (An alternative interpretation of gender inequality), *Shen bao*, November 8, 1912.

36. Xi, "Xinzhi koukuai."

37. Xi, "Xinzhi koukuai."

38. Cao and Gao, *Honglou meng*, chap. 11. For the translation, see Hawkes and Minford, *The Story*, 1:242.

39. For the reading of *yin-yang* numerology and how textual details in this chapter of *Honglou meng* invoke the stereotypical shrew narrative, see Epstein, *Competing Discourses*, 173–84.

40. Louise Edwards, "Representations of Women and Social Power in Eighteenth Century China: The Case of Wang Xifeng," *Late Imperial China* 14, no. 1 (1993): 39–41.

41. Some studies of *Honglou meng* imply that Wang Xifeng and her nephew Jia Rong might have had an illicit relationship. One commonly cited indicator is Wang Xifeng's unnatural speech and behavior in chapter 6 when Jia Rong comes to borrow a screen.

42. Xi, "Xinzhi koukuai."

43. Xiao 笑, "Xin Honglou meng" 新紅樓夢 (The new Dream of the Red Chamber), *Shi bao*, August 29, 1912. In fact, this was not the first time that Song was attacked. Other senators and suffragettes had struck him before on account of political disputes. See Strand, *An Unfinished Republic*, 124.

44. Strand, *An Unfinished Republic*, 127–28.

45. Cao and Gao, *Honglou meng*, chap. 74. For the translation, see Hawkes and Minford, *The Story*, 3:473.

46. Song Jiaoren met Tang Qunying in Japan. They both joined the Revolutionary Alliance in 1905 and had been conducting revolutionary activities together. Song supported the women's suffrage movement and wrote several statements for the women's newspapers including Tang's *Women's Vernacular Daily* and *East Asia Times*. See "Tang Qunying yu Song Jiaoren" 唐群英與宋教仁 (Tang Qunying and Song Jiaoren), in *Tang Qunying shiliao jicui* 唐群英史料集萃 (Historical materials on Tang Qunying), ed. Hengyang shi funü lianhehui 衡陽市婦女聯合會 (Hengyang: Funü lianhehui, 2006), 78–81. It was said that Song addressed Tang by the honorific "Elder Sister Tang" (*Tang dajie* 唐大姐), which indicates their closeness. See Louise Edwards, "Tang Qunying," in *Biographical Dictionary of Chinese Women: The Twentieth Century*, ed. Lily Xiao Hong Lee (New

York: M. E. Sharpe, 2003), 505; Strand, *An Unfinished Republic*, 104; "Tang Quny-ing yu Song Jiaoren," 78; Hershatter, *Women and China's Revolutions*, 90.

47. "Sun Zhongshan xiansheng ru jing hou zhi diyi dahui" 孫中山先生入京后之第一大會 (The first major meeting since Mr. Sun Zhongshan entered Bei-jing), *Minli bao*, August 31, 1912. Also see "Tang Qunying yu Song Jiaoren," 79.

48. The term appeared in Pu Songling's (1640–1715) "Jiang Cheng" 江城 (Jiang Cheng), in his volume *Liaozhai's Records of the Strange* (*Liaozhai zhiyi* 聊齋誌異; 1740). See Pu Songling 蒲松齡, "Jiang Cheng," in *Baihua qianzhu Liaozhai zhiyi* 白話淺注聊齋誌異 (Liaozhai's Records of the Strange: Annotated in ver-nacular Chinese) (Hong Kong: Shangwu yinshuguan, 1963), 340. Ye Zhifei (fl. 1644) wrote a play titled *The Tiger with Rouge* (*Yanzhi hu*; alternative title *Open Your Mouth and Laugh* [*Kaikou xiao* 開口笑]). Ye's play is based on Li Yu's (1610–1680) shrew story "Duqi shou youfu zhi gua" 妒妻守有夫之寡 (A jealous wife becomes a widow while her husband is still alive), in *Silent Operas* (*Wusheng xi* 無聲戲; ca. 1656–57). The Ming dynasty shrew play *The Lioness Roars* (*Shihou ji* 獅吼記), written by Wang Tingna (fl. 1596), also inspired Ye's play.

49. Hu Chi 虎癡, "Xinzhi koukuai" 心直口快 (Straight heart, fast mouth), *Shen bao*, September 3, 1912.

50. Wang Jiajian 王家儉, "Minchu de nüzi canzheng yundong" 民初的女子參政運動 (Women's suffrage movement in the early Republic), *Lishi xuebao*, no. 11 (1983): 163. According to Gail Hershatter, Tang's feet were never properly bound because she often removed the binding strips despite her mother's ef-forts. See Hershatter, *Women and China's Revolutions*, 89.

51. Wang Dungen, "Yingxiong jia" 英雄頰 (The cheeks of the hero), *Shen bao*, September 3, 1912.

52. Wang, "Yingxiong jia."

53. Wang Qisheng 王奇生, "Minguo chunian de nüxing fanzui (1914–1936)" 民國初年的女性犯罪 (Female crimes in early Republican China, 1914–1936), *Jindai Zhongguo funüshi yanjiu*, no. 1 (1993): 16–17; Bailey, "'Women Be-having Badly,'" 165. Bailey points out (167) that among homicide cases in years such as 1914 and 1919, the most typical offense was the murder of a husband by an adulterous wife, which reminds one of scenarios from the traditional Pan Jinlian story (see chapter 3). The Republican women, by murdering their hus-bands in pursuit of extramarital sexual pleasure, appear as nothing less than modern real-life versions of Pan.

54. Buxiao sheng 不肖生, *Liudong waishi* 留東外史 (An unofficial history of studying in Japan) (Beijing: Zhongguo huaqiao chubanshe, 1997), 446, 448.

55. Judge, *The Precious Raft of History*, 76–78; Bailey, *Gender and Education in China*, 43–44, 81, 101.

56. The letter refers to the Qing dynasty work *Traces of Flowers and the Moon* (*Huayue hen* 花月痕; 1888) as a device of persuasion. In that story, a prostitute even assists in the suppression of national enemies. Other late Qing writings that revolutionize the image of prostitutes include *A Flower in a Sinful Sea*, *The Stone of Goddess Nüwa* (*Nüwa shi* 女媧石; 1905), *Dreams of Shanghai Splendor* (*Hais-hang fanhua meng* 海上繁華夢; 1890–1908), and *New Camellia* (*Xin chahua* 新茶花; 1913), among others.

57. [Yan 嚴] Duhe 獨鶴, "Xini mou nüshi zhi bada hutong jijie shu" 戲擬某女士致八大胡同妓界書 (An imaginary playful letter from a certain lady to the prostitutes), *Shen bao*, November 22, 1912.

58. Xie Shengwei 諧聖韋, "Xini nüjie zizhihui jianzhang yuanqi" 戲擬女界自治會簡章緣起 (Bantering on the origin of the "brief program for the Women's Autonomous Association"), *Rizhi bao*, November 28, 1913.

59. Yan, "Xini."

60. Jin 津, "*Dangfu weixin*" 蕩婦維新 (A wanton woman joins the reform), *Aiguo bao*, October 1, 1912.

61. The statement first appeared in the ancient classic *Book of Odes* (*Shi jing* 詩經) to describe women's promiscuity.

62. Gai 匄, "Nannü pingquan jianzhang" 男女平權簡章 (Constitution for Equality between Men and Women), *Aiguo baihua bao*, September 17, 1913.

63. Yi He 一鶴, "Xin nüjie de xianxiang" 新女界的現像 (Phenomena in the new women's circles), *Aiguo baihua bao*, August 9–10, 1913.

64. In 1909 the American feminist Mrs. O. H. P. Belmont had proposed "a general female strike," asking women to "withdraw from every activity in which they are now associated with men." Belmont declared that "women will refuse to marry and will have nothing to do with the men, socially, industrially—any way." Years later, during the American and British suffrage campaigns, the play *Lysistrata* (originally performed in 411 BCE) by the ancient Greek playwright Aristophanes (ca. 460–ca. 380 BCE) was restaged to encourage noncooperation. The heroine, Lysistrata, leads Greek women to "stop the Peloponnesian war by deserting their homes, children and husbands, until the latter will hear reason." Western suffragettes found great inspiration in those ancient women's "denial of sex, words of love, kisses, or even kind looks" to their husbands or sweethearts. They called them "the first suffragettes" or "Greek suffragettes," and were excited by Lysistrata's bold claim that "if you make a man sufficiently uncomfortable, he will give up his own soul." See "Progress of Woman Suffrage," *New York Times*, September 24, 1909; "Sit in a Drizzle to See Greek Play: Courageous Suffragists in Outdoor Theatre Hear Aristophanes Plead Their Cause," *New York Times*, September 20, 1912; "First Suffragettes Seen in Greek Play: Aristophanes's Famous Comedy, 'Lysistrata,' Presented at Maxine Elliott's Theatre," *New York Times*, February 18, 1913. In the meantime, we should also note that manless women and sworn spinsters existed in Chinese society from imperial times to the modern era. For relevant scholarship on those women, see, for example, Hsiao-wen Cheng, *Divine, Demonic, and Disordered: Women without Men in Song Dynasty China* (Seattle: University of Washington Press, 2021); Janice E. Stockard, *Daughters of the Canton Delta: Marriage Patterns and Economic Strategies in South China, 1860–1930* (Stanford: Stanford University Press, 1989); Andrea Sankar, "Spinster Sisterhoods: *Jing Yih Sifu*: Spinster-Domestic-Nun," in *Lives: Chinese Working Women*, ed. Mary Sheridan and Janet W. Salaff (Bloomington: Indiana University Press, 1984); Emily Honig, *Sisters and Strangers: Women in the Shanghai Cotton Mills, 1919–1949* (Stanford: Stanford University Press, 1986); Kenneth Gaw, *Superior Servants: The Legendary Cantonese Amahs of the*

Far East (Singapore: Oxford University Press, 1991); Nicole Constable, *Maid to Order in Hong Kong: Stories of Migrant Workers* (Ithaca: Cornell University Press, 2007).

65. "Nüzi canzheng hui jishi" 女子參政會紀事 (A report on the women's suffrage meeting), *Minli bao*, September 27, 1912.

66. Mang Han 莽漢, "Xiyong Shen Peizhen" 戲詠沈佩貞 (Parodying Shen Peizhen), in *Shen Peizhen* 沈佩貞 (Shen Peizhen), ed. Fan Lang 飯郎 (Beijing: Xinhua shushe, 1915), 61.

67. Li San 立三, "Xinzhi koukuai" 心直口快 (Straight heart, fast mouth), *Shen bao*, October 18, 1912.

68. Xi Yinglu, "Wen Shen nüshi yanshuo ganyan" 聞沈女士演說感言 (Thoughts upon hearing Lady Shen's speech), *Shen bao*, October 23, 1912.

69. Bailey, *Gender and Education in China*, 190, n.35. The term *nüjie* was invented by late Qing male reformists. In the beginning, women writers of late Qing and early Republican China followed this discourse, denouncing *nüjie* as dark, backward, and sinful. Gradually they added new, positive, and subversive meanings to the notion, turning *nüjie* into a site of feminist solidarity. *Nüjie* contributed to the early Republican suffrage movement, wherein it signified the revolutionary collective opposing gender hierarchies and emboldening women in their political pursuits. For a trajectory of the development of the term, see Yun Zhang, "Nationalism and Beyond: Writings on *Nüjie* and the Emergence of a New Gendered Collective Identity in Modern China," *Nan Nü: Men, Women and Gender in China* 17, no. 2 (2015): 245–75.

70. Zhang Xiaofen 張孝芬, "Nüzi canzheng zhi taolun—Zhang Xiaofen nüshi laihan" 女子參政之討論—張孝芬女士來函 (Discussions on women's suffrage—A letter from Lady Zhang Xiaofen), *Minli bao*, March 18, 1912.

71. Li Jingye 李淨業, "Nüzi canzheng zhi taolun—Zhi Jiangnan Zhang Renlan tongzhi shu" 女子參政之討論—致江南張紉蘭同志書 (Discussions on women's suffrage—A letter to Zhang Renlan in Jiangnan), *Minli bao*, March 24, 1912.

72. The *Eastern Times* noted how "bizarre events and fanciful stories" often occurred because those new women never accepted libels in silence and frequently caused trouble in newspaper offices. Tang Qunying took down the signboard of the *Guoguang News* and smashed property at the office of the *Changsha Daily*. Shen Peizhen wrecked the office of the *Citizens' Daily* after it published her name alongside the names of the prostitute Jin Xiuqing and the opera performer Mei Lanfang (1894–1961). Another new woman, Pan Lianbi (dates unknown), who was said to have been a student of the famous late Qing and early Republican woman activist Lü Bicheng (1883–1943), severely beat a journalist from the *Eastern News* for his use of an erotic phrase when describing her appearance. See Ping Wu 平五, "Shen Peizhen wuda Guo Tong" 沈佩貞誤打郭同 (Shen Peizhen mistakenly hit Guo Tong), originally published in *Shi bao*, quoted from Fan, *Shen Peizhen*, 13–14.

73. Xu Zhiyan 許指嚴, "Nü weiren" 女偉人 (Great women), in *Xinhua miji* 新華秘記 (Secret notes about China) (1918; repr., Shanghai: Zhonghua shuju, 2007), 145.

74. Bao Tianxiao 包天笑, *Chuanying lou huiyilu* 釧影樓回憶錄 (Chuan-ying studio memoirs) (Hong Kong: Dahua chubanshe, 1971), 394.

75. Lin Shu 林紓, *Jinling qiu* 金陵秋 (The autumn in Nanjing), in vol. 5 of *Zhongguo jindai guben xiaoshuo jicheng* 中國近代孤本小說集成 (Collection of late imperial and modern Chinese fiction; only existing copy) (Beijing: Dazhong wenyi chubanshe, 1999), 3954.

76. Liu Chengyu 劉成禺, *Shizaitang zayi* 世載堂雜憶 (Miscellaneous memories from the Shizai studio), in *Jindai Zhongguo shiliao congkan* 近代中國史料叢刊, no. 717 (Series of source material on the history of modern China) (Taipei: Wenhai chubanshe, 1971), 220.

77. Bei An 悲菴, "Shen Peizhen da nao Xingchunju ji" 沈佩貞大鬧醒春居記 (Shen Peizhen causes a ruckus at Xingchun restaurant), *Shenzhou ribao*, June 1–2, 1915.

78. Rumor had it that Jiang Shuwan had earlier exposed her naked lower body on another public occasion. Bei, "Shen Peizhen."

79. Bei, "Shen Peizhen."

80. Ping, "Shen Peizhen," 16.

81. Wan Xiang 晚香, "Shen Peizhen ye da Shenzhou guan" 沈佩貞夜打神州館 (Shen Peizhen attacked the office of the Shenzhou ribao at night), originally published in *Shenzhou ribao*, quoted from Fan, *Shen Peizhen*, 20-26, see 24–25.

82. Wan, "Shen Peizhen," 25.

83. "Shen Peizhen sapo zhi guaixiang" 沈佩貞撒潑之怪象 (Strange phenomena of Shen Peizhen acting like a shrew and making a scene), originally published in *Beijing Guohua News*, quoted from Fan, *Shen Peizhen*, 19; Lao Tan 老談, "Wenming . . . kaitong . . . haha" 文明…開通…哈哈 (Civilization . . . open-mindedness . . . ha ha), in Fan, *Shen Peizhen*, 41.

84. Liu, *Shizaitang*, 222–23.

85. Wan, "Shen Peizhen," 23; "Juzhong daren zhi Shen Peizhen" 聚眾打人之沈佩貞 (Shen Peizhen who gathered a crowd to beat), in Fan, *Shen Peizhen*, 31; "Guo Shen shuangfang shensu zhi ciling" 郭沈雙方申訴之詞令 (The appeals of both Guo and Shen), in Fan, *Shen Peizhen*, 33.

86. Dan Fu 丹斧, "Nu ci yuan" 怒雌緣 (The fate of the angry females), in Fan, *Shen Peizhen*, 57.

87. Ping, "Shen Peizhen," 14.

88. Dan Fu, "Ni Shen Peizhen da Liangsan xiezui shu" 擬沈佩貞答良三謝罪書 (Shen Peizhen's reply to Liangsan's apology letter), in Fan, *Shen Peizhen*, 60.

89. "Shen Peizhen zhi an zhong an" 沈佩貞之案中案 (Cases inside the case of Shen Peizhen), in Fan, *Shen Peizhen*, 35; "Shen Peizhen an zhi yiwen zhongzhong" 沈佩貞案之軼聞種種 (Anecdotes surrounding Shen Peizhen's case), *Qunqiang bao*, July 8, 1915.

90. "Guo Shen shuangfang," 33.

91. "Shen Peizhen zhi ge baoguan shu" 沈佩貞致各報館書 (Shen Peizhen's letter to the newspapers), in Fan, *Shen Peizhen*, 38.

92. "Ben an zhi jieshu" 本案之結束 (The end of the case), in Fan, *Shen Peizhen*, 8.

93. Liu, *Shizaitang*, 223.

94. The quotations in this discussion are based on the 1990 reprint edition by the Zhejiang Ancient Books Publishing House, which keeps the novel's original content, commentaries, and the 120 illustrations by Hu Shouzhu (dates unknown).

95. Wei Lanshi 韋蘭史, preface to Tao Hancui 陶寒翠, *Minguo yanshi yanyi* 民國豔史演義 (repr., Hangzhou: Zhejiang guji chubanshe, 1990), 11.

96. See, for example, Edwards, *Gender, Politics, and Democracy*, 98–99; Madeleine Yue Dong, "Unofficial History and Gender Boundary Crossing in the Early Republic: Shen Peizhen and Xiaofengxian," in *Gender in Motion: Divisions of Labor and Cultural Change in Late Imperial and Modern China*, ed. Bryna Goodman and Wendy Larson (Lanham, MD: Rowman & Littlefield, 2005), 174–75.

97. Strand, *An Unfinished Republic*, 124.

98. Cao and Gao, *Honglou meng (sanjia pingben)*, 1:41. For the translation, see Hawkes and Minford, *The Story*, 1:90–91.

99. Tao, *Minguo*, 93.

100. For an analysis of the shrew and *yin-yang* symbolism through water imagery, see Epstein, *Competing Discourses*, 142–49.

101. Tao, *Minguo*, 96–98.

102. Tao, *Minguo*, 98.

103. Tao, *Minguo*, 95, 105.

104. Tao, *Minguo*, 99–100.

105. Sigmund Freud, *Three Contributions to the Theory of Sex* (New York: Nervous and Mental Disease Publishing Company, 1920), 19. Freud remarks in the note that "the shoe or slipper is accordingly a symbol for the female genitals." Also see Havelock Ellis, *Studies in the Psychology of Sex*, vol. 6 (Philadelphia: F. A. Davis Company, 1911), 101.

106. Zhang Ruohua 張若華, *Zhongguo chanzu lishi: Sancun jinlian yiqian nian* 中國纏足歷史：三寸金蓮一千年 (The history of foot-binding in China: The three-inch golden lotus in a thousand years) (Hong Kong: Zhonghua shuju, 2015), 119.

107. Tao, *Minguo*, 105–6.

108. McMahon, *Misers, Shrews, and Polygamists*, 55.

109. Tao, *Minguo*, 109–11.

110. McMahon, *Misers, Shrews, and Polygamists*, 55.

111. Freud mentioned the meaning of neckties as phallic symbols. In the tenth lecture of his *A General Introduction to Psychoanalysis*, delivered at the University of Vienna from 1915 to 1917, he said, "A tie, being an object which hangs down and is not worn by women, is clearly a male symbol." See Sigmund Freud, *A General Introduction to Psychoanalysis* (New York: Pocket Books, 1953), 165. Besides "the Freudian significance of ties" as a sexual symbol, scholars such as James Laver point out that there is also a dimension of "the Adlerian meaning" in ties, which defines them as a symbol of social power and hierarchy. See James Laver, *Modesty in Dress: An Inquiry into the Fundamentals of Fashion* (Boston: Houghton Mifflin Company, 1969), 124–25.

112. Dong, "Unofficial History," 184.

113. Dong, "Unofficial History," 182.

2. Jealous Shrew, Judicious New Woman: May Fourth Disputes on Female Jealousy and Virtue

1. Edwards, *Gender, Politics, and Democracy*, 109–10, 105.

2. Hildegard Baumgart, *Jealousy: Experiences and Solutions*, trans. Manfred Jacobson and Evelyn Jacobson (Chicago: University of Chicago Press, 1990), 121.

3. Wu, *The Chinese Virago*, 36. For an overview of female jealousy in Chinese history, see Chia-lin Pao Tao 鮑家麟, "Women and Jealousy in Traditional China," in vol. 1 of *Zhongguo jinshi shehui wenhuashi lunwenji* 中國近世社會文化史論文集 (Papers on society and culture of early modern China) (Taipei: Institute of History and Philology, Academia Sinica, 1992), 531–61. McMahon, *Misers, Shrews, and Polygamists,* also has a chapter on shrews and jealousy; see chap. 3 of that book.

4. For these accounts and some translated stories, see Wu, *The Chinese Virago* and *The Lioness Roars: Shrew Stories from Late Imperial China* (Ithaca: East Asia Program, Cornell University, 1995).

5. For analyses of the positive image of the shrewish wife in *A Pair of Male Phoenixes Flying Together* and other *tanci* works, see Wenjia Liu, "The *Tanci Feng Shuang Fei*: A Female Perspective on the Gender and Sexual Politics of Late-Qing China" (PhD diss., University of Oregon, 2010), 207–27; Maram Epstein, "Turning the Authorial Table: Women Writing Wanton ~~Women~~, Shame, and Jealousy in Two Qing *Tanci*," in Stevenson and Wu, *Wanton Women in Late-Imperial Chinese Literature*.

6. Zhang Xuan 張萱, "Dufu buke shao" 妒婦不可少 (Jealous women are indispensable), in vol. 2 of Zhang Xuan, *Yi yao* 疑耀 (Doubts and clarities) (Taipei: Yiwen yinshuguan, 1965), 4.

7. Hong Liangji 洪亮吉, *Beijiang shihua* 北江詩話 (Talks on poetry from the north window) (Beijing: Renmin wenxue chubanshe, 1998), 58–59.

8. Yu Zhengxie 俞正燮, "Du fei nüren ede lun" 妒非女人惡德論 (Jealousy is not women's vice), in vol. 13 of *Guisi leigao* 癸巳類稿 (Categorized manuscripts from the Guisi year [1833]), *Xuxiu Sikuquanshu* 續修四庫全書, no. 1159 (Siku quanshu continued) (Shanghai: Shanghai guji chubanshe, 2003), 542.

9. Xu Shupi 徐樹丕, "Xi jianke" 戲柬客 (Playful exchanges), in *Shixiao lu* 識小錄 (Records of small knowledge), *Hanfen lou miji diyi ji* 涵芬樓秘笈第一集 (Private texts from Hanfen Tower, vol. 1) (Shanghai: Shangwu yinshuguan, 1936), 75.

10. Hu Shi, "Zhongguo zuizao taolun funü wenti de yibu shu–Jinghua yuan" 中國最早討論婦女問題的一部書–鏡花緣 (Flowers in the Mirror: The earliest Chinese book on the women's question), *Funü nianjian* 婦女年鑒 (An almanac of women) 2 (1925): 243.

11. Gong Wei 龔煒, "Yuan du" 原妒 (The source of jealousy), in vol. 2 of *Chaolin bitan xubian* 巢林筆談續編 (Sequel to the occasional jottings of Chaolin), *Xuxiu Sikuquanshu* 續修四庫全書, no. 1177 (Siku quanshu continued) (Shanghai: Shanghai guji chubanshe, 2003), 374.

12. The Ming scholar Huang Daozhou (1585–1646) also discussed the root of jealousy in his "Xing wu jidu lun" 性無嫉妒論 (Jealousy is not rooted in

human nature), even though his opinion is irrelevant to *qing*. Grounding jealousy in the human desire for benefits, Huang rebutted criticism directed at jealous ministers and wives, and instead argued that it is the pursuit of status and fame by the innocent ministers and wives that gives rise to jealousy and danger.

13. Gong, "Yuan du," 374.

14. See scene 19, "A Visit to the Pavilion" (*Xu ge* 絮閣), in Hong Sheng 洪昇, *The Palace of Eternal Youth*, trans. Yang Xianyi and Gladys Yang (Beijing: Foreign Languages Press, 2010), 212–13.

15. When commenting on the love relationship between Lin Daiyu and Jia Baoyu, the commentator Zhi-yanzhai gave prominence to the role of jealousy in chapter 29 of *Honglou meng*: "*Qing* remains shallow before suspicion and jealousy; love turns genuine only after spoilt demeanor and pretended anger" (*wei xing caidu qing you qian, ken lu jiaochen ai shi zhen* 未形猜妒情猶淺, 肯露嬌嗔愛始真).

16. Wang Jiting 汪集庭, "Shishi nüzi yu shishi nüzi" 時式女子與時實女子 (The artificial new woman and the authentic new woman), *Funü zazhi* 3, no. 2 (1917): 16–17.

17. Xie Yuanding 謝遠定, "Duiyu qingnian funü de zhengyan" 對於青年婦女的諍言 (Admonitions to young women), *Funü zazhi* 11, no. 4 (1925): 624–27.

18. Wei Ming 微明, "Lun jidu" 論嫉妒 (said to be translated from Radjabnia's "On Jealousy"), *Xin nüxing* 4, no. 12 (1929): 1529–30.

19. Cao Guozhi 曹國智 et al., *Xin nüxing de dairenjiewu* 新女性的待人接物 (Manners of the new woman) (Hong Kong: Funü zhishi shushe, 1941), 27, 31.

20. Pan Guangdan 潘光旦, "Tao Liu dusha an de xinli beijing" 陶劉妒殺案的心理背景 (The psychological background of the Tao-Liu jealousy murder case), and "Tao Liu dusha an de shehui zeren" 陶劉妒殺案的社會責任 (The social responsibility of the Tao-Liu jealousy murder case), in *Pan Guangdan wenji* 潘光旦文集 (The works of Pan Guangdan) (Beijing: Beijing daxue chubanshe, 1993), 436–38, 440–42. Although jealousy does not apply only to homosexual relationships, Pan made it seem as if homosexual couples were more prone to jealousy, and their jealousy was usually so intense that it drove them to hallucinations and abnormal behaviors such as murder and self-harm. On this case, also see Peter J. Carroll, "'A Problem of Glands and Secretions': Female Criminality, Murder, and Sexuality in Republican China," in *Sexuality in China: Histories of Power and Pleasure*, ed. Howard Chiang (Seattle: University of Washington Press, 2018), 99–124. Carroll points out: "The murder and subsequent press coverage of the sequence of trials both helped corroborate existing prejudices and establish an ascendant popular perception of same-sex love relations as deviant, tinged with jealousy and insanity, and potentially violent and fatal" (100).

21. Mei 梅, "Women weishenme yao jiehun" 我們為什麼要結婚 (Why we marry), *Jiankang shenghuo* 1, no. 3 (1934): 115–16.

22. Xu Wuling 徐嫵靈, "Jidu zhexue: Dongwu zhi jidu" 嫉妒哲學：動物之嫉妒 (The philosophy of jealousy: Animal's jealousy), *Funü shibao* 1, no. 1 (1911): 12.

23. Feng Fei 馮飛, *Nüxing lun* 女性論 (Discussions on women) (Shanghai: Zhonghua shuju, 1919), 120.

24. Da Jue 大覺, "Du de" 妬德 (The virtue of jealousy), *Minguo ribao*, April 21–22, 1919; [Wang] Jiting, "Ai yu du" 愛與妬 (Love and jealousy), *Funü zazhi* 5, no. 12 (1919): 3–4.

25. "Nü xuesheng zhi you: Shuo du" 女學生之友：說妬 (The girl student's friend: Jealousy), *Zhonghua yingwen zhoubao* 中華英文週報 (Chung Hwa English Weekly) 4, nos. 102 and 103 (1921): 788–89, 820–22, see 788.

26. Xu Qinfu 許廑父, "Du" 妬 (Jealousy), *Xiaoshuo ribao*, December 4, 1922.

27. *After Returning Home* does not seem like other Nora plays because its wife character does not leave home. But the common scholarly opinion is that the play's heroine, Wu Zifang, exemplifies the Nora spirit nonetheless. See, for example, Xu Huiqi 許慧琦, *"Nala" zai Zhongguo: Xin nüxing xingxiang de suzao jiqi yanbian, 1900s–1930s* "娜拉"在中國：新女性形象的塑造及其演變 (Nora in China: The construction of the image of the new woman and its evolution, 1900s–1930s) (Taipei: Zhengzhi daxue shixue lishi xuexi, 2003), 126, n.594.

28. Hu Shi, *Zhongshen dashi* 終身大事 (The greatest event in life), *Xin qingnian* 6, no. 3 (1919): 78. For the translation, see Hu Shi and [Qin 秦] Yinren 蔭人, *Zhongshen dashi (Marriage)*, *Sizhong zhoukan*, nos. 58 and 71 (1929): 41.

29. According to Xiang Peiliang (1905–1959), besides Ouyang's *After Returning Home* and *The Shrew*, some of the 1920s "Nora plays" also include *The Sadness of Youth* (*Qingchun di beiai* 青春底悲哀) and *The Life of a New Man* (*Xinren de shenghuo* 新人的生活) by Xiong Foxi (1900–1965); *The Abandoned Woman* (*Qifu* 棄婦) and *A Revived Rose* (*Fuhuo de meigui* 復活的玫瑰) by Hou Yao (1903–1942); and *The Good Son* (*Hao erzi* 好兒子) by Wang Zhongxian (1888–1937). See Xiang Peiliang 向培良, *Zhongguo xiju gaiping* 中國戲劇概評 (Brief comments on Chinese drama) (Shanghai: Taidong tushuju, 1928). In addition, writers such as Guo Moruo (1892–1978), Bai Wei (1894–1987), Chen Dabei (1887–1944), Xia Yan (1900–1995), Cao Yu (1910–1996), Yu Shangyuan (1897–1970), Ding Xilin (1893–1974), Zhang Wentian (1900–1976), Pu Shunqing (1902–unknown), Xu Baoyan (dates unknown), and Xu Gongmei (1881–1950) all contributed Nora plays. For information about these writers and their Nora plays, see Zhang Chuntian 張春田, *Sixiangshi shiye zhong de "Nala": Wusi qianhou de nüxing jiefang huayu* 思想史視野中的 "娜拉"：五四前後的女性解放話語 ("Nora" from the perspective of intellectual history: The women's liberation discourse before and after May Fourth) (Taipei: Xinrui wenchuang, 2013), 92–93; Xu, *"Nala" zai Zhongguo*, 125.

30. The most sensational examples of female runaways were Li Chao (1895–1919), Zhao Wuzhen (1896–1919), and Li Xinshu (dates unknown). The 1919 cases of Li Chao and Zhao Wuzhen were notorious for symbolizing women's victimization in China. Li was a female student in Beijing who rejected her arranged marriage and went off to pursue her education. Falling ill at college, she died at the age of twenty-four after her family cut off her financial support. Leading male intellectuals including Hu Shi and Cai Yuanpei (1868–1940) wrote about Li's tragedy to advocate the liberation of Chinese women. Not long afterwards, Zhao Wuzhen, a young woman from Changsha, slit her throat on her wedding day while being carried in a sedan chair to the groom's home.

Zhao's shocking protest against arranged marriage elicited numerous articles in the press, among which were at least nine articles written by the young Mao Zedong. In the following year, another Changsha girl, Li Xinshu, left home to rebel against parental attempts to marry her off. She disclosed that she had been influenced by Ibsen's Nora. She was acclaimed by the public as more realistic and far-reaching as a Nora model than the radical Zhao Wuzhen. For public discussions of the three women as real-life Noras, see Zhang, *Sixiangshi*, 78–92.

31. For more biographical details, see Ouyang Yuqian 歐陽予倩, *Zi wo yanxi yilai* 自我演戲以來 (Since I started acting) (Beijing: Zhongguo xiju chubanshe, 1959).

32. According to the Republican critic A Ying, aka Qian Xingcun (1900–1977), Spring Willow Society had staged *A Doll's House* as *Wan'ou zhi jia* 玩偶之家 in 1914 in Shanghai. According to Ouyang Yuqian's memoir, however, this was only a wish that was never realized because of internal pressures and external objections. See A Ying 阿英, "Yibusheng de zuopin zai Zhongguo" 易卜生的作品在中國 (Ibsen's works in China), in vol. 2 of *A Ying wenji* 阿英文集 (The works of A Ying) (Hong Kong: Sanlian shudian, 1979), 668; Ouyang, *Zi wo*, 67, 68, 182. A clarification on this matter also appears in Zhang, *Sixiangshi*, 16, n.11.

33. Hu Jiwen 胡基文, "Ji Ouyang Yuqian xiansheng liushi dashou qing" 記歐陽予倩先生六十大壽慶 (On the celebration of Mr. Ouyang Yuqian's sixtieth birthday), *Ying ju* 1, no. 1 (1948), cited from *Ouyang Yuqian yanjiu ziliao* 歐陽予倩研究資料 (Research materials on Ouyang Yuqian), ed. Su Guanxin 蘇關鑫 (Beijing: Zhishi chanquan chubanshe, 2009), 81. Current scholarship also analyzes *Pan Jinlian* as a Nora play. As Yomi Braester notes, "The play should be counted among the 'new woman plays' inspired by Hu Shi's translation of Ibsen's *Et dukkehjem* (*A Doll's House*)." See Braester, *Witness against History*, 60.

34. Yang Lianfen 楊聯芬, "Wusi lihun sichao yu Ouyang Yuqian Huijia yihou 'benshi' kaolun" 五四離婚思潮與歐陽予倩《回家以後》"本事" 考論 (The divorce trend of the May Fourth generation and the "background story" of Ouyang Yuqian's After Returning Home), *Xin wenxue shiliao*, no. 1 (2010): 79.

35. Ouyang Yuqian, *Pofu* 潑婦 (The shrew), *Juben huikan* 劇本彙刊 (Selected works of drama), no. 1 (1925): 16–17.

36. Ouyang, *Pofu*, 23, 24.

37. Ouyang, *Pofu*, 26.

38. Carolyn FitzGerald argues that female entrapment is more visible than female empowerment in Ouyang Yuqian's early dramas. Her categorization of Suxin as an "oppressed" and "unsuccessful" Nora no different from other "tragic" female heroines in Ouyang's works seems to ignore the optimism and sense of (textual) escape grounded in the details of Suxin's characterization. See Carolyn FitzGerald, "Mandarin Ducks at the Battlefield: Ouyang Yuqian's Shifting Reconfigurations of Nora and Mulan," *Chinoperl* (Journal of Chinese oral and performing literature) 29, no. 1 (2010): 47, 50–51, 53.

39. Xu Gongmei 徐公美, "Yanle Pofu yihou" 演了潑婦以後 (After acting in The Shrew), in *Xiju duanlun* 戲劇短論 (Essays on drama) (Shanghai: Daguang shuju, 1936), 38.

40. Xu, "Yanle," 40.

41. See Yang, "Wusi lihun sichao," 79; and her later article Yang Lianfen, "'Nala' bu zou zenyang" "娜拉"不走怎樣 (What if Nora did not leave), *Wenyi zhengming*, no. 7 (2015): 39–42.

42. Ouyang Yuqian, *Huijia yihou* 回家以後 (After returning home), *Juben huikan*, no. 2 (1928): 74.

43. Ouyang, *Huijia*, 80, 51, 53–54.

44. For the debate, see, for example, Xue 雪, "Xiju xieshe de sanchu dumuju" 戲劇協社的三出獨幕劇 (The three one-act dramas by the Drama Association), *Wenxue*, December 15, 1924; Zhang Xichen 章錫琛, "Wu Zifang yu Nala yu A'erwen furen" 吳自芳與娜拉與阿爾文夫人 (Wu Zifang and Nora and Mrs. Alving), *Funü zhoubao*, December 21, 1924; [Zhou 周] Jianren建人, "Zhongguo de nüxingxing" 中國的女性型 (Types of women in China), *Funü zhoubao*, December 21, 1924, and January 11, 1925; [Zhou] Jianren, "Wu Zifang jiujing shi jiazuzhuyi xia de nüxingxing bushi?" 吳自芳究竟是家族主義下的女性型不是? (Is Wu Zifang a female type under familism?), *Funü zhoubao*, January 4, 1925; Xue, "Zai tantan Huijia yihou" 再譚譚《回家以後》(Talk about After Returning Home again), *Funü zhoubao*, January 4, 1925; Zhang Xichen, "Wu Zifang de lihun wenti" 吳自芳的離婚問題 (The divorce problem of Wu Zifang), *Funü zhoubao*, January 5, 1925; Gu Junzheng 顧均正, "Wu Zifang shi zenyang de yige ren" 吳自芳是怎樣的一個人 (What kind of person is Wu Zifang?), *Funü zhoubao*, January 5, 1925; Zhang Xichen, "Tao yi gui gao de 'Huijia yihou'" 逃易歸高的 "回家以後" (Easy to leave, hard to return: On After Returning Home), *Funü zhoubao*, February 9, 1925; Zhang Qichen 張其琛 [*sic*], "Wu Zifang yu dongfang de jiu daode" 吳自芳與東方的舊道德 (Wu Zifang and the old morals of the Orient), *Jue wu*, February 17, 1925.

45. Zhang, "Tao yi gui gao."

46. Zhou, "Zhongguo de nüxingxing." Zhou referred to stories in *Liaozhai's Records of the Strange* where the foxes often instruct the main wives to hold in their jealousy to earn their husbands' favor.

47. Zhou, "Wu Zifang jiujing."

48. Zhang, "Wu Zifang yu Nala."

49. Xue, "Zai tantan."

50. Edward M. Gunn, "Ouyang Yuqian—*Huijia yihou*," in *A Selective Guide to Chinese Literature, 1900–1949*, vol. 4, *The Drama*, ed. Bernd Eberstein (Leiden: E. J. Brill, 1990), 193.

51. Zhou Li 周立, "'Ziyou lihun' xiamian de xingui" "自由離婚"下面的新鬼 (The new ghost under "free divorce"), *Jue wu*, August 17, 1922.

52. Honma Hisao 本間久雄, *Funü wenti shijiang* 婦女問題十講 (Ten lectures on the women's question), trans. Zhang Xichen (Shanghai: Kaiming shudian, 1924), 227–29. The section on *yin* (promiscuity) and *du* (jealousy) is from the tenth lesson, authored by Zhang.

53. Honma, *Funü*, 222–23, 241–42.

54. Zhou Jianren, "Lixiang de nüxing" 理想的女性 (The ideal woman), *Funü zazhi* 11, no. 2 (1925): 312–15, see 314.

55. For relevant scholarship, see Lee, *Revolution of the Heart*; Wang, *Women in the Chinese Enlightenment*; Yuxin Ma, "Male Feminism and Women's Subjectivities:

Zhang Xichen, Chen Xuezhao, and The New Woman," *Twentieth-Century China* 29, no. 1 (2003): 1–37; Joshua Hubbard, "Queering the New Woman: Ideals of Modern Femininity in *The Ladies' Journal*, 1915–1931," *Nan Nü: Men, Women and Gender in China* 16, no. 2 (2014): 341–62; Mirela David, "Bertrand Russell and Ellen Key in China: Individualism, Free Love, and Eugenics in the May Fourth Era," in Chiang, *Sexuality in China*, 76–98.

56. [Chen 陳] Bainian 百年, "Yifuduoqi de xin hufu" 一夫多妻的新護符 (The new amulet for polygamy), in *Xin xingdaode taolunji* 新性道德討論集 (Discussions on the new sexual morality), ed. Zhang Xichen (Shanghai: Kaiming shudian, 1926), 39.

57. Zhang Xichen, "Xin xingdaode yu duoqi: Da Chen Bainian xiansheng" 新性道德與多妻：答陳百年先生 (The new sexual morality and polygamy: Answering Mr. Chen Bainian), in Zhang, *Xin xingdaode taolunji*, 46.

58. Chen Bainian, "Da Zhang Zhou er xiansheng lun yifuduoqi" 答章周二先生論一夫多妻 (Answering Mr. Zhang and Mr. Zhou about polygamy), in Zhang, *Xin xingdaode taolunji*, 61, 65–66.

59. Zhang Xichen, "Yu Chen jiaoshou tan meng" 與陳教授談夢 (Discussing dreams with Professor Chen), in Zhang, *Xin xingdaode taolunji*, 127.

60. Tian You 天游, "Du" 妒 (Jealousy), *Dongfang zazhi* 22, no. 13 (1925): 61–62. Also see Zhang, *Xin xingdaode taolunji*, 202.

61. Tian, "Du," 203.

62. Zhang Xichen, "Du fei nüren meide lun" 妒非女人美德論 (Jealousy is not women's virtue), *Xin nüxing* 1, no. 2 (1926): 12–17. Also see Zhang, *Xin xingdaode taolunji*, 212–13.

63. Zhang, "Du fei," 213.

64. Xu Huiqi, "1920 niandai de lian'ai yu xin xingdaode lunshu—Cong Zhang Xichen canyu de sanci lunzhan tanqi" 1920年代的戀愛與新性道德論述—從章錫琛參與的三次論戰談起 (Discourses on romantic love and the new sexual morality of the 1920s: Exemplified by three debates in which Zhang Xichen took part), *Jindai Zhongguo funüshi yanjiu*, no. 16 (2008): 50.

65. Fan Xianggu was known as a budding young intellectual who espoused Marxism. He was a member of the Blood Tide Society (*Xuechao she* 血潮社) and an editor of the *Taidong Monthly*. Exalting revolutionary art, the journal was very close to the leftist publications in theme and style, not to mention the fact that many established left-wing writers including Feng Xuefeng (1903–1976), Feng Xianzhang (1908/1910–1931), Meng Chao (1902–1976), and Qian Xingcun were all regular contributors. Fan was expelled from the CCP in 1929 for his Trotskyite tendencies, and his journal was subsequently shut down.

66. Fan Xianggu 范香谷, "Jidu shi e'de ma?" 嫉妒是惡德嗎？ (Is jealousy a vice?), *Xin nüxing* 1, no. 6 (1926): 82.

67. Fan, "Jidu," 83.

68. "Ellis on Jealousy" was translated by Yan Shi from a small section in Havelock Ellis's essay "The Art of Love" in *Psychology of Sex* and was published in *Funü zhoubao* on February 22, 1925. "Carpenter on Jealousy" was translated by Cong Yu and published in the same newspaper on June 7, 1925. Zhang Xichen referred to both articles sweepingly as a whole, despite the fact that they

contain different and even contradictory messages on jealousy. In Edward Carpenter's definition, there are two types of jealousy: natural jealousy and man-made jealousy; only the latter is described negatively as a "great disturber," a "chronic disease" that is "fearful and convulsive." In "The Art of Love," Havelock Ellis attacked jealousy for being "either atavistic or pathological," existing only "among animals, among savages, among children, in the senile, in the degenerate, and very specially in chronic alcoholics." See Havelock Ellis, *Studies in the Psychology of Sex*, vol. 6 (Philadelphia: F. A. Davis Company, 1911), 564. Although Ellis seems critical of jealousy, Yan Shi and Zhang Xichen dismissed his acknowledgment of the inseparability of love and jealousy. Yan Shi also removed many sources included in the original piece and added conjunctions to smooth the textual flow of his much-altered translation, making Ellis's writing read more like a negative rant on jealousy. Excluding positive and neutral voices, reducing polyvocality and polyvalence, Yan bolstered his own argument by falsely fashioning Ellis as an authority in judging jealousy as incompatible with modernity. Another problem of both translations is their eschewal of Ellis's and Carpenter's discussions of jealousy in same-sex love relationships. For how Ellis's theory (through Pan Guangdan's translation) dominated the discourse on homosexuality in China after the 1920s, see Tze-lan D. Sang, *The Emerging Lesbian: Female Same-Sex Desire in Modern China* (Chicago: University of Chicago Press, 2003), chap. 2. Unlike Ellis, Carpenter recognized the jealousy in homosexual societies as instinctive and natural, which he thought contrasted with the dishonest, property-oriented jealousy existing in heterosexual relationships, especially Western bourgeois monogamous families. See Edward Carpenter, "The Place of the Uranian in Society," in *The Intermediate Sex* (New York: M. Kennerley, 1921), chap. 5; "Marriage: A Retrospect" and "Marriage: A Forecast," in *Love's Coming of Age* (Chicago: Charles H. Kerr Publishing Company, 1902), 73-111.

69. Wu Moxi 吳墨西, "Ai de fangyu wu" 愛的防禦物 (The guard of love), *Funü zazhi* 16, no. 6 (1930): 57.

70. Zhou Jiawei 周家慰, "Jingyan zhi tan" 經驗之談 (Observation based on personal experience), *Funü zazhi* 16, no. 6 (1930): 62.

71. Lü Bo 綠波, "Shei shi fuxin zhe" 誰是負心者 (Who is the unfaithful one), *Funü zazhi* 16, no. 6 (1930): 58–61.

3. Reconfiguring Female Promiscuity in Love and Independence: Pan Jinlian, Nora, and Jiang Qing

For an earlier version of this chapter, see Shu Yang, "I Am Nora, Hear Me Roar: The Rehabilitation of the Shrew in Modern Chinese Theater," *Nan Nü: Men, Women and Gender in China* 18, no. 2 (2016): 291–325.

1. Epstein, "Turning the Authorial Table," 163.

2. A recent example can be found in the circulation of Liu Zhenyun's (1958–) novel *I Am Not Pan Jinlian* (*Wo bushi Pan Jinlian* 我不是潘金蓮; 2012) and its adaptation into a blockbuster movie in 2016.

3. For analyses on some rewritings of Pan Jinlian in film and literature, see, for example, Naifei Ding, *Obscene Things: Sexual Politics in Jin Ping Mei* (Durham:

Duke University Press, 2002), chap. 8, "Very Close to Yinfu and Enü; or, How Prefaces Matter for *Jin Ping Mei* (1695) and *Enü Shu* (Taipei, 1995)," 225–43; Yomi Braester, "History as the Absurd," in *Witness against History*, 72–76; Yau Ching, "Porn Power: Sexual and Gender Politics in Li Han-hsiang's *Fengyue* Films," in *As Normal As Possible: Negotiating Sexuality and Gender in Mainland China and Hong Kong*, ed. Yau Ching (Hong Kong: Hong Kong University Press, 2010), 122–29.

4. Martin W. Huang, *Desire and Fictional Narrative in Late Imperial China* (Cambridge: Harvard University Press, 2001), 111.

5. David Der-wei/Dewei Wang, *The Monster That Is History: History, Violence, and Fictional Writing in Twentieth-Century China* (Berkeley: University of California Press, 2004), 55.

6. Although *Pan Jinlian* is very much in tune with the May Fourth slogans and ideas, the scholar Yuan Guoxing argues that the play was likely produced earlier, between 1913 and 1915, in the form of a civilized play (*wenming xi* 文明戲, a genre of modern Chinese spoken drama of the 1900s and 1910s with a focus on civilizing the Chinese through Western-inspired theater), instead of during the May Fourth period as is widely believed. See Yuan Guoxing 袁國興, "Tan huaju Pan Jinlian de dansheng" 談話劇《潘金蓮》的誕生 (On the birth of the drama Pan Jinlian), *Dongbei shida xuebao*, no. 6 (1989): 100–101.

7. Wang, *The Monster That Is History*, 54; Chang-Tai Hung, "Female Symbols of Resistance in Chinese Wartime Spoken Drama," *Modern China* 15, no. 2 (1989): 153. Also see Edward M. Gunn, introduction to *Twentieth-Century Chinese Drama: An Anthology*, ed. Edward M. Gunn (Bloomington: Indiana University Press, 1983), xiii.

8. Ouyang Yuqian recalled in 1959 that *Pan Jinlian* was written in 1926, based on his opera script, which had been lost. See Ouyang Yuqian, preface to *Ouyang Yuqian xuanji* 歐陽予倩選集 (Selected works of Ouyang Yuqian) (Beijing: Renmin wenxue chubanshe, 1959), 1.

9. For records about the staging, see Tian Han 田漢, "Nanguo she shilüe" 南國社史略 (A brief history of the Southern Society), in *Zhongguo huaju yundong wushinian shiliaoji (diyi ji)* 中國話劇運動五十年史料集（第一輯） (Historical materials on fifty years of the Chinese drama movement, vol. 1), ed. Tian Han (Beijing: Zhongguo xiju chubanshe, 1958), 121–22; Tang Shuming 唐叔明, "Huiyi Nanguo she" 回憶南國社 (Recall the Southern Society), in Tian, *Zhongguo huaju*, 139.

10. Ouyang Yuqian, *Pan Jinlian* 潘金蓮 (Pan Jinlian), *Xin yue* 1, no. 4 (1928): 53. For the translation, see Catherine Swatek, trans., "P'an Chin-lien," in Gunn, *Twentieth-Century Chinese Drama*, 52.

11. Huang, *Desire and Fictional Narrative*, 113.

12. Swatek, "P'an Chin-lien," 56.

13. Swatek, "P'an Chin-lien," 56.

14. Swatek, "P'an Chin-lien," 53.

15. Swatek, "P'an Chin-lien," 54.

16. Swatek, "P'an Chin-lien," 59.

17. See, for example, Liang Qichao 梁啟超, "Lun qiangquan" 論強權 (On power), in *Yinbing shi ziyou shu* 飲冰室自由書 (The ice-drinker's studio: The

book on liberty) (Yangzhou: Jiangsu guangling guji keyinshe, 1990); "Xinmin shuo: Lun guojia sixiang" 新民說： 論國家思想 (On the new citizen: The idea of the nation), in vol. 2 of *Liang Qichao quanji* 梁啟超全集 (Complete works of Liang Qichao) (Beijing: Beijing chubanshe, 1999). It is also believed that Liang was the first Chinese scholar to introduce the German philosopher Friedrich Nietzsche (1844–1900) and his concept of the "Superman" to modern China. See Liang, "Jinhualun gemingzhe Jie De zhi xueshuo" 進化論革命者頡德之學說 (The theory of Benjamin Kidd, revolutionizer of evolution), in vol. 2 of *Liang Qichao quanji*, where he mentioned Nietzsche for the first time.

18. Ouyang, *Pan Jinlian*, 61. For the translation, see Swatek, "P'an Chin-lien," 57.

19. Swatek, "P'an Chin-lien," 72.

20. For analyses of the association of beauties with beasts in Ming-Qing literature, see, for example, Maram Epstein, "The Beauty Is the Beast: The Dual Face of Woman in Four Ch'ing Novels" (PhD diss., Princeton University, 1992), and *Competing Discourses*; chap. 5, "Seduction: Tiger and Yinfu," in Ding, *Obscene Things*, 143–64; Victoria Cass, "Predators," chap. 5 in *Dangerous Women: Warriors, Grannies, and Geishas of the Ming* (Lanham, MD: Rowman & Littlefield, 1999), 87–104.

21. For descriptions of the virtuous Wu Da, see Shi Nai'an 施耐庵 and Luo Guanzhong 羅貫中, *Shuihu quanzhuan* 水滸全傳 (The complete edition of Water Margin) (repr., Changsha: Yuelu shushe, 1988), chap. 24, 183–84; Lanling xiaoxiao sheng 蘭陵笑笑生, *Zhang Zhupo piping Jin Ping Mei* 張竹坡批評金瓶梅 (Zhang Zhupo annotating Plum in the Golden Vase) (repr., Ji'nan: Qilu shushe, 1991), chaps. 1 and 2, 31–33.

22. Ding, *Obscene Things*, 132.

23. Swatek, "P'an Chin-lien," 73.

24. Swatek, "P'an Chin-lien," 73.

25. Da Yin 大引, "Pan Jinlian zou le hongyun" 潘金蓮走了紅運 (Pan Jinlian got lucky), *Xi hai*, no. 1 (1937): 25.

26. Swatek, "P'an Chin-lien," 65, 73.

27. Ouyang Yuqian, "Pan Jinlian zixu" 《潘金蓮》自序 (Preface to Pan Jinlian), in Su, *Ouyang Yuqian yanjiu ziliao*, 119.

28. Shi and Luo, *Shuihu quanzhuan*, chap. 24, 189. For the translation, see *Outlaws of the Marsh*, trans. Sidney Shapiro, vol. 1 (Beijing: Foreign Languages Press, 1980), 373. In Lanling xiaoxiao sheng's *Zhang Zhupo piping Jin Ping Mei*, this passage appears the same. The commentator Zhang Zhupo (1670–1698) used words including "crying" (*ku* 哭) and "pain" (*tong* 痛) several times to highlight how much he empathized with the virtuous Wu Song when reading the dialogue between the brothers. See Lanling, *Zhang Zhupo piping*, 49–50.

29. Ouyang, *Pan Jinlian*, 75. For the translation, see Swatek, "P'an Chin-lien," 65.

30. Epstein, "Turning the Authorial Table," 157–58.

31. Ouyang, *Pan Jinlian*, 75. This line is left out in Swatek's translation.

32. Swatek, "P'an Chin-lien," 65.

33. Swatek, "P'an Chin-lien," 65.

34. Ding, *Obscene Things*, 148.

35. As Victoria Cass points out, Pan Jinlian's name—her surname Pan is a Chinese pun on the verb *pan* 判, which means "to judge"—serves to invoke the demonic judge (the adept Pan) from hell and "the sense of judging." See Cass, *Dangerous Women*, 102.

36. Ouyang, "Pan Jinlian zixu," 119.

37. Joshua Goldstein, *Drama Kings: Players and Publics in the Re-creation of Peking Opera, 1870–1937* (Berkeley: University of California Press, 2007), 180.

38. The Ming drama *The Noble Knight-Errant* (*Yixia ji* 義俠記; 1599) by Shen Jing (1553–1610) was probably the earliest extant text that grants Pan Jinlian the opportunity to tell her version of her life story. But in *Yixia ji*, Pan pushes the responsibility for Wu Da's murder onto Wang Po, another female victim, instead of protesting patriarchal society. For an account of *Yixia ji*'s adaptation of the *Shuihu* story, see Jing Shen, "Re-Visions of '*Shuihu*' Women in Chinese Theatre and Cinema," *China Review* 7, no. 1 (2007): 109–11.

39. Ouyang, *Pan Jinlian*, 89. For the translation, see Swatek, "P'an Chin-lien," 73.

40. Lanling, *Zhang Zhupo piping*, chap. 87, 1392. For the translation, see David Roy, trans., *The Plum in the Golden Vase or, Chin P'ing Mei*, vol. 5 (Princeton: Princeton University Press, 2013), 128.

41. For example, Jing Shen argues that "sexuality, usually associated with the seductress Pan Jinlian, is not a main issue in the play." See Shen, "Re-Visions," 119.

42. In *Pan Jinlian*, unprecedentedly, Jinlian is exposed to Ximen's head before her death. For more discussion of the plot adjustment, see the section "Head or Heart?" in Braester, *Witness against History*, 60–63.

43. For an analysis of how the male gaze empowers instead of objectifies Salome, see Linda Hutcheon and Michael Hutcheon, "'Here's Lookin' at You, Kid': The Empowering Gaze in 'Salome,'" *Profession* (1998): 11–22.

44. Ouyang, *Pan Jinlian*, 90. For the translation, see Swatek, "P'an Chin-lien," 74.

45. For example, Tian Han (1898–1968), one of the three founders of spoken drama in modern China (the other two being Hong Shen and Ouyang Yuqian), commented that this declaration makes Pan Jinlian a masochist (*bei nüedai kuang* 被虐待狂). See Tian Han, "Ta wei Zhongguo xiju yundong fendou le yisheng" 他為中國戲劇運動奮鬥了一生 (He struggled for the Chinese drama movement throughout his life), in Su, *Ouyang Yuqian yanjiu ziliao*, 105.

46. Ding, *Obscene Things*, xxiii.

47. Ding, *Obscene Things*, xx, xxxi, 196.

48. Swatek, "P'an Chin-lien," 74.

49. Wu Song's unfinished, ambiguous line "You love me? I . . . I. . ." was improvised during the premiere of the play into a complete and moralistic sentence: "You love me. I love my brother" (*ni ai wo, wo ai wode gege* 你愛我，我愛我的哥哥). Actor Zhou Xinfang adjusted Ouyang's Wu Song during his performance of the role because he insisted that Wu should always be a real hero.

In the 1960s Ouyang recalled Zhou's improvisation: "At the time we performed plays in a way different from today. We did not care much about themes. Lines were even added and revised during a performance. Wu Song was so impassioned that when it approached the end, he killed Pan Jinlian while saying 'You love me. I love my brother' under the witness of the neighbors. I remember very clearly that he was singing this line while thrusting the knife into Pan Jinlian's chest." See Liang Bingkun 梁秉堃, *Shijia hutong 56 hao: Wo qinli de renyi wangshi* 史家胡同 56 號：我親歷的人藝往事 (No. 56 on the shijia hutong: Past events of the Beijing People's Art Theater that I experienced) (Beijing: Jincheng chubanshe, 2010), 6. Zhou Xinfang's performance ensured the continuity of Wu Song's image as a rational, ruthless, and righteous hero, a characterization that Ouyang's script challenged.

50. Braester, *Witness against History*, 63.

51. David Der-wei Wang reads the ending as a forensic scene with renewed theatrics of law, justice, and violence. See Wang, *The Monster That Is History*, 55–56.

52. Ouyang, *Zi wo*, 291. Also see Hung, "Female Symbols," 154.

53. Piao Peng 飄蓬, "Cong Ouyang Yuqian shuodao Pan Jinlian" 從歐陽予倩說到《潘金蓮》(From Ouyang Yuqian to the drama Pan Jinlian), *Xinmin bao*, April 15, 1936.

54. Mei Ping 梅平, "Liangge Pan Jinlian jianmian" 兩個潘金蓮見面 (Two Pan Jinlians met), *Chun se* 2, no. 11 (1936): 22.

55. Man Yan 曼衍, "Yunnihui shang zhi Pan Jinlian: Ouyang Yuqian zuijin jiezuo" 雲霓會上之潘金蓮：歐陽予倩最近傑作 (On Pan Jinlian: The recent masterpiece of Ouyang Yuqian), *Xinwen bao*, January 5, 1928.

56. Da, "Pan Jinlian zou." For more current discussions on Ouyang's performance of Pan Jinlian, see Hu Ou 湖鷗, "Daoting tushuo: Ouyang Yuqian yu Pan Jinlian" 道聽途說：歐陽予倩與潘金蓮 (Hearsay: Ouyang Yuqian and Pan Jinlian), *Laoshi hua*, no. 38 (1934): 7; Fen Gong 芬公, "Ouyang Yuqian zhi Pan Jinlian" 歐陽予倩之潘金蓮 (Ouyang Yuqian's Pan Jinlian), *Jin'gang zuan*, November 9, 1928; "Ouyang Yuqian fanchuan yuanzi Pan Jinlian" 歐陽予倩反串原子潘金蓮 (Ouyang Yuqian played Pan Jinlian as a performance of gender role reversal), *Shanghai texie*, no. 17 (1946): 10; Yi Fang 一方, "Qiqing zhai suibi" 祈晴齋隨筆 (Qiqing studio essays), *Xianghai huabao*, no. 11 (1938): 1; Yin Fu 吟父, "Guan Ouyang Yuqian yan Pan Jinlian ganyan" 觀歐陽予倩演潘金蓮感言 (Thoughts after watching Ouyang Yuqian's performance of Pan Jinlian), *Xinwen bao*, January 14, 1928; Wu San 武三, "Pan Jinlian" 潘金蓮 (Pan Jinlian), *Xi bao*, no. 22 (1937): 2.

57. Xu Xiaotian 許嘯天, "Xu Xiaotian shuo" 許嘯天說 (Words from Xu Xiaotian), *Xinwen bao*, November 7, 1932; "Pan Jinlian shibushi yinfu?" 潘金蓮是不是淫婦 (Is Pan Jinlian a whore?), *Xinwen bao*, May 12, 1936.

58. Zhao Dan 趙丹, *Diyu zhi men* 地獄之門 (The gate of hell) (Shanghai: Wenhui chubanshe, 2005), 84.

59. Zhao, *Diyu*, 83.

60. Roxane Witke, *Comrade Chiang Ch'ing* (Boston: Little, Brown & Co., 1977), 102.

61. For leftist intellectuals such as Nie Gannu (1903–1986) and Mao Dun, the individualistic Nora serves as a foil to the nationalist heroine. Their re-definition of the new woman contains a direct attack on Nora as a cultural figure. Nie claimed: "Women in the new time will be totally unlike Nora. First, she is not necessarily a young lady from the gentry, bourgeois class; she feels the pains extending beyond her personal life; she does not resist in a passive way, much less go to the front on her own. As a member of the collectivity, she will fight bravely for all women and men under the intense pressure of life. She will become the woman hero of our time." See Nie Gannu 聶紺弩, "Tan Nala" 談《娜拉》(On Nora), written on January 27, 1935, in *She yu ta* 蛇與塔 (Snake and temple) (Beijing: Shenghuo dushu xinzhi sanlian shudian, 1999), 140.

62. Zang Jian, "'Women Returning Home'—A Topic of Chinese Women's Liberation," in Leutner, *Women in China*. See chapter 4 for further discussion of the issue of "women returning to the home."

63. In addition to the best-known *Yeyu juren xiehui*, other drama troupes also staged *A Doll's House* in 1935, including *Mofeng yishe* (Windmill Art Society) in Nanjing, *Minjiao guan* (People's Education House) in Ji'nan, and *Zhirenyong jushe* (Wisdom-Benevolence-Bravery Drama Society) and *Guanghua jushe* (Bright China Drama Society) in Shanghai. See Zhang, *Sixiangshi*, 157. Xu Maoyong (1911–1977) commented that the *Yeyu juren* version was the best among all the Nora performances he had seen. See Xu Maoyong 徐懋庸, "Kan le Nala zhi-hou" 看了娜拉之後 (After watching Nora), *Shishi xinbao*, June 30, 1935. Also see "Nala da zou hongyun" 娜拉大走鴻運 (Nora gets so lucky), *Shen bao*, June 21, 1935.

64. Xu, "*Nala" zai Zhongguo*, 3, 292. Gail Hershatter claims a bit differently: "*A Doll's House* was translated into Chinese in 1918, published and discussed in *New Youth* magazine, and widely performed in Chinese cities." See Hershatter, *Women and China's Revolutions*, 97.

65. Ross Terrill, *Madame Mao: The White-Boned Demon* (Stanford: Stanford University Press, 1999), 57.

66. Some rave reviews include Hai Shi 海士, "Kanguo Nala yihou" 看過《娜拉》以後 (After watching Nora), *Min bao*, June 28, 1935; Qi Lin 麒麟, "Ping Na'na zhi yanchu" 評娜那之演出 (Commenting on the performance of Nora), *Min bao*, June 29–30, 1935; "'Nala' di yanyuan" "娜拉"底演員 (The actors in Nora), *Shen bao*, June 21, 1935; You Na 尤娜, "Ping Nala de yanji" 評《娜拉》的演技 (On the acting of Nora), *Shen bao*, July 22, 1935; Bai Yan 白彥, "Dianxing de beiguo nüxing: Lan Ping" 典型的北國女性：藍蘋 (A typi-cal northern woman: Lan Ping), *Da wanbao*, January 7, 1937; Li Yi 李一, "Nala yeyu juren zai jincheng juyuan yanchu" 《娜拉》業餘劇人在金城劇院演出 (The Amateur Drama Association performed Nora at the Golden City The-ater), *Shishi xinbao*, June 28, 1935; Xu, "Kan."

67. Su Ge 蘇戈, "Cong Nala shuodao Yibusheng de chuangzuo fangfa" 從《娜拉》說到易卜生的創作方法 (From Nora to the writing methods of Ib-sen), *Min bao*, June 29, 1935; Li, "Nala yeyu."

68. You, "Ping Nala."

69. Ye Yonglie 葉永烈, *Jiang Qing zhuan* 江青傳 (Biography of Jiang Qing) (Beijing: Zuojia chubanshe, 1993), 71.

70. About his first impression of Lan Ping, Tang Na recalled: "Even in Shanghai, she was exceptional. Don't think of her as a timid Chinese girl. Perhaps you are used to Chinese girls being retiring. Well, Lan Ping was not like that. She was one who did not hesitate to go up and talk to a man, to take the initiative, to put herself in a man's path. Oh, she was a bold girl!" See Terrill, *Madame Mao*, 66.

71. It is alleged that the misunderstanding arose from press coverage about a joint wedding held at the Liuhe Pagoda in Suzhou for six Shanghai actresses and actors including Tang and Lan. Lan Ping was said to have attended only because of Tang's pressure. See Zhao, *Diyu*, 82; Ye, *Jiang Qing zhuan*, 88.

72. Ye, *Jiang Qing zhuan*, 96–99; Natascha Vittinghoff, "Jiang Qing and Nora: Drama and Politics in the Republican Period," in Leutner, *Women in China*, 225. Ross Terrill, however, believes that Tang Na did not get the letter from Zheng Junli until he and Lan Ping came back together from Ji'nan. See Terrill, *Madame Mao*, 83.

73. Vittinghoff, "Jiang Qing and Nora," 225. Vittinghoff's account of this matter is based on Ye's *Jiang Qing zhuan*, 91. In *Madame Mao*, Terrill states differently that what Tang Na took was "an overdose of sleeping pills" (82).

74. Vittinghoff, "Jiang Qing and Nora," 225.

75. "Lan Ping xiang chufengtou, yongde shi meiren ji" 藍蘋想出風頭，用的是美人計 (Lan Ping used the tactics of beauties for attracting attention), *Shidai bao*, June 15, 1937. See Ye, *Jiang Qing zhuan*, 131–33.

76. "Shiyi qingchang qiusi de yingxing Tang Na yujiu hou liuji hou jiayin" 失意情場求死的影星唐納遇救後留濟候佳音 (Failed at love, the movie star Tang Na was saved from suicide and waited in Ji'nan for good news), *Shi bao*, June 30, 1936.

77. Tu Yu 屠雨, "Tang Na, Lan Ping heli ji" 唐納、藍蘋合離記 (Separation and reunion between Tang Na and Lan Ping), *Xin bao*, July 1, 1936.

78. Xi Zi 系子, "Yingxing wowen lu: Lan Ping" 影星我聞錄：藍蘋 (Movie stars I know: Lan Ping), *Qingchun dianying* 3, no. 7 (1937): unpaginated.

79. Tu, "Tang Na, Lan Ping."

80. Lan Ping 藍蘋, "Jiang Qing xiegei Tang Na de jueqingshu" 江青寫給唐納的絕情書, written on June 23, 1936, first published in *Dao bao*, June 30–July 1, 1936, republished in *Mingbao yuekan*, no. 166 (1979): 42–43; in English, "Chiang Ch'ing's 'Farewell Letter' to T'ang Na," trans. William A. Wycoff, *Chinese Studies in History* 14, no. 2 (1980–81): 77. Lan also mentioned the discomfort of city life in another article titled "Cong Nala dao Da Leiyu" 從《娜拉》到《大雷雨》 (From Nora to The Big Storm), *Xin xueshi* 1, no. 5 (1937): 250-52.

81. Lan, "Chiang Ch'ing's 'Farewell Letter,'" 77–79.

82. As Natascha Vittinghoff points out: "The content of the play was reason for discriminating against women who played this role. Thus, the representation of a figure such as Nora on stage was directly linked to the social position of the actress in society." See Vittinghoff, "Jiang Qing and Nora," 230–31. Besides

the case of Lan Ping, there was also the widely discussed "Nora incident" (*Nala shijian* 娜拉事件), which took place in Nanjing in 1935. The incident concerned a schoolteacher, Wang Ping (1916–1990) (originally named Wang Guangzhen; the name Wang Ping reflects the influence of Lan Ping among the new women), who was dismissed from her position because she had performed as Nora in an amateur group. For further information, see Elisabeth Eide, *China's Ibsen: From Ibsen to Ibsenism* (London: Curzon Press, 1987), 95–96. All female students who played parts in the play were punished or expelled from school. See "Heri cai you guangming zhi lu, Nala wei yanju er shiye" 何日才有光明之路 娜拉為演劇而失業 (When will there be a bright path? Nora lost her job for her acting), *Xinmin bao*, February 2, 1935; Zhang Zhizhong 張致中, "Yishu de xishengzhe 'Nala' Wang Guangzhen jiezhi qianhou" 藝術的犧牲者"娜拉"王光珍解職前後 (Before and after "Nora" Wang Guangzhen got fired as a victim of the arts), *Da wanbao*, February 16, 1935; "Jingshi nüsheng yanju fengchao" 京市女生演劇風潮 (The incident of female students performing in Nanjing), *Da wanbao*, February 18, 1935.

83. "Lan Ping xiang," 132.

84. Terrill, *Madame Mao*, 78.

85. Ye, *Jiang Qing zhuan*, 92.

86. Lan Ping, "Yifeng gongkai xin" 一封公開信, written on May 31, 1937, first published in *Lianhua huabao* 9, no. 4 (1937): 94–96, republished as "Wo weishenme he Tang Na fenshou" 我為什麼和唐納分手, *Mingbao yuekan*, no. 166 (1979): 44–46; in English, "Why I Have Parted from T'ang Na," trans. William A. Wycoff, *Chinese Studies in History* 14, no. 2 (1980–81): 85.

87. Lan, "Why I Have," 86.

88. Lan, "Why I Have," 87, 90, 91.

89. Ye, *Jiang Qing zhuan*, 122.

90. Vittinghoff notes that even though the press lamented the suicide of another famous actress, Ruan Lingyu (1910–1935), in March 1935 as "tragic" and "unjust," they still anticipated Lan Ping's suicide because of the public criticism she faced. See Vittinghoff, "Jiang Qing and Nora," 228.

91. Lan, "Why I Have," 90.

92. Henrik Ibsen, *A Doll's House*, trans. Kenneth McLeish (London: Nick Hern Books, 1994), 96.

93. Lan, "Chiang Ch'ing's 'Farewell Letter,'" 82.

94. The identity of the shrew, even after the fall of the "Gang of Four," continued to haunt and frame representations of Jiang Qing in the socialist years. Her determination to assert an unconventionally strong womanhood continued to meet with social disapproval likening her to the shrew of traditional literature. For example, Roy Chan has discussed Jiang Qing's engagement with *Honglou meng* and her treatment as a modern-day Wang Xifeng in the post-Cultural Revolution tirades against her. See Roy Bing Chan, "Dream Fugue: Jiang Qing, the End of the Cultural Revolution, and Zong Pu's Fiction," chap. 5 in *The Edge of Knowing: Dreams, History, and Realism in Modern Chinese Literature* (Seattle: University of Washington Press, 2017), 147–75.

4. Popular Views on the Shrewish Wife: Henpecking Humor, Female Rule, and Family-State Metaphor

1. E. Perry Link, *Mandarin Ducks and Butterflies: Popular Fiction in Early Twentieth-Century Chinese Cities* (Berkeley: University of California Press, 1981), 55, 63, 208, 234.

2. *Secret Account of Henpecking* and *The East-of-the-River Lioness* declare in their prefaces that the goal of the stories is not to repress women's power (*fei eyi nüquan* 非遏抑女權), indicating that the author was aware of women's changing status in society.

3. Henpecking was also a hot topic in comedy movies at the time. *Poor Daddy* or *My Son Was a Hero* (*Pa laopo* 怕老婆; 1929) is an example (though not based on *Pa laopo riji*, discussed here).

4. The titles in this collection suggest that unconventional male and female models were popular objects of laughter. For the origin of the term *huaji xiaoshuo*, see Christopher Rea, *The Age of Irreverence: A New History of Laughter in China* (Oakland: University of California Press, 2015), 109–10. Note that the comic collections and the henpecking comedies analyzed in this chapter are not mentioned in Rea's book or listed under the "Selected Chinese Humor Collections, 1900–1937" in its appendix.

5. Popular writings on the joyful yet jeopardizing lifestyle in modern Shanghai with women-initiated hoaxes and parodies reached a climax in Xu Zhuodai's stories. For the section on tricksters, including female figures, see Rea, *The Age of Irreverence*, 118–24. Rea also points out that the tricksters "are rarely punished with comic justice" (130).

6. In addition to pictorials such as *Comic Pictorial* and *Funny World*, which presented continuous offerings under the topic of "wife-fearing" (*pa laopo*) or "tigress" (*ci laohu* 雌老虎) from the mid-1930s to the 1940s, magazines including *Universe Digest* also published cartoons on henpecking.

7. E. Perry Link, "Traditional-Style Popular Urban Fiction in the Teens and Twenties," in *Modern Chinese Literature in the May Fourth Era*, ed. Merle Goldman (Cambridge: Harvard University Press, 1977); Link, *Mandarin Ducks and Butterflies*, particularly chap. 6, "Fiction for Comfort."

8. Rea, *The Age of Irreverence*, 107, 130.

9. Yan Sanlang 燕三郎, *Yanzhi hu* 胭脂虎 (Tiger with rouge) (n.p., 1916), 72.

10. Yan, *Yanzhi*, 1.

11. Huaji Sanlang 滑稽三郎, *Pa laopo riji* 怕老婆日記 (The diary of a henpecked husband) (Hong Kong: Siti yinyeshe, 1920), 2.

12. Echoing the plot of cousin love or cousin marriage typified by the late imperial novel *Dream of the Red Chamber*, modern Chinese literature saw a great number of works depicting overt or latent love relationships between male protagonists and their younger female cousins (*biaomei* 表妹). The *biaomei* figure appears frequently in works of modern popular fiction and the May Fourth canon including Ba Jin's (1904–2005) *Family* (*Jia* 家; 1933).

13. Link, *Mandarin Ducks and Butterflies*, 208.

14. For an analysis of the use of the female models in *Jade Pear Spirit*, see Link, *Mandarin Ducks and Butterflies*, 41–54, 199–208.

15. Peng Xiaofeng 彭曉豐, "Mao Dun xiaoshuo zhong shidai nüxing xingxiang de yanhua jiqi gongneng fenxi" 茅盾小說中時代女性形象的衍化及其功能分析 (An analysis of the evolution and function of images of the new woman in Mao Dun's works), *Zhongguo xiandai wenxue yanjiu congkan*, no. 3 (1992): 213–20.

16. For an illustration in the Republican popular press in 1923 of a similar two-faced woman who lures men to their doom, see Rea, *The Age of Irreverence*, 121.

17. While the new women in Republican Shanghai were often criticized for their ostentatious dress, the standard clothing for modern female students was quite plain. Girl students were supposed to wear the so-called "civilized new clothes" (*wenming xinzhuang* 文明新裝), which included a plain shirt, non-patterned long black skirt, and little to no jewelry. See Zheng Yongfu 鄭永福 and Lü Meiyi 呂美頤, *Jindai Zhongguo funü shenghuo* 近代中國婦女生活 (Women's lives in modern China) (Zhengzhou: Henan renmin chubanshe, 1993), 100.

18. Huaji, *Pa*, 13. Similar points of view on the benefits of having a shrewish wife are also mentioned in chapter 2 on jealousy.

19. *Plum in the Golden Vase* and *Marriage Bonds to Awaken the World* include plenty of animal imagery. Cats and dogs are naturally and allegorically associated with the shrew. For readings of images of cats and dogs, see Epstein, *Competing Discourses*, 129, 136–37, 140, 147–48; Ding, *Obscene Things*, chap. 7, "A Cat, a Dog, and the Killing of Livestock," 195–223.

20. Huaji, *Pa*, 10, 13, 20.

21. Ding, *Obscene Things*, 200, 222.

22. Even the way Ximen Qing kills the cat is quite like Xingshi's. For an analysis of that episode in *Plum in the Golden Vase*, see Ding, *Obscene Things*, 211.

23. Huaji, *Pa*, 51.

24. Wu, *The Chinese Virago*, 161.

25. New-style divorce in China started in the late Qing, when Westernized figures such as Qiu Jin experimented with Western-style conduct. Because of its procedural simplicity and professed fairness across gender, it quickly became a "category of scandal," condemned for the liberty it granted people to divorce "on a whim, shuffle some papers with a new-style lawyer, and falsely pretend to believe that nothing serious had happened." See Link, *Mandarin Ducks and Butterflies*, 222. During the May Fourth era, the New Cultural intellectuals denounced old-style divorce in traditional China as sanctioning men's superiority over women. They advocated new-style divorce to promote women's equal rights in marriage. See Mao Dun [Shen Yanbing 沈雁冰], "Lihun yu daode wenti" 離婚與道德問題 (Divorce and the issue of morality), *Funü zazhi* 8, no. 4 (1922): 13–16.

26. Link, *Mandarin Ducks and Butterflies*, 223.

27. Huaji, *Pa*, 76.

28. Cheng Zhanlu 程瞻廬, "Danqiu huazuo nü'er shen" 但求化作女兒身 (I wish to transform myself into a woman), in *Zhanlu xiaoshuoji* 瞻廬小說集 (Collection of Cheng Zhanlu) (Shanghai: Shijie shuju, 1924), 55.

29. Jiang Hongjiao 江紅蕉, "Miyue lüxing xiaoshi" 蜜月旅行笑史 (The laughable history of honeymoon travel), in *Hongjiao xiaoshuoji* 紅蕉小說集 (Collection of Jiang Hongjiao) (Shanghai: Shijie shuju, 1924), 91.

30. Link, *Mandarin Ducks and Butterflies*, 189–95.

31. The 1920s saw the publication of various how-to books, from guides to brothels, to manuals on household management, to books about dating and marriage tips. For example, *Sachet* (*Xiang nang* 香囊; 1920), edited by the male Butterfly writer Qiandu Liulang, groups women into over 140 categories and lists under each category the ways in which men should cope with them. It gives concrete advice on how to tame the shrew types. A new edition of *Sachet* appeared in 1921 under the editorship of an educated woman named Xu Guifang (dates unknown). This edition leaves out more than half of the 140-plus categories and adds a new section on how to deal with different types of husbands, with a total of 53 categories. It contains an appeal to women to rein in their husbands through violence and sex. The shrewish wife is the object of transformation in the first part of the new edition on dealing with women while being the desirable model in the second part on disciplining husbands. This juxtaposition points to public interest and struggle in integrating the shrew into the new woman debate. See Qiandu Liulang 前度劉郎 and Xu Guifang 徐桂芳, eds., *Xiang nang* 香囊 (Sachet) (Hong Kong: Huaxin shuju, 1920–21).

32. Yu Xuelun 喻血輪 and Wang Zuidie 王醉蝶, *Junei qushi* 懼內趣史 (The funny history of henpecking) (Shanghai: Dadong shuju, 1925), 95–96.

33. For analyses of carnivalistic Shanghai, see Rea, *The Age of Irreverence*, 130; Yue Meng, *Shanghai and the Edges of Empires* (Minneapolis: University of Minnesota Press, 2005), "Part II. The Carnival and the Radical."

34. Catherine Vance Yeh, "Shanghai Leisure, Print Entertainment, and the Tabloids, *xiaobao* 小報," in *Joining the Global Public: Word, Image, and City in Early Chinese Newspapers, 1870–1910*, ed. Rudolf G. Wagner (Albany: State University of New York Press, 2007), 204.

35. Sarah Appleton Aguiar, *The Bitch Is Back: Wicked Women in Literature* (Carbondale: Southern Illinois University Press, 2001), 50–56. On the image of the American bitch, also see Delores Barracano Schmidt, "The Great American Bitch," *College English* 32, no. 8 (1971): 900–5.

36. Aguiar, *The Bitch Is Back*, 50.

37. For some recent mentions of this phrase, see Jana Rosker, *Following His Own Path: Li Zehou and Contemporary Chinese Philosophy* (Albany: State University of New York Press, 2019), 169; Zhaoguang Ge, *What Is China? Territory, Ethnicity, Culture, and History* (Cambridge: Harvard University Press, 2018), 86–87; Tianyu Cao et al., eds., *Culture and Social Transformations: Theoretical Framework and Chinese Context* (Leiden: Brill, 2014), 78.

38. The conservatives, exemplified by the so-called Warring State Strategies school (*Zhanguoce pai* 戰國策派, a group of writers advocating *Strategies of the Warring States* during World War II), demanded that women return to the home instead of continuing their pursuit of public life, reasoning that giving birth to children is the first and foremost task for women. Pan Guangdan,

the well-known sociologist and eugenicist, denounced the women's movement from as early as the 1920s and advocated motherhood. During the Second Sino-Japanese War, Pan further emphasized the urgency of applying science to child rearing for Chinese new women/mothers. See Lü Wenhao 呂文浩, "'Funü huijia'—Pan Guangdan yizai tiaoqi lunzheng de guandian" "婦女回家"—潘光旦一再挑起論爭的觀點 ("Women returning to the home": An idea Pan Guangdan repeatedly brought up for debate), *Wenshi xuekan* 1 (2014): 177–91; Pan Guangdan, *Yousheng yu kangzhan* 優生與抗戰 (Eugenics and the war of resistance), vol. 5 of *Pan Guangdan wenji* 潘光旦文集 (Collected works of Pan Guangdan) (Beijing: Beijing daxue chubanshe, 2000).

39. For example, Chen Yi (1883–1950), the chairman of the Fujian provincial government, wrote several articles stressing women's roles within the family as mothers and housewives. Starting from 1938, the Fujian government continuously laid off female workers and limited enrollment of women in companies and schools, provoking intense responses in society. For details about the incidents in Fujian and competing discourses on women's public and private roles during the time of the anti-Japanese war, see Lü Fangshang 呂芳上, "Kangzhan shiqi de nüquan lunbian" 抗戰時期的女權論辯 (Women's rights controversies in the Sino-Japanese conflict period), *Jindai zhongguo funüshi yanjiu* 2 (1994): 81–115.

40. "China's Womankind at the Crossroad," *The China Critic* 5, no. 50 (1932): 1322.

41. For women's rising visibility, vitality, and villainy in the popular imagination and real-life situations during the mid- to late Republican period, see Rea, *The Age of Irreverence*; Jin Jiang, *Women Playing Men: Yue Opera and Social Change in Twentieth-Century Shanghai* (Seattle: University of Washington Press, 2009). For how Chinese women seized opportunities in the anti-Japanese war in the 1930s and 1940s for their own benefit, see Diana Lary, *The Chinese People at War: Human Suffering and Social Transformation, 1937–1945* (Cambridge: Cambridge University Press, 2010). Lary discusses how "the war lifted some of the age-old pressures against women being involved outside the home," providing women with "the possibility and the necessity of emancipation from the domestic prisons" (97).

42. For the rise and fall of humor culture in the 1930s, see Rea, *The Age of Irreverence*, 12 and chap. 6.

43. Lin Yutang 林語堂, "Rang niang'er men gan yixia ba" 讓娘兒們幹一下吧 (Let women do it), *Shen bao*, August 18, 1933.

44. After the publication of Lin Yutang's article, Lu Xun immediately issued a flat denial of the possibility of female rule in his response. "Women only know how to breed [*yangsheng* 養生], not bleed [*songsi* 送死, as in sacrificing their lives in conflicts and battles]. How can we count on them to govern the world?" See Lu Xun [Yu Ming 虞明], "Niang'er men ye buxing" (Women couldn't do it either), *Shen bao*, August 21, 1933, in Lu Xun, *Jiwaiji shiyi bubian* 集外集拾遺補編 (A supplement to the collection of addenda, second collection) (Beijing: Renmin wenxue chubanshe, 2006), 357–59. Lu Xun might have taken women's (in)capacity too literally, and his exaggeration of the obstacles stemming from

female reproductivity appears misogynistic. Lu also coded bad human traits and failures in negative feminine terms. For instance, he saw global problems as arising not from the fact that "men are the rulers" but because "men are ruling in a womanly way" (*nanzi zai nüren de tongzhi* 男子在女人地統治), which illustrates his stigmatization of the female sex or how he saw any associations with the term "woman" as inferior and insane. He took the infamous Ming eunuch Wei Zhongxian (1568–1627) as an extreme example of womanly governance and ended his article with a warning about the risk of letting women rule: "Even a half-woman's rule is so appalling, not to mention that of any real, complete woman!"

45. Lin Yutang's criticism of men extended to his defense of Chinese girls against Western men such as Maurice Dekobra (1885–1973), who Lin believed had abused their privilege as white men in observing, judging, and consuming the beauty of modern Chinese women. See Lin Yutang, "An Open Letter to M. Dekobra: A Defense of the Chinese Girl," *The China Critic* 6, no. 51 (1933): 1237–38. Yet Lin's discourses on women failed to win the hearts of some new women at the time. The most well-known case is the response of a pseudonymous "Cassandra" (said to be a female writer) to Lin's articles including "I Like to Talk with Women" in 1932. See Cassandra, "Men Are So Wonderful!," *The China Critic* 5, no. 49 (1932): 1304–5.

46. Jun Qian, "Lin Yutang: Negotiating Modernity Between East and West" (PhD diss., University of California, Berkeley, 1996), 5.

47. Lin Yutang, *The Vigil of a Nation* (New York: John Day Company, 1944), 57.

48. A recent example can be seen in Qiliang He, *Feminism, Women's Agency, and Communication in Early Twentieth-Century China: The Case of the Huang–Lu Elopement* (New York: Palgrave Macmillan, 2018), 144.

49. Qian, "Lin Yutang," 9.

50. Diran John Sohigian, "The Life and Times of Lin Yutang" (PhD diss., Columbia University, 1991), 454.

51. Lin Yutang, "Hunjia yu nüzi zhiye" 婚嫁與女子職業 (Marriage and women's occupation), in *Lin Yutang ji* 林語堂集 (The works of Lin Yutang) (Guangzhou: Huacheng chubanshe, 2007), 118. For how this piece stirred anger among some Chinese new women against gendered conservatism, see Motoe Sasaki, *Redemption and Revolution: American and Chinese New Women in the Early Twentieth Century* (Ithaca: Cornell University Press, 2016), 155.

52. For references to the cases of personal help, career support, and editorial assistance that Lin Yutang provided to young women, see Amy D. Dooling, ed., *Writing Women in Modern China: The Revolutionary Years, 1936–1976* (New York: Columbia University Press, 2005), 18; Xie Bingying, *A Woman Soldier's Own Story: The Autobiography of Xie Bingying*, trans. Lily Chia Brissman and Barry Brissman (New York: Columbia University Press, 2001), vii, 184; Xie Bingying/ Hsieh Pingying, *Girl Rebel: The Autobiography of Hsieh Pingying*, trans. Adet Lin and Anor Lin (repr., New York: Da Capo Press, 1975), with an introduction by Lin Yutang.

53. Xie, *Girl Rebel*, xiii–xiv.

54. "Lin Yutang's Letter to Richard Walsh (November 18, 1934)," in Qian Suoqiao, *Lin Yutang and China's Search for Modern Rebirth* (New York: Palgrave Macmillan, 2017), 178.

55. Lin Yutang, "Confucius as I Know Him," *The China Critic*, January 1, 1931.

56. Diran John Sohigian, "Confucius and the Lady in Question: Power Politics, Cultural Production and the Performance of *Confucius Saw Nanzi* in China in 1929," *Twentieth-Century China* 36, no. 1 (2011): 24.

57. Lin, "Confucius." For the sources Lin studied in writing the play, see Lin Yutang, "Guanyu 'Zijian Nanzi' de hua: Da Zhao Yuchuan xiansheng" 關於"子見南子"的話：答趙譽船先生 (About Confucius Saw Nanzi: Answering Mr. Zhao Yuchuan), in *Dahuang ji* 大荒集 (The great wilderness collection) (Taipei: Zhiwen chubanshe, 1966), 173–75.

58. Lu Xun, "Zai xiandai Zhongguo de Kong fuzi" 在現代中國的孔夫子 (Confucius in present-day China), in vol. 6 of *Lu Xun quanji* 魯迅全集 (The complete works of Lu Xun) (Beijing: Renmin wenxue chubanshe, 1981), 318. For the translation, see Sohigian, "The Life," 431.

59. See, for example, Sohigian, "The Life," 428–45, 502; Fang Lu, "Constructing and Reconstructing Images of Chinese Women in Lin Yutang's Translations, Adaptations and Rewritings" (PhD diss., Simon Fraser University, 2008), 88–99; Olivia Milburn, "Gender, Sexuality, and Power in Early China: The Changing Biographies of Lord Ling of Wei and Lady Nanzi," *Nan Nü: Men, Women and Gender in China* 12 (2010): 1–29; Gao Fang 高方, "Nanzi yu Zhongguo zaoqi nüxingzhuyi xingtai" 南子與中國早期女性主義形態 (Nanzi and Chinese early feminism), *Journal of Harbin University* 35, no. 6 (2014): 41–44.

60. One scholar notes only that *Confucius Saw Nancy* was "perhaps inspired by Ibsen." See Sohigian, "The Life," 502. The play has also been studied as an instance of "historical drama" or "women's theater" together with Ouyang Yuqian's *Pan Jinlian* and Guo Moruo's *Sange panni de nüxing* 三個叛逆的女性 (Three rebellious women), rewriting the historical women Wang Zhaojun, Zhuo Wenjun, and Nie Ying. See Sohigian, "Confucius," 27; Xiaomei Chen, *Occidentalism: A Theory of Counter-Discourse in Post-Mao China* (New York: Oxford University Press, 1995), chap. 6; Lu, "Constructing," 91. Although these plays all convey modern ideas through ancient female figures, there is one fundamental difference: the three heroines in Guo's plays were not labeled "shrews" but were deemed quite positive in history. These plays are not discussed in this book for they do not demonstrate the tension brought by the shrew's rehabilitation as in the works of Ouyang Yuqian and Lin Yutang.

61. Milburn, "Gender, Sexuality," 27. About Nanzi's notoriety, also see Sohigian, "The Life," 432, and "Confucius," 25; Siegfried Englert and Roderich Ptak, "Nan-Tzu, or Why Heaven Did Not Crush Confucius," *Journal of the American Oriental Society* 106, no. 4 (1986): 684; Duan Zongshe 段宗社, "'Zijian Nanzi': Lishi gong'an yu xiandai xiangxiang" "子見南子"：歷史公案與現代想象 (Confucius Saw Nanzi: Historical facts and modern imagination), *Qilu xuekan*, no. 226 (2012): 134–35. Scholars normally conclude that there was

no solid evidence to support Nanzi's so-called disgraceful behavior, and her infamy might be the result of misogyny.

62. Lin, "Confucius," 6. For other references to Nanzi as the real power behind the throne, see Englert and Ptak, "Nan-Tzu," 680; Milburn, "Gender, Sexuality," 5; Sohigian, "Confucius," 29, and "The Life," 433.

63. Gao, "Nanzi," 41.

64. Sohigian, "The Life," 433; Milburn, "Gender, Sexuality," 3.

65. For analyses of the positive description of Nanzi's thoughts and words in *Lienü zhuan*, see Milburn, "Gender, Sexuality," 25–27; Englert and Ptak, "Nan-Tzu," 684. Note that Nanzi's name was intentionally omitted in this positive record.

66. Lin, *Zi jian Nanzi* 子見南子 (Confucius saw Nanzi), *Benliu* 1, no. 6 (1928): 927. For the translation, see Lin Yutang, trans., *Confucius Saw Nancy: A One-Act Tragicomedy*, in *Confucius Saw Nancy and Essays about Nothing* (Shanghai: Commercial Press, 1936), 9. Lin Yutang translated this play into English "in response to the request of the Chinese students at Columbia University who enacted it at the International House in December 1931." See Lin, preface to *Confucius Saw Nancy*, v.

67. Lin, *Confucius Saw Nancy*, 41. The details about revealing an undergown and the word "flirting" do not appear in the Chinese script, in which there is only a brief line, *jieyi qiwu* 解衣起舞 (untie one's clothes and start dancing). See Lin, *Zi jian Nanzi*, 949.

68. Lin, *Confucius Saw Nancy*, 44–45.

69. Lin, *Confucius Saw Nancy*, 45.

70. Sohigian, "The Life," 437–55, and "Confucius," 32–42.

71. Lu Xun, "Guanyu Zijian Nanzi" 關於《子見南子》, no. 2 (About Confucius Saw Nanzi; document no. 2), in Lu, *Jiwaiji*, 316. The use of the term "whore" is from Sohigian, "The Life," 439. Those who supported the performance, however, thought the performer who played Nanzi was dressed elegantly and decorously (*guzhuang xiuya juzhi dafang* 古裝秀雅舉止大方). See Lu, "Guanyu," document no. 3, 318.

72. Milburn, "Gender, Sexuality," 25.

73. Lin, *Zi jian Nanzi*, 928. The translation of *yinyan huixing* is mine since Lin Yutang rendered it only as "perfectly disgraceful" in his translation. See Lin, *Confucius Saw Nancy*, 12.

74. Lin, *Zi jian Nanzi*, 932. For the translation, see Lin, *Confucius Saw Nancy*, 17.

75. A late imperial scholar, Liu Baonan (1791–1855), had a similar interpretation of the oath. He read Nanzi as the real subject, instead of a vague "Heaven" that would strike or destroy Confucius if he failed to attend the meeting. Liu did not concern himself about Nanzi's being a woman but based his reading on the idea that she was the one holding power. See Liu Baonan 劉寶楠, *Lunyu zhengyi* 論語正義 (Collected commentaries on the Analects) (Beijing: Zhonghua shuju, 1990), 245.

76. Lin, *Zi jian Nanzi*, 930. For the translation, see Lin, *Confucius Saw Nancy*, 14.

77. Lin, *Confucius Saw Nancy*, 4.

78. *T'ien Hsia Monthly* (1935-1941) was a prestigious English-language journal where Lin Yutang served as editor and contributor. Aiming to promote "international cultural understanding" by an "attempt more at an interpretation of China to the West" (see the "Foreword" of the journal), the monthly introduced positive aspects of Chinese culture as well as negative petty figures during the war, such as opportunists and false patriots. Volume 3 in 1936 included a story titled "The Patriot" which pours scorn on a Mr. Yu for being a coward in his roles as schoolteacher, husband, father, and citizen. His wife, domineering and directly described as a "shrew" in the story, is rendered in a comparatively favorable light. Compared to her vision of wartime reality and her resoluteness in taking care of the family, the image of the man is pathetic. This story can be taken as more evidence for the social preference for strong wifehood in wartime or the charm of the Chinese shrew for an intended Western audience. See Wenping Hsieh 謝文炳 and Richard L. Jen 任玲遜, trans., "The Patriot," *T'ien Hsia Monthly* 3, no. 2 (1936): 168-86.

79. Lin Yutang, *My Country and My People* (New York: John Day Company, 1935), 144.

80. Lin, *My Country*, 144-46.

81. Qian, "Lin Yutang," 185.

82. Lin Yutang, "Feminist Thought in Ancient China," *T'ien Hsia Monthly* 1, no. 2 (1935): 150.

83. He, *Feminism*, 144.

84. Ji Ping 寄萍, "Youmo dashi Lin Yutang fufu fangwen ji (xia)" 幽默大師林語堂夫婦訪問記（下） (Interview of humor master Lin Yutang and his wife: Second half), *Shen bao*, February 22, 1936.

85. For an analysis of these women, see Lu, "Constructing," chap. 4.

86. Lu, "Constructing," 88.

87. Lin Yutang, preface to *Lady Wu: A True Story* (Melbourne: William Heinemann, 1957), vii-xii.

88. Wang Jingzhi (a mutual friend of Hu Shi and Cao Chengying) and Cheng Fade (son of Hu Shi's nephew) both recalled the detail about the kitchen knife. Shi Yuangao, a distant cousin of Hu Shi, also said that he even saw Jiang Dongxiu try to stab Hu with a pair of scissors when she could not fully vent her anger through words. See Shen Weiwei 沈衛威, *Hu Shi zhouwei* 胡適周圍 (Hu Shi's surroundings) (Beijing: Gongren chubanshe, 2003).

89. Tang Degang 唐德剛, *Hu Shi zayi* 胡適雜憶 (Miscellaneous recollections of Hu Shi) (Beijing: Huawen chubanshe, 1990), 39.

90. According to Shi Yuangao, Jiang Dongxiu not only managed to secure her own marriage but also defended Liang Shiqiu's (1903-1987) wife in court when Liang filed for divorce.

91. Jiang Dongxiu may be widely considered a shrewish wife who was so threatening that Hu Shi dared not leave her. Yet there has been another interpretation of the relationship between the two. Some studies have pointed out Hu's romantic propensity and his affairs with several women in China and abroad, indicating that taking on the persona of a weak henpecked husband

might have been a ruse. For accounts of Hu's love affairs, see Lynn Pan, *When True Love Came to China* (Hong Kong: Hong Kong University Press, 2015), 132–34; Susan Chan Egan and Chih-p'ing Chou, *A Pragmatist and His Free Spirit: The Half-Century Romance of Hu Shi and Edith Clifford Williams* (Hong Kong: Chinese University Press, 2009); Jiang Yongzhen 江勇振, *Xingxing, yueliang, taiyang: Hu Shi de qinggan shijie* 星星·月亮·太陽：胡適的情感世界 (The stars, the moon, and the sun: The women in Hu Shi's life) (Beijing: Xinxing chubanshe, 2012). For Hu's confirmation of a newspaper commentary saying that his being henpecked was a sham and Jiang was in fact more like a powerless monarch, see Hu Songping 胡頌平, *Hu Shizhi xiansheng wannian tanhualu* 胡適之先生晚年談話錄 (A record of conversations with Mr. Hu Shi in his later life) (Taipei: Lianjing chuban shiye gongsi, 1984), 171.

92. While this book focuses on discourses and constructions, it is still interesting to note that the Republican period witnessed many celebrity couples, in addition to Hu Shi and Jiang Dongxiu, in which the wife had the upper hand over her famous husband. To list a few: Liu Shipei (1884–1919) and He Zhen (1884–1920), Feng Yuxiang (1882–1948) and Li Dequan (1896–1972), Zhou Zuoren (1885–1967) and his Japanese wife, and Wang Jingwei (1883–1944) and Chen Bijun (1891–1959). In *The Birth of Chinese Feminism*, He Zhen is acclaimed as a central female theorist, while the connection between her public feminism and her domestic shrewishness is not mentioned. In Chinese scholarship and (historical) fiction, by contrast, He is described as using the banner of gender equality to validate her unequal treatment of Liu. She is criticized for writing radical pieces about abolishing marriage only to justify her extramarital affair. See Lydia Liu, Rebecca Karl, and Dorothy Ko, eds., *The Birth of Chinese Feminism: Essential Texts in Transnational Theory* (New York: Columbia University Press, 2013); Shi Zhixuan 石之軒, *Huanghua fu: Gongheguo qianye fengyunlu* 黃花賦：共和國前夜風雲錄 (Huanghua rhapsody: Record of the vicissitudes on the eve of the Republic) (Beijing: Zhongguo wenlian chubanshe, 2006); Zhang Ming 張鳴, *Lishi de digao: Wanjin Zhongguo de linglei guancha* 歷史的底稿：晚近中國的另類觀察 (Manuscript of history: An alternative observation of modern and contemporary China) (Beijing: Zhongguo dang'an chubanshe, 2006). About Li Dequan, see Kate Merkel-Hess, "A New Woman and Her Warlord: Li Dequan, Feng Yuxiang, and the Politics of Intimacy in Twentieth-Century China," *Frontiers of History in China* 11, no. 3 (2016): 431–57.

93. Hu Shi, *The Chinese Renaissance* (New York: Paragon Book Reprint Corp., 1963), 104–5.

94. Luo Jialun, "Events Leading to Hu Shi's Becoming Chinese Ambassador to the United States," *Chinese Studies in History* 42, no. 1 (2008): 66–67. This is a translation by Sylvia Chia from the original Chinese text (abridged and revised) published in vol. 2 of *Recollections of Mr. Hu Shi*, ed. Yu-ning Li (New York: Outer Sky Press, 1997).

95. Luo, "Events," 67.

96. Hu Shi, preface to *Japanese Sense of Humor*, by Hollington K. Tong, in vol. 3 of *A Collection of Hu Shih's English Writings* 胡適英文文存, ed. Chih-p'ing Chou 周質平 (Taipei: Yuanliu chuban gongsi, 1995), iv.

97. K. P. S. Menon, *Journey Round the World* (Bombay: Bharatiya vidya bhavan, 1966), 166.

98. Hu Shi collected French telephone tokens with the letters "PTT" (Postes, Télégraphes et Téléphones) for the pun on the Chinese phrase *pa taitai*. See Hu Songping, *Hu Shizhi xiansheng nianpu changbian chugao* 胡適之先生年譜長編初稿 (A draft chronological biography of Mr. Hu Shi), vols. 5, 7, 10 (Taipei: Lianjing chuban gongsi, 1990), 1782–83, 2502–3, 3543–45; Hu, *Hu Shizhi xiansheng wannian*, 3–4; Li Ao 李敖, ed., *Hu Shi yucui* 胡適語粹 (Cream of Hu Shi's words) (Shanghai: Wenhui chubanshe, 2003), 146–47; Li Ao, *Li Ao da quanji 18: Hu Shi yu wo* 李敖大全集 18：胡適與我 (The great collection of Li Ao: Hu Shi and I, vol. 18) (Beijing: Zhongguo youyi chuban gongsi, 1999), 20–22; Egan and Chou, *A Pragmatist*, 124, 407, 408; "Hu Resting Well; To Be Hospitalized 2 Weeks," *China News*, February 26, 1961.

99. Hu, preface, 1480.

100. Hu, preface, 1480–81.

101. Yin 音, "Taitai wansui" 太太萬歲 (Long live the missus), *Beiping ribao*, May 6, 1948.

102. Yin, "Taitai."

103. [Nie] Gannu, "Lun pa laopo" 論怕老婆 (On wife-fearing), *Yecao wencong*, no. 10 (1948): 36–37.

104. Nie, "Lun," 39.

105. See, for example, Cai Yibai 蔡夷白, "Pa laopo" 怕老婆 (Wife-fearing), *Tie bao*, November 13, 1947; "Pa laopo lun" 怕老婆論 (The idea of wife-fearing), *Yisiqi huabao* 19, no. 10 (1948): 9; Yu Shi 玉士, "Pa laopo lun" 怕老婆論 (The idea of wife-fearing), *Zhen hua* 5, no. 1 (1948): 5; Heng Gong 恆公, "Pa laopo neng cujin heping minzhu lun" 怕老婆能促進和平民主論 (The idea that wife-fearing can facilitate peace and democracy), *Xiangxuehai zhoubao* 1, no. 5 (1949): 2. Note that the last three publications, though titled differently, are nearly identical in content. Also note that the relationship between the situation of wife-fearing in a country and its democratic level or wartime stance had been brought up by another writer in 1936, before Hu Shi's public pronouncement on it. See Wen Bi 問筆, "Pa laopo lun" 怕老婆論 (The idea of wife-fearing), *Yuzhou feng*, no. 14 (1936): 109.

106. Xu Zhimo 徐志摩, "Xingshi yinyuan zhuan xu" 《醒世姻緣傳》序 (Preface to Marriage Bonds to Awaken the World), originally published in *Xin yue* 4, no. 1, in vol. 3 of *Hu Shi wencun (disi ji)* 胡適文存（第四集）(Collection of Hu Shi's essays, no. 4) (Taipei: Yuanliu chuban gongsi, 1986), 180.

107. Xu, "Xingshi," 181.

108. Ching-kiu Stephen Chan, "The Language of Despair: Ideological Representations of the 'New Woman' by May Fourth Writers," in *Gender Politics in Modern China: Writing and Feminism*, ed. Tani Barlow (Durham: Duke University Press, 1993), 13–14.

109. Even in the Western world, *Thick Black Theory* is considered a strategy treatise, hailed as the Chinese counterpart to Machiavelli's *The Prince*.

110. Li Zongwu 李宗吾, *Pa laopo de zhexue* 怕老婆的哲學 (The philosophy of wife-fearing) (Chengdu: Chenzhong shuju, 1946), 12.

111. Li, *Pa*, 6, 13, 18.

112. Li, *Pa*, 14.

113. Given the fact that *The Philosophy* was written during the Second Sino-Japanese War, when Li Zongwu was in Sichuan working for the provincial government, Communist scholars in mainland China tend to read the text as Li's mockery of the nonresistance policy of the KMT government out of its "fear" of Japan. As analyzed by an article published in the CCP's mouthpiece magazine *Seeking Truth*, however, the message is not monolithic. See Li Fei 李飛 et al., "Lun Li Zongwu Pa laopo zhexue zhi lishi beijing" 論李宗吾《怕老婆哲學》之歷史背景 (Historical background of Li Zongwu's The Philosophy of Wife-Fearing), *Qiu shi*, no. 2 (2008): 99–101.

114. Chen Yuan 陳遠, *Zheng shuo Li Zongwu: Xiandai sixiangshi shang de houhei jiaozhu* 正說李宗吾：現代思想史上的厚黑教主 (Li Zongwu in a positive light: The thick black founder in modern intellectual history) (Taipei: Xiuwei zixun keji gufen youxian gongsi, 2009), 186–87.

115. In contrast to Li Zongwu's *Classic of Wife-Fearing*, which exercises defiance against the classics, Hu Shi's "new three followings and four virtues" (*xin sancong side* 新三從四德) speaks more to marital mundanity: a husband should follow his wife when she goes out (*taitai waichu yao gencong* 太太外出要跟從), obey his wife when she gives orders (*taitai mingling yao fucong* 太太命令要服從), have the virtue of endurance when his wife beats and curses him (*taitai dama yao rende* 太太打罵要忍得/德); and more. See Chen, *Zheng shuo*, 185; "Hu Shi tan junei" 胡適談懼內 (Hu Shi talking about henpecking), originally published in *Zhongyang ribao*, April 14, 1961, later included in Li, *Li Ao da quanji*, 18.

116. Li, *Li Ao da quanji*, 21.

117. Li, *Pa*, 17–18.

118. Lu, "Constructing," 83.

119. Reviews include Hu Ke 胡珂, "Shu fen" 抒憤 (Expressing anger), *Shidai ribao* (*Xinsheng*), December 12, 1947; Dongfang Didong 東方蝃蝀, "Taitai Wansui de taitai" 《太太萬歲》的太太 (The wife in Long Live the Missus), *Dagong bao* (*Da gongyuan*), December 13, 1947; Fang Cheng 方澄, "Suowei 'fushi de beiai'–Taitai Wansui guanhou" 所謂"浮世的悲哀"–《太太萬歲》觀後 (The so-called "sadness of the floating world": After watching Long Live the Missus), *Dagong bao* (*Da gongyuan*), December 14, 1947; Xu Ceng 徐曾, "Zhang Ailing he ta de Taitai Wansui" 張愛玲和她的《太太萬歲》 (Zhang Ailing and her Long Live the Missus), *Xin min bao* (*Ye huayuan*), December 15, 1947; Sha Yi 沙易, "Ping Taitai Wansui" 評《太太萬歲》 (Commenting on Long Live the Missus), *Zhongyang ribao* (*Ju yi*), December 19, 1947; Wang Rong 王戎, "Shi Zhongguo de you zenmeyang?–Taitai Wansui guanhou" 是中國的又怎麼樣？–《太太萬歲》觀後 (From China, then what? After watching Long Live the Missus), *Xin min bao* (*Xin yingju*), December 28, 1947; Shen Xie 莘薤, "Women bu qiqiu ye bu shishe lianjia de lianmin–Yige 'taitai' kan le Taitai Wansui" 我們不乞求也不施捨廉價的憐憫–一個"太太"看了《太太萬歲》 (We don't beg or give cheap mercies: After a "wife" watching Long Live the Missus), *Dagong bao* (*Xiju yu dianying*), January 7, 1948; Hong Shen 洪深, "Shu wo buyuan lingshou zhefan shengqing–Yige zhangfu duiyu Taitai Wansui de huida" 恕我不願領受這

番盛情—一個丈夫對於《太太萬歲》的回答 (Forgive me for not being willing to accept the great kindness: A husband's answer to Long Live the Missus), *Dagong bao* (*Xiju yu dianying*), January 7, 1948. Except for Dongfang Didong's comment, which is more neutral, other articles are all critical.

120. Kenny K. K. Ng, "The Screenwriter as Cultural Broker: Travels of Zhang Ailing's Comedy of Love," *Modern Chinese Literature and Culture* 20, no. 2 (2008): 131–84, see 146. For how *Long Live the Missus* defies the melodramatic norm of female suffering by appropriating screwball characterizations to grant the heroine the advantage, see 140–45.

121. Shen, "Women." Zhang Ailing did not follow the trend of writing the husband as following his wife, but she did not seem to sing the praises of wifely submission either. According to Zhang's account, her intention was to record moments of mundane life and depict an ordinary *taitai* who is lowbrow, parochial, and vain. The term *wansui* might simply register the author's general uncritical attitude toward common life and petty nonentities. See Zhang Ailing 張愛玲, "'Taitai Wansui' tiji" "太太萬歲"題記 (Preceding notes on Long Live the Missus), *Dagong bao*, December 3, 1947.

122. Shen, "Women."

123. Hong, "Shu."

124. Wu Xiaoli 巫小黎, "'Zhanhou' Shanghai wentan: Yi Taitai Wansui de pipan wei ge'an" "戰後"上海文壇：以《太太萬歲》的批判為個案 (The "postwar" Shanghai literary scene: A case study of the criticisms of Long Live the Missus), *Xiandai zhongwen xuekan*, no. 5 (2013): 39–45, see 44.

5. Revolutionary Views on the Shrewish Wife: From Husband-Disciplining to Early Communist State-Building

1. For an overview of post–May Fourth Nora stories, dramas, and films, see Xu, "*Nala*" *zai Zhongguo*, 293–96, 302–5; Zhang, *Sixiangshi*, 153–54.

2. There were two influential discussions in the 1930s. The *National News Weekly* launched a discussion in 1934 titled "What Happened After All since Nora Left Home" (*Nala zouhou jiujing zenyang* 娜拉走後究竟怎樣), which lasted for over two months. In 1935 *Women's Life* organized talks and publications on the topic of "Nora after leaving home" (*chuzou hou de Nala* 出走後的娜拉). For further information, see Xu, "*Nala*" *zai Zhongguo*, 258–65, 301–2.

3. Meng Yue 孟悅 and Dai Jinhua 戴錦華, *Fuchu lishi dibiao: Xiandai funü wenxue yanjiu* 浮出歷史地表：現代婦女文學研究 (Emerging on the horizon of history: Modern Chinese women's literature) (Beijing: Zhongguo renmin daxue chubanshe, 2004), 107.

4. Mao Dun, "Chuangzao" 創造 (Creation), *Dongfang zazhi* 25, no. 8 (1928): 114.

5. Mao Dun, "Chuangzuo shengya de kaishi—huiyilu (shi)" 創作生涯的開始—回憶錄（十）(The beginning of a career in writing: A memoir, no. 10), originally published in *Xin wenxue shiliao*, no. 1 (1981), in vol. 1 of *Mao Dun zhuanji* 茅盾專集 (Critical anthology of Mao Dun), ed. Tang Jinhai 唐金海 et al. (Fuzhou: Fujian renmin chubanshe, 1983), 620.

6. Jianhua Chen, "An Archaeology of Repressed Popularity: Zhou Shou-juan, Mao Dun, and Their 1920s Literary Polemics," in *Rethinking Chinese Popular Culture: Cannibalizations of the Canon*, ed. Carlos Rojas and Eileen Cheng-yin Chow (London: Routledge, 2009), 106; David Der-Wei Wang, *Fictional Realism in Twentieth-Century China: Mao Dun, Lao She, Shen Congwen* (New York: Columbia University Press, 1992), 81.

7. Mao, "Chuangzuo," 620.

8. Zheng Jian 鄭堅, "Cong geming de 'youwu' dao geming de nüshen: Yi Mao Dun xiaoshuo zhong shidai nüxing xingxiang suzao weili" 從革命的"尤物"到革命的女神：以茅盾小說中時代女性形象塑造為例 (From a revolutionary "stunner" to a revolutionary goddess: The feminine images in the novels of Mao Dun), *Hebei shifan daxue xuebao (zhexue shehui kexue ban)* 30, no. 3 (2007): 88–92.

9. For such criticism, see Wang, *Fictional Realism*, 81; Jin Feng, *The New Woman in Early Twentieth-Century Chinese Fiction* (West Lafayette: Purdue University Press, 2004), 120; Li Li, "Female Bodies as Imaginary Signifiers in Chinese Revolutionary Literature," in *Chinese Revolution and Chinese Literature*, ed. Tao Dongfeng et al. (Newcastle upon Tyne: Cambridge Scholars Publishing, 2009), 103.

10. Chen Xinyao 陳欣瑤, "Chongdu 'Li Shuangshuang'–Lishi yujing zhong de 'nongcun xin nüxing' jiqi zhuti xushu" 重讀"李雙雙"–歷史語境中的"農村新女性"及其主體敘述 (Rereading "Li Shuangshuang": The "rural new woman" in the historical context and her subjective narration), *Zhongguo xiandai wenxue yanjiu congkan*, no. 1 (2014): 113–16.

11. Before *Roaring*, there were a few published stories on the peasant movement during the Northern Expedition. *Roaring* is recognized as the first literary text with a positive image of the peasants. See Xiaorong Han, *Chinese Discourses on the Peasant, 1900–1949* (Albany: State University of New York Press, 2005), 64.

12. Wang, *The Monster That Is History*, 61.

13. In later works such as *The White-Haired Girl* (*Baimao nü* 白毛女; 1945) and *Wang Gui and Li Xiangxiang* (*Wang Gui yu Li Xiangxiang* 王貴與李香香; 1945), the wickedness of the landlord class is explicitly grounded in its violence against innocent rural women. Among characters of the peasant class, there are either no traces of oppression or mild instances of domestic violence without particular significance.

14. Jiang Guangci 蔣光慈, *Paoxiao le de tudi* 咆哮了的土地 (The roaring earth), in vol. 2 of *Jiang Guangci wenji* 蔣光慈文集 (Collection of Jiang Guangci's works) (Shanghai: Shanghai wenyi chubanshe, 1983), 181.

15. For examples of the *suku* practice by peasant women during the land reform, see Ono, *Chinese Women*, 172. Note the similar acts of crying and accusing between Hejie and the peasant women that Ono refers to.

16. Jiang, *Paoxiao*, 229–30.

17. Jiang, *Paoxiao*, 230.

18. Jiang, *Paoxiao*, 231.

19. Jiang, *Paoxiao*, 382.

20. Jiang, *Paoxiao*, 384.

21. For a historical overview of the interplay between the politics of gender and the early Communist movements, see Christina K. Gilmartin, *Engendering the Chinese Revolution: Radical Women, Communist Politics, and Mass Movements in the 1920s* (Berkeley: University of California Press, 1995).

22. Wu Sihong 吳似鴻, "Jiang Guangci huiyilu" 蔣光慈回憶錄 (The memoir of Jiang Guangci), in *Jiang Guangci yanjiu ziliao* 蔣光慈研究資料 (Research materials on Jiang Guangci), ed. Fang Ming 方銘 (Beijing: Zhishi chanquan chubanshe, 2010), 91; Fan Boqun 范伯群 and Zeng Huapeng 曾華鵬, "Jiang Guangchi lun" 蔣光赤論 (On Jiang Guangchi), in Fang, *Jiang Guangci yanjiu ziliao*, 324.

23. Before "Report," Mao Zedong had written extensively on women's issues. He wrote "The Strength of the Heart" (*Xin zhi li* 心之力) in 1917 emphasizing women's role in raising new citizens. In 1919 Mao became more radical. His "Women's Revolutionary Army" (*Nüzi geming jun* 女子革命軍) and "The Great Union of the Populace" (*Minzhong de da lianhe* 民眾的大聯合) promote women's equal rights. After the shocking incident in which Zhao Wuzhen killed herself in her bridal sedan to protest her arranged marriage, Mao published about ten articles within a matter of days, denouncing society's sin in killing the free will of individuals. For Mao's earlier writings, see Stuart R. Schram and Nancy J. Hodes, eds., *Mao's Road to Power: Revolutionary Writings, 1912–1949*, vol. 1 (Armonk, NY: M. E. Sharpe, 1992).

24. Mao Zedong 毛澤東, "Hunan nongmin yundong kaocha baogao" 湖南農民運動考察報告 (Report on an investigation of the peasant movement in Hunan), in vol. 1 of *Mao Zedong xuanji* 毛澤東選集 (Selected works of Mao Zedong) (Beijing: Renmin chubanshe, 1951), 33. For a translation, see "Report on an Investigation of the Peasant Movement in Hunan," in *Selected Works of Mao Tse-tung*, vol. 1 (Peking: Foreign Languages Press, 1965), 44.

25. Mao, "Report," 23, 44–45.

26. Ono, *Chinese Women*, 149.

27. Mao, "Report," 46.

28. Women's freedom to divorce was also included in the family law of the Nationalist government. Ono Kazuko writes that the Nationalist law seems to lack honesty in relation to women's real power in divorce. See Ono, *Chinese Women*, 153. For a summary of the Nationalist "family law," see M. J. Meijer, *Marriage Law and Policy in the Chinese People's Republic* (Hong Kong: Hong Kong University Press, 1971), 26–29.

29. Hershatter, *Women and China's Revolutions*, 168.

30. Mao Zedong, "Xingguo diaocha" 興國調查 (Xingguo Investigation), in *Mao Zedong nongcun diaocha wenji* 毛澤東農村調查文集 (Collected writings of Mao Zedong on rural investigations) (Beijing: Renmin chubanshe, 1982), 222–23. For a translation, see "Xingguo Investigation," in Schram and Hodes, *Mao's Road to Power*, 3:594–655.

31. Zhang Huaiwan 張懷萬, "Zhang Huaiwan xunshi ganxi'nan baogao" 張懷萬巡視贛西南報告 (A report on Zhang Huaiwan's investigation in southwest Jiangxi), in vol. 1 of *Zhongyang geming genjudi shiliao xuanbian* 中央革命根據

地史料選編 (Selected historical documents on the Central Revolutionary Base Area), ed. *Jiangxi sheng dang'an guan* 江西省檔案館 (Nanchang: Jiangxi renmin chubanshe, 1982), 180–212, see 192–93; Mao Zedong, "Xunwu diaocha" 尋烏調查 (Xunwu Investigation), in *Mao Zedong nongcun*, 177–81. For a translation, see "Xunwu Investigation," in Schram and Hodes, *Mao's Road to Power*, 3:296–418.

32. "Xiangganbian suqu funü gongzuo jue'an" 湘贛邊蘇區婦女工作決案 (Resolution of women's work in the Hunan-Jiangxi Border Soviet Area), in *Zhongguo funü yundong lishi ziliao (1927–1937)* 中國婦女運動歷史資料 (Historical source materials of the Chinese women's movement), ed. *Quanguo fulian fuyun shi* 全國婦聯婦運室 (Beijing: Zhongguo funü chubanshe, 1991), 157; Zhu Xiaodong 朱曉東, "Tongguo hunyin de zhili—1930 nian-1950 nian geming shiqi de hunyin he funü jiefang faling zhong de celüe yu shenti" 通過婚姻的治理—1930年-1950年革命時期的婚姻和婦女解放法令中的策略與身體 (Governance through marriage: Marital situations in the revolutionary 1930s to 1950s and the strategies and the body in decrees on women's liberation), *Beida falü pinglun* 4, no. 2 (2001): 398; Hershatter, *Women and China's Revolutions*, 170.

33. Pu Anxiu 浦安修, "Wunian lai huabei kangri minzhu genjudi funü yundong de chubu zongjie" 五年來華北抗日民主根據地婦女運動的初步總結 (A preliminary summary of the women's movement in the Anti-Japanese Democratic Base Areas of North China in the past five years), in *Quanguo, Zhongguo funü yundong lishi ziliao (1937–1945)*, 711.

34. He Youliang 何友良, *Zhongguo Suweiai quyu shehui biandongshi* 中國蘇維埃區域社會變動史 (History of social changes in the Chinese Soviet Areas) (Beijing: Dangdai Zhongguo chubanshe, 1996), 183. For more cases illustrating rural women's autonomy and their negotiations between state rules and personal interests, see Xiaoping Cong, *Marriage, Law, and Gender in Revolutionary China, 1940–1960* (Cambridge: Cambridge University Press, 2016), chap. 2.

35. Cai Chang 蔡暢, "Yingjie funü gongzuo de xin fangxiang" 迎接婦女工作的新方向 (Welcoming the new direction of women's work), in *Quanguo, Zhongguo funü yundong lishi ziliao (1937–1945)*, 650.

36. Hershatter, *Women and China's Revolutions*, 170; Schram and Hodes, *Mao's Road to Power*, 4:616.

37. Pu, "Wunian," 685.

38. Pu, "Wunian," 685.

39. Meng Zhaoyi 孟昭毅 and Wang Qing 王清, "Dangqian funü yundong zhong liangge xuyao zhuyi de shiji wenti (jielu)" 當前婦女運動中兩個需要注意的實際問題（節錄） (Two practical problems requiring attention in the current women's movement, an extract), originally published in *Qiqi yuekan* 1, no. 5 (1941), in *Quanguo, Zhongguo funü yundong lishi ziliao (1937–1945)*, 528.

40. Meng and Wang, "Dangqian," 529–30.

41. Meng and Wang, "Dangqian," 530.

42. About the notion of "the Yan'an Way," see Mark Selden, *The Yenan Way in Revolutionary China* (Cambridge: Harvard University Press, 1971), and *China in Revolution: The Yenan Way Revisited* (Armonk, NY: M. E. Sharpe, 1995).

43. *Zhongguo funü da fanshen* 中國婦女大翻身 (The great turning over/transformation of Chinese women) (Hong Kong: Xin minzhu chubanshe, 1949),

2. This shift is also mentioned in Peng Dehuai 彭德懷, "Guanyu huabei gen-judi gongzuo de baogao" 關於華北根據地工作的報告 (A report of the work in the Base Areas of North China), in vol. 3 of *Gongfei huoguo shiliao huibian* 共匪禍國史料彙編 (Collection of historical source materials on the Communist bandits' scourge to the nation) (Taipei: Zhonghua minguo kaiguo wushinian wenxian bianzuan weiyuanhui, 1964), 346–406; Anna Louise Strong, *The Chinese Conquer China* (Garden City, NY: Doubleday & Company, 1949), 170; Pu, "Wunian," 701–2.

44. Ono, *Chinese Women*, 166.

45. Zhu, "Tongguo," 389–91. Cong Xiaoping also discusses misunderstandings, complaints, and opposition from male peasants in the 1940s in response to the marriage reform and women's new status. See Cong, *Marriage, Law, and Gender*, chap. 1 and primarily chap. 5.

46. Although there were shifts in policies, as Cong Xiaoping notes, it is simplistic or even incorrect to argue that the CCP knowingly sacrificed women's rights to win the support of male peasants. See Cong, *Marriage, Law, and Gender*, introduction and chap. 1.

47. Zhou Enlai 周恩來, "Lun 'xianqi liangmu' yu muzhi" 論"賢妻良母"與母職 (On "good wife wise mother" and motherly duties), originally published in *Xinhua ribao*, September 27, 1942, in *Quanguo, Zhongguo funü yundong lishi ziliao (1937–1945)*, 608–11.

48. "Zhongguo gongchandang zhongyang weiyuanhui guanyu ge kangri genjudi muqian funü gongzuo fangzhen de jueding" 中國共產黨中央委員會關於各抗日根據地目前婦女工作方針的決定 (Decisions of the Central Committee of the Chinese Communist Party on guiding principles for the current women's work in the Anti-Japanese Base Areas), in *Quanguo, Zhongguo funü yundong lishi ziliao (1937–1945)*, 648.

49. Cong, *Marriage, Law, and Gender*, 69.

50. Jack Belden, *China Shakes the World* (New York: Harper and Brothers, 1949), 289–90.

51. Belden, *China*, 290.

52. Belden, *China*, 293, 301.

53. Belden, *China*, 302.

54. Belden, *China*, 290, 303.

55. Belden, *China*, 305.

56. Belden, *China*, 307.

57. For an analysis of how the Gold Flower story points to typical features of Communist radical feminism, see He Guimei 賀桂梅, "'Yan'an daolu' zhong de xingbie wenti—Jieji yu xingbie yiti de lishi sikao" "延安道路"中的性別問題—階級與性別議題的歷史思考 (The sex of "Yan'an road": A historical thinking of class and sex), *Nankai xuebao*, no. 6 (2006): 16–22, see 18.

58. Belden, *China*, 276.

59. For more information on the fear among poor peasants about the loss of wives due to rural Communist reform, see Hershatter, *Women and China's Revolutions*, 168–69.

60. "The Township Head and His Wife" (*Xiangzhang fufu* 鄉長夫婦; 1941), published in the *Liberation Daily*, is a piece that projects conservative

perspectives on gender images. In the story, the wife is sexually attractive and cares less about Communism than about her family. She is associated by her husband, the township head, with the category of reactionary "dirty matters" (*zang dongxi* 髒東西). See Hong Liu 洪流, "Xiangzhang fufu" 鄉長夫婦 (The township head and his wife), in vol. 2 of *Yan'an wenyi congshu* 延安文藝叢書 (Anthology of literature and the arts from Yan'an) (Changsha: Hunan renmin chubanshe, 1984), 26–31.

61. Liang Yan 梁彥, "Mo mai nü" 磨麥女 (The wheat-grinding girl), in *Yan'an wenyi congshu*, 2:158, 164.

62. Liu Qing 柳青, "Xishi" 喜事 (The wedding), in *Yan'an wenyi congshu*, 2:443.

63. Liu, "Xishi," 2:451.

64. For discussions of actual women who ran away and their tactical manipulation of social and political changes of this time period and beyond, see the section "Resistance to the Patriarchy: Women Running Away and 'Being Kidnapped,'" in Cong, *Marriage, Law, and Gender*, 79–84; the section "Women and the Rise of Rural Communism: The Jiangxi Soviet," in Hershatter, *Women and China's Revolutions*, 166–71; Zhao Ma, *Runaway Wives, Urban Crimes, and Survival Tactics in Wartime Beijing, 1937–1949* (Cambridge: Harvard University Press, 2015).

65. Zhuang Qidong 莊啟東, "Fufu" 夫婦 (The husband and wife), in *Yan'an wenyi congshu*, 2:227.

66. Kong Jue 孔厥, "Yige nüren fanshen de gushi" 一個女人翻身的故事 (The story of a woman's turning over/transformation), in *Yan'an wenyi congshu*, 3:38–57.

67. Pan Zhiting 潘之汀, "Manzi fufu" 滿子夫婦 (The Manzi couple), in *Yan'an wenyi congshu*, 3:294, 296.

68. Gu Jin 古今, "Xin guiju" 新規矩 (The new rule), in *Yan'an wenyi congshu*, 3:446.

69. Gu, "Xin," 3:450.

70. Gu, "Xin," 3:452–53.

Epilogue: Shrews in the Great Leap Forward

For an earlier version of this chapter, see Shu Yang, "Shrews Rehabilitated in Women's Liberation? Li Shuangshuang, *Pola* Womanhood, and the Great Leap Forward Heroines," *Chinese Literature: Essays, Articles, Reviews* 41 (2019): 113–27.

1. For more on the implementation and impact of the Marriage Law of 1950, see Ono, *Chinese Women*, 176–86; Neil J. Diamant, *Revolutionizing the Family: Politics, Love, and Divorce in Urban and Rural China, 1949–1968* (Berkeley: University of California Press, 2000); Hershatter, *Women and China's Revolutions*, 221–26.

2. "Zhongguo funü yundong dangqian renwu de jueyi" 中國婦女運動當前任務的決議 (Resolution of current tasks of the Chinese women's movement), passed in the first Chinese women's all-China representative meeting (*Zhongguo funü diyici quanguo daibiao dahui* 中國婦女第一次全國代表大會) in April 1949, *Xin minzhu funü yuekan*, no. 1 (1949): 25–26.

3. Tina Mai Chen, "Female Icons, Feminist Iconography? Socialist Rhetoric and Women's Agency in 1950s China," *Gender & History* 15, no. 2 (2003): 268–95, see 271. For a case study on producing the women models, see Gail Hershatter, "Getting a Life: The Production of 1950s Women Labor Models in Rural Shaanxi," in *Beyond Exemplar Tales: Women's Biography in Chinese History*, ed. Joan Judge and Hu Ying (Berkeley: University of California Press, 2011), 36–51. For a study on the socialist molding of representations of female tractor drivers, see Daisy Yan Du, "Socialist Modernity in the Wasteland: Changing Representations of the Female Tractor Driver in China, 1949–1964," *Modern Chinese Literature and Culture* 29, no. 1 (2017): 55–94.

4. For earlier scholarship on this maxim, see Otto Braun, *A Comintern Agent in China, 1932–1939* (Stanford: Stanford University Press, 1982), 54–55; Chang Kuo-t'ao, *The Rise of the Chinese Communist Party: 1928–1938* (Lawrence: University Press of Kansas, 1972), 378; Harrison E. Salisbury, *The Long March: The Untold Story* (New York: McGraw-Hill, 1985), 83. For writings on the relation between food, taste, and revolution, see Hanchao Lu, "The Tastes of Chairman Mao: The Quotidian as Statecraft in the Great Leap Forward and Its Aftermath," *Modern China* 41, no. 5 (2015): 539–72; Andrew Leonard, "Why Revolutionaries Love Spicy Food," *Nautilus*, April 6, 2016, last accessed April 15, 2022, http://nautil.us/issue/35/boundaries/why-revolutionaries-love-spicy-food.

5. Wang Wenshi 王汶石, *Hei Feng* 黑鳳 (Hei Feng) (Beijing: Zhongguo qingnian chubanshe, 1963), 11.

6. Wang Wenshi, "Xin jieshi de huoban" 新結識的夥伴 (The newly made friends), *Renmin wenxue*, no. 12 (1958): 19, 22.

7. Wang, "Xin jieshi," 19; Duan Quanfa 段荃法, "Xueying xuechui" 雪英學炊 (Xueying learns to cook), in *Xueying xuechui* (Beijing: Zuojia chubanshe, 1959), 58.

8. According to the interviews conducted by Richard King, Li Zhun "believed that the story was reprinted over 400 times in numerous editions and read by 300 million people." See Richard King, ed., *Heroes of China's Great Leap Forward: Two Stories* (Honolulu: University of Hawai'i Press, 2010), 8.

9. Li Zhun 李準, "Li Shuangshuang xiaozhuan" 李雙雙小傳 (A brief biography of Li Shuangshuang), *Renmin wenxue*, no. 3 (1960): 12, 13.

10. Scholarly discussions have centered on the variations across the three media forms of fiction, film, and comics instead of the changes between the two fiction texts. For comparisons of adaptations across media, see Richard King, *Milestones on a Golden Road: Writing for Chinese Socialism, 1945–80* (Vancouver: UBC Press, 2013), 79–80, 85–90; King, *Heroes*, 8; Krista Van Fleit Hang, *Literature the People Love: Reading Chinese Texts from the Early Maoist Period (1949–1966)* (New York: Palgrave Macmillan, 2013), 58–69. For a brief comparison of the two written stories of 1959 and 1960, see King, *Milestones*, 79–80.

11. Li, "Li Shuangshuang," 12. For the 1959 version, see Li Zhun, "Li Shuangshuang xiaozhuan," in *Li Shuangshuang xiaozhuan* 李雙雙小傳 (A brief biography of Li Shuangshuang) (Beijing: Renmin wenxue chubanshe, 1977), 333.

12. Li, "Li Shuangshuang," 14. For the translation (with slight modification), see Li Zhun, "A Brief Biography of Li Shuangshuang," trans. Richard King, in King, *Heroes*, 24.

13. Li, "Li Shuangshuang," 14. For the translation, see Li, "A Brief Biography," 25.

14. King, *Milestones*, 87.

15. According to Richard King, Shuangshuang's laughing can be linked to the transgressive laughter of at least two traditional female characters: Li Cuilian and Yingning. See King, *Milestones*, 82–84. On reading women's unruly laughter, also see Kathleen Rowe, *The Unruly Woman: Gender and the Genres of Laughter* (Austin: University of Texas Press, 1995).

16. Li, "Li Shuangshuang," 23. Xiwang starts to address his wife by her name, instead of using terms including "the one in my home" (*an nage wuli ren* 俺那個屋裡人), "Little Chrysanthemum's mother" (*an Xiaoju ta ma* 俺小菊她媽), or "the one that cooks for me" (*an zuofan de* 俺做飯的). The change of language indicates that Xiwang comes to embrace Shuangshuang's independence and public identity.

17. Li, "Li Shuangshuang," 27. For the translation, see Li, "A Brief Biography," 61.

18. For details of the author's encounter with the village woman, see King, *Heroes*, 7, and *Milestones*, 81–82.

19. Li Zhun, "Wo xi'ai nongcun xinren" 我喜愛農村新人 (I love the new people in the countryside), and "Xiang xin renwu jingshen shijie xuexi tansuo" 向新人物精神世界學習探索 (Learning from and exploring the spiritual world of the new people), in *Li Shuangshuang—Cong xiaoshuo dao dianying* 李雙雙—從小說到電影 (Li Shuangshuang: From fiction to film) (Beijing: Zhongguo dianying chubanshe, 1963), 202, 214.

20. Li, "Xiang," 214.

21. Li Cuilian, the defiant daughter and wife originally appearing in a Tang dynasty transformation text (*bianwen* 變文), is satirized in *Kuaizui Li Cuilian ji* for her unwomanly qualities, including garrulity, irascibility, and violence. For the plot and a brief analysis of the Li Cuilian story, see Wu, *The Chinese Virago*, 166–69. For a translation of the story, see H. C. Chang, "The Shrew," in *Chinese Literature: Popular Fiction and Drama* (Edinburgh: Edinburgh University Press, 1973), 32-55. Yingning, the giggling heroine in the eighteenth-century *Liaozhai*, though delightful for her childlike, mirthful, and filial nature, is a fox-spirit considered "a threat to male dominance." See King, *Milestones*, 84. Aigu in Lu Xun's "Divorce" is controversial for her simultaneous attacks on and submission to social and gender norms.

22. King, *Heroes*, 8. According to King, Li Zhun first admitted that he was inspired by Li Cuilian in a 1993 interview. Given that Li had clearly mentioned these sources in the essay I have cited from the 1963 collection, King either is unaware of that essay or is referring to some undefined events during the 1960s that might have silenced Li, making him unable to admit to the seemingly unlikely sources for decades.

23. Li Xiujian 李修建, "Gongheguo qianqi dianying zhong de nüxing xingxiang" 共和國前期電影中的女性形象 (Female images in early PRC cinema), *Changsha ligong daxue xuebao (sheke ban)* 23, no. 1 (2008): 43–48.

24. Chen Sihe 陳思和, *Zhongguo dangdai wenxueshi jiaocheng* 中國當代文學史教程 (A course in contemporary Chinese literary history) (Shanghai: Fudan

daxue chubanshe, 2004), 49–50. Chen's idea is also acknowledged in Hang, *Literature the People Love*, 67, 71–72; and King, *Milestones*, 49, 90.

25. Lu Ren 魯韌, "Li Shuangshuang de daoyan fenxi he gousi" 《李雙雙》的導演分析和構思 (On directing and constructing the film Li Shuangshuang), in *Li Shuangshuang—Cong xiaoshuo dao dianying*, 222.

26. Xiaoning Lu, "Zhang Ruifang: Modelling the Socialist Red Star," in *Chinese Film Stars*, ed. Mary Farquhar and Yingjin Zhang (New York: Routledge, 2010), 103.

27. Zhang Ruifang 張瑞芳, "Banyan Li Shuangshuang de jidian tihui" 扮演李雙雙的幾點體會 (Some thoughts and feelings about my performance of Li Shuangshuang), in *Li Shuangshuang—Cong xiaoshuo dao dianying*, 264; "Li Shuangshuang gei women dailai le shenme?" 《李雙雙》給我們帶來了什麼？ (What does the film Li Shuangshuang bring to us?), published in *Renmin ribao*, November 29, 1962, in *Li Shuangshuang—Cong xiaoshuo dao dianying*, 412.

28. Zhang, "Banyan," 264.

29. Zhang, "Banyan," 233, 240, 248–49.

30. Zhang, "Banyan," 240, 242.

31. For more about the comic films produced in the interlude between the Great Leap Forward and the more intense movements in the late 1960s, see King, *Milestones*, 86; Krista Van Fleit Hang, "Zhong Xinghuo: Communist Film Worker," in Farquhar and Zhang, *Chinese Film Stars*, 109; Hang, *Literature the People Love*, 20–21, 63, 123.

32. Zhang, "Banyan," 245.

33. The quality of *pola* in Li Shuangshuang's characterization has caught the attention of very recent Chinese feminist scholarship and been viewed in a politically positive light. See Li Na 李娜, "Li Shuangshuang: Cong gengshen de tu li 'pola' chulai—Shitan 20 shiji wuliushi niandai 'xinxing funü' de yizhong shengchengshi" 李雙雙：從更深的土裡"潑辣"出來—試探20世紀五六十年代"新型婦女"的一種生成史 (Li Shuangshuang, boldly arising from deep roots: A historical investigation of the emergence of "new women" in the 1950s–1960s), *Funü yanjiu luncong*, no. 2 (2022): 33–56.

34. For a reading on how the trajectory of women's activism in the PRC intertwined with socialist state feminism, see Wang Zheng, *Finding Women in the State: A Socialist Feminist Revolution in the People's Republic of China, 1949–1964* (Oakland: University of California Press, 2017).

35. Sandy To, *China's Leftover Women: Late Marriage among Professional Women and Its Consequences* (Abingdon: Routledge, 2015), 51.

BIBLIOGRAPHY

A Ying 阿英. "Yibusheng de zuopin zai zhongguo" 易卜生的作品在中國 (Ibsen's works in China). In vol. 2 of *A Ying wenji* 阿英文集 (The works of A Ying), 667–72. Hong Kong: Sanlian shudian, 1979.

Adams, Jad. *Women and the Vote: A World History*. Oxford: Oxford University Press, 2014.

Aguiar, Sarah Appleton. *The Bitch Is Back: Wicked Women in Literature*. Carbondale: Southern Illinois University Press, 2001.

Bai Yan 白彥. "Dianxing de beiguo nüxing: Lan Ping" 典型的北國女性：藍蘋 (A typical northern woman: Lan Ping). *Da wanbao*, January 7, 1937.

Bailey, J. Paul. *Women and Gender in Twentieth-Century China*. New York: Palgrave Macmillan, 2012.

———. *Gender and Education in China: Gender Discourses and Women's Schooling in the Early Twentieth Century*. London: Routledge, 2007.

———. "'Women Behaving Badly': Crime, Transgressive Behaviour and Gender in Early Twentieth Century China." *Nan Nü: Men, Women, and Gender in China* 8, no. 1 (2006): 156–97.

Bao Tianxiao 包天笑. *Chuanying lou huiyilu* 釧影樓回憶錄 (Chuan-ying studio memoirs). Hong Kong: Dahua chubanshe, 1971.

Barlow, Tani E. *The Question of Women in Chinese Feminism*. Durham: Duke University Press, 2004.

———, ed. *Gender Politics in Modern China: Writing and Feminism*. Durham: Duke University Press, 1993.

Baumgart, Hildegard. *Jealousy: Experiences and Solutions*. Translated by Manfred and Evelyn Jacobson. Chicago: University of Chicago Press, 1990.

Bei An 悲菴. "Shen Peizhen da nao Xingchunju ji" 沈佩貞大鬧醒春居記 (Shen Peizhen causes a ruckus at Xingchun restaurant). *Shenzhou ribao*, June 1–2, 1915.

Belden, Jack. *China Shakes the World*. New York: Harper and Brothers, 1949.

"Ben an zhi jieshu" 本案之結束 (The end of the case). In Fan, *Shen Peizhen*, 1–14.

Benedict, Carol. *Golden-Silk Smoke: A History of Tobacco in China, 1550–2010*. Berkeley: University of California Press, 2011.

Braester, Yomi. *Witness against History: Literature, Film, and Public Discourse in Twentieth-Century China*. Stanford: Stanford University Press, 2003.

Braun, Otto. *A Comintern Agent in China, 1932–1939*. Stanford: Stanford University Press, 1982.

Buxiao sheng 不肖生. *Liudong waishi* 留東外史 (An unofficial history of studying in Japan). Beijing: Zhongguo huaqiao chubanshe, 1997.

Cai Chang 蔡暢. "Yingjie funü gongzuo de xin fangxiang" 迎接婦女工作的新方向 (Welcoming the new direction of women's work). In *Quanguo, Zhongguo funü yundong lishi ziliao (1937–1945)*, 650–54.

Cai Yibai 蔡夷白. "Pa laopo" 怕老婆 (Wife-fearing). *Tie bao*, November 13, 1947.

Cao Guozhi 曹國智 et al. (anonymous). *Xin nüxing de dairenjiewu* 新女性的待人接物 (Manners of the new woman). Hong Kong: Funü zhishi shushe, 1941.

Cao, Tianyu, Xueping Zhong, Kebin Liao, and Ban Wang, eds. *Culture and Social Transformations: Theoretical Framework and Chinese Context*. Leiden: Brill, 2014.

Cao Xueqin 曹雪芹 and Gao E 高鶚. *Honglou meng (sanjia pingben)* 紅樓夢 (三家評本) (The three commentaries edition of Dream of the Red Chamber). 2 Vols. Shanghai: Shanghai guji chubanshe, 1988.

Carpenter, Edward/Jiabende 賈本德. "Lun Jidu" 論嫉妒 (Carpenter on jealousy). Translated by Cong Yu 從予. *Funü zhoubao*, June 7, 1925.

——. *The Intermediate Sex*. New York: M. Kennerley, 1921.

——. *Love's Coming of Age*. Chicago: Charles H. Kerr Publishing Company, 1902.

Carroll, Peter J. "'A Problem of Glands and Secretions': Female Criminality, Murder, and Sexuality in Republican China." In Chiang, *Sexuality in China*, 99–124.

Cass, Victoria. *Dangerous Women: Warriors, Grannies, and Geishas of the Ming*. Lanham, MD: Rowman & Littlefield, 1999.

Cassandra. "Men Are So Wonderful!" *The China Critic* 5, no. 49 (1932): 1304–5.

Chan, Ching-kiu Stephen. "The Language of Despair: Ideological Representations of the 'New Woman' by May Fourth Writers." In Barlow, *Gender Politics in Modern China*, 13–32.

Chan, Roy Bing. *The Edge of Knowing: Dreams, History, and Realism in Modern Chinese Literature*. Seattle: University of Washington Press, 2017.

Chang, H. C., trans. "The Shrew." In *Chinese Literature: Popular Fiction and Drama*, 32–55. Edinburgh: Edinburgh University Press, 1973.

Chang, Kuo-t'ao. *The Rise of the Chinese Communist Party: 1928–1938*. Lawrence: University Press of Kansas, 1972.

Chen Bainian 陳百年. "Da Zhang Zhou er xiansheng lun yifuduoqi" 答章周二先生論一夫多妻 (Answering Mr. Zhang and Mr. Zhou about polygamy). In Zhang Xichen, *Xin xingdaode taolunji*, 55–66.

——. "Yifuduoqi de xin hufu" 一夫多妻的新護符 (The new amulet for polygamy). In Zhang Xichen, *Xin xingdaode taolunji*, 35–40.

Chen, Jianhua. "An Archaeology of Repressed Popularity: Zhou Shoujuan, Mao Dun, and Their 1920s Literary Polemics." In Rojas and Chow, *Rethinking Chinese Popular Culture*, 91–114.

Chen Sihe 陳思和. *Zhongguo dangdai wenxueshi jiaocheng* 中國當代文學史教程 (A course in contemporary Chinese literary history). Shanghai: Fudan daxue chubanshe, 2004.

Chen, Tina Mai. "Female Icons, Feminist Iconography? Socialist Rhetoric and Women's Agency in 1950s China." *Gender & History* 15, no. 2 (2003): 268–95.

Chen, Xiaomei. *Occidentalism: A Theory of Counter-Discourse in Post-Mao China*. New York: Oxford University Press, 1995.

Chen Xinyao 陳欣瑤. "Chongdu 'Li Shuangshuang'—Lishi yujing zhong de 'nongcun xin nüxing' jiqi zhuti xushu" 重讀"李雙雙"—歷史語境中的"農村新女性"及其主體敘述 (Rereading "Li Shuangshuang": The "rural new woman" in the historical context and her subjective narration). *Zhongguo xiandai wenxue yanjiu congkan*, no. 1 (2014): 113–16.

Chen Yuan 陳遠. *Zheng shuo Li Zongwu: Xiandai sixiangshi shang de houhei jiaozhu* 正說李宗吾：現代思想史上的厚黑教主 (Li Zongwu in a positive light: The thick black founder in modern intellectual history). Taipei: Xiuwei zixun keji gufen youxian gongsi, 2009.

Chen Zhengyuan 陳姃湲. "Jianjie jindai Yazhou de 'xianqi liangmu' sixiang—Cong huigu Riben, Hanguo, Zhongguo de yanjiu chengguo tanqi" 簡介近代亞洲的"賢妻良母"思想—從回顧日本、韓國、中國的研究成果談起 (A brief introduction to the idea of "good wives and wise mothers" in modern Asia: Research findings from Japan, South Korea, and China). *Jindai zhongguo funüshi yanjiu*, no. 10 (2002): 199–219.

Cheng, Hsiao-wen. *Divine, Demonic, and Disordered: Women without Men in Song Dynasty China*. Seattle: University of Washington Press, 2021.

Cheng Zhanlu 程瞻廬. "Danqiu huazuo nü'er shen" 但求化作女兒身 (I wish to transform myself into a woman). In *Zhanlu xiaoshuoji* 瞻廬小說集 (Collection of Cheng Zhanlu), 47–56. Shanghai: Shijie shuju, 1924.

Chiang, Howard, ed. *Sexuality in China: Histories of Power and Pleasure*. Seattle: University of Washington Press, 2018.

"China's Womankind at the Crossroad." *The China Critic* 5, no. 50 (1932): 1322–23.

Ching, Yau, ed. *As Normal as Possible: Negotiating Sexuality and Gender in Mainland China and Hong Kong*. Hong Kong: Hong Kong University Press, 2010.

——. "Porn Power: Sexual and Gender Politics in Li Han-hsiang's *Fengyue* Films." In Ching, *As Normal as Possible*, 113–31.

Chou Chih-p'ing 周質平, ed. *A Collection of Hu Shih's English Writings* 胡適英文文存. Taipei: Yuanliu chuban gongsi, 1995.

Chow, Rey. *Woman and Chinese Modernity: The Politics of Reading between West and East*. Minneapolis: University of Minnesota Press, 1991.

Cong, Xiaoping. *Marriage, Law, and Gender in Revolutionary China, 1940–1960*. Cambridge: Cambridge University Press, 2016.

Constable, Nicole. *Maid to Order in Hong Kong: Stories of Migrant Workers*. Ithaca: Cornell University Press, 2007.

Croissant, Doris, Catherine Vance Yeh, and Joshua S. Mostow, eds. *Performing "Nation": Gender Politics in Literature, Theater, and the Visual Arts of China and Japan, 1880–1940*. Leiden: Brill, 2008.

Croll, Elisabeth. *Feminism and Socialism in China*. London: Routledge & Kegan Paul, 1978.

Da Jue 大覺. "Du de" 妒德 (The virtue of jealousy). *Minguo ribao*, April 21–22, 1919.

Da Yin 大引. "Pan Jinlian zou le hongyun" 潘金蓮走了紅運 (Pan Jinlian got lucky). *Xi hai*, no. 1 (1937): 25.

Dan Fu 丹斧. "Ni Shen Peizhen da Liangsan xiezui shu" 擬沈佩貞答良三謝罪書 (Shen Peizhen's reply to Liangsan's apology letter). In Fan, *Shen Peizhen*, 60.

———. "Nu ci yuan" 怒雌緣 (The fate of the angry females). In Fan, *Shen Peizhen*, 45–58.

David, Mirela. "Bertrand Russell and Ellen Key in China: Individualism, Free Love, and Eugenics in the May Fourth Era." In Chiang, *Sexuality in China*, 76–98.

Diamant, Neil J. *Revolutionizing the Family: Politics, Love, and Divorce in Urban and Rural China, 1949–1968*. Berkeley: University of California Press, 2000.

Ding, Naifei. *Obscene Things: Sexual Politics in Jin Ping Mei*. Durham: Duke University Press, 2002.

Dong, Madeleine Yue. "Unofficial History and Gender Boundary Crossing in the Early Republic: Shen Peizhen and Xiaofengxian." In Goodman and Larson, *Gender in Motion*, 169–87.

Dongfang Didong 東方蝃蝀. "Taitai Wansui de taitai" 《太太萬歲》的太太 (The wife in Long Live the Missus). *Dagong bao (Da gongyuan)*, December 13, 1947.

Dooling, Amy D. *Women's Literary Feminism in Twentieth-Century China*. New York: Palgrave Macmillan, 2005.

———, ed. *Writing Women in Modern China: The Revolutionary Years, 1936–1976*. New York: Columbia University Press, 2005.

Du, Daisy Yan. "Socialist Modernity in the Wasteland: Changing Representations of the Female Tractor Driver in China, 1949–1964." *Modern Chinese Literature and Culture* 29, no. 1 (2017): 55–94.

Duan Quanfa 段荃法. "Xueying xuechui" 雪英學炊 (Xueying learns to cook). In *Xueying xuechui*, 47–60. Beijing: Zuojia chubanshe, 1959.

Duan Zongshe 段宗社. "'Zijian Nanzi': Lishi gong'an yu xiandai xiangxiang" "子見南子": 歷史公案與現代想象 (Confucius Saw Nanzi: Historical facts and modern imagination). *Qilu xuekan*, no. 226 (2012): 134–38.

Eberstein, Bernd, ed. *A Selective Guide to Chinese Literature, 1900–1949*. Vol. 4. *The Drama*. Leiden: E. J. Brill, 1990.

Edwards, Louise. *Women Warriors and Wartime Spies of China*. Cambridge: Cambridge University Press, 2016.

———. *Gender, Politics, and Democracy: Women's Suffrage in China*. Stanford: Stanford University Press, 2008.

———. "Opposition to Women's Suffrage in China: Confronting Modernity in Governance." In Leutner and Spakowski, *Women in China*, 107–28.

———. "Tang Qunying." In Lee, *Biographical Dictionary of Chinese Women*, 505.

———. "Representations of Women and Social Power in Eighteenth Century China: The Case of Wang Xifeng." *Late Imperial China* 14, no. 1 (1993): 34–59.

Egan, Susan Chan, and Chih-p'ing Chou. *A Pragmatist and His Free Spirit: The Half-Century Romance of Hu Shi and Edith Clifford Williams*. Hong Kong: Chinese University Press, 2009.

Eide, Elizabeth. *China's Ibsen: From Ibsen to Ibsenism*. London: Curzon Press, 1987.

Ellis, Havelock/Ailisi 藹理斯. "Jidu lun" 嫉妒論 (Ellis on jealousy). Translated by Yan Shi 晏始. *Funü zhoubao*, February 22, 1925.

———. *Studies in the Psychology of Sex*. Vol. 6. Philadelphia: F. A. Davis Company, 1911.

Englert, Siegfried, and Roderich Ptak. "Nan-Tzu, or Why Heaven Did Not Crush Confucius." *Journal of the American Oriental Society* 106, no. 4 (1986): 679–86.

Epstein, Maram. "Turning the Authorial Table: Women Writing Wanton Women, Shame, and Jealousy in Two Qing *Tanci*." In Stevenson and Wu, *Wanton Women in Late-Imperial Chinese Literature*, 157–83.

———. *Competing Discourses: Orthodoxy, Authenticity, and Engendered Meanings in Late Imperial Chinese Fiction*. Cambridge: Harvard University Press, 2001.

———. "The Beauty Is the Beast: The Dual Face of Woman in Four Ch'ing Novels." PhD diss., Princeton University, 1992.

Fan Boqun 范伯群 and Zeng Huapeng 曾華鵬. "Jiang Guangchi lun" 蔣光赤論 (On Jiang Guangchi). In Fang, *Jiang Guangci yanjiu ziliao*, 309–28.

Fan Lang 飯郎, ed. *Shen Peizhen* 沈佩貞 (Shen Peizhen). Beijing: Xinhua shushe, 1915.

Fan Xianggu 范香谷. "Jidu shi e'de ma?" 嫉妒是惡德嗎 (Is jealousy a vice?). *Xin nüxing* 1, no. 6 (1926): 82–83.

Fang Cheng 方澄. "Suowei 'fushi de beiai'—Taitai Wansui guanhou" 所謂"浮世的悲哀"—《太太萬歲》觀後 (The so-called "sadness of the floating world": After watching Long Live the Missus). *Dagong bao* (*Da gongyuan*), December 14, 1947.

Fang Ming 方銘, ed. *Jiang Guangci yanjiu ziliao* 蔣光慈研究資料 (Research materials on Jiang Guangci). Beijing: Zhishi chanquan chubanshe, 2010.

Farquhar, Mary, and Yingjin Zhang, eds. *Chinese Film Stars*. New York: Routledge, 2010.

Fen Gong 芬公. "Ouyang Yuqian zhi Pan Jinlian" 歐陽予倩之潘金蓮 (Ouyang Yuqian's Pan Jinlian). *Jin'gang zuan*, November 9, 1928.

Feng Fei 馮飛. *Nüxing lun* 女性論 (Discussions on women). Shanghai: Zhonghua shuju, 1919.

Feng, Jin. *The New Woman in Early Twentieth-Century Chinese Fiction*. West Lafayette: Purdue University Press, 2004.

"First Suffragettes Seen in Greek Play: Aristophanes's Famous Comedy, 'Lysistrata,' Presented at Maxine Elliott's Theatre." *New York Times*, February 18, 1913.

FitzGerald, Carolyn. "Mandarin Ducks at the Battlefield: Ouyang Yuqian's Shifting Reconfigurations of Nora and Mulan." *Chinoperl* (Journal of Chinese oral and performing literature) 29, no. 1 (2010): 45–104.

Freud, Sigmund. *A General Introduction to Psychoanalysis*. New York: Pocket Books, 1953.

———. *Three Contributions to the Theory of Sex*. New York: Nervous and Mental Disease Publishing Company, 1920.

Gai 句. "Nannü pingquan jianzhang" 男女平權簡章 (Constitution for Equality between Men and Women). *Aiguo baihua bao*, September 17, 1913.

Gao Fang 高方. "Nanzi yu Zhongguo zaoqi nüxingzhuyi xingtai" 南子與中國 早期女性主義形態 (Nanzi and Chinese early feminism). *Journal of Harbin University* 35, no. 6 (2014): 41–44.

Gao Muzi 槁木子. "Nannü bu pingquan zhi biejie" 男女不平權之別解 (An alternative interpretation of gender inequality). *Shen bao*, November 8, 1912.

Gaw, Kenneth. *Superior Servants: The Legendary Cantonese Amahs of the Far East*. Singapore: Oxford University Press, 1991.

Ge, Zhaoguang. *What Is China? Territory, Ethnicity, Culture, and History*. Cambridge: Harvard University Press, 2018.

Gilmartin, Christina K. *Engendering the Chinese Revolution: Radical Women, Communist Politics, and Mass Movements in the 1920s*. Berkeley: University of California Press, 1995.

Glosser, Susan L. *Chinese Visions of Family and State, 1915–1953*. Berkeley: University of California Press, 2003.

Goldman, Merle, ed. *Modern Chinese Literature in the May Fourth Era*. Cambridge: Harvard University Press, 1977.

Goldstein, Joshua. *Drama Kings: Players and Publics in the Re-creation of Peking Opera, 1870–1937*. Berkeley: University of California Press, 2007.

Gong Wei 龔煒. "Yuan du" 原妒 (The source of jealousy). In vol. 2 of Gong Wei, *Chaolin bitan xubian* 巢林筆談續編 (Sequel to the occasional jottings of Chaolin), *Xuxiu Sikuquanshu* 續修四庫全書, no. 1177 (Siku quanshu continued), 374–75. Shanghai: Shanghai guji chubanshe, 2003.

Goodman, Bryna, and Wendy Larson, eds. *Gender in Motion: Divisions of Labor and Cultural Change in Late Imperial and Modern China*. Lanham, MD: Rowman & Littlefield, 2005.

Gu Jin 古今. "Xin guiju" 新規矩 (The new rule). In vol. 3 of *Yan'an wenyi congshu*, 437–53.

Gu Junzheng 顧均正. "Wu Zifang shi zenyang de yige ren" 吳自芳是怎樣的一個人 (What kind of person is Wu Zifang?). *Funü zhoubao*, January 5, 1925.

Gunn, Edward M. "Ouyang Yuqian--*Huijia yihou*." In Eberstein, *A Selective Guide*, 191–93.

———, ed. *Twentieth-Century Chinese Drama: An Anthology*. Bloomington: Indiana University Press, 1983.

———. Introduction to *Twentieth-Century Chinese Drama*, vii–xxiii.

Guo Moruo 郭沫若. *Sange panni de nüxing* 三個叛逆的女性 (Three rebellious women). Shanghai: Guanghua shuju, 1926.

"Guo Shen shuangfang shensu zhi ciling" 郭沈雙方申訴之詞令 (The appeals of both Guo and Shen). In Fan, *Shen Peizhen*, 32–35.

Hai Shi 海士. "Kanguo Nala yihou" 看過《娜拉》以後 (After watching Nora). *Min bao*, June 28, 1935.

Han, Xiaorong. *Chinese Discourses on the Peasant, 1900–1949*. Albany: State University of New York Press, 2005.

Hang, Krista Van Fleit. *Literature the People Love: Reading Chinese Texts from the Early Maoist Period (1949–1966)*. New York: Palgrave Macmillan, 2013.

———. "Zhong Xinghuo: Communist Film Worker." In Farquhar and Zhang, *Chinese Film Stars*, 108–18.

Harris, Kristine. "The New Woman: Image, Subject, and Dissent in 1930s Shanghai Film Culture." *Republican China* 20, no. 2 (1995): 55–79.

Harrison, Henrietta. *The Making of the Republican Citizen: Political Ceremonies and Symbols in China, 1911–1929.* New York: Oxford University Press, 2000.

Hawkes, David, and John Minford, trans. *The Story of the Stone.* 5 Vols. Harmondsworth: Penguin Books, 1973–1986.

He Guimei 賀桂梅. "'Yan'an daolu' zhong de xingbie wenti—Jieji yu xingbie yiti de lishi sikao" "延安道路"中的性別問題—階級與性別議題的歷史思考 (The sex of "Yan'an road": A historical thinking of class and sex). *Nankai xuebao,* no. 6 (2006): 16–22.

He, Qiliang. *Feminism, Women's Agency, and Communication in Early Twentieth-Century China: The Case of the Huang–Lu Elopement.* New York: Palgrave Macmillan, 2018.

He Youliang 何友良. *Zhongguo Suweiai quyu shehui biandongshi* 中國蘇維埃區域社會變動史 (History of social changes in the Chinese Soviet Areas). Beijing: Dangdai Zhongguo chubanshe, 1996.

Hegel, Robert E., and Katherine Carlitz, eds. *Writing and Law in Late Imperial China: Crime, Conflict, and Judgment.* Seattle: University of Washington Press, 2007.

Heng Gong 恆公. "Pa laopo neng cujin heping minzhu lun" 怕老婆能促進和平民主論 (The idea that wife-fearing can facilitate peace and democracy). *Xiangxuehai zhoubao* 1, no. 5 (1949): 2.

"Heri cai you guangming zhi lu, Nala wei yanju er shiye" 何日才有光明之路娜拉為演劇而失業 (When will there be a bright path? Nora lost her job for her acting). *Xinmin bao,* February 2, 1935.

Hershatter, Gail. *Women and China's Revolutions.* Lanham, MD: Rowman & Littlefield, 2019.

———. "Getting a Life: The Production of 1950s Women Labor Models in Rural Shaanxi." In Judge and Hu, *Beyond Exemplar Tales,* 36–51.

Hong Liangji 洪亮吉. *Beijiang shihua* 北江詩話 (Talks on poetry from the north window). Beijing: Renmin wenxue chubanshe, 1998.

Hong Liu 洪流. "Xiangzhang fufu" 鄉長夫婦 (The township head and his wife). In vol. 2 of *Yan'an wenyi congshu,* 26–31.

Hong Shen 洪深. "Shu wo buyuan lingshou zhefan shengqing—Yige zhangfu duiyu Taitai Wansui de huida" 恕我不願領受這番盛情—一個丈夫對於《太太萬歲》的回答 (Forgive me for not being willing to accept the great kindness: A husband's answer to Long Live the Missus). *Dagong bao* (*Xiju yu dianying*), January 7, 1948.

Hong Sheng 洪昇. *The Palace of Eternal Youth.* Translated by Yang Xianyi and Gladys Yang. Beijing: Foreign Languages Press, 2010.

Honig, Emily. *Sisters and Strangers: Women in the Shanghai Cotton Mills, 1919–1949.* Stanford: Stanford University Press, 1986.

Honma, Hisao 本間久雄. *Funü wenti shijiang* 婦女問題十講 (Ten lectures on the women's question). Translated by Zhang Xichen. Shanghai: Kaiming shudian, 1924.

Hsieh, Wen-ping 謝文炳, and Richard L. Jen 任玲遜, trans. "The Patriot." *T'ien Hsia Monthly* 3, no. 2 (1936): 168–86.

Hu Chi 虎癡. "Xinzhi koukuai" 心直口快 (Straight heart, fast mouth). *Shen bao*, September 3, 1912.

Hu Jiwen 胡基文. "Ji Ouyang Yuqian xiansheng liushi dashou qing" 記歐陽予倩先生六十大壽慶 (On the celebration of Mr. Ouyang Yuqian's sixtieth birthday). In Su, *Ouyang Yuqian yanjiu ziliao*, 78–81.

Hu Ke 胡珂. "Shu fen" 抒憤 (Expressing anger). *Shidai ribao* (*Xinsheng*), December 12, 1947.

Hu Ou 湖鷗. "Daoting tushuo: Ouyang Yuqian yu Pan Jinlian" 道聽途說：歐陽予倩與潘金蓮 (Hearsay: Ouyang Yuqian and Pan Jinlian). *Laoshi hua*, no. 38 (1934): 7.

"Hu Resting Well; To Be Hospitalized 2 Weeks." *China News*, February 26, 1961.

Hu Shi 胡適. "Hu Shi tan junei" 胡適談懼內 (Hu Shi talking about henpecking). In Li Ao, *Li Ao da quanji 18*, 20–22.

——. Preface to *Japanese Sense of Humor*, by Hollington K. Tong, iii–vii. In vol. 3 of Chou, *A Collection*, 1478–83.

——. *The Chinese Renaissance*. New York: Paragon Book Reprint Corp., 1963.

——. "Zhongguo zuizao taolun funü wenti de yibu shu—Jinghua yuan" 中國最早討論婦女問題的一部書—鏡花緣 (Flowers in the Mirror: The earliest Chinese book on the women's question). *Funü nianjian* 婦女年鑒 (An almanac of women) 2 (1925): 231–55.

——. "Meiguo de furen: Zai Beijing nüzi shifan xuexiao jiangyan" 美國的婦人：在北京女子師範學校講演 (Women in America: A speech at Beijing Women's Normal School). In vol. 4 of *Hu Shi wencun* 胡適文存 (Collection of Hu Shi's writings), 39–61. Shanghai: Yadong tushuguan, 1921.

——. *Zhongshen dashi* 終身大事 (The greatest event in life). *Xin qingnian* 6, no. 3 (1919): 70–78.

Hu Shi 胡適 and [Qin 秦] Yinren 蔭人. *Zhongshen dashi (Marriage)*. *Sizhong zhoukan*, nos. 58 and 71 (1929): 27–29, 35–41.

Hu Songping 胡頌平. *Hu Shizhi xiansheng nianpu changbian chugao* 胡適之先生年譜長編初稿 (A draft chronological biography of Mr. Hu Shi). Vols. 5, 7, 10. Taipei: Lianjing chuban gongsi, 1990.

——. *Hu Shizhi xiansheng wannian tanhualu* 胡適之先生晚年談話錄 (A record of conversations with Mr. Hu Shi in his later life). Taipei: Lianjing chuban shiye gongsi, 1984.

Hu, Ying. *Tales of Translation: Composing the New Woman in China, 1899–1918*. Stanford: Stanford University Press, 2000.

Huaji Sanlang 滑稽三郎. *Pa laopo riji* 怕老婆日記 (The diary of a henpecked husband). Hong Kong: Siti yinyeshe, 1920.

Huang, Martin W. *Negotiating Masculinities in Late Imperial China*. Honolulu: University of Hawai'i Press, 2006.

——. *Desire and Fictional Narrative in Late Imperial China*. Cambridge: Harvard University Press, 2001.

Hubbard, Joshua. "Queering the New Woman: Ideals of Modern Femininity in *The Ladies' Journal*, 1915–1931." *Nan Nü: Men, Women and Gender in China* 16, no. 2 (2014): 341–62.

Hung, Chang-Tai. "Female Symbols of Resistance in Chinese Wartime Spoken Drama." *Modern China* 15, no. 2 (1989): 149–77.

Hutcheon, Linda, and Michael Hutcheon. "'Here's Lookin' at You, Kid': The Empowering Gaze in 'Salome.'" *Profession* (1998): 11–22.

Ibsen, Henrik. *A Doll's House*. Translated by Kenneth McLeish. London: Nick Hern Books, 1994.

Ji Ping 寄萍. "Youmo dashi Lin Yutang fufu fangwen ji (xia)" 幽默大師林語堂夫婦訪問記 (下) (Interview of humor master Lin Yutang and his wife: Second half). *Shen bao*, February 22, 1936.

Jiang Guangci 蔣光慈. *Paoxiao le de tudi* 咆哮了的土地 (The roaring earth). In vol. 2 of *Jiang Guangci wenji* 蔣光慈文集 (Collection of Jiang Guangci's works), 155–421. Shanghai: Shanghai wenyi chubanshe, 1983.

Jiang Hongjiao 江紅蕉. "Miyue lüxing xiaoshi" 蜜月旅行笑史 (The laughable history of honeymoon travel). In *Hongjiao xiaoshuoji* 紅蕉小說集 (Collection of Jiang Hongjiao), 87–104. Shanghai: Shijie shuju, 1924.

Jiang, Jin. *Women Playing Men: Yue Opera and Social Change in Twentieth-Century Shanghai*. Seattle: University of Washington Press, 2009.

Jiang Yongzhen 江勇振. *Xingxing, yueliang, taiyang: Hu Shi de qinggan shijie* 星星·月亮·太陽：胡適的情感世界 (The stars, the moon, and the sun: The women in Hu Shi's life). Beijing: Xinxing chubanshe, 2012.

Jin 津. "Dangfu weixin" 蕩婦維新 (A wanton woman joins the reform). *Aiguo bao*, October 1, 1912.

Jin Tianhe 金天翮. *Nüjie zhong* 女界鐘 (The women's bell). Shanghai: Shanghai guji chubanshe, 2003.

"Jingshi nüsheng yanju fengchao" 京市女生演劇風潮 (The incident of female students performing in Nanjing). *Da wanbao*, February 18, 1935.

Judge, Joan. *The Precious Raft of History: The Past, the West, and the Woman Question in China*. Stanford: Stanford University Press, 2008.

Judge, Joan, and Hu Ying, eds. *Beyond Exemplar Tales: Women's Biography in Chinese History*. Berkeley: University of California Press, 2011.

"Juzhong daren zhi Shen Peizhen" 聚眾打人之沈佩貞 (Shen Peizhen who gathered a crowd to beat). In Fan, *Shen Peizhen*, 31–32.

King, Richard. *Milestones on a Golden Road: Writing for Chinese Socialism, 1945–80*. Vancouver: UBC Press, 2013.

———, ed. *Heroes of China's Great Leap Forward: Two Stories*. Honolulu: University of Hawai'i Press, 2010.

Kong Jue 孔厥. "Yige nüren fanshen de gushi" 一個女人翻身的故事 (The story of a woman's turning over/transformation). In vol. 3 of *Yan'an wenyi congshu*, 38–57.

Lan Ping 藍蘋/Jiang Qing 江青. "Cong Nala dao Da Leiyu" 從《娜拉》到《大雷雨》 (From Nora to The Big Storm). *Xin xueshi* 1, no. 5 (1937): 250-52.

———. "Yifeng gongkai xin" 一封公開信/"Wo weishenme he Tang Na fenshou" 我為什麼和唐納分手. *Lianhua huabao* 9, no. 4 (1937): 94-96. *Mingbao yuekan*, no. 166 (1979): 44–46. Translated by William A Wycoff as "Why I Have Parted from T'ang Na." *Chinese Studies in History* 14, no. 2 (1980–81): 83–91.

———. "Jiang Qing xiegei Tang Na de jueqingshu" 江青寫給唐納的絕情書. *Dao bao*, June 30–July 1, 1936. *Mingbao yuekan*, no. 166 (1979): 42–43. Translated by William A Wycoff as "Chiang Ch'ing's 'Farewell Letter' to T'ang Na." *Chinese Studies in History* 14, no. 2 (1980–81): 77–82.

"Lan Ping xiang chufengtou, yongde shi meiren ji" 藍蘋想出風頭，用的是美人計 (Lan Ping used the tactics of beauties for attracting attention). *Shidai bao*, June 15, 1937. In Ye, *Jiang Qing zhuan*, 131–33.

Lanling xiaoxiao sheng 蘭陵笑笑生. *Zhang Zhupo piping Jin Ping Mei* 張竹坡批評金瓶梅 (Zhang Zhupo annotating Plum in the Golden Vase). Reprint. Ji'nan: Qilu shushe, 1991.

Lao She 老舍. "Liutun de" 柳屯的 (A woman from the Liu village). In *Lao She mingzuo xinshang* 老舍名作欣賞 (Appreciations of Lao She's masterpieces), edited by Fan Jun 樊駿, 463–88. Beijing: Zhongguo heping chubanshe, 1995.

Lao Tan 老談. "Wenming . . . kaitong . . . haha" 文明…開通…哈哈 (Civilization . . . open-mindedness . . . ha ha). In Fan, *Shen Peizhen*, 41.

Lary, Diana. *The Chinese People at War: Human Suffering and Social Transformation, 1937–1945*. Cambridge: Cambridge University Press, 2010.

Laver, James. *Modesty in Dress: An Inquiry into the Fundamentals of Fashion*. Boston: Houghton Mifflin Company, 1969.

Lee, Haiyan. *Revolution of the Heart: A Genealogy of Love in China, 1900–1950*. Stanford: Stanford University Press, 2007.

Lee, Lily Xiao Hong. *Biographical Dictionary of Chinese Women: The Twentieth Century*. New York: M. E. Sharpe, 2003.

Leonard, Andrew. "Why Revolutionaries Love Spicy Food." *Nautilus*, April 6, 2016. Last accessed April 15, 2022, http://nautil.us/issue/35/boundaries/why-revolutionaries-love-spicy-food.

Leutner, Mechthild, and Nicola Spakowski, eds. *Women in China: The Republican Period in Historical Perspective*. Berlin: Lit Verlag, 2005.

Li Ao 李敖, ed. *Hu Shi yucui* 胡適語粹 (Cream of Hu Shi's words). Shanghai: Wenhui chubanshe, 2003.

——. *Li Ao da quanji 18: Hu Shi yu wo* 李敖大全集 18：胡適與我 (The great collection of Li Ao: Hu Shi and I, vol. 18). Beijing: Zhongguo youyi chuban gongsi, 1999.

Li Fei 李飛, Zhao Shaocheng 趙紹成, Tang Zili 唐自力, and Guo Ping 郭萍. "Lun Li Zongwu Pa laopo zhexue zhi lishi beijing" 論李宗吾《怕老婆哲學》之歷史背景 (Historical background of Li Zongwu's The Philosophy of Wife-Fearing). *Qiu shi*, no. 2 (2008): 99–101.

Li Jingye 李淨業. "Nüzi canzheng zhi taolun–Zhi Jiangnan Zhang Renlan tongzhi shu" 女子參政之討論–致江南張紉蘭同志書 (Discussions on women's suffrage–A letter to Zhang Renlan in Jiangnan). *Minli bao*, March 24, 1912.

Li, Li. "Female Bodies as Imaginary Signifiers in Chinese Revolutionary Literature." In Tao, Yang, Roberts, and Yang, *Chinese Revolution and Chinese Literature*, 93–118.

Li Na 李娜. "Li Shuangshuang: Cong gengshen de tu li 'pola' chulai–Shitan 20 shiji wuliushi niandai 'xinxing funü' de yizhong shengchengshi" 李雙雙：從更深的土裡"潑辣"出來–試探20世紀五六十年代"新型婦女"的一種生成史 (Li Shuangshuang, boldly arising from deep roots: A historical investigation of the emergence of "new women" in the 1950s–1960s). *Funü yanjiu luncong*, no. 2 (2022): 33–56.

Li San 立三. "Xinzhi koukuai" 心直口快 (Straight heart, fast mouth). *Shen bao*, October 18, 1912.

Li Shuangshuang—Cong xiaoshuo dao dianying 李雙雙—從小說到電影 (Li Shuangshuang: From fiction to film). Beijing: Zhongguo dianying chubanshe, 1963.

"Li Shuangshuang gei women dailai le shenme?" 《李雙雙》給我們帶來了什麼？ (What does the film Li Shuangshuang bring to us?). In *Li Shuangshuang—Cong xiaoshuo dao dianying*, 409-12.

Li, Wai-yee. *Women and National Trauma in Late Imperial Chinese Literature*. Cambridge: Harvard University Press, 2014.

Li Xiujian 李修建. "Gongheguo qianqi dianying zhong de nüxing xingxiang" 共和國前期電影中的女性形象 (Female images in early PRC cinema). *Changsha ligong daxue xuebao (sheke ban)* 23, no. 1 (2008): 43-48.

Li Yi 李一. "Nala yeyu juren zai jincheng juyuan yanchu" 《娜拉》業餘劇人在金城劇院演出 (The Amateur Drama Association performed Nora at the Golden City Theater). *Shishi xinbao*, June 28, 1935.

Li Youning 李又寧 and Zhang Yufa 張玉法, eds. *Jindai Zhongguo nüquan yundong shiliao (1842–1911)* 近代中國女權運動史料 (Source materials on the women's rights movement in modern China, 1842-1911). Taipei: Zhuanji wenxueshe, 1975.

Li, Yu-ning, ed. *Recollections of Mr. Hu Shi*. Vol. 2. New York: Outer Sky Press, 1997.

Li Zhun 李準. "A Brief Biography of Li Shuangshuang." In King, *Heroes of China's Great Leap Forward*, 15-61.

——. "Li Shuangshuang xiaozhuan." In *Li Shuangshuang xiaozhuan* 李雙雙小傳 (A brief biography of Li Shuangshuang), 332-66. Beijing: Renmin wenxue chubanshe, 1977.

——. "Wo xi'ai nongcun xinren" 我喜愛農村新人 (I love the new people in the countryside). In *Li Shuangshuang—Cong xiaoshuo dao dianying*, 198-206.

——. "Xiang xin renwu jingshen shijie xuexi tansuo" 向新人物精神世界學習探索 (Learning from and exploring the spiritual world of the new people). In *Li Shuangshuang—Cong xiaoshuo dao dianying*, 207-16.

——. "Li Shuangshuang xiaozhuan" 李雙雙小傳 (A brief biography of Li Shuangshuang). *Renmin wenxue*, no. 3 (1960): 11-27.

Li Zongwu 李宗吾. *Pa laopo de zhexue* 怕老婆的哲學 (The philosophy of wife-fearing). Chengdu: Chenzhong shuju, 1946.

Liang Bingkun 梁秉堃. *Shijia hutong 56 hao: Wo qinli de renyi wangshi* 史家胡同56號：我親歷的人藝往事 (No. 56 on the shijia hutong: Past events of the Beijing People's Art Theater that I experienced). Beijing: Jincheng chubanshe, 2010.

Liang Qichao 梁啟超. "Xinmin shuo: Lun guojia sixiang" 新民說：論國家思想 (On the new citizen: The idea of the nation). In vol. 2 of *Liang Qichao quanji* 梁啟超全集 (Complete works of Liang Qichao), 663-67. Beijing: Beijing chubanshe, 1999.

——. "Jinhualun gemingzhe Jie De zhi xueshuo" 進化論革命者頡德之學說 (The theory of Benjamin Kidd, revolutionizer of evolution). In vol. 2 of *Liang Qichao quanji* 2, 1026-29.

——. "Lun qiangquan" 論強權 (On power). In *Yinbing shi ziyou shu* 飲冰室自由書 (The ice-drinker's studio: The book on liberty), 44–51. Yangzhou: Jiangsu guangling guji keyinshe, 1990.

Liang Yan 梁彥. "Mo mai nü" 磨麥女 (The wheat-grinding girl). In vol. 2 of *Yan'an wenyi congshu*, 148–71.

Lin Shu 林紓. *Jinling qiu* 金陵秋 (The autumn in Nanjing). In vol. 5 of *Zhongguo jindai guben xiaoshuo jicheng* 中國近代孤本小說集成 (Collection of late imperial and modern Chinese fiction; only existing copy), 3905–66. Beijing: Dazhong wenyi chubanshe, 1999.

Lin Yutang 林語堂. "Hunjia yu nüzi zhiye" 婚嫁與女子職業 (Marriage and women's occupation). In *Lin Yutang ji* 林語堂集 (The works of Lin Yutang), 115–18. Guangzhou: Huacheng chubanshe, 2007.

——. "Guanyu 'Zijian Nanzi' de hua: Da Zhao Yuchuan xiansheng" 關於"子見南子"的話：答趙譽船先生 (About Confucius Saw Nanzi: Answering Mr. Zhao Yuchuan). In Lin Yutang, *Dahuang ji* 大荒集 (The great wilderness collection), 173–75. Taipei: Zhiwen chubanshe, 1966.

——. *Lady Wu: A True Story*. Melbourne: William Heinemann, 1957.

——. *The Vigil of a Nation*. New York: John Day Company, 1944.

——, trans. *Confucius Saw Nancy: A One-Act Tragicomedy*. In Lin Yutang, *Confucius Saw Nancy and Essays about Nothing*, 1–46. Shanghai: Commercial Press, 1936.

——. Preface to Lin, *Confucius Saw Nancy*, v–vi.

——. "Feminist Thought in Ancient China." *T'ien Hsia Monthly* 1, no. 2 (1935): 127–50.

——. *My Country and My People*. New York: John Day Company, 1935.

——. "Lin Yutang's Letter to Richard Walsh (November 18, 1934)." In Qian, *Lin Yutang and China's Search*, 178.

——. "An Open Letter to M. Dekobra: A Defense of the Chinese Girl." *The China Critic* 6, no. 51 (1933): 1237–38.

——. "Rang niang'er men gan yixia ba" 讓娘兒們幹一下吧 (Let women do it). *Shen bao*, August 18, 1933.

——. "Confucius as I Know Him." *The China Critic*, January 1, 1931.

——. *Zi jian Nanzi* 子見南子 (Confucius saw Nanzi). *Benliu* 1, no. 6 (1928): 921–53.

Link, E. Perry. *Mandarin Ducks and Butterflies: Popular Fiction in Early Twentieth-Century Chinese Cities*. Berkeley: University of California Press, 1981.

——. "Traditional-Style Popular Urban Fiction in the Teens and Twenties." In Goldman, *Modern Chinese Literature in the May Fourth Era*, 327–49.

Liu Baonan 劉寶楠. *Lunyu zhengyi* 論語正義 (Collected commentaries on the Analects). Beijing: Zhonghua shuju, 1990.

Liu Chengyu 劉成禺. *Shizaitang zayi* 世載堂雜憶 (Miscellaneous memories from the Shizai studio). In *Jindai Zhongguo shiliao congkan* 近代中國史料叢刊, no. 717 (Series of source material on the history of modern China). Taipei: Wenhai chubanshe, 1971.

Liu, JeeLoo. *Neo-Confucianism: Metaphysics, Mind, and Morality*. Hoboken, NJ: Wiley, 2018.

Liu, Lydia, Rebecca Karl, and Dorothy Ko, eds. *The Birth of Chinese Feminism: Essential Texts in Transnational Theory.* New York: Columbia University Press, 2013.

Liu Qing 柳青. "Xishi" 喜事 (The wedding). In vol. 2 of *Yan'an wenyi congshu*, 437–51.

Liu Tieleng 劉鐵冷. *Hedong shi* 河東獅 (The east-of-the-river lioness). Hong Kong: Siti yinyeshe, 1922.

———. *Junei miji* 懼內秘記 (Secret account of henpecking). Shanghai: Xiaoshuo congbaoshe, 1920.

Liu, Wenjia. "The *Tanci Feng Shuang Fei*: A Female Perspective on the Gender and Sexual Politics of Late-Qing China." PhD diss., University of Oregon, 2010.

Lowy, Dina. *The Japanese "New Woman": Images of Gender and Modernity.* New Brunswick: Rutgers University Press, 2007.

Lu, Fang. "Constructing and Reconstructing Images of Chinese Women in Lin Yutang's Translations, Adaptations and Rewritings." PhD diss., Simon Fraser University, 2008.

Lu, Hanchao. "The Tastes of Chairman Mao: The Quotidian as Statecraft in the Great Leap Forward and Its Aftermath." *Modern China* 41, no. 5 (2015): 539–72.

Lu Ren 魯韌. "Li Shuangshuang de daoyan fenxi he gousi" 《李雙雙》的導演分析和構思 (On directing and constructing the film Li Shuangshuang). In *Li Shuangshuang—Cong xiaoshuo dao dianying*, 217–32.

Lu, Xiaoning. "Zhang Ruifang: Modelling the Socialist Red Star." In Farquhar and Zhang, *Chinese Film Stars*, 97–107.

Lu Xun 魯迅/Yu Ming 虞明. "Niang'er men ye buxing" 娘兒們也不行 (Women couldn't do it either). *Shen bao*, August 21, 1933. In Lu Xun, *Jiwaiji shiyi bubian* 集外集拾遺補編 (A supplement to the collection of addenda, second collection), 357–59. Beijing: Renmin wenxue chubanshe, 2006.

———. "Guanyu Zijian Nanzi" 關於《子見南子》, no. 2 (About Confucius Saw Nanzi; document no. 2). In Lu, *Jiwaiji*, 314–34.

———. "Zai xiandai Zhongguo de Kong fuzi" 在現代中國的孔夫子 (Confucius in present-day China). In vol. 6 of *Lu Xun quanji* 魯迅全集 (The complete works of Lu Xun), 313–21. Beijing: Renmin wenxue chubanshe, 1981.

"Lun nüzi yaoqiu canzhengquan wenti" 論女子要求參政權問題 (On the issue of women's demand for suffrage). *Shen bao*, March 25, 1912.

"Lun she nüfan xiyi suo" 論設女犯習藝所 (On building vocational training centers for women criminals). *Shuntian shibao*, June 12–13, 1906. In Li and Zhang, *Jindai Zhongguo nüquan yundong shiliao*, 709–12.

Lunceford, Brett. *Naked Politics: Nudity, Political Action, and the Rhetoric of the Body.* Lanham, MD: Lexington Books, 2012.

Luo, Jialun. "Events Leading to Hu Shi's Becoming Chinese Ambassador to the United States." Translated by Sylvia Chia. *Chinese Studies in History* 42, no. 1 (2008): 61–67. In vol. 2 of Li Yu-ning, *Recollections of Mr. Hu Shi*, 85–94.

Lü Bo 綠波. "Shei shi fuxin zhe" 誰是負心者 (Who is the unfaithful one). *Funü zazhi* 16, no. 6 (1930): 58–61.

Lü Fangshang 呂芳上. "Kangzhan shiqi de nüquan lunbian" 抗戰時期的女權論辯 (Women's rights controversies in the Sino-Japanese conflict period). *Jindai zhongguo funüshi yanjiu* 2 (1994): 81–115.

Lü Wenhao 呂文浩. "'Funü huijia'–Pan Guangdan yizai tiaoqi lunzheng de guandian" "婦女回家"–潘光旦一再挑起論爭的觀點 ("Women returning to the home": An idea Pan Guangdan repeatedly brought up for debate). *Wenshi xuekan* 1 (2014): 177–91.

Ma, Yuxin. *Women Journalists and Feminism in China: 1898–1937*. Amherst, NY: Cambria Press, 2010.

——. "Male Feminism and Women's Subjectivities: Zhang Xichen, Chen Xuezhao, and The New Woman." *Twentieth-Century China* 29, no. 1 (2003): 1–37.

Ma, Zhao. *Runaway Wives, Urban Crimes, and Survival Tactics in Wartime Beijing, 1937–1949*. Cambridge: Harvard University Press, 2015.

Man Yan 曼衍. "Yunnihui shang zhi Pan Jinlian: Ouyang Yuqian zuijin jiezuo" 雲霓會上之潘金蓮：歐陽予倩最近傑作 (On Pan Jinlian: The recent masterpiece of Ouyang Yuqian). *Xinwen bao*, January 5, 1928.

Mang Han 莽漢. "Xiyong Shen Peizhen" 戲詠沈佩貞 (Parodying Shen Peizhen). In Fan, *Shen Peizhen*, 60–62.

Mao Dun 茅盾. "Chuangzuo shengya de kaishi–huiyilu (shi)" 創作生涯的開始–回憶錄（十） (The beginning of a career in writing: A memoir, no. 10). In vol. 1 of *Mao Dun zhuanji* 茅盾專集 (Critical anthology of Mao Dun), edited by Tang Jinhai 唐金海, Kong Haizhu 孔海珠, Zhou Chundong 周春東, and Li Yuzhen 李玉珍, 611–26. Fuzhou: Fujian renmin chubanshe, 1983.

——. "Lu" 路 (The road). In vol. 2 of *Mao Dun wenji* 茅盾文集 (Collected works of Mao Dun), 277–390. Hong Kong: Jindai tushu gongsi, 1966.

——. "Chuangzao" 創造 (Creation). *Dongfang zazhi* 25, no. 8 (1928): 99–114.

——. Shen Yanbing 沈雁冰. "Lihun yu daode wenti" 離婚與道德問題 (Divorce and the issue of morality). *Funü zazhi* 8, no. 4 (1922): 13–16.

Mao Zedong 毛澤東. "Xingguo Investigation." In vol. 3 of Schram and Hodes, *Mao's Road to Power*, 594–655.

——. "Xunwu Investigation." In vol. 3 of Schram and Hodes, *Mao's Road to Power*, 296–418.

——. "Xingguo diaocha" 興國調查 (Xingguo investigation). In *Mao Zedong nongcun diaocha wenji* 毛澤東農村調查文集 (Collected writings of Mao Zedong on rural investigations), 182–251. Beijing: Renmin chubanshe, 1982.

——. "Xunwu diaocha" 尋烏調查 (Xunwu investigation). In *Mao Zedong nongcun*, 41–181.

——. "Report on an Investigation of the Peasant Movement in Hunan." In vol. 1 of *Selected Works of Mao Tse-tung*, 23–59. Peking: Foreign Languages Press, 1965.

——. "Hunan nongmin yundong kaocha baogao" 湖南農民運動考察報告 (Report on an investigation of the peasant movement in Hunan). In vol. 1 of *Mao Zedong xuanji* 毛澤東選集 (Selected works of Mao Zedong), 13–46. Beijing: Renmin chubanshe, 1951.

McMahon, R. Keith. *Polygamy and Sublime Passion: Sexuality in China on the Verge of Modernity*. Honolulu: University of Hawai'i Press, 2010.

——. "Love Martyrs and Love Cheaters at the End of the Chinese Empire." In Croissant, Yeh, and Mostow, *Performing "Nation,"* 135–42.

——. *Misers, Shrews, and Polygamists: Sexuality and Male-Female Relations in Eighteenth-Century Chinese Fiction*. Durham: Duke University Press, 1995.

Mei 梅. "Women weishenme yao jiehun" 我們為什麼要結婚 (Why we marry). *Jiankang shenghuo* 1, no. 3 (1934): 115–16.

Mei Ping 梅平. "Liangge Pan Jinlian jianmian" 兩個潘金蓮見面 (Two Pan Jinlians met). *Chun se* 2, no. 11 (1936): 22.

Meijer, M. J. *Marriage Law and Policy in the Chinese People's Republic*. Hong Kong: Hong Kong University Press, 1971.

Meng Huan 夢幻. "Lun nüzi yaoqiu canzhengquan zhi guaixiang" 論女子要求參政權之怪象 (On the strange phenomenon of women demanding suffrage). *Dagong bao*, March 30, 1912.

Meng, Yue. *Shanghai and the Edges of Empires*. Minneapolis: University of Minnesota Press, 2005.

Meng, Yue 孟悅, and Dai Jinhua 戴錦華. *Fuchu lishi dibiao: Xiandai funü wenxue yanjiu* 浮出歷史地表：現代婦女文學研究 (Emerging on the horizon of history: Modern Chinese women's literature). Beijing: Zhongguo renmin daxue chubanshe, 2004.

Meng Zhaoyi 孟昭毅 and Wang Qing 王清. "Dangqian funü yundong zhong liangge xuyao zhuyi de shiji wenti (jielu)" 當前婦女運動中兩個需要注意的實際問題（節錄）(Two practical problems requiring attention in the current women's movement, an extract). In *Quanguo, Zhongguo funü yundong lishi ziliao (1937–1945)*, 521–30.

Menon, K. P. S. *Journey Round the World*. Bombay: Bharatiya vidya bhavan, 1966.

Merkel-Hess, Kate. "A New Woman and Her Warlord: Li Dequan, Feng Yuxiang, and the Politics of Intimacy in Twentieth-Century China." *Frontiers of History in China* 11, no. 3 (2016): 431–57.

Milburn, Olivia. "Gender, Sexuality, and Power in Early China: The Changing Biographies of Lord Ling of Wei and Lady Nanzi." *Nan Nü: Men, Women and Gender in China* 12 (2010): 1–29.

"Nala da zou hongyun" 娜拉大走鴻運 (Nora gets so lucky). *Shen bao*, June 21, 1935.

"'Nala' di yanyuan" "娜拉" 底演員 (The actors in Nora). *Shen bao*, June 21, 1935.

Ng, Kenny K. K. "The Screenwriter as Cultural Broker: Travels of Zhang Ailing's Comedy of Love." *Modern Chinese Literature and Culture* 20, no. 2 (2008): 131–84.

Nie Gannu 聶紺弩. "Tan Nala" 談《娜拉》(On Nora). In Nie Gannu, *She yu ta* 蛇與塔 (Snake and temple), 137–40. Beijing: Shenghuo dushu xinzhi sanlian shudian, 1999.

——. "Lun pa laopo" 論怕老婆 (On wife-fearing). *Yecao wencong*, no. 10 (1948): 34–40.

"Nü xuesheng zhi you: Shuo du" 女學生之友：說妒 (The girl student's friend: Jealousy). *Zhonghua yingwen zhoubao* 中華英文週報 (Chung Hwa English Weekly) 4, nos. 102 and 103 (1921): 788–89, 820–22.

"Nüquan pengzhang" 女權膨脹　(The expansion of women's rights). *Beijing nübao*, April 21, 1907.

"Nüshi da ma canyiyuan" 女士大罵參議員　(Ladies tongue-lashing the senators). *Aiguo bao*, December 11, 1912.

"Nüzi canzheng hui jishi" 女子參政會紀事 (A report on the women's suffrage meeting). *Minli bao*, September 27, 1912.

"Nüzi canzheng zhi zhang'ai" 女子參政之障礙 (Obstacles to women's suffrage) [illustration]. *Zhongguo ribao*, November 9, 1912.

"Nüzi da nao canyiyuan ji" 女子大鬧參議院記 (A report on the ruckus caused by the women at the senate). *Shengjing shibao*, March 31, 1912.

"Nüzi yaoqiu canzhengquan" 女子要求參政權　(Women ask for suffrage). *Minli bao*, March 23, 1912.

"Nüzi yi wuli yaoqiu canzhengquan" 女子以武力要求參政權 (Women ask for suffrage by force). *Shen bao*, March 24, 1912.

Ono, Kazuko. *Chinese Women in a Century of Revolution, 1850–1950*. Edited by Joshua A. Fogel. Stanford: Stanford University Press, 1978.

Ouyang Yuqian 歐陽予倩. "Pan Jinlian zixu" 《潘金蓮》自序 (Preface to Pan Jinlian). In Su, *Ouyang Yuqian yanjiu ziliao*, 118–19.

———. *Ouyang Yuqian xuanji* 歐陽予倩選集 (Selected works of Ouyang Yuqian). Beijing: Renmin wenxue chubanshe, 1959.

———. Preface to *Ouyang Yuqian xuanji*, 1–3.

———. *Zi wo yanxi yilai* 自我演戲以來 (Since I started acting). Beijing: Zhongguo xiju chubanshe, 1959.

———. *Huijia yihou* 回家以後　(After returning home). *Juben huikan* 劇本彙刊 (Selected works of drama), no. 2 (1928): 41–86.

———. *Pan Jinlian* 潘金蓮 (Pan Jinlian). *Xin yue* 1, no. 4 (1928): 53–90.

———. *Pofu* 潑婦 (The shrew). *Juben huikan*, no. 1 (1925): 1–26.

"Ouyang Yuqian fanchuan yuanzi Pan Jinlian" 歐陽予倩反串原子潘金蓮 (Ouyang Yuqian played Pan Jinlian as a performance of gender role reversal). *Shanghai texie*, no. 17 (1946): 10.

Ouyang Yuqian performing as Pan Jinlian [illustration]. *Tianjin shangbao huakan* 6, no. 37 (1932): 3.

"Pa laopo lun" 怕老婆論　(The idea of wife-fearing). *Yisiqi huabao* 19, no. 10 (1948): 9.

Paderni, Paola. "Between Constraints and Opportunities: Widows, Witches, and Shrews in Eighteenth-Century China." In Zurndorfer, *Chinese Women in the Imperial Past*, 258–85.

Pan Guangdan 潘光旦. *Yousheng yu kangzhan* 優生與抗戰　(Eugenics and the war of resistance). Vol. 5 of *Pan Guangdan wenji* 潘光旦文集 (Collected works of Pan Guangdan). Beijing: Beijing daxue chubanshe, 2000.

———. "Tao Liu dusha an de xinli beijing" 陶劉妒殺案的心理背景 (The psychological background of the Tao–Liu jealousy murder case) and "Tao Liu dusha an de shehui zeren" 陶劉妒殺案的社會責任 (The social responsibility of the Tao–Liu jealousy murder case). In *Pan Guangdan wenji* 潘光旦文集 (The works of Pan Guangdan), 436–38, 440–42. Beijing: Beijing daxue chubanshe, 1993.

Pan, Lynn. *When True Love Came to China*. Hong Kong: Hong Kong University Press, 2015.

Pan Zhiting 潘之汀. "Manzi fufu" 滿子夫婦 (The Manzi couple). In vol. 3 of *Yan'an wenyi congshu*, 292–97.

Peng Dehuai 彭德懷. "Guanyu huabei genjudi gongzuo de baogao" 關於華北根據地工作的報告 (A report of the work in the Base Areas of North China). In vol. 3 of *Gongfei huoguo shiliao huibian* 共匪禍國史料彙編 (Collection of historical source materials on the Communist bandits' scourge to the nation), 346–406. Taipei: Zhonghua minguo kaiguo wushinian wenxian bianzuan weiyuanhui, 1964.

Peng Xiaofeng 彭曉豐. "Mao Dun xiaoshuo zhong shidai nüxing xingxiang de yanhua jiqi gongneng fenxi" 茅盾小說中時代女性形象的衍化及其功能分析 (An analysis of the evolution and function of images of the new woman in Mao Dun's works). *Zhongguo xiandai wenxue yanjiu congkan*, no. 3 (1992): 213–20.

Piao Peng 飄蓬. "Cong Ouyang Yuqian shuodao Pan Jinlian" 從歐陽予倩說到《潘金蓮》 (From Ouyang Yuqian to the drama Pan Jinlian). *Xinmin bao*, April 15, 1936.

Ping Wu 平五. "Shen Peizhen wuda Guo Tong" 沈佩貞誤打郭同 (Shen Peizhen mistakenly hit Guo Tong). In Fan, *Shen Peizhen*, 13–16.

"Progress of Woman Suffrage." *New York Times*, September 24, 1909.

Pu Anxiu 浦安修. "Wunian lai huabei kangri minzhu genjudi funü yundong de chubu zongjie" 五年來華北抗日民主根據地婦女運動的初步總結 (A preliminary summary of the women's movement in the Anti-Japanese Democratic Base Areas of North China in the past five years). In *Quanguo, Zhongguo funü yundong lishi ziliao (1937–1945)*, 684–716.

Pu Songling 蒲松齡. *Baihua qianzhu Liaozhai zhiyi* 白話淺注聊齋誌異 (Liaozhai's Records of the Strange: Annotated in vernacular Chinese). Hong Kong: Shangwu yinshuguan, 1963.

Qi Lin 麒麟. "Ping Na'na zhi yanchu" 評娜那之演出 (Commenting on the performance of Nora). *Min bao*, June 29–30, 1935.

Qian, Jun. "Lin Yutang: Negotiating Modernity Between East and West." PhD diss., University of California, Berkeley, 1996.

Qian, Suoqiao. *Lin Yutang and China's Search for Modern Rebirth*. New York: Palgrave Macmillan, 2017.

Qiandu Liulang 前度劉郎 and Xu Guifang 徐桂芳, eds. *Xiang nang* 香囊 (Sachet). Hong Kong: Huaxin shuju, 1920–21.

Quanguo fulian fuyun shi 全國婦聯婦運室, ed. *Zhongguo funü yundong lishi ziliao* 中國婦女運動歷史資料 (Historical source materials of the Chinese women's movement). Beijing: Zhongguo funü chubanshe, 1991.

Raphals, Lisa. *Sharing the Light: Representations of Women and Virtue in Early China*. Albany: State University of New York Press, 1998.

Rea, Christopher. *The Age of Irreverence: A New History of Laughter in China*. Oakland: University of California Press, 2015.

Rojas, Carlos, and Eileen Cheng-yin Chow, eds. *Rethinking Chinese Popular Culture: Cannibalizations of the Canon*. London: Routledge, 2009.

Rosker, Jana. *Following His Own Path: Li Zehou and Contemporary Chinese Philosophy*. Albany: State University of New York Press, 2019.

Rowe, Kathleen. *The Unruly Woman: Gender and the Genres of Laughter*. Austin: University of Texas Press, 1995.

Roy, David Tod. *The Plum in the Golden Vase or, Chin P'ing Mei*. Vol. 5. Princeton: Princeton University Press, 2013.

Salisbury, Harrison E. *The Long March: The Untold Story*. New York: McGraw-Hill, 1985.

Sang, Tze-lan D. "Failed Modern Girls in Early-Twentieth-Century China." In Croissant, Yeh, and Mostow, *Performing "Nation,"* 179–202.

——. *The Emerging Lesbian: Female Same-Sex Desire in Modern China*. Chicago: University of Chicago Press, 2003.

Sankar, Andrea. "Spinster Sisterhoods: *Jing Yih Sifu*: Spinster-Domestic-Nun." In Sheridan and Salaff, *Lives*, 51–70.

Sasaki, Motoe. *Redemption and Revolution: American and Chinese New Women in the Early Twentieth Century*. Ithaca: Cornell University Press, 2016.

Schmidt, Delores Barracano. "The Great American Bitch." *College English* 32, no. 8 (1971): 900–5.

Schram, Stuart R., and Nancy J. Hodes, eds. *Mao's Road to Power: Revolutionary Writings, 1912–1949*. Vols. 1–4. Armonk: M. E. Sharpe, 1992–1997.

Selden, Mark. *China in Revolution: The Yenan Way Revisited*. Armonk: M. E. Sharpe, 1995.

——. *The Yenan Way in Revolutionary China*. Cambridge: Harvard University Press, 1971.

Sha Ting 沙汀. "Shou dao" 獸道 (The way of the beast). In *Sha Ting xuanji* 沙汀選集 (Selected works of Sha Ting), 114–24. Hong Kong: Wenxue chubanshe, 1957.

Sha Yi 沙易. "Ping Taitai Wansui" 評《太太萬歲》 (Commenting on Long Live the Missus). *Zhongyang ribao (Ju yi)*, December 19, 1947.

Shakespeare, William. *The Taming of the Shrew*. Edited by Elizabeth Schafer. Cambridge: Cambridge University Press, 2002.

Shapiro, Sidney, trans. *Outlaws of the Marsh*. Beijing: Foreign Languages Press, 1980.

She Zi 舍子. "Wuqi buyou" 無奇不有 (Nothing is too strange). *Shi bao*, March 23, 1912.

Shen, Jing. "Re-Visions of '*Shuihu*' Women in Chinese Theatre and Cinema." *China Review* 7, no. 1 (2007): 105–27.

"Shen Peizhen an zhi yiwen zhongzhong" 沈佩貞案之軼聞種種 (Anecdotes surrounding Shen Peizhen's case). *Qunqiang bao*, July 8, 1915.

"Shen Peizhen sapo zhi guaixiang" 沈佩貞撒潑之怪象 (Strange phenomena of Shen Peizhen acting like a shrew and making a scene). In Fan, *Shen Peizhen*, 16–19.

"Shen Peizhen zhi an zhong an" 沈佩貞之案中案 (Cases inside the case of Shen Peizhen). In Fan, *Shen Peizhen*, 35–39.

"Shen Peizhen zhi ge baoguan shu" 沈佩貞致各報館書 (Shen Peizhen's letter to the newspapers). In Fan, *Shen Peizhen*, 37–39.

Shen Weiwei 沈衛威. *Hu Shi zhouwei* 胡適周圍 (Hu Shi's surroundings). Beijing: Gongren chubanshe, 2003.

Shen Xie 莘薤. "Women bu qiqiu ye bu shishe lianjia de lianmin—Yige 'taitai' kan le Taitai Wansui" 我們不乞求也不施捨廉價的憐憫—一個"太太"看了《太太萬歲》 (We don't beg or give cheap mercies: After a "wife" watching Long Live the Missus). *Dagong bao* (*Xiju yu dianying*), January 7, 1948.

Shenjing bing 神經病. "Wuti" 無題 (No title). *Shi bao*, March 27, 1912.

Sheridan, Mary, and Janet W. Salaff, eds. *Lives: Chinese Working Women*. Bloomington: Indiana University Press, 1984.

Shi Nai'an 施耐庵 and Luo Guanzhong 羅貫中. *Shuihu quanzhuan* 水滸全傳 (The complete edition of Water Margin). Reprint. Changsha: Yuelu shushe, 1988.

Shi Zhixuan 石之軒. *Huanghua fu: Gongheguo qianye fengyunlu* 黃花賦：共和國前夜風雲錄 (Huanghua rhapsody: Record of the vicissitudes on the eve of the Republic). Beijing: Zhongguo wenlian chubanshe, 2006.

"Shiyi qingchang qiusi de yingxing Tang Na yujiu hou liuji hou jiayin" 失意情場求死的影星唐納遇救後留濟候佳音 (Failed at love, the movie star Tang Na was saved from suicide and waited in Ji'nan for good news). *Shi bao*, June 30, 1936.

"Sit in a Drizzle to See Greek Play: Courageous Suffragists in Outdoor Theatre Hear Aristophanes Plead Their Cause." *New York Times*, September 20, 1912.

Sohigian, Diran John. "Confucius and the Lady in Question: Power Politics, Cultural Production and the Performance of *Confucius Saw Nanzi* in China in 1929." *Twentieth-Century China* 36, no. 1 (2011): 23–43.

———. "The Life and Times of Lin Yutang." PhD diss., Columbia University, 1991.

Stevenson, Mark, and Wu Cuncun, eds. *Wanton Women in Late-Imperial Chinese Literature: Models, Genres, Subversions and Traditions*. Leiden: Brill, 2017.

Stockard, Janice E. *Daughters of the Canton Delta: Marriage Patterns and Economic Strategies in South China, 1860–1930*. Stanford: Stanford University Press, 1989.

Strand, David. *An Unfinished Republic: Leading by Word and Deed in Modern China*. Berkeley: University of California Press, 2011.

Strong, Anna Louise. *The Chinese Conquer China*. Garden City, NY: Doubleday & Company, 1949.

Su Ge 蘇戈. "Cong Nala shuodao Yibusheng de chuangzuo fangfa" 從《娜拉》說到易卜生的創作方法 (From Nora to the writing methods of Ibsen). *Min bao*, June 29, 1935.

Su Guanxin 蘇關鑫, ed. *Ouyang Yuqian yanjiu ziliao* 歐陽予倩研究資料 (Research materials on Ouyang Yuqian). Beijing: Zhishi chanquan chubanshe, 2009.

"Sun Zhongshan xiansheng ru jing hou zhi diyi dahui" 孫中山先生入京后之第一大會 (The first major meeting since Mr. Sun Zhongshan entered Beijing). *Minli bao*, August 31, 1912.

Swatek, Catherine. "P'an Chin-lien." In Gunn, *Twentieth-Century Chinese Drama*, 52–75.

Tam, Kwok-kan. *Chinese Ibsenism: Reinventions of Women, Class and Nation.* Springer Nature Singapore, 2019.

——. *Ibsen in China, 1908–1997: A Critical-Annotated Bibliography of Criticism, Translation and Performance.* Hong Kong: Chinese University Press, 2001.

Tang Degang 唐德剛. *Hu Shi zayi* 胡適雜憶 (Miscellaneous recollections of Hu Shi). Beijing: Huawen chubanshe, 1990.

"Tang Qunying yu Song Jiaoren" 唐群英與宋教仁 (Tang Qunying and Song Jiaoren). In *Tang Qunying shiliao jicui* 唐群英史料集萃 (Historical materials on Tang Qunying), edited by *Hengyang shi funü lianhehui* 衡陽市婦女聯合會, 78–81. Hengyang: Funü lianhehui, 2006.

Tang Shuming 唐叔明. "Huiyi Nanguo she" 回憶南國社 (Recall the Southern Society). In Tian, *Zhongguo huaju*, 139–46.

Tao, Chia-lin Pao 鮑家麟. "Women and Jealousy in Traditional China." In vol. 1 of *Zhongguo jinshi shehui wenhuashi lunwenji* 中國近世社會文化史論文集 (Papers on society and culture of early modern China), 531–61. Taipei: Institute of History and Philology, Academia Sinica, 1992.

Tao, Dongfeng, Yang Xiaobin, Rosemary Roberts, and Yang Ling, eds. *Chinese Revolution and Chinese Literature.* Newcastle upon Tyne: Cambridge Scholars Publishing, 2009.

Tao Hancui 陶寒翠. *Minguo yanshi yanyi* 民國豔史演義 (An unofficial erotic history of the Republic). Reprint. Hangzhou: Zhejiang guji chubanshe, 1990.

Terrill, Ross. *Madame Mao: The White-Boned Demon.* Stanford: Stanford University Press, 1999.

Theiss, Janet. "Explaining the Shrew: Narratives of Spousal Violence and the Critique of Masculinity in Eighteenth-Century Criminal Cases." In Hegel and Carlitz, *Writing and Law in Late Imperial China*, 44–63.

——. *Disgraceful Matters: The Politics of Chastity in Eighteenth-Century China.* Berkeley: University of California Press, 2004.

Tian Han 田漢. "Ta wei Zhongguo xiju yundong fendou le yisheng" 他為中國戲劇運動奮鬥了一生 (He struggled for the Chinese drama movement throughout his life). In Su, *Ouyang Yuqian yanjiu ziliao*, 99–115.

——, ed. *Zhongguo huaju yundong wushinian shiliaoji (diyi ji)* 中國話劇運動五十年史料集 (第一輯) (Historical materials on fifty years of the Chinese drama movement, vol. 1). Beijing: Zhongguo xiju chubanshe, 1958.

——. "Nanguo she shilüe" 南國社史略 (A brief history of the Southern Society). In *Zhongguo huaju*, 113–38.

Tian You 天游. "Du" 妒 (Jealousy). *Dongfang zazhi* 22, no. 13 (1925): 61–62.

To, Sandy. *China's Leftover Women: Late Marriage among Professional Women and Its Consequences.* Abingdon: Routledge, 2015.

Tu Yu 屠雨. "Tang Na, Lan Ping heli ji" 唐納、藍蘋合離記 (Separation and reunion between Tang Na and Lan Ping). *Xin bao*, July 1, 1936.

Vittinghoff, Natascha. "Jiang Qing and Nora: Drama and Politics in the Republican Period." In Leutner and Spakowski, *Women in China*, 208–41.

Wagner, Rudolf G., ed. *Joining the Global Public: Word, Image, and City in Early Chinese Newspapers, 1870–1910.* Albany: State University of New York Press, 2007.

Wan Xiang 晚香. "Shen Peizhen ye da Shenzhou guan" 沈佩貞夜打神州館 (Shen Peizhen attacked the office of the Shenzhou ribao at night). In Fan, *Shen Peizhen*, 20–26.

Wang, Dewei/David Der-Wei 王德威. *The Monster That Is History: History, Violence, and Fictional Writing in Twentieth-Century China*. Berkeley: University of California Press, 2004.

———. *Xiangxiang Zhongguo de fangfa: Lishi, xiaoshuo, xushi* 想像中國的方法：歷史，小說，敘事 (Ways to imagine China: History, fiction, and narration). Beijing: Shenghuo dushu xinzhi sanlian shudian, 1998.

———. "Pan Jinlian, Sai Jinhua, Yin Xueyan: Zhongguo xiaoshuo shijie zhong 'huoshui' zaoxing de yanbian" 潘金蓮、賽金花、尹雪豔：中國小說世界中"禍水"造型的演變 (Pan Jinlian, Sai Jinhua, Yin Xueyan: The transformation of "femme fatale" images in the world of Chinese fiction). In *Xiangxiang Zhongguo de fangfa*, 256–69.

———. *Fictional Realism in Twentieth-Century China: Mao Dun, Lao She, Shen Congwen*. New York: Columbia University Press, 1992.

Wang Dungen 王鈍根. "Yingxiong jia" 英雄頰 (The cheeks of the hero). *Shen bao*, September 3, 1912.

———. A Chinese suffragette kicking a policeman during a protest in Nanjing in 1912 [illustration]. *Shen bao*, March 30, 1912.

———. "Bo bo nüzi canzhengquan" 駁駁女子參政權 (Opposition to the opposition to women's suffrage). *Shen bao*, March 18, 1912.

Wang Jiajian 王家儉. "Minchu de nüzi canzheng yundong" 民初的女子參政運動 (Women's suffrage movement in the early Republic). *Lishi xuebao*, no. 11 (1983): 149–71.

Wang Jiting 汪集庭. "Ai yu du" 愛與妬 (Love and jealousy). *Funü zazhi* 5, no. 12 (1919): 3–4.

———. "Shishi nüzi yu shishi nüzi" 時式女子與時實女子 (The artificial new woman and the authentic new woman). *Funü zazhi* 3, no. 2 (1917): 16–17.

Wang Qisheng 王奇生. "Minguo chunian de nüxing fanzui (1914–1936)" 民國初年的女性犯罪 (Female crimes in early Republican China, 1914–1936). *Jindai Zhongguo funüshi yanjiu*, no. 1 (1993): 5–18.

Wang Rong 王戎. "Shi Zhongguo de you zenmeyang?—Taitai Wansui guanhou" 是中國的又怎麼樣？—《太太萬歲》觀後 (From China, then what? After watching Long Live the Missus). *Xin min bao* (*Xin yingju*), December 28, 1947.

Wang Wenshi 王汶石. *Hei Feng* 黑鳳 (Hei Feng). Beijing: Zhongguo qingnian chubanshe, 1963.

———. "Xin jieshi de huoban" 新結識的夥伴 (The newly made friends). *Renmin wenxue*, no. 12 (1958): 19–23.

Wang, Zheng. *Finding Women in the State: A Socialist Feminist Revolution in the People's Republic of China, 1949–1964*. Oakland: University of California Press, 2017.

———. *Women in the Chinese Enlightenment: Oral and Textual Histories*. Berkeley: University of California Press, 1999.

Wei Lanshi 韋蘭史. Preface to *Minguo yanshi yanyi*, by Tao Hancui, 11. Hangzhou: Zhejiang guji chubanshe, 1990.

Wei Ming 微明. "Lun jidu" 論嫉妒 (said to be translated from Radjabnia's "On Jealousy"). *Xin nüxing* 4, no. 12 (1929): 1529–30.

Wen Bi 問筆. "Pa laopo lun" 怕老婆論 (The idea of wife-fearing). *Yuzhou feng*, no. 14 (1936): 107–9.

Widmer, Ellen. "Review of *The Chinese Virago: A Literary Theme*," by Yenna Wu. *Chinese Literature: Essays, Articles, Reviews* 20 (1998): 185–88.

Witke, Roxane. *Comrade Chiang Ch'ing*. Boston: Little, Brown & Co., 1977.

Wu Moxi 吳墨西. "Ai de fangyu wu" 愛的防禦物 (The guard of love). *Funü zazhi* 16, no. 6 (1930): 57–58.

Wu San 武三. "Pan Jinlian" 潘金蓮 (Pan Jinlian). *Xi bao*, no. 22 (1937): 2.

Wu Sihong 吳似鴻. "Jiang Guangci huiyilu" 蔣光慈回憶錄 (The memoir of Jiang Guangci). In Fang, *Jiang Guangci yanjiu ziliao*, 89–131.

Wu Xiaoli 巫小黎. "'Zhanhou' Shanghai wentan: Yi Taitai Wansui de pipan wei ge'an" "戰後"上海文壇：以《太太萬歲》的批判為個案 (The "postwar" Shanghai literary scene: A case study of the criticisms of Long Live the Missus). *Xiandai zhongwen xuekan*, no. 5 (2013): 39–45.

Wu, Yenna. *The Chinese Virago: A Literary Theme*. Cambridge: Harvard University Press, 1995.

——. *The Lioness Roars: Shrew Stories from Late Imperial China*. Ithaca: East Asia Program, Cornell University, 1995.

——. "The Inversion of Marital Hierarchy: Shrewish Wives and Henpecked Husbands in Seventeenth-Century Chinese Literature." *Harvard Journal of Asiatic Studies* 48, no. 2 (1988): 363–82.

"Wuhan nüjie qutan lu" 武漢女界趣談錄 (Interesting anecdotes about women in Wuhan). *Shen bao*, October 14, 1912.

Xi Yinglu 息影廬. "Wen Shen nüshi yanshuo ganyan" 聞沈女士演說感言 (Thoughts upon hearing Lady Shen's speech). *Shen bao*, October 23, 1912.

——. "Xinzhi koukuai" 心直口快 (Straight heart, fast mouth). *Shen bao*, October 16, 1912.

Xi Zi 系子. "Yingxing wowen lu: Lan Ping" 影星我聞錄：藍蘋 (Movie stars I know: Lan Ping). *Qingchun dianying* 3, no. 7 (1937): unpaginated.

Xiang Peiliang 向培良. *Zhongguo xiju gaiping* 中國戲劇概評 (Brief comments on Chinese drama). Shanghai: Taidong tushuju, 1928.

"Xiangganbian suqu funü gongzuo jue'an" 湘贛邊蘇區婦女工作決案 (Resolution of women's work in the Hunan–Jiangxi Border Soviet Area). In *Quanguo, Zhongguo funü yundong lishi ziliao (1927–1937)*, 157–60.

"Xianping er (Nanjing)" 閒評二 (南京) (Random comments, no. 2, from Nanjing). *Dagong bao*, March 30, 1912.

Xiao 笑. "Xin Honglou meng" 新紅樓夢 (The new Dream of the Red Chamber). *Shi bao*, August 29, 1912.

Xie, Bingying. *A Woman Soldier's Own Story: The Autobiography of Xie Bingying*. Translated by Lily Chia Brissman and Barry Brissman. New York: Columbia University Press, 2001.

——. Hsieh, Pingying. *Girl Rebel: The Autobiography of Hsieh Pingying*. Translated by Adet Lin and Anor Lin. Reprint. New York: Da Capo Press, 1975.

Xie Shengwei 諧聖韋. "Xini nüjie zizhihui jianzhang yuanqi" 戲擬女界自治會簡章緣起 (Bantering on the origin of the "brief program for the Women's Autonomous Association"). *Rizhi bao*, November 28, 1913.

Xie Yuanding 謝遠定. "Duiyu qingnian funü de zhengyan" 對於青年婦女的諍言 (Admonitions to young women). *Funü zazhi* 11, no. 4 (1925): 624–27.

Xu Ceng 徐曾. "Zhang Ailing he ta de Taitai Wansui" 張愛玲和她的《太太萬歲》 (Zhang Ailing and her Long Live the Missus). *Xin min bao* (*Ye huayuan*), December 15, 1947.

Xu Gongmei 徐公美. "Yanle Pofu yihou" 演了潑婦以後 (After acting in The Shrew). In *Xiju duanlun* 戲劇短論 (Essays on drama), 37–40. Shanghai: Daguang shuju, 1936.

Xu Huiqi 許慧琦. "1920 niandai de lian'ai yu xin xingdaode lunshu—Cong Zhang Xichen canyu de sanci lunzhan tanqi" 1920年代的戀愛與新性道德論述—從章錫琛參與的三次論戰談起 (Discourses on romantic love and the new sexual morality of the 1920s: Exemplified by three debates in which Zhang Xichen took part). *Jindai Zhongguo funüshi yanjiu*, no. 16 (2008): 29–90.

——. "Nala" zai Zhongguo: Xin nüxing xingxiang de suzao jiqi yanbian, 1900s–1930s "娜拉" 在中國：新女性形象的塑造及其演變 (Nora in China: The construction of the image of the new woman and its evolution, 1900s–1930s). Taipei: Zhengzhi daxue shixue lishi xuexi, 2003.

Xu Maoyong 徐懋庸. "Kan le Nala zhihou" 看了娜拉之後 (After watching Nora). *Shishi xinbao*, June 30, 1935.

Xu Qinfu 許廑父. "Du" 妒 (Jealousy). *Xiaoshuo ribao*, December 4, 1922.

Xu Shupi 徐樹丕. "Xi jianke" 戲柬客 (Playful exchanges). In *Shixiao lu* 識小錄 (Records of small knowledge), *Hanfen lou miji diyi ji* 涵芬樓秘笈第一集 (Private texts from Hanfen Tower, vol. 1), 74–75. Shanghai: Shangwu yinshuguan, 1936.

Xu Wuling 徐嫵靈. "Jidu zhexue: Dongwu zhi jidu" 嫉妒哲學：動物之嫉妒 (The philosophy of jealousy: Animal's jealousy). *Funü shibao* 1, no. 1 (1911): 11–16.

Xu Xiaotian 許嘯天. "Pan Jinlian shibushi yinfu?" 潘金蓮是不是淫婦 (Is Pan Jinlian a whore?). *Xinwen bao*, May 12, 1936.

——. "Xu Xiaotian shuo" 許嘯天說 (Words from Xu Xiaotian). *Xinwen bao*, November 7, 1932.

Xu Zhimo 徐志摩. "Xingshi yinyuan zhuan xu" 《醒世姻緣傳》序 (Preface to Marriage Bonds to Awaken the World). In vol. 3 of *Hu Shi wencun (disi ji)* 胡適文存（第四集） (Collection of Hu Shi's essays, no. 4), 175–90. Taipei: Yuanliu chuban gongsi, 1986.

Xu Zhiyan 許指嚴. "Nü weiren" 女偉人 (Great women). In *Xinhua miji* 新華秘記 (Secret notes about China), 145–49. Reprint. Shanghai: Zhonghua shuju, 2007.

Xue 雪. "Zai tantan Huijia yihou" 再譚譚《回家以後》 (Talk about After Returning Home again). *Funü zhoubao*, January 4, 1925.

——. "Xiju xieshe de sanchu dumuju" 戲劇協社的三出獨幕劇 (The three one-act dramas by the Drama Association). *Wenxue*, December 15, 1924.

Yan Duhe 嚴獨鶴. "Xini mou nüshi zhi bada hutong jijie shu" 戲擬某女士致八大胡同妓界書 (An imaginary playful letter from a certain lady to the prostitutes). *Shen bao*, November 22, 1912.

Yan Sanlang 燕三郎. *Yanzhi hu* 胭脂虎 (Tiger with rouge). N.p.: 1916.

Yan'an wenyi congshu 延安文藝叢書 (Anthology of literature and the arts from Yan'an). Changsha: Hunan renmin chubanshe, 1984.

Yang Lianfen 楊聯芬. "'Nala' bu zou zenyang" "娜拉" 不走怎樣 (What if Nora did not leave). *Wenyi zhengming*, no. 7 (2015): 39–42.

——. "Wusi lihun sichao yu Ouyang Yuqian Huijia yihou 'benshi' kaolun" 五四離婚思潮與歐陽予倩《回家以後》"本事"考論 (The divorce trend of the May Fourth generation and the "background story" of Ouyang Yuqian's After Returning Home). *Xin wenxue shiliao*, no. 1 (2010): 79–85.

Yang, Shu. "Wrestling with Tradition: Early Chinese Suffragettes and the Modern Remodeling of the Shrew Trope." *Modern Chinese Literature and Culture* 34, no. 1 (2022): 128–69.

——. "Shrews Rehabilitated in Women's Liberation? Li Shuangshuang, *Pola Womanhood*, and the Great Leap Forward Heroines." *Chinese Literature: Essays, Articles, Reviews* 41 (2019): 113–27.

——. "I Am Nora, Hear Me Roar: The Rehabilitation of the Shrew in Modern Chinese Theater." *Nan Nü: Men, Women and Gender in China* 18, no. 2 (2016): 291–325.

"Yaoqiu nüzi canzhengquan zhi wuli" 要求女子參政權之武力 (The force of those asking for women's suffrage). *Shi bao*, March 23, 1912.

Ye Yonglie 葉永烈. *Jiang Qing zhuan* 江青傳 (Biography of Jiang Qing). Beijing: Zuojia chubanshe, 1993.

Yeh, Catherine Vance. "Shanghai Leisure, Print Entertainment, and the Tabloids, *xiaobao* 小報." In Wagner, *Joining the Global Public*, 201–33.

——. *Shanghai Love: Courtesans, Intellectuals, and Entertainment Culture, 1850–1910*. Seattle: University of Washington Press, 2006.

Yi Fang 一方. "Qiqing zhai suibi" 祈晴齋隨筆 (Qiqing studio essays). *Xianghai huabao*, no. 11 (1938): 1.

Yi He 一鶴. "Xin nüjie de xianxiang" 新女界的現像 (Phenomena in the new women's circles). *Aiguo baihua bao*, August 9–10, 1913.

Yin 音. "Taitai wansui" 太太萬歲 (Long live the missus). *Beiping ribao*, May 6, 1948.

Yin Fu 吟父. "Guan Ouyang Yuqian yan Pan Jinlian ganyan" 觀歐陽予倩演潘金蓮感言 (Thoughts after watching Ouyang Yuqian's performance of Pan Jinlian). *Xinwen bao*, January 14, 1928.

"Yingguo nüzi zhi baoheng" 英國女子之暴橫 (The cruelty of English women). *Minli bao*, April 23, 1912.

You Na 尤娜. "Ping Nala de yanji" 評《娜拉》的演技 (On the acting of Nora). *Shen bao*, July 22, 1935.

Yu Shi 玉士. "Pa laopo lun" 怕老婆論 (The idea of wife-fearing). *Zhen hua* 5, no. 1 (1948): 5.

Yu Xuelun 喻血輪 and Wang Zuidie 王醉蝶. *Junei qushi* 懼內趣史 (The funny history of henpecking). Shanghai: Dadong shuju, 1925.

Yu Zhengxie 俞正燮. "Du fei nüren ede lun" 妒非女人惡德論 (Jealousy is not women's vice). In vol. 13 of Yu Zhengxie, *Guisi leigao* 癸巳類稿 (Categorized manuscripts from the Guisi year [1833]), *Xuxiu Sikuquanshu* 續修四庫全書, no. 1159 (Siku quanshu continued), 542. Shanghai: Shanghai guji chubanshe, 2003.

Yuan Guoxing 袁國興. "Tan huaju Pan Jinlian de dansheng" 談話劇《潘金蓮》的誕生 (On the birth of the drama Pan Jinlian). *Dongbei shida xuebao*, no. 6 (1989): 100–101.

Zang, Jian. "'Women Returning Home'—A Topic of Chinese Women's Liberation." In Leutner and Spakowski, *Women in China*, 376–95.

Zhan Xiaobai 湛晓白. "Beijing Nübao yu Qingmo Beijing nüzi jiaoyu chutan" 《北京女報》與清末北京女子教育初探 (Studies of Beijing Women's News and Beijing's female education in the late Qing). *Beijing shehui kexue*, no. 5 (2012): 96–101.

——. "Cong yulun dao xingdong: Qingmo Beijing Nübao jiqi shehui zitai" 從輿論到行動：清末《北京女報》及其社會姿態 (From public opinion to action: Beijing Women's News and its social attitude in the late Qing dynasty). *Shi lin*, no. 4 (2008): 37–48.

Zhang Ailing 張愛玲. "'Taitai Wansui' tiji" "太太萬歲"題記 (Preceding notes on Long Live the Missus). *Dagong bao*, December 3, 1947.

Zhang Chuntian 張春田. *Sixiangshi shiye zhong de "Nala": Wusi qianhou de nüxing jiefang huayu* 思想史視野中的"娜拉"：五四前後的女性解放話語 (Nora from the perspective of intellectual history: The women's liberation discourse before and after May Fourth). Taipei: Xinrui wenchuang, 2013.

Zhang Huaiwan 張懷萬. "Zhang Huaiwan xunshi ganxi'nan baogao" 張懷萬巡視贛西南報告 (A report on Zhang Huaiwan's investigation in southwest Jiangxi). In vol. 1 of *Zhongyang geming genjudi shiliao xuanbian* 中央革命根據地史料選編 (Selected historical documents on the Central Revolutionary Base Area), edited by *Jiangxi sheng dang'an guan* 江西省檔案館, 180–212. Nanchang: Jiangxi renmin chubanshe, 1982.

Zhang Ming 張鳴. *Lishi de digao: Wanjin Zhongguo de linglei guancha* 歷史的底稿：晚近中國的另類觀察 (Manuscript of history: An alternative observation of modern and contemporary China). Beijing: Zhongguo dang'an chubanshe, 2006.

Zhang Qichen 張其琛 [*sic*]. "Wu Zifang yu dongfang de jiu daode" 吳自芳與東方的舊道德 (Wu Zifang and the old morals of the Orient). *Jue wu*, February 17, 1925.

Zhang Ruifang 張瑞芳. "Banyan Li Shuangshuang de jidian tihui" 扮演李雙雙的幾點體會 (Some thoughts and feelings about my performance of Li Shuangshuang). In *Li Shuangshuang—Cong xiaoshuo dao dianying*, 233–69.

Zhang Ruohua 張若華. *Zhongguo chanzu lishi: Sancun jinlian yiqian nian* 中國纏足歷史：三寸金蓮一千年 (The history of foot-binding in China: The three-inch golden lotus in a thousand years). Hong Kong: Zhonghua shuju, 2015.

Zhang Xiaofen 張孝芬. "Nüzi canzheng zhi taolun—Zhang Xiaofen nüshi laihan" 女子參政之討論——張孝芬女士來函 (Discussions on women's suffrage—A letter from Lady Zhang Xiaofen). *Minli bao*, March 18, 1912.

Zhang Xichen 章錫琛, ed. *Xin xingdaode taolunji* 新性道德討論集 (Discussions on the new sexual morality). Shanghai: Kaiming shudian, 1926.

——. "Xin xingdaode yu duoqi: Da Chen Bainian xiansheng" 新性道德與多妻：答陳百年先生 (The new sexual morality and polygamy: Answering Mr. Chen Bainian). In *Xin xingdaode taolunji*, 41–48.

——. "Yu Chen jiaoshou tan meng" 與陳教授談夢 (Discussing dreams with Professor Chen). In *Xin xingdaode taolunji*, 105–38.

——. "Du fei nüren meide lun" 妬非女人美德論 (Jealousy is not women's virtue). *Xin nüxing* 1, no. 2 (1926): 12–17.

——. "Tao yi gui gao de 'Huijia yihou'" 逃易歸高的 "回家以後" (Easy to leave, hard to return: On After Returning Home). *Funü zhoubao*, February 9, 1925.

——. "Wu Zifang de lihun wenti" 吳自芳的離婚問題 (The divorce problem of Wu Zifang). *Funü zhoubao*, January 5, 1925.

——. "Wu Zifang yu Nala yu A'erwen furen" 吳自芳與娜拉與阿爾文夫人 (Wu Zifang and Nora and Mrs. Alving). *Funü zhoubao*, December 21, 1924.

Zhang Xuan 張萱. "Dufu buke shao" 妒婦不可少 (Jealous women are indispensable). In vol. 2 of Zhang Xuan, *Yi yao* 疑耀 (Doubts and clarities), 4. Taipei: Yiwen yinshuguan, 1965.

Zhang, Yun. *Engendering the Woman Question: Men, Women, and Writing in China's Early Periodical Press*. Leiden: Brill, 2020.

——. "Nationalism and Beyond: Writings on *Nüjie* and the Emergence of a New Gendered Collective Identity in Modern China." *Nan Nü: Men, Women and Gender in China* 17, no. 2 (2015): 245–75.

Zhang Zhizhong 張致中. "Yishu de xishengzhe 'Nala' Wang Guangzhen jiezhi qianhou" 藝術的犧牲者 "娜拉" 王光珍解職前後 (Before and after "Nora" Wang Guangzhen got fired as a victim of the arts). *Da wanbao*, February 16, 1935.

Zhao Dan 趙丹. *Diyu zhi men* 地獄之門 (The gate of hell). Shanghai: Wenhui chubanshe, 2005.

Zheng Jian 鄭堅. "Cong geming de 'youwu' dao geming de nüshen: Yi Mao Dun xiaoshuo zhong shidai nüxing xingxiang suzao weili" 從革命的 "尤物" 到革命的女神: 以茅盾小說中時代女性形象塑造為例 (From a revolutionary "stunner" to a revolutionary goddess: The feminine images in the novels of Mao Dun). *Hebei shifan daxue xuebao (zhexue shehui kexue ban)* 30, no. 3 (2007): 88–92.

Zheng Yongfu 鄭永福 and Lü Meiyi 呂美頤. *Jindai Zhongguo funü shenghuo* 近代中國婦女生活 (Women's lives in modern China). Zhengzhou: Henan renmin chubanshe, 1993.

Zhongguo funü da fanshen 中國婦女大翻身 (The great turning over/transformation of Chinese women). Hong Kong: Xin minzhu chubanshe, 1949.

"Zhongguo funü yundong dangqian renwu de jueyi" 中國婦女運動當前任務的決議 (Resolution of current tasks of the Chinese women's movement). *Xin minzhu funü yuekan*, no. 1 (1949): 25–26.

"Zhongguo gongchandang zhongyang weiyuanhui guanyu ge kangri genjudi muqian funü gongzuo fangzhen de jueding" 中國共產黨中央委員會關於各抗日根據地目前婦女工作方針的決定 (Decisions of the Central

Committee of the Chinese Communist Party on guiding principles for the current women's work in the Anti-Japanese Base Areas). In *Quanguo, Zhongguo funü yundong lishi ziliao (1937–1945)*, 647–49.

Zhou Enlai 周恩來. "Lun 'xianqi liangmu' yu muzhi" 論"賢妻良母"與母職 (On "good wife wise mother" and motherly duties). In *Quanguo, Zhongguo funü yundong lishi ziliao (1937–1945)*, 608–11.

Zhou Jianren 周建人. "Lixiang de nüxing" 理想的女性 (The ideal woman). *Funü zazhi* 11, no. 2 (1925): 312–15.

——. "Wu Zifang jiujing shi jiazuzhuyi xia de nüxingxing bushi?" 吳自芳究竟是家族主義下的女性型不是 (Is Wu Zifang a female type under familism?). *Funü zhoubao*, January 4, 1925.

——. "Zhongguo de nüxingxing" 中國的女性型 (Types of women in China). *Funü zhoubao*, December 21, 1924, and January 11, 1925.

Zhou Jiawei 周家慰. "Jingyan zhi tan" 經驗之談 (Observation based on personal experience). *Funü zazhi* 16, no. 6 (1930): 61–62.

Zhou Li 周立. "'Ziyou lihun' xiamian de xingui" "自由離婚"下面的新鬼 (The new ghost under "free divorce"). *Jue wu*, August 17, 1922.

Zhou Shoujuan 周瘦鵑, trans. "Funü zhi yuanzhi" 婦女之原質 (The original qualities of women). *Funü shibao*, no. 8 (1912): 24.

Zhu, Ping. *Gender and Subjectivities in Early Twentieth-Century Chinese Literature and Culture*. New York: Palgrave Macmillan, 2015.

Zhu Xiaodong 朱曉東. "Tongguo hunyin de zhili—1930 nian-1950 nian geming shiqi de hunyin he funü jiefang faling zhong de celüe yu shenti" 通過婚姻的治理—1930年-1950年革命時期的婚姻和婦女解放法令中的策略與身體 (Governance through marriage: Marital situations in the revolutionary 1930s to 1950s and the strategies and the body in decrees on women's liberation). *Beida falü pinglun* 4, no. 2 (2001): 383–401.

Zhuang Qidong 莊啟東. "Fufu" 夫婦 (The husband and wife). In vol. 2 of *Yan'an wenyi congshu*, 221–31.

Zurndorfer, Harriet, ed. *Chinese Women in the Imperial Past: New Perspectives*. Leiden: Brill, 1999.

Index

adultery, committed by Pan Jinlian, 67, 70, 74–75

After Returning Home (Ouyang Yuqian), 51, 52, 55–59, 168n27

agency
female, in *Pan Jinlian*, 71–72
jealousy and, 60
Liu Mali as symbolic of women's, 59
sexual, in Chinese writing tradition, 66–67

Autumn in Nanjing, The, 32

Bailey, Paul J., 161n53
Beijing Women's News, 11–13, 17
Belden, Jack, 132, 135
Belmont, Mrs. O. H. P., 162n64
Benedict, Carol, 154n12
biaomei figure, 180n12
bodily functions, female, 19–21, 159n27
Braester, Yomi, 169n33
breastfeeding, 19–20, 159n27
Brief Biography of Li Shuangshuang, A (film, 1962), 148–51. *See also* Li Shuangshuang (fictional character)
"Brief Biography of Li Shuangshuang, A" (Li Zhun), 144–48, 197n8. *See also* Li Shuangshuang (fictional character)
Butterfly stories, new woman as shrewish wife in, 91–98

Cai Yuanpei, 168n30
Carpenter, Edward, 171n68
Carroll, Peter J., 167n20
Cass, Victoria, 175n35
castration, violence as displaced form of, 41
cats, 94–95, 181nn19,22
Chan, Roy, 179n94
"Cheeks of the Hero, The" (Wang Dungen), 26–27
Chen Bainian (Chen Daqi), 60–61
Chen Daqi (Chen Bainian), 60–61
Chen Sizhen (fictional character), 116–17

Chen Yi, 183n39
Chen Yuan, 115
Chinese Nora plays
After Returning Home as, 168n27
jealousy in, 51–59
Pan Jinlian as, 169n33
See also *Pan Jinlian* (Ouyang Yuqian)
cigarettes and cigarette smoking, 154n12
Classic of Wife-Fearing (Li Zongwu), 114
clothing, 181n17
comic stories
new woman as shrewish wife in, 91–98
shrewish wife in post-May Fourth, 100
Communism
appeal of, 135
and Nora's shaping into revolutionary icon, 119–26
and "the Yan'an Way," 131–36
in Yan'an literature, 139–41
Communist radical feminism
and prevalence of shrews, 127–31, 137
shift to family harmony from, 131, 136
and "the Yan'an Way," 131–36
in Yan'an literature, 137–38
concubinage, 31–32, 34, 47, 48, 51, 53–55, 71–72. *See also* polygamy
Confucian culture and ideology, 2, 6, 45, 46, 67, 68, 78, 101, 103, 114, 120, 150
neo-Confucianism, 2–3, 115
Confucius Saw Nancy (Lin Yutang), 102–6, 185n60, 186nn66,75
Cong Xiaoping, 195nn45–46
conservatism, 6, 93, 99, 108, 182n38, 183n39
Constitution for Equality between Men and Women, 30
cousin love/cousin marriage, 180n12
"Creation" (Mao Dun), 120–22

Dan Fu, 33–34
Dekobra, Maurice, 184n45
Diary of a Henpecked Husband, The, 91, 92–96